Praise for
JERI SMITH-READY
and the ASPECT OF CROW series

EYES
OF
CROW

"There's an abundance of riches in this book, and Smith-Ready handles them all so well. The cultures and customs are well thought out and rendered, the connections with the spirit guides are wonderfully magical and filled with mystery, and the complicated relationships of the tribespeople are handled with a realistic flair."
—Award-winning author Charles de Lint,
Fantasy & Science Fiction

"Ms. Smith-Ready has woven an exquisite tapestry of a world, filled with texture and richness. Beware, reader!
You may never want to return..."
—*New York Times* bestselling author P.C. Cast

"A spellbinding plot and smooth-flowing narrative draw the reader into a world of myth and magic...lovers of fantasy are about to embark on a great new series."
—*Romantic Times BOOKreviews*, 4 1/2 stars Top Pick
(Reviewers' Choice Award, Best Fantasy Novel)

"Smith-Ready's *Eyes of Crow* is just the first installment in what could be an entertaining and profoundly moving series. Jean M. Auel meets Mercedes Lackey."
—Barnes & Noble *Explorations*

"Mystical, magical, romantic, suspenseful and action-packed, *Eyes of Crow* is an excellent example of what a fantasy novel should be."
—*Coffee Time Romance*

"The first installment in this magical series is an emotional, engaging, and appealing fantasy. Smith-Ready is a born storyteller."
—*Book Loons*

VOICE OF CROW

THE REAWAKENED

JERI SMITH-READY

LUNA™
www.LUNA-Books.com

LUNA™

THE REAWAKENED

ISBN-13: 978-0-373-80271-5
ISBN-10:   0-373-80271-4

Copyright © 2008 by Jeri Smith-Ready

First trade printing November 2008

Author photo copyright © 2006 by Szemere Photography

www.LUNA-Books.com

Printed in U.S.A.

In memory of Francisca "Paqui" Martin,
whose Spirit lives on—in the wind,
in the mountains, in our hearts.

Acknowledgments:

Many invaluable resources helped me build the story and world of *The Reawakened,* including *Learning to Eat Soup with a Knife* by John A. Nagl and *Guerrilla Warfare* by Mao Tse-Tung (translated by Samuel B. Griffith II). Lycas's concept of the "war of the flea" was borrowed from Robert Taber's landmark publication, *The War of the Flea: The Classic Study of Guerrilla Warfare.*

Many thanks to my family, for all their love and faith from the beginning.

I'm indebted, as always, to my beta readers, for seeing what I couldn't: Adrian Pastore, Terri Prizzi, Cecilia Ready and Rob Staeger. Kudos to the hardworking folks behind the scenes at Luna Books who brought the book to life: Tracy Farrell, Mary-Theresa Hussey, Margo Lipschultz, Marianna Ricciuto and Kathleen Oudit.

Thanks to my amazing, intrepid editor Stacy Boyd, who helped me whittle and trim the Amazing Colossal Manuscript into a novel that can be comfortably held with two hands. My agent, Ginger Clark of Curtis Brown, Ltd., is the sweetest, strongest advocate I could have ever hoped for. I am beyond blessed to have both these ladies in my life.

Thanks most of all to my husband, Christian Ready, for his love and inspiration, and for keeping the Flying Fear Monkeys at bay.

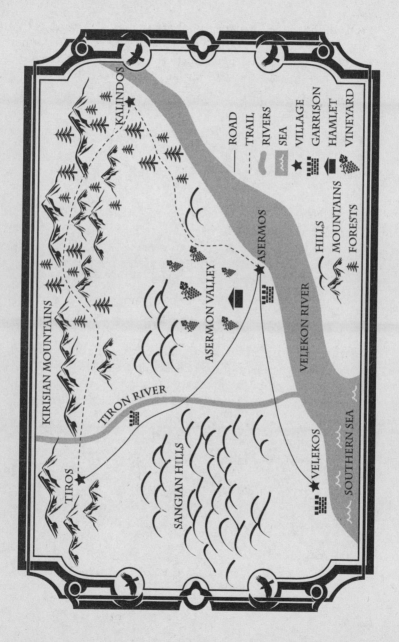

You might as well expect the rivers to run backward as that any man who is born a free man should be contented when penned up and denied liberty to go where he pleases.

—In-mut-too-yah-lat-lat ("Chief Joseph"),
Nimiputimt (Nez Perce) tribe

PART ONE

01

Tiros

Dust gritted between Rhia's teeth as she buried another dead soldier. She tugged the rough cloth covering her mouth and nose, securing its bottom edge inside her collar. As the hot wind changed direction, she shifted, keeping her back to the scouring gusts to protect her eyes.

A warm hand touched her elbow. "Rhia, let me finish."

She squinted up into the early evening light, at the ruddy face of her husband, Marek. "I need to occupy my mind as much as you do today. Besides, I'm the only one who can deliver them."

"But you're not the only one who can shovel." His blue-gray eyes smiled at her over his own cloth mask, crinkling the lines at their corners. "Save your strength for dancing."

She wiped the sweat from her temple and looked behind her

at the road leading into Tiros. "It's hard to imagine celebrating in this place."

Trees had been razed for a mile outside the village's perimeter to avoid giving cover to the enemy. Their trunks and branches had been used to build watchtowers, two of which loomed behind her, one on either side of the road leading into town. Inside the towers, Eagle lookouts and Cougar archers kept guard.

Few people left Tiros unseen. Fewer entered Tiros unshot.

At Rhia's feet, the Ilion soldier lay in a hole deep enough to keep the vultures away but shallow enough that the Ilions—or "Descendants," as Rhia's people called them—could retrieve the bodies the next time they arrived on a "diplomatic mission."

In a line stretching to her right lay the soldier's five comrades—dressed in plainclothes rather than their typical red-and-yellow uniforms—along with the spy who'd brought them. Other Tirons had dug the graves this morning; it was up to Marek and Rhia to fill them in and send the soldiers to the Other Side. No one joined them to pay respects to the dead, for the enemy and its spy had done nothing to earn it.

Marek tossed a shovelful of dust over the Descendant's face. "If Lycas were here, he'd want to put their heads on pikes on the road to Asermos."

She sighed at the reminder of her brother's brutality. "And give the Descendants an excuse for a full-scale invasion. At least with an honorable burial, we can claim our archers killed them defending the town—which is the truth."

"Doesn't mean they didn't enjoy it." His shovel clanked against a rock hidden in the dust. "Gave them a chance to practice the unofficial village motto: 'Keep Outsiders Outside.'"

They shared a grim look at the rows of tents sitting on the edge of the village. Tiros, built to hold perhaps a thousand people, had swollen to three times its original size with refugees from the villages of Velekos and Asermos, as the Ilion army pressed northward. The same aspects that made Tiros easy to defend—no immediate water access and flat, dry terrain surrounded on three sides by steep, rugged hills—also made survival difficult. In the twelve years since the Descendant invasion, Tiros had suffered growing pains that threatened to tear it apart.

Marek tapped down the dust over the last soldier with the toe of his boot, then marked the grave with a makeshift Ilion flag—a long stick with a red-and-yellow cloth attached.

Rhia knelt beside the grave, closed her eyes and raised her palms. In the span of one deep breath, she drew a shroud between herself and this world of vigilance. The next breath brought an awareness of Crow, her Guardian Spirit Animal, whose presence had hovered close to her for nearly all of her thirty-seven years. Now He waited to take what was His.

With her third breath, she called the crows.

The chant rumbled low in her throat, and as soon as it left her mouth it was swept away by the wind. No matter, for in this song her voice traveled to the Other Side, where all places were one. She could have whispered it or even sung it inside her mind. They would hear. They would come.

Within moments they approached, their caws riding the wind, whose roar obscured the rush of their heavy wings. Seven birds, one for each death.

Rhia wondered how the Descendants felt about being carried off by Crow, a Spirit they didn't believe in. Did they search for Xenia, their goddess of Death, lament her absence and finally her nonexistence?

The souls of these soldiers passed quickly, without reluctance. Though their deaths had been violent, they believed they had died for the greater glory of Ilios, just as they'd desired.

The young Asermon spy, on the other hand, resisted. The ache of his regret skewered her as he tried to escape Crow's embrace. The man, whose name she didn't know, had betrayed his own people.

His own people. Generations ago, the citizens of the four villages—Asermos, Velekos, Kalindos and Tiros—had divided themselves, focusing on their differences and long-standing tribal rivalries. The disunity had made them easy prey for the Ilions. But now, with their common oppression by the Spirit-shunning Descendants, they stood as one people.

Crow took the spy, completing His passage to the Other Side. Rhia worried the Asermon would linger, full of bitterness and sorrow, in the gloomy Gray Valley between here and there.

The cries of the crows faded, and Rhia lowered her hands. Marek's fingers under her elbow steadied her as she stood, her knees aching and heart thumping from the last soul's perilous journey.

He brushed the dust off the crow feather around her neck, then did the same for his own fox- and wolf-tail fetishes. Then he unbuckled the waterskin from his belt and offered it to her. As usual, it was nearly empty.

She squinted at the angle of the sun. "It's almost time."

"Nilik could come back tomorrow, or the next day. A Bestowing might take longer if Raven claims him."

"Hush." She rubbed the back of her neck, which always prickled at the mention of the greatest Spirit. "Don't assume anything. It shows arrogance."

"No." He put an arm around her shoulders. "It shows faith."

Rhia clamped her lips tight. She couldn't blame Marek for wanting to believe that Raven would deliver them from occupation. Raven was the only Spirit who had never bestowed a human with an Aspect—a combination of power and wisdom reflecting traits of that animal. An ancient legend said that Raven would one day bestow Her Aspect when the Spirit-people faced their most harrowing hour. Rhia hated to imagine an hour more harrowing than those they lived in now.

Before her son Nilik's birth eighteen years ago, a deluge of dreams foretold that the Raven child would be born to a Crow like Rhia. Most of her people believed it. Some even hoped this event would spark another Reawakening, when the Spirits would all appear together in this world, to save the people who had served Them for thousands of years.

Some days, the only alternative to faith was despair.

As Rhia and Marek walked hand in hand into the village, a shout came from the watchtower above.

"South!"

They stopped and looked up. Sani the Eagle woman pointed to their left. All five Cougars in her watchtower scrambled into position. Rhia saw the silhouettes of their bows against the azure sky.

"Someone's coming." Marek dropped the shovels and ran in the direction Sani was pointing.

"Wait!" Rhia rushed to keep up with him, and only succeeded because he waited for her at the foot of the watchtower. "It could be more Descendants."

She stood on tiptoe and strained to see what had provoked the alert. The only sign was a rising cloud of dust, small enough that she could block it with her outstretched thumb. It created a tan puff against the darker browns and greens of the background hills.

"It can't be Nilik." Marek shaded his right temple against the glare of the setting sun. "Near as I can tell, this person's on horseback."

"And it's the wrong direction from the Bestowing." The site for this sacred three-day quest lay to the west of Tiros—far from Descendant-occupied territories. Despite the Ilions' best efforts—negotiations, bribes and escalating shows of force—Tiros remained a free village, as did Kalindos, Marek's birthplace in the high mountain forest two weeks' travel away.

How long this freedom would last, no one knew.

Another shout came from the tower. Rhia looked up to see Sani leaning over the rough wooden railing.

"It's Lycas!"

Rhia yelped with joy and bounced on her toes. Her brother's continued survival amazed her. As the leader of the guerrilla fighting forces, Lycas was the Ilions' favorite target. She feared it was only a matter of time before they found a way to counteract his Wolverine savagery, wiliness and inhuman strength.

"Nilik will be glad," Marek said in typical understated fashion.

Rhia smiled, imagining her son's face when he came back from his Bestowing to see his uncle waiting. During Lycas's sporadic visits to Tiros, he treated Nilik like his own son.

Small wonder. Rhia had named him in memory of their brother Nilo, Lycas's twin who had died in the first battle against the Ilions nearly twenty years ago.

She rubbed her breastbone, as if she could feel the wound herself. No death before or since had carved such a gouge in her and Lycas.

Her brother waved one of his immense arms as he approached at an easy trot. His long black hair streamed in the wind despite the tie binding it at his nape. Even at a distance, his size and strength were intimidating. She didn't envy the Descendants whose last living sight was Lycas's face.

He slowed the horse to a cooling walk, and the cloud of dust around him diminished. Unable to wait any longer, Rhia ran to greet him.

Lycas dismounted, his posture showing no symptoms of a long ride or a long life. He gave a casual wave, as if he'd been gone eight hours instead of eight months.

"You made it!" Rhia hurtled into her brother's arms, dwarfing herself in his enormous embrace. His dark bay mare snorted and danced at the end of the reins, startled by the sudden movement.

"Good, I'm not too late, then." Lycas let go of Rhia and picked up the wide-brimmed hat that had toppled from her head. He tugged her auburn braid, then tossed it back over her shoulder, as if to confirm that it hadn't been cut in mourning for anyone in her immediate family.

Marek stepped forward and embraced Lycas, thumping him on the back. Lycas returned the gesture—less heartily, of course, to avoid cracking his brother-in-law's ribs.

"Nilik should be back tonight," Marek said. "Big party, all of Tiros is coming."

Lycas merely nodded and clucked to his horse to lead her into the village. Rhia studied his black-and-gray-stubbled face, which looked unusually drawn and somber.

She stopped in her tracks. "You have bad news."

He took a deep breath, wrinkling his nose. No doubt his

Wolverine sense of smell was assaulted by the stench of Tiros, of too many people and not enough latrines.

"Jula's at home?" he asked.

"Yes." Rhia's voice filled with caution. "Why?"

"I'll wait until we get there to tell you. I don't want to have to repeat it twice."

They passed the watchtower, collected the shovels and set off for the center of the village. A gust of wind blew up, and Rhia raised the cloth around her neck to cover her mouth and nose.

Dust danced in small tornados over the street, which was empty of life except for a few wandering dogs. Most Tirons were at the other end of the village, dragging tables, benches and lantern posts to the center of the westernmost intersection for Nilik's feast.

Lycas jerked his thumb over his shoulder. "What are the red-and-yellow flags for?"

Marek held up the shovels. "Descendant grave markers. Six men last night, with pitch-soaked rags in bottles."

"Fire starters." Lycas hissed in a breath. "A place this dry, with the homes so close together, they could burn the whole village."

"Vara's working on that," Rhia said. "She's having the Tirons add brick and stone to the walls between the houses to slow the spread of fire."

"Vara the Snake is here? Why?"

"She had to leave Asermos about seven months ago, just after you were here last." She shook her head in disgust. "The new grandparent laws."

The older she got, the more Rhia questioned the progression of her people's magic powers. They moved from first to second phase of their Aspects by conceiving a child, which caused many painful social and personal complications.

Third-phase Aspects, bestowed when a person became a grandparent, included such formidable powers as shapeshifting, long-distance telepathy—and in Rhia's case—resurrecting the dead. She was in no hurry to take on that ultimate burden.

Because the Ilions rejected the Spirits and created gods in their own image, they possessed no magic. To protect themselves, they required all third-phase Asermons to be registered. Last year, registration had turned to exile.

Lycas's voice returned her mind to the present. "How did the soldiers get so close to the village?"

"The lookouts recognized the man with them," Marek said, "someone from Asermos."

"A spy." Lycas let out a harsh breath. "Was he killed?"

"They shot him," Rhia said. Some said it was in defense of the village, but others claimed it was in cold blood. Either way, his soul had drowned in regret.

"He might have had information we could use," Lycas said.

They left the horse at a ramshackle stable where a gruff old man refused Lycas's Ilion coins. Rhia had to barter her stall-mucking services in exchange for the boarding.

A short trudge later, they reached Rhia and Marek's home. She opened the gate to a waist-high wooden fence, which led to a small yard. White and brown chickens scattered as they passed. Rhia nudged one aside before pushing open the front door.

Her daughter Jula sat at the table in the center of the main room, brown hair veiling her face as she bent over a piece of parchment. She looked up as Lycas ducked his head to enter the house.

"Uncle!" She popped out of her chair and ran in three strides to give him a leaping embrace. At sixteen, she was still tiny, like

Rhia herself, and Lycas lifted her as if she weighed no more than a bird.

When he set her down, she grasped his hands. "Did Papa tell you my news?"

Marek grinned at her on his way to the stove. "Thought we'd let you surprise him."

"I had my Bestowing!"

Lycas looked at Rhia, his eyes filled with sudden hope.

Jula grabbed his arm. "No, I'm not Raven, but we always knew that, since the prophecy said it would be a hard labor, and my birth was easy."

Rhia grunted. "That was the last day you gave me no trouble." As she moved to shut the door behind her, a brown chicken slipped through. A sharp bark shot from under the table, and the chicken scampered outside.

Jula turned back to Lycas. "So guess what I am? And no looking at the fetish hanging by the door."

Lycas sighed, heightening Rhia's fear. Usually he indulged his niece in all her teasing and tricks. Instead he pointed at the two parchment sheets on the table. "What's that?"

"A project." Jula hurried to tuck one sheet behind the other. "And maybe a short letter for Corek."

Lycas's face turned graver, which Rhia hadn't thought possible. Had something happened to Corek? Growing up, Jula and Nilik had spent summers with the family of Rhia's Crow-brother Damen, including his son Corek and stepdaughter Lania. The four children had been inseparable. Rhia and Marek and Damen had not-so-secretly speculated on the likelihood of a romance between Jula and Corek, and between Nilik and Lania.

Oblivious to Lycas's dark mood, Jula picked up the parchment and heaved a dramatic sigh. "Father's making me help him and Galen with the code to fool the Descendants. They test it on me."

"She acts like she hates it." Marek squeezed her shoulder. "But she won't let us forget that she writes better than we do."

"Even though she'd rather talk." Rhia turned to hang her black feather fetish on a nail by the door.

"Even though she'd rather talk," Rhia heard her own voice say again.

She turned and glared at Jula. "Stop that."

"Stop that," her daughter said in a perfect imitation of Rhia's voice. Jula covered an impish grin with her hand. "Sorry," she said in her own voice.

Lycas shook his head in sympathy at Rhia. "A Mockingbird girl. Could a Crow mother be any more cursed?"

Rhia smiled. Though she and Jula bickered, like their feathered counterparts, she was lucky her children were alive and safe. She knew Lycas worried about his own daughter Sura, who remained in occupied Asermos, where her mother Mali led the resistance. His crusade against the Ilions had taken him away from his family when Sura was only two weeks old. He'd said it was more important for his daughter to grow up in a land of freedom than to have a father.

Now she had neither. It was too dangerous for the outlaw Lycas to show his face in Asermos. Rhia hoped her own children filled at least part of the void in his life.

He ruffled Jula's hair. "Congratulations on your Bestowing."

"Thank you!" She rolled up the parchment sheets. "Nilik will be so happy you're here to see him become Raven."

Rhia pulled out a chair for Lycas. "Sit. Drink. Talk."

He obliged, sinking into the chair so heavily she feared it would break. She set a full mug of ale in front of him. He gulped the contents in one long swallow, let her refill it, then took a deep breath.

"Last month I set up a camp near Velekos so I could work with the resistance there, such as it is."

"Good," Marek said. "It's been weeks since we've gotten a direct message from Velekos, since Damen told us magic had been outlawed there, like in Asermos."

"The Ilions have been tightening their grip so slowly, most of the Velekons hardly even noticed." He opened and closed his fist around the clay mug, in a gesture Rhia recognized as a wish for a Descendant neck. "Last week, they noticed."

"What happened?" she asked, dreading the answer.

"There was an incident." Lycas stared straight ahead at the steps leading to the upper floor. "Lania went for her Bestowing, in a remote area in the hills northwest of Velekos. A squadron of Ilion soldiers came upon her."

Rhia's stomach twisted. Beside her, Jula gave a soft gasp.

Lycas continued. "They said they were just having fun. Harassing her, calling her names. Then she became violent, delirious, babbling something about the power of a Wasp. They say she stabbed one in the thigh."

Rhia winced. "So they arrested her?"

He made a bitter noise in his throat. "They beat her. They raped her." His lips tightened. "They murdered her."

"No…" With a low moan, Jula dropped into the chair across from Lycas. She put her face in her hands and started to cry.

Rhia opened her mouth, but even she, a Crow, couldn't find

the words to express her sorrow. If anything like that had happened to her own children…

Lycas spoke again. "They desecrated Lania's body so that—" His voice lost its flatness, coming closer to breaking than she'd heard in years. "It took a week to find all of her, to give her a proper burial."

Rhia's legs trembled, and she sank into the chair beside Jula, who was sobbing now. She put her arms around her daughter. For once, Jula didn't rebuff her, just clutched her like a frightened child.

"Lania was only sixteen," Lycas whispered.

"Monsters," Marek spat as he paced behind the table. "What happened to the soldiers?"

"Suspended without pay," Lycas replied, "and jailed at the garrison until their trial. Spirits know when that'll be. The military says it's an isolated incident, a few bad boys run amuck." He squeezed the mug again, then set it aside quickly as if to avoid crushing it. "Velekos has exploded. Riots, vandalism, mass arrests. By now there's probably a curfew."

A whimper came from under the table. Rhia looked down to see Hector, their nut-brown terrier, trying to climb into their laps. She boosted him up, wincing as his claws scratched her legs. Jula hugged the dog and sobbed into his shaggy coat.

"We hadn't heard any of this," Marek said.

"It happened last week." Lycas looked each of them in the eye. "That's why I'm here, not just for Nilik's Bestowing. Velekos is ready to revolt, but they need help. Not just soldiers and archers. Messengers, healers for the wounded, builders to create secret passageways from home to home." He looked at Marek and Jula. "Code-breakers."

Rhia felt a cold dread slither through her veins. She couldn't let Nilik go to Velekos, but she also couldn't tell anyone why.

Marek looked out the window. "Something's happening." He opened the front door. Rhia heard distant shouting and the pounding of feet.

Someone called their names, and Rhia recognized the voice of one of their neighbors.

"Nilik's coming!" the man shouted. Hector began to yap.

Jula dumped the dog off her lap and brushed the heels of her hands hard against her wet eyes. "When he hears about Lania—" Her voice choked.

"We'll be there for him." Rhia fetched the pitcher of water and poured her daughter a mug.

Jula slurped down the water, wincing as she swallowed. Then she slammed down the cup. "Let's go. We want to be in the front of the crowd."

They hurried down the dusty main road, Hector leading the way. Rhia's heart pounded, and not just from exertion in the late summer heat. Her people needed Raven now more than ever, after what had happened to Lania.

When they finally reached the front of the throng, Nilik was little more than a moving spot on the horizon to Rhia's eyes. She folded her arms and stood her ground. It would undermine Nilik's dignity to have his mother rush forward and clamp him in a smothering embrace.

Her toes twitched with impatience inside her boots, and her mind ran through all the possibilities, every Spirit Nilik could have. He'd shown no particular talents growing up—or rather, he'd displayed a wide range of skills, proudly honing each to extreme competence, though not brilliance. He proved equally deadly with sword and dagger and had worked beside Bear and Wolverine warriors to repel more than one Descendant attack. He could hunt most prey with a bow and arrow, though not with a Wolf or Cougar's preternatural skill and patience. He could read and write as nimbly as any Fox, Hawk or Mockingbird; Marek had seen to both children's literacy at a young age.

Perhaps his wide-ranging but less-than-luminous skills meant that Raven would choose him. As the Spirit of Spirits, She was connected to them all.

Rhia could see Nilik now, and hear the whispers of speculation behind her:

"He's walking so upright and proud. Must be a Bear."

"But look at the swiftness of his gait. Could surprise everyone and be a Spider."

Someone snickered. "The boy can't draw a stick figure with the right number of legs, and you think he'll be an artist? He looks quick and strong because he's a Deer. That's my wager."

"You're all fools," a fourth voice whispered. "He's got to be the Raven. Got to be. He'll deliver us all."

Rhia closed her eyes, wishing it weren't too late to pray for such an event. She'd thought it audacious before, to ask the Spirit Above All Others to bestow Her Aspect upon Nilik—or anyone, for that matter.

"Please," she whispered softly. "We need You. Accept my son as Your servant."

She opened her eyes to see Nilik stride across the dusty plain. His posture gave no clue he'd just spent three days without food, water and sleep; that he had been visited by Spirits both benevolent and terrifying.

As he came closer, his pace slowed and he removed his hat,

revealing a sunburned, sweat-streaked face. His light brown hair, which had never felt a mourning blade, hung down his back and blew in the evening breeze.

He scanned the faces of those in the front of the crowd, keeping his own visage inscrutable. When his gaze alighted on Lycas, he stopped short.

"Uncle!"

Nilik's dignity and serenity shattered as he ran forward, past his parents, and embraced Lycas, who returned the hug with a misty look in his eyes.

Nilik drew back, gave Lycas's wolverine claw fetish a long look, then clutched it in his fist. Rhia gasped. It was exceedingly rude to touch the fetish of an Animal one didn't share, a show of disrespect for that person's Spirit.

Which could only mean one thing…

Rhia's heart thudded, then seemed to stop.

Nilik opened his hand and gazed at the claw. "I'll be needing one of these now."

A sigh of disappointment spread through the crowd. As increasingly loud murmurs carried the news backward through the throng, Rhia stood as if frozen.

No.

She wanted to throw herself at her son, beat her fists against his chest until he took it back, until he told the truth. That he was Raven. That he was Fox, or Horse, or Butterfly or Otter.

Anything but Wolverine. Anything but a warrior.

The crowd dispersed, making their way to the tables. Several well-muscled men lingered. Rhia recognized them as the close-knit band of Tiron Wolverines. They were no doubt waiting to "welcome" their new Spirit-brother with their usual ritual, which involved a thorough beating to demonstrate how much violence he could endure without pain or injury.

Nilik finally looked at Rhia and Marek. "I know you wanted me to be Raven. I'm sorry I let you down."

Rhia stepped toward him. "Nilik, it's not your fault."

He looked at Jula, whose face was still red and puffy. "Were you crying?"

She covered her cheeks and squeaked out his name.

Nilik turned back to Rhia. "What's going on?"

She took his hand. "It's Lania." A hundred times or more she had appeared on a neighbor's doorstep with these terrible words, ready to counsel and console. Why was it so hard to speak them to her son? "She's dead."

He stepped back, yanking his hand out of hers. "Our Lania?" He touched his chest as if to say, *My Lania?*

Nilik turned away, lifting his face toward the tendrils of red and orange clouds stretching across the sky. He stood motionless for a long moment, hands on his hips, drawing deep, quaking breaths.

Finally he turned back to Lycas, his face contorted. "Descendants?" he hissed.

Lycas nodded, then told the story of Lania's death, which pained Rhia even more upon the second hearing.

As his uncle spoke, Nilik hunched over, running both hands over his scalp, squeezing his head tight between them as if he could press the pain away. His breath came faster, and he swallowed several times, each one harder than the last.

When the story was finished, Nilik slowly pulled back his shoulders, lowered his hands, then turned his haunted blue-gray gaze upon Lycas. "When you leave, I'm going with you. I'm going to Velekos."

Rhia shivered at the sound of the village's name slipping from her son's mouth.

Velekos. The place she could never let him go, not after the vision she'd received at his birth.

Velekos was the place where Nilik would die.

02

Asermos

"**W**ake up!"

Sura felt a chill as blankets were whipped off her. A pack was shoved into her arms, jamming her middle finger.

"Ow."

"Shh!" A cool, thin hand covered her mouth. "They're coming," Mali whispered. "You know what to do."

Sura sat up, eyes searching the dark and seeing only her mother's pale face. "Soldiers?"

"Down the road. Torynna just came to warn me. Five men, all armed." Mali pulled aside the chair that sat between their beds, then yanked up the rug.

Sura shuddered at the thought of going into the tunnel, but a decade of running this drill pushed her limbs into automatic action. She grabbed her boots and shoved her feet into them. "Come with me."

"We've discussed this a hundred times." Mali started pulling up the floorboards. "If I run, I'll be admitting my guilt. They'll kill us both."

"Not if we escape."

"They'll follow. If I let them take me, they won't search for you. They don't care about you."

They will, Sura thought as she put on her pack, jerking the straps tight against her shoulders. One day the Descendant scum would pay for everything. They would all burn.

Mali lifted the last board. "Go. Now."

Sura lowered herself into the hole, stepping quickly down the ladder that had been nailed into the side of it. With her chest at floor level, she stopped.

"What are you waiting for?"

"Maybe I should go to the hills to find my father."

Her mother put down the board and grabbed Sura's shoulders. *"What did we say?"* She shook her so hard, Sura thought her teeth would fall out. "What's the plan?"

"Kalindos."

"So where are you going?"

"Kalindos," Sura whispered.

"But first?"

"Get a horse from Bolan."

Mali pulled her close and kissed her forehead. "I love you."

"I love you, too." When her mother released her, Sura clutched her wrist. "Please come. They might kill you."

Mali shook her head. "They don't want another martyr on their hands. They'll imprison me, discredit me to our people."

She cupped Sura's chin. "Tell the Kalindons the truth. That's your job. Don't try to be a hero."

"But my father could be—"

"Your father could be under the ground or at the bottom of the river for all we know. If you want to survive, you stay far away from him. Understand?"

Sura nodded.

"Remember, if Lycas cared about us, he wouldn't have left in the first place."

A knock came at the door. Sura's heart slammed her chest, but Mali didn't even blink.

"Go."

Sura moved down the ladder and took one more look up. Shadows sharpened the angles of her mother's rigid face.

"You know what to do," Mali whispered, then slid the boards back over the hole.

Everything went dark. Sura swallowed hard and lowered herself to the floor of the tunnel. She began to crawl.

Her pack scraped the ceiling, triggering a rain of moist dirt that tickled her skin where her shirt had ridden above her waist. Earthworms and beetles skittered off her, as well, and a distant part of her mind hoped none of them fell down her trousers.

She listened for a struggle in the house above her, though she knew she was too deep to hear. The only sounds were her own pounding heartbeat and the scrambling of tiny claws. A mole or shrew, no doubt.

She crawled faster. *Pretend it's another drill,* she told herself. *Pretend the walls aren't closing in.* She closed her eyes, since there was no light, anyway, and focused on keeping her breath steady.

Soon her knee hit a wooden slab, signaling the end of the tunnel. She put a hand out to avoid banging her skull. Her fingers scraped another ladder.

Though her lungs longed for fresh air, she forced herself to climb slowly and quietly. When the top of her head tapped the hole cover, she stopped and listened.

Voices, distant, arguing. Her ears strained for a closer sound, one that would tell her a soldier was waiting outside her hiding place, like a fox watching a rabbit hole.

No leaves rustled nearby except those shifted by the faint breeze. Descendants had no talent for covering their footfalls. Even their raspy breath seemed to fill the air for miles, belying their presence as well as a shout.

Sura took a handful of mud from the tunnel wall and smeared it over her face. With her black hair and dark clothes, it would complete her night camouflage. She slowly lifted the wooden cover, far enough to peek.

It was a cloudy, moonless night, but after the total darkness of the hole, the world seemed bright and clear. She had emerged in the woods across the lane from her mother's house. The front door was open, but she couldn't see Mali behind the group of soldiers, two of whom flanked the doorway, facing Sura. She stayed low and slitted her eyes to keep them from reflecting the torch.

Another soldier came from around the back of the house, where he had no doubt been guarding against Mali and Sura's retreat. The other two stood inside the front doorway. As the voices rose in argument, the leader grabbed the guard's torch and waved the flame toward the walls, as if threatening to burn down the house.

Sura's fist clenched the edge of the hole, fingers sinking into the mud. She'd spent all eighteen years of her life there. They couldn't settle for stealing her mother, they had to take her home, too?

Mali just needed the element of surprise to overcome these soldiers. Her second-phase Wasp powers gave her the fighting skill and strength of three normal men. In the dark, she could probably overcome all five. Then she and Sura could flee together to Kalindos.

Sura rested the hole cover on the crown of her head, then cupped her hands to her mouth, ready to strike.

They led her mother out of the house. The torch-wielding soldier held his light near Mali so that two of the others could bind her. They pulled her arms behind her back and wrapped a thin rope around her wrists.

Mali kept her chin up and her jaw set. She had always planned to surrender without fighting, to counter her reputation as the fierce leader of the Asermon resistance. The less trouble she caused them in custody, the sooner the authorities would let her go, and the sooner she could get back to planning their assassinations.

Mali's posture stiffened suddenly, just as the breeze died. In the silence, Sura heard one of the men say, "Now she won't be able to hit us back."

Before the soldier could finish the knot, Sura focused on the torch, called upon her Spirit, then sucked in her breath, hard and swift.

The torch snuffed out.

The men shouted, and Mali broke free. She whirled on them, fists and feet flying. Two collapsed, moaning and clutching their groins.

Mali turned to run. A soldier grabbed her long dark braid and slammed her onto her back. The other two moved quickly to point the tips of their swords at her throat and stomach. She froze, panting.

Sura gritted her teeth in frustration, and at the torch's searing heat that careened within her now.

The largest soldier—the one who had caught Mali—flipped her over, then planted a knee in the small of her back as he bound her wrists. He lifted her to stand and turned her to face him.

"Are you going to be good?" he said.

She spit at his feet.

"Sorry, I didn't hear you." He punched Mali in the mouth. She staggered back only a step, then spit again. He struck her once more. Mali didn't even flinch this time, just smiled as she spit in his face.

They repeated the process over and over, until Sura knew her mother's saliva must have been dark with blood. Still Mali said nothing, and her legs did not give way.

Sura shook her head. Surely the soldier had been told that Mali's Wasp defenses allowed little injury and even less pain. She was a warrior in body and Spirit. He might as well be punching a tree.

Grunting in frustration, he struck her in the gut, then the side. Mali laughed.

His punches turned flailing, yet he refused the others' offers of help. By now, Sura knew, his knuckles would be raw, maybe even broken from the impact against Mali's tough exterior.

Finally he tottered back and raised his arm, then lost his balance and tipped backward into the mud. The others laughed—at least, the two who weren't still curled up on the ground in agony.

The large soldier rolled over and lurched to his feet. He tugged down the end of his red-and-yellow jacket, as if a crooked uniform were the most embarrassing part of the situation.

"Let's take her in and be rid of her," he said. "Let her plague the prison guards."

The two injured soldiers were roused, reluctantly. They all proceeded down the lane, and Sura noticed that even after the beating, her mother walked taller than the rest.

03

Tiros

Rhia tugged her hood farther over her forehead against the rain sweeping the Tiron streets. The wind was harshest out here at the end of town where no buildings stood to block it.

Lycas's horse grunted and shook her head, jerking Rhia's arm. Drops cascaded from her forelock onto the broad white stripe on her face.

Tiros needed the rain—the cisterns were nearly empty—but no messenger pigeons from Kalindos would arrive in such weather. The birds would hunker down in a tree until the storm passed. Rhia wished she could attach a message to a crow, who would fly undaunted through a hurricane if it meant finding a sure source of food.

"Speaking of undaunted..." she murmured as her brother appeared, striding down the street to the place where the horses waited. He wore no hood and didn't even hunch his shoulders against the rain slashing his face.

Four Tiron Wolverines flanked him, looking slightly more daunted by the storm, though they did a fair job of imitating Lycas's effortless swagger. Behind them strode four Bear men with swords at their waists; two second-phase Cougars (a male and female) with bows strung over their shoulders; Sani the Eagle woman, who needed no weapon but her own eyes; an Otter with a healer's pack strapped to her back; and lastly a young Horse man, lugging a pair of large covered cages, each containing two Tiron messenger pigeons.

Looking past them into the town, Rhia saw most of the Tirons standing on their porches to bid the travelers farewell. She was glad she couldn't see the pain in the parents' eyes as they sent their children off to battle.

When Lycas reached her, Rhia hugged him goodbye, taking care not to stab herself on one of the five daggers on his belt and sash. At least one more lurked inside each of his boots. For all she knew, he had one hidden in his long, thick black hair.

"I hate the thought of you traveling in this weather," she said.

"Me, too, but only because I'd rather be fighting in it." He let her go, more quickly than usual. "You sure you won't let Nilik come to Velekos?"

She looked away and tried to sound like a worried mother, instead of a death-glimpsing Crow. "It's too dangerous."

"It's his calling," he said, for what seemed like the thirty-seventh time in the last four days. "It's his destiny."

If only you knew how true that was. "I realize he's a warrior now," she said through gritted teeth. "He can be a warrior right here, defending Tiros."

Lycas gave a harsh sigh. "I don't mean just any kind of fighting. He cared about Lania. Wolverines live for vengeance."

"Not all Wolverines." He started to turn away from her, and she grabbed his arm. "You treat every Descendant you meet as if they personally killed Nilo. Nineteen years' worth of corpses, and it'll never be enough."

"You're right," he snapped, "it won't. Not until every last Descendant leaves our soil, or until I'm rotting under it."

Rhia closed her eyes and shook her head, wishing Lycas could find half the peace in this world as their brother had found on the Other Side.

"Where is Nilik, anyway?" Lycas asked.

"Probably off sulking. He'll hear it from me for his rudeness."

"Don't. It hurts his honor to watch other warriors leave without him." Lycas gave her another accusatory glare.

"He might follow you."

Her brother's gaze wavered, and he moderated his tone. "If he does, I promise I'll send him home, unless I know you've changed your mind."

"I won't."

"But if you do, give him a password. Use the dog's name."

She nodded, just to let the issue lie. "Send word when you arrive."

"If I can. You know how it is." He ruffled her hair through her hood, causing water to cascade over her face.

She smacked his hand away. "Ow!" she groaned at the impact. It was like whacking a boulder. Lycas let out a booming laugh, and she was filled with a mixture of sorrow and annoyance.

Rhia turned away to adjust her hood and saw Marek and Jula standing with Galen the Hawk under the awning of the corner store. They hunched over a lengthy piece of parchment, on which Galen was making a few last-minute marks. In the four days since Lycas's arrival, the three of them had slept little, finishing a coded language that was similar enough to the Descendants' writing to fool them. A disinformation campaign could wreak as much havoc as a hundred dagger-bearing Wolverines.

Marek rolled up the parchment and placed it in a long leather satchel. He and Galen hurried over to Rhia and Lycas, followed by a pair of Badger bodyguards.

Third-phase Hawks like Galen could send instant thoughts to each other over long distances. Unfortunately, Galen was the only one of his kind, but as soon as another Hawk entered the third phase, he would be a powerful weapon against the Ilions—hence the need for the hulking Badger guards.

Marek gave Lycas a long, hard hug goodbye, while Galen turned his gaze northeast toward the mountain pass.

"No pigeons," Rhia told him. "I get nervous when we don't hear from my father for over a month."

Galen sighed and smoothed a long gray hair back under his hat. "One day Thera will enter the third phase, and we'll be able to communicate instantly. Then we could finally coordinate our efforts to help Asermos."

"We're ready to leave," Lycas said. He gave Galen a quick bow, then stood up just in time to be slammed with a hug from Jula.

"Take me with you," she said.

He laughed and peeled her arms from around his waist. "Funny girl. I promise I'll personally escort you to Velekos the moment it's liberated."

"And I can swim in the bay? And eat oysters?"

"Until you vomit."

She kicked the toe of her boot into the muddy ground. "You better not die and break your promise."

Lycas laughed. Rhia didn't. Biting back the words "Be careful," she watched her only living brother strap his supplies to the back of the dark bay mare, then lead the horse to the head of the line.

He looked back at the last moment and gave the crowd a mocking version of the Ilion salute—putting his fist to his groin instead of his heart.

Rhia let out a sigh when the troupe headed for the scrub of the nearby hills. Trouble always followed Lycas, so maybe it would leave with him, too.

A movement in the corner of her eye caught her attention. Nilik stood alone, away from the rest of the crowd. Like his uncle, he wore no hood to fend off the driving rain. Water streamed over his shoulders and long, pale brown hair. He watched Lycas and his troupe ride away, his own face frozen in a stoic sculpture that made Rhia uneasy.

In the last two years, Nilik had looked like a younger, taller version of his father, with the same animated blue-gray eyes that showed every passing emotion. Now he looked like a stranger.

"Don't despair about Raven," Marek murmured. "It could still be one of our children."

"How?"

"She might claim one of them later. I have two Spirits, why couldn't Nilik or Jula?"

"True." She looked at the bits of fox and wolf tails hanging from Marek's neck. He was the only person she'd ever known with two Spirits. "But Fox helped you survive when Wolf couldn't. I wouldn't wish your ordeal on them."

"Me, neither." Marek followed her gaze to their son. "He'll feel better once he starts training here in Tiros."

"I don't think either of our children will ever speak to me again." She jutted her chin in the direction of Jula, who was still bouncing on her toes, waving to the departing troupe.

"They can't understand," he said.

"No, they—" His words struck her as odd. "Why can't they?"

Marek didn't reply, just watched Lycas's caravan move across the plain toward the Sangian Hills.

Rhia felt as though a stone were stuck in her throat. Marek knew. Had her words revealed her secret vision of Nilik's death? All these years, she'd been so careful not to let on, to keep a Crow's most sacred confidence. She'd pretended that she was worried for Nilik's safety for all the mundane reasons. But Marek must have figured out why she insisted on keeping their son away from Velekos.

She could see her vision now, as clearly as if she were nineteen again, gazing down at a newborn Nilik.

His breath, nonexistent at first, had just started. In her exhaustion, she had reached forward with Crow magic to witness the end of his life, on a beach near Velekos, a young man dressed for battle. The waves washed his blood out to sea as Crow carried his soul to the Other Side.

As his mother wept.

Kalindos

Sura's feet were killing her—or at least, she wished they would. Death would at least stop the soreness in her thighs and backside from three days of riding.

Her pony snorted with impatience as she led him—or rather, as *he* led *her*—through the forest of pines, spruces and hickories. Judging by the overgrown path, few people traveled between Kalindos and Asermos anymore. Twice she had been forced to double back and pick up a lost trail, and even now she wasn't certain how far it was to the village. She only knew that the way was getting steeper.

The gelding snorted again and shook his head. She let a few more inches of reins slip through her hands, hoping the slack would appease him. He quieted, but his ears continued to twitch and swivel. Worried that he sensed danger, Sura scanned their surroundings for bears and cougars, seeing nothing but birds and a few squirrels. The fat, gray rodents ignored her in their haste to bury nuts under the thick carpet of needles and leaves. It made her realize how far north and how high she'd traveled: Kalindos was already edging into autumn.

She returned her focus to the ground. Left foot, right foot, she recited to herself. Left foot, right foot. Maybe the rhythm would help her forget the sensation of daggers jabbing into her soles.

The horse suddenly jerked up his chin and whinnied. She cursed—now her arm and shoulder would be sore, too.

"What is it now?" she said. "Spirits, you're a complete—"

The next word faded in her throat as she saw what stood before her on the trail.

Or rather, *who*. Three humans, the middle one tall and male with long red hair. He appeared unarmed but was flanked by two women holding taut bows with nocked arrows. All three wore trousers, vests and long-sleeved shirts that blended with the forest. Dark green paint slathered their faces.

"Who are you?" the man's voice boomed. "Stand still and answer fast. Only takes a second for them to aim and fire."

"Half a second," growled the tall blonde on his left.

Sura raised both hands, palms forward. "Don't shoot. I come from Asermos. I'm one of you."

The women snickered. "Those two statements don't match," said the shorter one. A dark brown curl flopped over her eye, and she gave an irritated jerk of her head. "We don't take refugees unless they're kin to a Kalindon."

"My stepgrandfather is Tereus the Swan."

"He's not a real Kalindon," the short woman said, "he only married one."

Sura swallowed. Her next answer could get her welcomed or killed. "My blood grandfather is—was—Razvin the Fox."

The women hissed and raised their bows to aim for her heart. "That traitor's name is poison here," said the blonde.

"Wait." The man held up his hand, and they reluctantly changed the angle of their bows, but kept them taut. "If Razvin's your grandfather," he asked Sura, "whose daughter are you?"

Sura forced the name out of her mouth. "Lycas."

Their jaws dropped, and so did the blond woman's bow.

"Lycas the Wolverine?" she said with awe. "Lycas the liberator?"

"He hasn't liberated much of anything yet," Sura muttered.

"Why should we believe you?" said the brunette. "Anyone could claim to be his child." The haughty look in her blue eyes turned Sura's mouth sour.

"I have proof." She reached for her saddlebag.

"Hold on, hold on." The man sauntered over. "Let me get it." He gave her a wink as he passed. "These two are a little jumpy today," he whispered.

"Careful, Etarek," the unpleasant one said. "She's probably lying."

"She's not lying, Daria. And *you* be careful. Stop pointing that thing at us." He glared at her, then opened the flap on the saddlebag. "What am I looking for?" he asked Sura.

"A letter from Bolan the Horse. My mother said you would trust his word." She glanced over her shoulder at the women— at their weapons in particular.

Etarek pulled out a folded piece of parchment, held shut by

a dab of blue wax shaped like a horse's head. "That's his seal."
He tucked the letter into an inside vest pocket. "Come with us."

"Aren't you going to read it?"

"We don't read." He took the reins of her horse. Sura stepped
to the other side so he could lead from the left. The blond woman
moved off the trail out of the way. The other, Daria, merely
folded her arms and stood in Sura's path.

"Care to share your name?" she said.

"Sura." She brushed past Daria, bumping her shoulder.

"Sura the what?" Daria bounced alongside her. "What Animal
are you, or is that against occupation law?"

"It is against the law, but I have one, anyway." She didn't feel
inclined to share it on demand—not with this woman, at least.

"Let me guess." Daria circled around to examine her from behind. Sura turned to watch her, and promptly tripped over a root.
Daria cackled. "Not a Cougar, that's for sure, unless you can do
this." She ran behind the horse and leaped over him lengthwise,
performing a perfect somersault in the air before landing on her
feet on the path in front of them. The gelding balked and pinned
back his ears.

"Show-off," said the other woman, who turned a friendly
smile on Sura. "I'm Kara the Wolf. Etarek's a Deer." She turned
to pat his cheek. "A dear, dear boy."

"I've never met a Deer," Sura said. "What's your magic?"

Etarek shrugged. "I hear things."

"Modest." Kara gave his shoulder a playful slap. "He hears
what isn't said. Not as words, though, not until his second phase.
But he can read people's feelings from their voices. For detect-
ing lies, he's the next best thing to an Owl."

"But a slightly better dancer." Daria smirked at him, then

turned to walk backward, examining Sura head to foot. "You're a Badger. Or a Bobcat. No, too clumsy. But definitely an Animal that can be mean. I sense that in you."

"Sense what?" Sura said. "A kindred spirit?"

Kara chortled. "Ouch. Daria, you've met your match."

Sura added, "Some of us only bite when provoked." Kara and Etarek shared a hearty laugh, while Daria just scowled at them and turned away with a *Hmmph!*

"Don't mind her," Etarek said to Sura with a smile that warmed the back of her neck. "She just doesn't like to be outnastied."

Just then the trail curved up and to the left, rounding a boulder half the size of Sura's house. About fifty paces ahead, the trees ended suddenly in front of a long, high structure.

Sura gasped. "What's that?"

"Fire ring," Etarek said. "Keeps out intruders and stops forest fires from destroying the village."

"It goes all the way around Kalindos?"

"Wouldn't be much point if it didn't," Daria said.

The ring—which stretched as far as she could see in both directions—stood at least twice her height, made of interlocking wooden slats to form a thick wall.

She looked for an opening. "How do we get through with the horse?"

Daria sighed as she withdrew a pair of thick leather gloves from her back pocket. "We have to take it apart. The boards have to be pulled out in a certain order that only we guards know."

Etarek handed the reins to Sura. "Daria's brother, Dravek, will put it back together. He's our Snake, the fire expert."

Sura sighed with relief at the thought of a possible mentor. "I'll help him."

"Please don't." Daria pulled a pair of boards from the wall and tossed them to Etarek. "I can't bear the thought of anyone making his life easier."

"No, I mean, I'll help him because I'm a Snake."

They all stared at her, especially Etarek, who fumbled the boards in his arms. They spilled onto the ground with a clatter. Kara covered her mouth and giggled.

Daria turned to Etarek. "For your sake, I hope she's nothing like Dravek."

"Hey," Kara said, "watch what you say about him around me."

"No accounting for taste." Daria tossed a slat to her.

Sura noticed an intricate pattern forming as the wood was withdrawn from the wall. The boards and limbs were notched so that it required a unique sequence of moves to dismantle it.

"How do you keep the ring from burning Kalindos?" she asked.

"There's a firebreak on the other side," Kara said, "plus a stone trench." She tossed the boards into a pile. "When the ring burns, it heats the stones, which'll stay hot long after the wood has smoldered, and singe anyone who makes it through. Not enough to kill them, but to wound, at least, and maybe make their horses balk."

"Clever."

Etarek nodded to her. "It was an Asermon Snake who thought of it. Do you know Vara?"

"I did, but she moved to Tiros before I knew I was a Snake, so I've never had a mentor."

"You've had your Bestowing, though, right?" Kara asked.

"No. It's forbidden."

"Then how do you know you're a Snake?" Etarek said.

Sura met his gaze. "I just know."

He raised his eyebrows and smiled as he turned back to the wall. Through the remaining slats, Sura saw a wide trench made of thousands of pale, fist-size stones. She wondered how her horse could maneuver over such an unstable surface.

Etarek slipped through a gap in the wall, strode several paces to their left and bent down next to a brush pile. He withdrew a wide wooden panel, which he dragged toward them, then laid across the trench as a bridge.

These Kalindons were smarter than their reputations.

Sura led the horse across the makeshift wooden bridge, which was just wide enough for the animal. "Can anyone—I mean, does anyone in Kalindos read?" she asked them.

"A few," Kara said.

"We're not stupid," Daria added. "We just have more important things to do than act like Descendants."

Sura turned to her, taking care not to twist her ankles on the rocks. "Knowing how to read and write isn't acting like a Descendant. It helps us fight them."

Daria uttered a skeptical grunt.

"You two keep patrolling," Etarek said. "I'll take her from here."

"I'm sure you will." Daria gave him a sly grin. "And get my brother out of bed so he can fix this wall."

Etarek took back the reins, and Sura let her pace lag so she could walk slightly behind him—to examine him for menace, of course. As they passed through the treeless firebreak, the late-morning sunlight glinted off his long, red ponytail. His face was obscured by the green camouflage paint, but his smile seemed genuine and a quickness sparked within his bright blue eyes.

What she noticed most was the way he walked, with his shoulders back and chin high. In the streets of Asermos, such a posture would get him beaten. The Descendants preferred Sura's people to slink.

They entered the cover of deep forest again, and her eyes strained to adjust in the shadows.

"What did Daria mean," Sura asked, "you should hope I'm nothing like Dravek?"

Etarek laughed. "You know what Snakes are known for."

Her face heated. "It's not true. I mean—not always."

"Which part, setting fires or having an unnaturally high sex drive?"

"Uh…" She pushed down her embarrassment, remembering that Kalindons were more open about these matters than Asermons.

"Just remember, it's a small village." They rounded another large boulder. "Speaking of which."

Sura had heard many tales of Kalindos, but the sight of it made her feet stop fast, her right toe clipping her left heel. She pitched forward, and Etarek grabbed her elbow to keep her from falling.

"Don't worry." He patted her shoulder. "It happens to every newcomer."

She wiped her rapidly warming cheeks and looked up. Far above her head lay a network of wooden homes, built against and even around the tree trunks. Some stood alone and some were connected by wooden bridges to other houses. Most were half the size of the home she'd lived in with her mother, but a few looked like they held several rooms. Above and to her right, a man and a woman stood together on a porch watching a young boy climb the rope ladder to their home.

Sura's neck grew stiff from looking up. She rubbed it and squinted down the main path. "Where can I find Tereus?"

"He's at the weekly Council meeting. His wife Elora's the Council leader." He handed her Bolan's letter. "I'll stable your horse, and you go to the meeting." He pointed through the trees at a small group of people gathered in a distant clearing. "Good luck."

She gave him a grateful nod and hurried off. By the time she reached the clearing, some of the people had seated themselves in a ring formed by seven flat stones. A few dozen stood on the outskirts, leaning against trees with their arms crossed, as though prepared to wait a long time.

Sura wasn't prepared to wait at all. She pushed through the crowd, ignoring their surprised gasps. Certainly she made a ragged appearance, with her disheveled clothes and mud-streaked face and hair.

When Sura reached the edge of the circle, a woman with blond-gray hair—Elora, she assumed—was standing in the center, addressing the Council. Sura stepped between two stones to enter the circle.

The woman merely blinked. "Hello. Please introduce yourself and state your business."

"My name is Sura." She heard a man behind her gasp. "My father is Lycas the Wolverine and my mother is Mali the Wasp."

The murmurs increased in volume. Several pairs of eyes shot her skeptical looks.

She pulled out Bolan's letter. "I have proof."

"I don't need proof." A man with a long gray braid moved in front of her. "I'm Tereus the Swan. Your father is my stepson." He examined her face and smiled. "It's been ten years, but I'd know those eyes anywhere, granddaughter."

She stared at him, her throat tightening. She remembered Tereus from her earliest memories—which, not coincidentally, were also her best memories.

"*I'd* like proof," said a younger Council member to her left, a lanky man with thinning light brown hair. He snatched the letter from Sura's hand and tore it open, wrinkling his nose at her. She became more aware than ever of not having bathed in four days.

"What does it say, Adrek?" asked a woman with dark red hair sitting on his other side.

He squinted at the letter for several seconds, then tossed it to the inquiring woman. "Bolan has bad handwriting."

She rolled her eyes and unfolded the letter. "It says this girl is who she says." She kept reading, then her jaw dropped. "Your mother's been captured?"

Another round of gasps, even louder.

"Come." Elora stepped aside and beckoned Sura to the circle's center. "Let everyone hear."

Sura recounted the story of Mali's arrest. Her voice cracked when she told the part about her mother's beating, but she just lifted her chin higher and kept her breath steady.

When she had finished, Tereus came to her and placed his hands on her shoulders. "I'm sorry for all you've suffered. You're among family now."

She stared into his deep blue eyes, crinkled with age and long-ago laughter. Her own eyes grew hot and blurry. She pulled away.

"Before I can help her, I need my Bestowing. I need to train to use my Snake powers."

At the mention of her Spirit, the crowd members exchanged

glances and a few cocked eyebrows. She felt like throwing a sack over her body, but she put her hands on her hips and challenged their gazes. "I need to find Dravek."

The afternoon light angled gold and silver through the pine branches as Sura made her way toward the fire ring. After meeting dozens of Kalindons—friendly and not-so-friendly—she relished having a few moments alone. Even when she'd taken a bath at Elora and Tereus's house, where she would be staying, the two had hovered outside her room, asking her questions about the situation in Asermos.

The breeze blew her clean, damp curls in front of her face. She rarely wore her hair down, but her scalp was sore after being tormented by a tight braid for four days.

She heard a rustle behind her and jerked her head to look over her shoulder. Nothing but a sparrow rooting among the pinecones for its lunch. Sura let out a deep breath, reminding herself that here, no soldiers monitored her every move.

The fire ring appeared in the distance, past the place where the trees ended. A clatter of boards told her someone was there. She put on her thin leather gloves—to protect from splinters, she told herself, knowing the gesture was actually to hide the sweat covering her palms.

What if Dravek wanted her to prove her powers? She couldn't create fire and couldn't control its spread. All she could do was extinguish it. Though she knew that many people never exhibited any magic at all before their Bestowing, her lack of skills made her feel inadequate.

A tall figure dressed in black stepped through the opening in the fire ring. He flung an armful of wood into the stone trench, then turned back through the gap without noticing her. His shoulders hunched and his fists clenched as he stomped out of sight. Her steps slowed for a moment at the sight of his menacing posture, until she reminded herself she'd faced much more dire threats in Asermos than an eighteen-year-old tantrum-tossing Snake.

Sura stood next to the trench, listening to him gather wood on the other side, muttering to himself.

"Either they're idiots, or they're trying to make my life miserable. Wouldn't put it past Daria, but Kara, what's her issue now? What have I done this time, what did I say, who did I look at for one too many moments and how long am I going to have to hear about—"

He rounded the corner of the gap, arms full of wood, and stopped short when he saw Sura.

She stared at him across the rocky trench. Her toes curled in her boots as if they could clutch the ground that seemed to sway beneath her.

Everything about him was black—his clothes, his gloves, his eyes, his short, spiky hair. Everything but his face, which was rapidly reddening.

"Sorry." He glanced back at the place he'd just come from, as if a different person had stood there. "Didn't mean for you to hear that."

"Hear—" Sura cleared her throat. "Hear what?"

A corner of his mouth twitched, and her heart squirmed in her chest.

"Right." He winked. "Sura?"

"Yes? I mean, yes. I'm Sura. And you're Dravek."

"I am. Dravek."

They stared at each other for several long moments, and she thought she saw him swallow.

She replanted her feet to maintain her balance. "Would you like some help moving the wood?"

He didn't speak or move, just stared at her, absorbing her with his dark gaze. She had the sensation of being tasted, sipped like an unfamiliar but enticing drink.

"Are you sure you're a Snake?" he said finally.

"I'm sure."

"Etarek said you haven't been Bestowed."

"Do you think I'm lying?"

"I can't tell without touching you."

She stepped back, her stomach quivering. "What do you mean?"

"When people lie, sometimes their hands get cold, but it's not foolproof. Sometimes it just means they're afraid."

"Afraid of you?"

He opened his mouth a fraction of an inch, and she could see his tongue run over the inside of his bottom teeth. "I'm a Snake, aren't I?"

She let out a deep breath and smiled. *Someone who knows what it's like to be me.*

He set the wood down on a pile to his right. "There's a bit more to gather. Come on." He held out his hand. "Watch your step."

She lurched forward, as if drawn by an invisible cord, completely failing to heed his advice. The first rock she stepped on turned over. She lost her balance and pitched forward.

With inhuman speed, he reached out and caught her arm before she could fall. A flash of heat danced around the place where they touched, flaring back and forth between them.

She blinked hard, trying to clear her head, as he raised her to her feet. Dravek took her other arm, more gently, and the hot sensation flowed stronger, smoother, like a river unfettered by twisting banks. She stared down at his gloved hands, then looked up at his face.

The forest seemed to darken around her. His black eyes reflected the sunlight, flickering like a torch. She wondered if they lit up like that in the dark.

"Come here." He drew her up and over the ridge of the trench with him until they passed outside the fire ring onto level ground. Still gripping one of her wrists, he tugged off one of his gloves with his teeth and tossed it away. Then he motioned for her to do the same.

She wanted to put her free hand behind her back, so his flesh couldn't touch it. But something told her that if she didn't give it to him, Dravek would seize it, anyway.

Without taking her eyes off his, Sura put the tip of her middle finger in her mouth. The glove tasted of pine pitch and mink oil. She withdrew her hand easily, then without hesitation, took Dravek's.

The heat spiked, and flames leaped behind her eyes.

She gasped, and the glove fell from her mouth. "What just happened?" She felt his gaze sear hers but feared to turn away, lest it burn another part of her.

"I don't know." His voice shook. "Maybe it's because we're Snakes."

"I've never met another one since I had my powers."

"Me, neither."

Their fingers intertwined, and their palms pressed together. She had to concentrate to keep her breath even and slow.

This was her Spirit-brother. She should feel as much desire

for him as she would a member of her own family. But for the first time in months, every inch of her skin felt alive.

A long moment passed, empty of words.

Finally she whispered, "Now what?"

His arm tensed, as if to pull her closer. Then he blinked rapidly and let her go. "Uh." He brushed his bare hand over his shirt, then put his glove on. "Help me. That is, you can help me put the ring back together." He unhooked a flask from his belt and held it out. "Water?"

"Thank you," she said quickly. The container was nearly full, and she took a deep draught, hoping it would cool her skin from the inside out.

She handed the flask back to him, careful not to touch his fingers. He emptied it in two long gulps. They looked at each other again, then simultaneously jerked their gazes to the ring.

Dravek cleared his throat. "First I need to bring all the wood to the interior and sort it. They left it on the wrong side and just threw it all into one pile. That's what I was griping about when you walked up." He wiped his mouth, then his forehead, which was beaded with sweat.

"I'm sure they just forgot."

"No." He shook the empty flask and frowned. "My sister loves to plague me."

"I think she loves to plague everyone."

He grinned at her, giving his face a boyish, less treacherous cast. "You picked up on that, then?"

Feeling her face flush, Sura turned to the pile of boards and put her glove back on. "But Kara seems lovely." She grasped as many boards as she could carry. "Why would she want to cause you trouble?"

He snorted and reached his long arms around the rest of the wood. "To make me call off the wedding?"

"Oh. Congratulations." Sura hoped her voice disguised her odd sense of disappointment. She made her way carefully over the rocky trench. "I heard Kalindons didn't marry anymore, that everyone just, you know—"

"Sleeps with everyone else?"

She dropped the wood on the pile. "Yes."

"Exaggeration." He chose a pair of long boards. "Mostly." He fastened the boards to the sides of the ring, then locked them together with their notches.

Sura put her hands in her pockets, for lack of any task to occupy them, and to hide her nervousness. "When's the wedding?"

"Next week. You should come. I've heard Kalindon feasts are quite an experience for outsiders." He glanced at her as he picked up another, shorter pair of boards. "Is it true that in Asermos, parties only last one night?"

"There's not much to celebrate these days."

"All the more reason to do it." He stopped and looked at her. "After the Descendants invaded, killed all our elders and stole half the population, including—" His voice tightened, and he took a breath. "Kalindos went back to the old ways. The Spirits protect us as long as we follow Their wishes."

"Which are?" She'd heard tales of Kalindon excesses.

He swept his arm toward the forest around him. "Living close to the trees. Taking care of each other, whether we share blood or not." His eyes met hers. "Indulging our appetites."

She wanted to look away but forced herself to hold his gaze. "What do appetites have to do with honoring the Spirits?"

"We give thanks for our lives by living them, every moment."

He rested the other end of his board on a rock and spun it on the tip. "We live as if life is more important than survival."

"Nothing's more important than survival. You'd know that if you lived in Asermos."

He snorted. "You have more food, more healers, no wild animals big enough to eat you. Seems to me Asermos is—"

"They've outlawed grandparents."

He stopped spinning the board. "Outlawed?"

"Last year. The Ilions are afraid of our third-phase powers. When they find out someone's pregnant, they make their parents move to Tiros." She rubbed her arms. "So women don't get pregnant anymore, or if they do, they don't stay that way."

"I hadn't heard that." He turned and shoved the board into its proper place. "I'm sorry. Guess we're pretty isolated out here. Did you tell the Council about this?"

"I told Elora."

He stopped suddenly and looked at her. "Is that the real reason they put your mother in prison? You're pregnant?"

"No," she hurried to say. "It's because of the resistance." She tugged on the tips of her gloved fingers. The topic veered too close to parts of her life she didn't want to think about, much less discuss with this strange new acquaintance.

Dravek's voice softened. "Did you leave a mate behind in Asermos?"

"Not really." She looked at the dark soil at her feet and ran her thumb over the scar beneath her shirt. "He died."

"I'm sorry." He took a step closer, so that he was almost within reach. "Descendants?"

"Of course," she said, as if no one ever died of another cause. But few had, in her memory.

Dravek inhaled as if to say something, but didn't speak, perhaps waiting for her to explain. But she couldn't, not until she trusted him with the whole truth. Anyone could be an Ilion spy, even here in Kalindos.

"Can I help you with the wall?" she asked him. "I could hand you the pieces."

He stepped back and took a breath, as if she'd released him from a spell. "It'll go faster if I do it alone." He gestured to the sloppy pile. "Every minute this gap is open, the village is vulnerable."

"Of course." She turned away. "I'll go now."

"Sura, wait."

Dravek touched her arm. Another jolt of heat seared her, stronger than before. He hissed and let go.

She stared at him. "Did that hurt?"

"No." He looked at his hand, then back at her. "You?"

"No." She examined her skin where he'd touched her. "It wasn't painful, just..." Her voice trailed off.

"Hot," he whispered.

Another flush of heat crawled over her scalp, from nape to forehead. "I really should go." *Far, far away,* she thought. *Now.*

"You could help me sort the wood." He blinked hard, then shook his head. "What am I saying? You're probably tired from your journey."

At the moment, with her blood singing and skin tingling, she felt not a shred of exhaustion. "Do you want me to stay?"

He started to shrug, then gave a crooked smile that squeezed her heart. "Yes?"

In the last of a series of arduous thrusts, Dravek finally spent himself inside Kara. She went rigid, then limp in his arms, murmuring his name in a long, laughing moan that accentuated his silence.

He rolled off her, more relieved than gratified, and made a late effort to echo her sounds of satisfaction. His own ears weren't convinced.

He looked across her sweat-streaked body at the window on the other side of his tree house. The moonlight's angle had changed since she'd arrived. "You should hurry," he told her, "or you'll be late."

She turned to face him and curled one leg around both of his. "Can't throw me out so quick once we're married."

He wiped his face and forced a smile onto it. "I can if you're still hunting. Kalindos needs to eat."

Kara turned toward the window, then gasped. "Look at the moon." She sat up and reached for her shirt. "I had no idea it was so late."

"Sorry it took me so long." Dravek slid to the edge of the bed and stood up. "I don't know what it was." He moved away from her and went to the basin of water on his dresser.

"I wouldn't normally complain," she said with a laugh. She padded to the corner where her trousers and underclothes lay in a rumpled pile. "Were you distracted?"

Dravek splashed water on his face and pretended he didn't hear her. "Hmm?"

"A bit rougher than usual. Again, I'm not complaining." She picked up her clothes and hissed a breath through her teeth. "Ow. Not complaining too much." She approached him as he dried his face and hands on a semiclean cloth. "Is something wrong?"

"Of course not." He leaned over and kissed her cheek, hoping his tone sounded cajoling instead of defensive.

She pulled away with an exasperated sigh. "Why is, 'of course not' always a man's answer to that question?"

"Because it's the wrong question to ask."

Kara yanked up her trousers, then sat on the bed to put on her socks. "I'll be more specific, then. What happened today that made you think about something besides my body?" She picked up her moccasins, then set them in her lap. "Is it another woman?" Before he could answer, she shook her head, bouncing dark blond curls against her cheeks. "No, I swore I'd never ask you that."

He held up a hand. "Stop torturing yourself, and I'll tell you." Not *everything,* of course. Absolute honesty would never be their friend. "It's Sura."

Her eyes widened, and her lower lip trembled. "But she's your Spirit-sister."

"That's not what I meant," he said, perhaps a little too hastily. "On the way home, she told me what's been happening in Asermos. Horrible things my father's people have done."

"Dravek…" Kara came forward and placed a soft hand on his chest. "Adrek's your father, not that Ilion slavemaster."

He shook his head. "Adrek raised me, and I'm grateful. But his blood doesn't flow through me like it does Daria." His fist tightened on the towel, and he wanted to rip it in two. "What flows through me is evil."

"And good, too, like every one of us." She wrapped her arms around his waist. "I'm glad you're not like Adrek and Daria. You're a lot nicer."

"I'm not nice."

"No, but you're not-nice in a much nicer way." Her hands slipped down to squeeze the sides of his hips, as she had when he'd made love to her. "Do you still want to marry me?"

His heartbeat spiked. "Why do you ask that?"

She tilted her head. "The way we got engaged wasn't completely…fair. I wouldn't blame you for feeling trapped. If you change your mind, even a minute before the wedding, I'll understand."

Her words sounded sincere, and her eyes were round and unblinking, but he could feel her skin grow cold with apprehension.

"Don't be silly. Of course I want to marry you." He gently removed her hands from his hips, where her nails were digging into his flesh. "Now stop, or I'll keep you here another hour or two."

"Won't Mother love that." Balancing on one foot at a time, she tugged on her moccasins. "It's wretched having a parent with the same Spirit."

"Daria and Adrek are both Cougars. She doesn't mind."

"Cougars hunt alone. Wolves have to hunt in packs, take orders from their leaders." She pulled her mass of curls back and began to braid her hair. "Wish I had my own pack."

"One day you will."

She gasped. "We'll go to Tiros, then, after we get married? So you can train with Vara?"

Dravek's stomach sank, though he didn't understand why. He hadn't been eager to leave Kalindos before, but now the thought filled him with dread, a dread connected to Sura.

"I can't leave now that I have an apprentice."

"But if you train with Vara, you can come back and be an even better mentor. Especially after you make the second phase." She slid her hand over her belly and put on a serene smile.

Dravek suddenly wanted to get dressed—another unusual impulse. He grabbed the closest shirt and yanked it over his head, though he suspected it was inside out. "I should at least take her for her Bestowing. There's time before the wedding." He knelt and skimmed his hands along the rug near the bed, searching for his drawers and trousers.

"Good, then." She dashed for the door. "See you tomorrow!"

He grunted a reply, still seeking the rest of his clothes and cursing his lack of night vision.

Kara put her hand on the latch, then stopped and turned slowly. "You didn't do it."

He looked up. "Do what?"

"Grab me. Every time I leave your house, you snatch me up and steal one more kiss. This time you let me go."

"Oh." His hand finally met cloth, and he pulled his trousers from under the bed. "Sorry."

She waited a moment, then turned the latch. "Good night, then."

Kara was halfway across the threshold before he darted across the room and seized her by the waist. She released a shriek of delight as he wrestled her back inside and onto his bed. He gripped her wrists and spread his body over hers.

"One more," he whispered against her lips. "So you won't forget me."

The kiss was long and languid, and soon she was squirming beneath him, her skin heating and pulsing.

Finally he scooped Kara into his arms and carried her to the porch, where he planted her back on her feet. She stumbled a little, her eyes dark and dazed with desire.

"Good night," she whispered.

He smiled at her as he shut the door.

When her footsteps reached the ladder, he let himself inhale.

When the ladder's creaks faded, he let out a long, tightly held breath. He looked down and was relieved to see that his shirt-tail hid his complete lack of arousal.

He stripped off his shirt before sinking back into bed. Kara's scent covered the pillow and blanket, but failed to stoke his passion.

Perhaps he was ill, Dravek wondered as he stared up at the pine branch that bisected his one-room tree house. He'd wanted almost every woman he'd ever met, and more than half the men. But after meeting Sura, those previous desires felt as stale as week-old bread. He craved her, inexplicably, with body and soul. The hours since they'd parted felt like endless gray days, like the ones at the end of winter.

He sat up. *No. This doesn't happen.* She was supposed to be like a sister to him.

Dravek drew both hands through his hair, rubbing his temples with the insides of his wrists. Maybe Sura wasn't really a Snake. That would explain it. If a different Spirit claimed her at the Bestowing, he'd deal with these feelings then. If Snake claimed her, he'd marry Kara and leave for Tiros. By the time he returned, either Sura or this bizarre attraction would be gone.

Anything to avoid hurting Kara. If he ever saw those beautiful blue eyes fill with tears on his account again…no, he'd felt like a monster long enough.

Dravek lay down facing the wall, determined to sleep. He closed his eyes and forced his mind to think of stones, trees, birds—anything but the image of Sura standing straight and strong before him, long black curls streaming across her face, over her neck, then falling to caress her breasts.

He shifted his body to ease the new ache in his groin, but

kept his hands under the pillow. He wouldn't touch himself and think of Sura.

That way lay a path more treacherous than any he'd ever walked. It dizzied him, like looking out over a great height, one from which he'd surely fall like a stone.

Tiros

Rhia woke suddenly, as if yanked from sleep by a rope tied around her mind. She turned to look for Marek, but he wasn't there. The morning light was brighter than when she usually woke.

She tottered into the kitchen, rubbing her sticky eyes. Jula was sitting at the table with a mug of tea that was no longer steaming. Her mud-brown hair draped over the parchment she was writing on.

"Where's your father?"

"Chickens," Jula said without looking up.

Rhia shuffled to the stove and picked up the teakettle. Some chicory would banish her yawns. "Nilik's still in bed?"

"No."

"He left early?"

"Yes."

"To go to work?"

Jula hesitated, then quietly set down her quill pen. "To go to Velekos."

A cold sensation dribbled down Rhia's spine. "That's not funny."

"I'm not laughing."

"He followed your uncle?"

"Yes."

Rhia swept a hand over her clammy forehead and fought to catch her breath. "Lycas will turn him back. He promised, unless Nilik knew the password."

"You mean, 'Hector'?"

Rhia dropped the teakettle. It bounced off the edge of the stove and clanged against the wooden floor. "What did you say?"

"I saw you and Papa talking about it, here last night."

"I never told him the password."

"No, but while you were telling him *about* the password, you picked up Hector and cuddled him. Did I guess right?"

Rhia stared at her daughter's satisfied face as the vision of Nilik's death flared in her mind. "You have no idea what you've done," she whispered.

"Yes, I do." Jula turned back to her paper. "I made Nilik happy. I let him fulfill his destiny."

"That's just it." Rhia grabbed Jula's shoulder and made her look up. "You don't know what that destiny is."

Jula shifted out of Rhia's grip. "And you do?"

"Yes!"

The color drained from Jula's face.

"I mean, no." Rhia gritted her teeth. "I don't know his destiny. I'm just afraid, that's all."

"Why didn't you tell me you knew?" Jula slid out of her chair and backed away. "Why would you let me send him away to die?" Her voice pitched higher. "How could you be so cruel?"

"You know I can't break Crow's sacred law."

"Even to save your own son?"

"I tried to save him!" She advanced on Jula. "I tried to keep him here. But you had to spite me, didn't you? You had to prove how clever you are. You don't care about Nilik's destiny, you only care about yourself."

Jula's eyes narrowed slowly. "Somebody has to care about me, because you sure don't."

"That's not true." Rhia laid a hand on her daughter's arm as gently as her anger would allow. "I love you."

Jula turned away. "I don't want the love of a freak like you."

Rhia's stomach dropped. She watched her daughter march toward the stairs to make her usual dramatic exit to her room.

The front door slammed open, and Marek strode in, blocking Jula's path. "I heard what you said to her." He jutted his thumb at the open window. "Apologize. Now."

Jula backed up and bowed her head. "I'm sorry, Papa."

"To her!" Marek roared. "If you ever speak to your mother like that again, don't bother speaking to me at all."

Jula gasped and raised wet eyes to meet his. Her lower lip trembled, and she slowly turned to Rhia. "I'm sorry, Mother. I ruined everything."

Marek's expression and voice softened. "What are you talking about, ruined everything?"

Jula looked at Rhia, who shook her head.

"Tell your father what you did."

Jula stared at the floor. "I gave Nilik the password so he could join Uncle Lycas."

Marek's face grayed as he looked at Rhia. "How did she know the password? I don't even know the password."

"She guessed."

"But—he can't go to Velekos, right? Because of—"

"Don't say it."

"Rhia, you're the one who hates keeping secrets." He looked at Jula, then back at her. "Nilik will die there, won't he?"

Rhia closed her eyes. The word *"Yes"* wouldn't come. Every bit of Crow in her kept it in. But her silence seemed to satisfy Marek.

He strode to the closet and pulled out their traveling packs. "Let's go get our son."

Sangian Hills

Nilik ran through the night.

His legs raced with unprecedented strength and speed, devouring the dusty miles. His arms pumped to drive him along, and he wished he could run on all four limbs like his Spirit's real-life counterpart.

He let his lungs expand, savoring the new Wolverine power. He'd never felt weak or fragile, but compared to now, the man of just ten days ago was little more than a mouse. So what if Raven had passed him by? He wouldn't trade this feeling for anything.

Especially now. When his legs began to ache from the hours of running, he only had to think of Lania's face lit with laughter, or her long red curls blazing in the sunset. And then think of how her killers' necks would feel, shattered between his hands.

They'd called her a Wasp, said she'd turned on them in a fury. But Nilik knew from the beauty she molded out of scraps of cloth and clay that Lania was—would have been—a Spider woman, an artist. She'd felt the unmistakable calling since they were children.

Trees blocked the bright moonlight as he entered a steeply sloped ravine. The tracks of Lycas's team led down a gentle trail to his left, no doubt because of the pack horses, which meant Nilik could make up ground by climbing straight down and up the other side of the ravine. Maybe he'd even catch them before the end of the night. Then on to Velekos, and vengeance.

He clambered down the steep wall, grasping rocks and shrubs to keep from falling into the streambed. By the time he reached the bottom, his knees ached from the strain, and his strength was beginning to ebb. Wolverines weren't made for climbing, he reminded himself.

The stream was nearly dry, unusual even for this time of year. Everything seemed to be dying. It was as if the presence of the Ilions had made the land lose its will to live.

A short hop took him over the stream, and after a moment to catch his breath, Nilik climbed, letting the memories stoke his strength.

He'd wrangled every detail of Lania's death out of his uncle, horrors Lycas hadn't told the rest of the family. The Descendant monsters had strewn parts of her body all around Velekos, displaying them on street corners. At the entrance to her own neighborhood, the Acrosia, the place where the revolution was coming to a boil, her head had been placed on a pike.

Nilik's foot slipped. His hands scrabbled for a grip but seized only loose soil. He slid several feet before a jutting stone knocked him off balance, backward into nothing.

He yelped, anticipating the bone-crushing impact on the streambed. But as he fell, his body took over, twisting and bending by instinct, then relaxing just before the ground slammed into him.

Nilik stared at the damp soil beneath his face. Nothing hurt. Last month such a fall would have broken his limbs, maybe even killed him.

Kneeling on all fours, struggling for breath, he thought of Lania. No one knew what they'd meant to each other. No one knew how a year ago, on her family's last visit, they'd stolen three hours alone in the drafty tent of one of his friends. No one knew how Nilik had begged her to stay in Tiros where it was safe, how he'd sworn to marry her after their Bestowings.

He pressed his forehead into the mud. They hadn't made love, though they'd come close. Now he regretted stopping, regretted his stupid assumption that someday they'd have another chance, another time when he could make it perfect for her.

He thought of the pale, freckled skin on Lania's shoulders, the gleam in her green eyes as she'd touched him and held him with the urgency of the besieged. The Descendants had carved that skin and extinguished that gleam forever.

Nilik's fingers dug deep into the soil, and he swallowed a shriek of anguish. They would pay. If it took his last breath, they would pay.

He got to his feet, stretching cautiously, feeling for sprains or wounds from the fall. Nothing. He checked his dagger belt to make sure his weapons were fastened into their sheaths.

As he passed his hand over the hilt of each blade, a surge of power coursed through him. Wolverine had altered more than Nilik's body. His mind was now calmed only by thoughts of cutting, twisting, ripping. The bloodlust was like a constant tang on the back of his tongue.

This time instead of climbing the rocks, he loped up the path, following the trail of Lycas's troupe.

Hundreds of steps later, he reached the top of the ravine, panting. He stumbled as he stepped onto the flat land, and he longed to sink down and rest his screaming legs.

"Halt!"

Nilik froze at the sound of the unfamiliar voice from above.

"Put your hands over your head," the voice boomed. "Now!"

Nilik hesitated. With his new strength, he could take on several Descendant soldiers, but not without his weapons. He raised one hand over his head, while letting the other drift past his dagger belt. His thumb opened the clasp that held his favorite blade, the one Lycas had given him last year, as if he'd known they would someday be Spirit-brothers.

One thing was for certain: he wouldn't be taken alive.

Standing in the tree's shadow, he could hide his movement from weak Descendant eyes. His fingers slipped around the hilt.

"I saw that." The voice took on a new edge. "Step forward, hands up—both of them—or you'll be shot."

Shot? Descendants didn't use bows and arrows; they thought the weapons were cowardly, womanly, without honor.

Nilik raised his other palm and walked out from under the trees. A rocky ridge loomed before him, a dark mass against the starry sky.

"Nilik?" came another, older voice. "What are you doing here?"

He let out a breath. Uncle Lycas.

"Hector!" Nilik shouted, hoping Jula had guessed the password correctly.

A short silence followed, then Lycas called, "Stay. I'll come down."

While he waited for his uncle to appear, Nilik fought to steady his breath. If his sister had misled him, he'd be in for a long, possibly unconscious ride home to Tiros. At the top of the ridge, two archers stood with their arrows trained upon him, no doubt suspecting him of being a decoy.

Finally Lycas appeared from a hidden trail at the bottom of the ridge. Behind him strode a slightly younger man with a dark, thick beard and the same carved wolverine claw that hung around Lycas's and Nilik's necks.

"I thought your mother wouldn't let you go." Lycas handed Nilik a water skin.

Nilik took a deep draught and wiped the sweat from his face. "I knew the password, didn't I?"

Lycas grinned and raised his arms as if to embrace Nilik, then seemed to reconsider. He turned to the other man. "This is Sirin, my executive officer and second-in-command."

Nilik bowed, feeling his calves and hamstrings quiver at the strain. "It's an honor."

Sirin examined him, then nodded and returned the bow. "Welcome to our band of bandits."

"Bandits?" Nilik furrowed his brow at Lycas. "What's he mean?"

"It's what the Ilions call us. They won't recognize a rebellion, because that would admit weakness, so they treat us like criminals, even though we've never attacked a civilian."

"Thugs, they also call us." Sirin scratched his chin. "What's the other one I like?"

"Hooligans," Lycas added. "Ruffians."

"Brigands." Sirin snapped his fingers. "That's my favorite. I'd never even heard that word before I found out I was one."

Lycas gestured for them to follow him up the ridge. "It serves us well," he said to Nilik. "They won't deploy enough soldiers against us to do the job right, because that would mean we were a threat. They send just enough men to donate arms and horses to our cause."

"And uniforms," Sirin added. "Which make good disguises once the blood's washed out."

Nilik chuckled, then realized Sirin wasn't joking. He feigned a cough to cover his embarrassment.

Lycas glanced back at them. "Now it's to the point where even if they tried a major military operation to stop us, we'd still likely win. We fight on uneven terrain where their horses are useless, we wait in ambush instead of marching in the open like idiots, we fight at night or in bad weather whenever possible. Above all, we're not afraid to retreat."

"I don't understand," Nilik admitted, his mind as tired as his legs.

Lycas paused on a level part of the trail and waited for them to catch up. "We're not fighting the same kind of war as the Ilions. They're still locked into notions of a warrior's honor and glory. We have no honor except loyalty to the cause, no glory other than survival."

Nilik made a frustrated noise in his throat. "Then how are we ever going to win?"

"Listen to me." Lycas put his hands on Nilik's shoulders. "We don't need to win. We need to not lose." He cut off Nilik's scoff with a light shake. "Let me finish."

Chastised, Nilik sobered his face. "Sorry. Go on."

"Imagine a dog. That dog has one flea. Is it in any danger?" Nilik shook his head, and Lycas continued. "Now imagine that same dog with a hundred fleas." He tightened his grip on Nilik's shoulders. "A thousand fleas."

Nilik resisted the urge to scratch his own arms at the thought.

"A dog with a thousand fleas," Lycas said, "is bleeding to death, little by little. The fleas can't kill it directly, but they can drive it mad. It thinks about nothing but scratching and biting its own skin. Can a dog kill a flea by scratching?"

Nilik shrugged. "No. The flea just jumps to another part of the dog."

"Exactly." Lycas let go of him. "We're the fleas. Not a glorious image, but it's the only way we can stand against their superior numbers and arms."

"So we just annoy them into ending the occupation?" Nilik tried to sound sincere instead of obnoxious.

"Even a thousand fleas can't kill a dog," Lycas said patiently. "But one day, when it has a disease, or a wound, it'll be too weak to survive." He smiled. "We will have sucked too much blood."

"So what's the disease?" Nilik asked. "What's the wound?"

"The disease is in Asermos, where our people have resisted the occupation since its first days. They've turned the Ilions into unwilling tyrants. Martial law is expensive, not to mention a political disaster." He turned back to the path. "The wound, I hope, will be in Velekos."

They continued up the ridge in silence. Nilik burned to inflict that wound, and a thousand others, on the Ilion army who had taken his home, enslaved his father and murdered the woman he loved.

* * *

Lycas watched Nilik across the campfire and wished the boy were anywhere else. Any*thing* else.

He didn't care so much that Raven hadn't come for his nephew—Lycas had never put much stock in prophecies, or anything else he couldn't see and touch. But why not Hawk or Horse or Fox? Lycas would have been happy for any other Guardian Spirit to claim Nilik, as long as it wasn't one of the warriors, Bear or his own Wolverine. The thought of watching his nephew die in battle made the blood pound behind Lycas's eyes.

His fingers twitched at the memory of his own twin's death and the moments afterward. The look of agony on Nilo's face, fading to blank. Then a skull crumbling in Lycas's hands like an eggshell, brains oozing between his knuckles onto the blood-slicked battleground. The scream of Nilo's killer rising to a higher pitch than a man should be capable of, only to be cut short when his throat left his body. Lycas's sole regret was that he could only kill the Descendant soldier once.

He couldn't remember the rest of that afternoon, but others said he'd gone mad with grief and fury, savaging the enemy, both the living and the dead. He wished he could remember. It would have been a good memory.

Lycas studied Nilik's face as the young man focused on the words and plans of his new platoon leader, a first-phase but battle-tested Bear from Velekos. In the old days, Bears tended to be in charge of strategy, while Wolverines made up the masses of troops. But in this sort of warfare, a Wolverine's wiliness could take a man further in the army than a Bear's meticulous planning.

Lycas sighed. Though he wished it weren't so, Nilik had all the attributes of a Wolverine—intelligence, discipline and courage that teetered just on the sane side of recklessness. Spirits knew he had the will to fight—maybe too much.

Sirin approached and sat next to Lycas, balancing two plates of food in one hand while he unscrewed the top of a water flask with the thumb of the other. "I can't get used to seeing you clean-shaven, my friend. Almost didn't recognize you when you got here yesterday." He rubbed his own dark brown beard, which was thick and ragged from months in the wilderness.

Lycas accepted the extra plate and spoke without taking his eyes off Nilik. "Can you use him here?"

"Your nephew? I thought you were bringing him to the camp near Velekos."

"I'd rather not." He couldn't explain why, not even to himself. Nilik knew the password, but Rhia had been so adamant about keeping him in Tiros.

Sirin examined Nilik as he gnawed a strip of dried venison. "What experience has he got?"

"Basic weapons? Some. Mountain warfare? None. But you always say, the greener they come, the easier they are to train."

Sirin grimaced and scratched the back of his neck. "I'm up to my ears in recruits."

"Success will do that."

"Every company in the battalion is full. More recruits means we have to add a fourth company. That would put us at regiment strength, which adds a whole other level of command that we can't handle."

Lycas took the water flask. "You can handle it."

"We've got problems with discipline, training. Half the Bears leading these platoons couldn't persuade a dog to lick its own balls. Then there are the logistical issues."

"None of which will be made worse by taking Nilik."

Sirin let out a harsh sigh, then lowered his voice. "I thought the whole point of Nilik being here was to go to Velekos, find the thugs who killed that girl. He's a motivated fighter."

"Too motivated. His thirst for vengeance will make him careless."

"It sure hasn't hurt *your* judgment."

Slowly Lycas turned his gaze on his executive officer. Though his eyes were narrowed in contemplation of Sirin's words, the younger Wolverine took it as a glare of intimidation.

Sirin glanced away, cowed. "As you wish, sir. I'll reassign him before you leave tomorrow."

"Thank you, as always, for your candor." Lycas made himself add, "This time it worked."

Sirin cocked his head. "So you don't want me to reassign Nilik?"

"I'll take him to Velekos and train him myself. You were right."

"I was?" Sirin blinked rapidly. "Wait. Explain this, so I can remember it for future reference, and so I know I'm not hallucinating."

"I wanted you to keep Nilik here so I wouldn't have to watch him die like my brother. That's a bad way to make a decision." He took a gulp of water and handed back the flask, already missing the taste of Tiron bitter ale. "Besides, you're in charge of personnel. I trust your advice."

Sirin chuckled. "A year ago, you would've pounded my face into the dust for questioning you. You're getting old, Lycas."

"I think the word is *wise.*"

From behind them came the slap of small boots against stone. Lycas turned to see Sani, the third-phase Eagle woman he'd brought from Tiros as a lookout.

"Sir, Ilion soldiers," she said. "Twenty men, plus an officer on horseback."

Lycas hurried to the eastern edge of the ridge, Sirin and Sani on his heels. He squinted at the dusky rolling hills that lay between here and Asermos. Though gifted with excellent night vision, he couldn't discern details at such a distance.

"Are they headed this way?" Lycas asked Sani.

"No, they're passing south to north, far enough there's no way they can see us." She shoved the strands of gray-brown hair out of her pale face and focused on the passing Ilions. "Looks like they're on the road to Tiros, probably to the northwest garrison."

"Twenty-one, you said."

"Correct, sir."

He tallied up the number of fighters at his and Sirin's disposal. They were nearly equally matched with the Ilions, not even counting the Tirons Lycas had brought.

"Release the bait," he told Sani.

When she was gone, he turned to see Nilik approach.

"Descendants?" his nephew asked him. "Coming here?"

"Maybe. Our archers will drop them, but it's up to us to finish them off, up close." He put a hand on Nilik's shoulder. "If you need to debrief afterward, come to me."

Nilik swallowed, and Lycas knew immediately that the boy had never killed before. He nodded and choked out a, "Thank you, sir."

A Cougar hurried to the farthest edge of the ridge to their right, a flaming arrow nocked in his longbow. A sheet of parchment fluttered, attached to the shaft.

The arrow arced across the darkening sky like a meteor, leaving a green afterglow on Lycas's vision. It would only land halfway to the Ilion soldiers, but they might come to investigate it. When they did, they'd find a note with nothing but Lycas's initial in bold blue paint next to a Wolverine paw print.

"Few can resist," Sirin told Nilik. "Junior officers are so ambitious." He turned to Lycas. "I can only imagine what reward they'd receive for capturing or killing you."

"Or you."

"Pah. I'd be a consolation prize." He shifted his shoulders. "By the way, the bait worked while you were in Tiros, so at least the lower-level Ilion commanders believed you never left the hills."

"Good."

Lycas had no desire to be a celebrity. But by fixating on him, the Descendants spent all their energy trying to find and defeat one person. He understood what the Ilions did not: that his death would make no difference.

It wasn't *his* revolution, after all. It was everyone's.

Kalindos

"Forgive my bluntness, but who died?"

Dravek didn't answer right away, which made Sura even more nervous. They were approaching a clearing about an hour's walk from Kalindos, a clearing filled with hundreds of boulders of all sizes. They looked as if they had rolled there centuries before, gathering for a great boulder meeting that had never adjourned. On the other side of the field loomed the gray-brown ridges of Mount Beros.

As he walked, Dravek juggled two short torches, which unfortunately were lit. When they reached the edge of the clearing, Dravek stepped out onto the closest boulder, tossed the last torch high in the air and caught it behind his back.

"No one died," he said.

"Then why is your hair so short?"

"I work with fire." He shoved the unlit end of one torch into a chest-high hollow post between two boulders. "Prefer to keep the flames from engulfing my head."

She stepped onto the flattest stone she could find and set down the pack he'd given her to carry. "You could wear it long, just tie it back."

"I think it looks good like this." He ran a hand over his head in both directions. The short strands sprang back into place. "Don't you?"

His smile almost made her lose her balance as she shifted to the next stone.

"You shouldn't cut your hair unless someone's died. It's a sacred privilege, not a matter of vanity."

"Don't assume you know all about me." He crossed over several boulders to where the other hollow post stood. He inserted the torch, then pointed to a flat boulder halfway between the two flames. "Let's sit."

She made her way over to join him, stepping carefully to keep her balance so he wouldn't touch her again. They weren't wearing gloves today, and the thought of his skin against hers did not enhance her concentration.

They sat cross-legged on the rock, facing each other.

"Let's see if you're really a Snake." He nodded at the torch to his left. "Make that one flare."

"I can't. All I can do is snuff." A nervous laugh escaped her throat. "I'm just a lowly snuffer."

He smirked. "Then show me how you snuff."

Sura swallowed hard, then with no small effort, tore her gaze from him and stood to face the torch. She cupped her hands around her mouth, forming a tunnel that she aimed at the base of the flame. Her mind brought forth an image of a wet blanket descending, wrapping, smothering.

She sucked in a hard breath, and the torch snuffed out.

Sura feigned nonchalance as she turned back to Dravek, her limbs tingling with the torch's heat.

"Good," he said. "Now try it again without looking."

The flame burst forth from the end of the torch. She gasped. His eyes had never left her face, nor had he given the slightest twitch.

"How did you do that?"

"With my mind," he said, "the way you'll learn to do."

"But I thought Snakes could only *control* fire, not make it out of nothing."

"It wasn't out of nothing. The torch was still hot, so I just brought it back to life. Now try it again without looking."

Sura set her jaw and faced the torch again, this time with her eyes shut. Her mind reached out, calculating the distance, trying to see the flame's position.

"No need to scrunch up your face," Dravek said.

"Shh. I'm trying to see it."

She heard the rustle of his clothes as he stood and drew near. The heat under her skin continued to build.

"Don't try to see it." His whisper caressed the top of her ear. "Just feel it."

She shifted away a few inches and extended her hand toward the torch. "I can't."

"I'll help you." Touching her waist, he turned her around. She drew in a sharp breath and reached for his arms to steady herself.

"I won't let you fall." He turned her in place, spinning her slowly one way, then the other, until she no longer knew which way was which. "And no using the sun to get your bearings…" He covered her eyes with his palm and began to turn with her. She let her body relax against his, surrendering to this disorienting dance.

After a few more rotations, Dravek held her still, his hand over her eyes. "Try it now, Sura. If you're really a Snake, you should feel the fire wherever it is. It calls to you."

She settled her mind, noticing how cool his hand felt against her brows and the bridge of her nose. Perhaps he had released his own heat by reigniting the torch a minute ago. She wanted do the same, to stop the burning within that begged her to reach for him, to do the wrongest thing in the world.

She drew a deep breath, and the fire appeared in her mind—not as an orange flame dancing in the breeze, but as a pulsing white core of heat. It wanted to be inside her, swallowed and consumed like prey. She coiled her awareness around it and squeezed, gently but without mercy. The fire sighed as it died.

"Yes," Dravek breathed. "Now bring it back."

"I can't."

"You can. Quickly, before the torch cools. Let the heat flow back all at once. Count to three and then release."

"One," Sura said under her breath. The heat twitched within her, wanting to take form in flame again. If she didn't send it out, it would devour her.

"Two," she whispered. Dravek was right. It would be easy. Make it burn.

An image slammed her mind, the one she'd been fighting all morning, the one that Dravek's intoxicating presence had banished for a few moments.

An Asermon farm, burning. Flames licking the thatched roof, ripping it, until it collapsed on the shrieking people within.

She tightened her mental grip on the torch's embers, smothering them to cold hard nothingness.

Dravek let her go. "You almost had it. What happened?"

She tried to speak, but the heat seared her lungs so that she couldn't even catch a breath. She bent over and gripped her knees.

Dravek reached for her.

"Don't touch me!" she choked.

"You're burning up," he said. "If you don't let it out, it'll hurt you."

"I can handle it." She sat down hard on the boulder. Red circles danced before her eyes.

Dravek knelt beside her. "You don't have to handle it." He took her wrist. "Give it to me."

As if he'd opened the spout of a well pump, the heat rushed from every part of her body, down her arm toward the place where they touched. He gasped and went rigid. His eyes bulged, showing more white than black.

"What's wrong?" She tried to pull her arm out of his grip, which had tightened like a muskrat trap. "Dravek?"

A sudden sweeping *whoosh!* came from behind her. She turned to see the extinguished torch flare toward the sky. The flame reached higher than the tallest tree, its core shining with blue-white heat.

Dravek let go of her wrist and collapsed on the boulder. Sweat soaked his scarlet face, which was quickly paling.

The torch cracked in half, then toppled over onto the rocks. They watched in silence as it slowly burned itself out, the ashes falling in clumps and scattering across the rock in the steady breeze.

"Did we do that?" she whispered, though she knew the answer.

Dravek sat up slowly, turning away from her. He put his head in his hands and murmured, "There must be a reason for this."

She looked at the broken torch. "We made a lot of heat."

"It was you," he said. "I was just channeling it."

"But if I took the heat from the first torch and gave it to you, then the second flame should have only been twice as big. But it was easily ten times the size. That means we multiply each other's powers, not add to them. But why?"

"Why," Dravek whispered, but didn't answer or even look at her. Finally he let out a long breath before getting to his feet. He stepped over the boulders until he reached the broken torch. She watched him bend down next to the foot-long piece of wood, watched the muscles of his back shift as he reached forward to grasp it, watched his long fingers curl around the splintered shaft.

Sura knew she shouldn't stare. He was another woman's mate. He was her mentor. Most of all, he was her Spirit-brother. But her eyes refused to blink as he lifted the torch and brought his other hand toward it.

The flame burst forth, small and orange and controlled again. His shoulders relaxed, as if he'd just released a great source of tension.

Dravek turned to her. "I think you're a Snake. But it's not up to me." He stepped to the next boulder and pulled a small pack out of the one they'd brought. "Here's everything you need."

"For what?"

"Your Bestowing. A change of clothes, a few blankets, a bit of food and water to break your fast in three days, before you return."

"My Bestowing?" She stood up and almost backed off the side of the boulder. "Now? Where?"

He looked at Mount Beros, then back at her. "The sooner you go, the sooner you'll have full control of your powers, and the sooner you can help your mother."

"But—"

"I'm leaving," he said. "After the wedding, Kara and I are moving to Tiros. You and I don't have much time together." He looked away, then back at her. "To train."

Sura hid her flinch at this news. "I didn't know that." She climbed up onto his boulder and took the pack from his hand. "Where on the mountain do I go?"

"Just keep walking until you find the place that feels right."

I already have, she thought, and wanted to slap herself. She slung the pack over her shoulder. "Dravek, what if I'm not a Snake?" She attempted a smile. "Can we still be friends?"

His gaze was deadly serious as he moved closer. "If you're not a Snake…" Dravek touched her cheek with the barest tip of his fingers. "We can be anything you want."

08

Sangian Hills

"I think I've finally got it," Marek said, rustling the papers behind Rhia as they rode south on their journey from Tiros. "Alanka's son's a crafty one when it comes to code. A Fox after my own heart."

"Read it, read it." Rhia had been eager to hear the latest news from Alanka. She hadn't seen her sister in almost twenty years, since she and her husband Filip had decided to stay in Ilios to complete the rescue of nearly two hundred captured Kalindons scattered across the nation. Letters came once a year at the most. Rhia had tried not to pester Marek every night this week during his painstaking code interpretation.

He cleared his throat. "'Dear everyone, I hope this finds you well and happy, as much as can be expected. Filip and I are thrilled to be grandparents, though I torment him by disappearing and reappearing when he's trying to give a speech. The people here in Ilios think it's fun, though. All the political talk and military efforts by Filip and Kiril don't impress people nearly as much as a third-phase Wolf's invisibility. Hee-hee.'"

Rhia smiled, though she missed her sister so much it hurt. She wondered if the landscape in that part of Ilios were anything like the red-brown hills they rode through now. She found it ironic that the more remote sections of Ilios were freer than Asermos and Velekos when it came to practicing magic.

"'As you might have heard,'" Marek continued reading, "'we've sent most of the surviving Kalindon captives back home to the Reawakened lands. Once the Ilions found out the children in the army camp didn't develop magic no matter how deep the wilderness, they started selling them off at slave auctions. It felt strange to purchase people I used to baby-sit, but at least they're free now.'"

"Why do you think they don't develop powers?" Rhia asked Marek.

"Maybe the Spirits won't give magic to those who'd use it against us. Let me finish before I get motion sick." He flipped a page. "'Arcas and Koli send their love. They finally had a child after all these years of trying. I call her my little sunbeam. I'd never tell my own children this, but I secretly always hoped one of them would have Filip's blond hair instead of taking after my—'" Marek cut himself off. "What's that smell?"

"Is that part of the letter?"

"No. Stop for a moment." He slid off the horse's back and rushed around the next bend in the trail.

"What is it?" She rode forward and turned the corner. "What did you—" The stench hit her nose, an odor she knew all too well.

Rhia urged the horse to the edge of the ridge and looked out upon the sort of slaughter that could only be the work of her brother.

And now her son, she realized with a thudding heart.

A platoon of Descendants lay in the wide ravine. The late-morning sun revealed not even a twitch of life. A sea of vultures, ravens and crows shared a macabre feast.

She dismounted slowly, her body weighted with dread.

"No," Marek said. "Let's move on. There's nothing you can do here."

"I have a duty to the dead."

"It's not safe." His eyes narrowed at the bodies. "Besides, they're just Descendants."

"They're all the same to Crow."

Marek scoffed. "I wish I could be so broad-minded." He pointed back into the ravine. "I hear a stream that way. I'll water the horse while you're taking care of the enemy." He jerked the reins out of her hand.

She sighed as she watched him lead the horse away. His treatment in Ilion captivity had hardened his heart against them. She couldn't blame him. It was all she could do herself not to walk away and leave the soldiers to the scavengers.

As she neared the scene of battle, the birds took flight in a rush of thumping wings. The ravens and crows alighted on the rocky outcrops and trees of the hill, while the vultures glided in the sky above, biding their time until their meal resumed. Rhia stepped carefully among the bodies, checking for signs of life. Though she had no healing magic, her mother had taught her first aid, and she'd unfortunately had many occasions to whet that skill.

All twenty corpses wore the scarlet-and-yellow uniform of the Descendants. Though many had round red arrow wounds in their arms and legs, and a few appeared to have sword slashes in their sides, every throat was slit from ear to ear. Each had died in his enemy's embrace.

In the center of the carnage lay a Descendant flag. Its red-and-yellow tatters fluttered in the wind. As she knelt to examine it, she caught the distinct scent of human urine.

She wrinkled her nose. "Lycas, was that necessary?"

Perhaps it was. She'd never understand a warrior's mind, never grasp the need to turn the enemy into something less than human. When she released their souls to Crow, He gladly accepted each one.

As the vultures' shadows swept the ground, Rhia walked the area's perimeter in search of more clues.

A mass of footprints led south toward Velekos, including sets of hoofprints with boot prints beside them, as if someone were leading the horses at a leisurely pace. Probably Lycas's troupe on their way to Velekos. More footprints led west, deeper into the hills—Sirin's fighters returning to the guerrilla headquarters.

She quickened her pace, reaching the eastern end of the perimeter. What she saw stopped her breath.

A set of horse tracks pointed east, toward Asermos. They were deep and widely spaced as if the animal were running.

Rhia quickly knelt beside the first body and murmured the prayer of passage. When Marek appeared with the pony, she called out to him.

"Keep a listen to the east. A horse ran away."

"We should leave now."

Fear tugged at her. If a Descendant had escaped on that horse, he could return with reinforcements. But it wouldn't be the first time she'd risked her life for her Crow duties.

"Just a few more minutes," she told Marek.

When she had said a prayer over each body, she found a clean spot in the center of the bloodbath—away from the flag—and knelt to call the crows. Before closing her eyes, she glanced at Marek. His own eyes were blank as he tuned his mind to his better senses of hearing and scent.

The crows came at once, circling the sky, one for each dead. Their rasping, croaking voices filled her mind, creating a whirlwind of sound. She sank into it, feeling the presence of Crow flow through her.

Marek's voice reached through the cacophony. He was the best part of her real life, but these moments between worlds were precious to her.

"Rhia!" He shook her shoulder hard, jolting her out of the reverie.

"What? What?" She wiped her face with her sleeve and looked up into his wide gray eyes.

"Call them off." Marek took her elbow and hauled her to her feet. "I hear something."

She waved her arms at the birds. "Go!" They dispersed with a few stray grok!s, returning to the hillside.

In the crows' silence came the sound of many hooves.

She turned to dash for their horse, but Marek grabbed her.

"They'll catch us if we run," he said. "We have to hide."

"We can't hide our horse."

"We'll send him home."

He stuffed Alanka's letter into their saddlebag as Rhia tied the reins in a knot so the horse wouldn't trip on them.

"Yahh!" Together they smacked the horse's rump, and he took off in the direction of Tiros.

Marek grabbed her hand, and they dashed deeper into the ravine. The rock walls echoed with approaching hooves, making it sound as if they were being chased by hundreds.

They came to a dead end, with nowhere to go but up. As they climbed the ridge's steep trail, the hooves silenced. The Descendants had found the massacre.

Rhia and Marek reached a flat part of the ridge. They dropped to their bellies and peered over the edge at the new Ilion platoon.

Most of the soldiers were caring for their dead—wrapping them and placing them on skids, which were being attached to the horses. From a distance, their sad, heavy postures made them look like any other men in mourning. One knelt next to his fallen comrade, face turned down but palms to the sky.

"He's praying," she whispered.

Marek followed her gaze. "To Xenia, the death goddess."

"Look." She pointed to a pair of soldiers who were studying the tracks of their horse. "Maybe they'll think we went back to Tiros."

One of the soldiers called over several more, and they all headed into the ravine, fully armed, following what must be fresh footprints. Marek cursed and pulled Rhia to her feet. They ran.

The trail twisted and narrowed as it climbed the hill, which provided no caves or crevices for shelter.

They rounded the corner of a large red rock wall, and the trail suddenly shrank to a narrow ledge. Rhia skidded, nearly slipping over the edge of the cliff. Marek grabbed her around the waist. Panting, she peered into an enclosed ravine at least twenty feet deep.

"Careful." He stepped sideways along the ledge, his back to the cliff. "Don't look down."

Rhia heard voices on the trail behind them. She took a deep breath and followed Marek, keeping her eyes on him and the other edge of the ravine, where the trail widened.

She reached the other side and gave a heavy exhale. Marek took her hand.

They rushed around the next bend, and her heart sank.

A dead end.

Marek swept aside the branches of a thick bush. "Get down."

"There's no room for you."

"Doesn't matter." He pushed her, gently but firmly, inside the shrub. "Whatever happens, don't make a sound."

She shook her head. "You can use your Fox camouflage."

"If I hide, they'll find you. They've seen our footprints. They know there are two of us."

"Then what good does it do me to hide?"

"So you'll be out of the way while I kill them." He put his fingers to her lips. "They won't take me alive."

She clutched his hand and held back a sob. "Don't do this."

Marek kissed her softly. "I love you."

He stood, unstrapped the bow from his back and moved the hunting knife in his boot to the back of his waistband.

Rhia shrank back into the brush and waited.

With a rush of feet and clanging swords, the Descendants appeared. She heard the wooden squeak of a bow stretched taut.

"Get out," Marek snarled to them. "This is your one warning."

"Throw down your weapon!" one of the soldiers yelled.

A snap, then a whistle, and someone gave a strangled yelp.

"That *was* your one warning," Marek said.

Someone shouted the order to charge. Marek's bow snapped again and again, but Rhia heard only the thump of arrows hitting shields as the soldiers advanced.

He backed up until his feet were next to the bush where Rhia hid. The soldiers were almost upon him. She wouldn't let them take him from her again.

Just as she was preparing to leap out and shove his attackers into thin air, one of Marek's heels slipped. He backpedaled, kicking up dust and small stones, then tumbled over the edge of the ravine. His scream lengthened and faded, cut off by a sickening thud.

Her heart slammed to a halt. No sound came from below.

No. He couldn't be dead. Not Marek.

She clutched her hair and held in her shriek, longing to hurl herself over the edge, to join Marek forever on the Other Side. Her heart demanded it, but her legs remained frozen in place, the weight of the silence crushing her into the hard, cold earth.

Rhia opened her eyes. *The silence.*

She listened with the depths of her soul, but heard no wings. Crow wasn't coming.

Marek was alive.

"Is he dead?" one of the soldiers said.

"You two, go find out," said another with a commanding voice. "If he's alive, he'll have information."

"Sergeant, there's no way down except jumping off the edge ourselves."

A pair of feet came close to the bush, boot toes brushing the bottom leaves. "The tracks stop here."

The branches swept back, and Rhia stared up at the face of a blue-eyed soldier.

"Look what I found." He gave her a satisfied smile, then grasped her under the armpits and yanked her from the bush. He dragged her to the edge of the ridge and dumped her on her knees.

"No!" she shrieked when she saw Marek lying sprawled on the rocks below. He looked so lifeless, she didn't have to fake her fear.

She spit on the boots of the closest Descendants. "Murderers!"

Another man seized her braid and yanked her head back. "How do you know he's dead?" His voice belonged to the one they'd called "Sergeant."

She tugged the crow feather out of the front of her shirt. "I hear Him fly."

The sergeant let go of her and twisted his well-lined face. "Filthy beast. We'll take her instead."

Someone yanked Rhia's hands behind her and bound them with a rope.

A younger soldier with a boyish face said, "Sergeant, you still want us to get the body?"

The sergeant peered over the edge. "Might as well let the crows take care of him." He nudged Rhia with the tip of his boot. "It's not worth the risk now that we've got this one."

She started to weep, repeating Marek's name through her tears to reinforce the lie of his death.

They led her down the rocky path toward the rest of the troupe, two of them carrying their wounded comrade, the one Marek had shot in the knee. Rhia struggled against her bindings enough to be convincing, but not enough to slow them down. The sooner they could leave, the sooner Marek could return to Tiros and get help.

Assuming he could walk. Assuming he ever woke up. Her

eyes overflowed again, and genuine tears dripped in streams off her chin.

They led Rhia to a tall, thin Ilion who was supervising the transport of the dead. The sergeant gave the officer a brief salute.

"Sir." He pushed Rhia forward. "We found this one. And a man with a hunting bow, but he fell and died. Extracting him would have been too treacherous, in my judgment."

The officer raked a skeptical glare over the sergeant. "Indeed. We wouldn't want anyone getting hurt now, would we?" He gestured to the mass of corpses behind them.

"As you say, sir," the sergeant replied with a clenched jaw.

The officer glanced at Rhia, then stopped to examine her. He stepped up and yanked her feather fetish so hard the leather chain bit into her skin.

"Those crows we saw," he whispered. "Circling, not landing to feast." His gaze on her softened. "You were guiding home the souls of our men?"

She nodded.

He struck her hard across the face. A sharp pain stabbed her neck as it snapped back, and red sparks danced across her vision.

The officer loomed over her, eyes tight with fury. "It's not enough you people have to slaughter us, piss on our flag? You have to desecrate our dead, too? Curse them to an eternity of emptiness with your Spirits?"

"It's not empty." She spit a line of blood and drool. Her tongue felt for loose teeth and found none. "The Spirits are for everyone."

He smacked her again, but this time she anticipated it, and ducked so that his blow glanced off the side of her cheek, his nails raking her skin.

"This one's more valuable than we thought." He smiled at her. "I know who you are, Rhia of Asermos. There aren't many Crows among your people."

Her blood froze, but she kept her face indignant. "I'm from Tiros, a free village, and my name is—"

"Don't bother. Your brother is what we call a 'man of interest.' Perhaps he'd be *interested* in your arrest."

She kept the panic from her face. Did they know she'd been coordinating the smuggling of weapons from Tiros to Asermos for years? "Arrest for what?"

"We found you at the scene of massive human casualties."

"A scene that clearly took place over a day ago. A scene requiring more manpower and weapons than my husband and I had."

"Evidence of anything can be provided."

"But not believed in court. Last I heard, Ilios still held to the rule of law, such as it is."

"All we need is enough evidence to hold you until your brother comes to set you free." He reached forward to grasp her crow feather, which he used to pull her closer to him. "Besides, you were doing magic." With his other hand, he drew a knife. She jerked back, expecting to feel the blade at her throat.

He slashed the leather band that held her fetish. Though her hands were bound, instinct drove them to reach for the feather. The sergeant yanked her back by the wrists, sending shooting pains into her shoulders.

"Magic," the officer said, "is illegal in Ilion territories."

"I'm not standing on Ilion territory."

"Again, a detail that can be established when you have your day in court. Until then, you can sit in detention."

"As bait for someone you think is my brother. I don't even have a brother."

"Hmm." He tossed her feather on the ground and crushed it under his boot. "You won't for long."

Kalindos

Sura stared through the fire into eternity.

The fire was Dravek's, burning at the far edge of the boulder field below, where she had left him. From her perch outside a small cave on Mount Beros she could see a wide swath of valley. A few hours before, the sun had set, glistening yellow and orange over the distant Velekon River. Thus began the first night of her Bestowing.

The Descendant authorities in Asermos had banned this coming-of-age ritual, as they had all other forms of magic. A few Asermons dared to sneak away for their Bestowing, but those caught were made examples of. Mali had wanted Sura to keep a low profile to avoid scrutiny of her own activities, like raiding armories and planning assassinations.

But Sura had always known that her destiny could only be

delayed, not denied. She was meant to be here right now, waiting for her Guardian Spirit.

She wondered how long Dravek's fire would burn. Surely he would put it out before going to sleep. The night wasn't cold enough to need the warmth of a flame, so perhaps he was only using the light to perform some task.

She should probably pray or something, Sura realized. Her mother had taught her chants to honor and call upon dozens of Spirits—always quietly, in the privacy of their home, of course. But at the moment nothing seemed right except silence.

Silence, and fire. Her eyes unfocused further, her gaze adhered to the flame. The sensation of cold, hard stone beneath her legs began to fade, and she floated. It seemed as if she could hear the torch's sparks, that she could rise with them all the way to the sky.

She'd lived the last half of her life afraid. Yet now, on the verge of confronting something more powerful than the entire Ilion army, she felt no fear, only peace.

So much so that when she felt a strange, dark presence at her back, she merely acknowledged its existence. It loomed closer, yet she did not look away from the flame. It rasped a cold breath on the back of her neck, then inhaled hard, as if to pull something out of her. Her strength? Her courage? Her soul?

"Get out," she whispered, and away it slunk.

Sura watched the fire as it burned all night.

"Stop that," the eagle said.

"I've got to keep up my strength." Sura flexed her biceps, lifting a round rock the size of her fist. "Never know when I'll need to defend myself." She nodded to the eagle. "Go on, I'm listening."

"And I'm speaking." Its sharp male voice cut the crisp morning air. "I said to put that down. You're safe here, so stop trying to be your mother."

As if I could ever be that strong. Sura dropped the rock and folded her arms. "Can I ask you a question first?" When the bird tilted his cloud-white head, she said, "The Eagles I know call their Spirit *She*, but you speak to me with a man's voice. Why?"

"The Spirits are neither male nor female."

"Even Raven?"

"Especially Raven." The eagle preened his gleaming brown wing feathers. "We manifest as male or female according to whichever we think you'll respond to best."

Sura cocked her head, wondering why the Spirits assumed she would listen better to a man. She'd had so few of them in her life.

The eagle continued. "But we stay consistent with those who serve us, which is why all Eagles refer to me as *She*. Humans confuse so easily."

"I can't deny that." Something about his words made her glance toward the boulder field. In the bright sunshine she could no longer see the torch, if it still burned, and she definitely couldn't see Dravek. Her lack of distance vision alone told her that she wasn't an Eagle.

"If you're not my Guardian Spirit," she said to the bird, "why are you here?"

"Because I have something to teach you."

Sura waited. The eagle shifted his position to stare off into the distance toward the western horizon.

Finally she grew impatient. "When do we begin?"

He clicked his sharp yellow beak. "Oh, you want it in words?"

Sura closed her mouth and thought hard about what Eagle represented. Seeing far, not just in space but time, as well. Third-phase Eagles had the power of prophecy, but their vision only encompassed details. An Eagle might receive a premonition as mundane as a piece of cloth lying in a basket. Understanding its context often required the logic of a Hawk or the intuition of a Swan—preferably both.

Finally she said, "If I receive a vision, I should see it as an event that will really happen, and not just a symbol, no matter how strange it seems. Is that right?"

"Hmm." The eagle turned to her. "You don't confuse as easily as most."

As he spread his wings, she couldn't resist one last question. "Will Raven come soon and bestow Her Aspect?"

"If I had a fresh rat for each time someone asked me that question." The eagle shook his head. "Only She knows."

He took off and soared into the valley below, fading slowly, as if passing into an invisible mist.

Sura watched the space where the eagle had disappeared, to see if another Spirit would emerge. She heard footsteps behind her, and turned to see two deer with expansive sets of antlers clop up the trail to the ridge where she sat. She scrambled to her feet.

"Greetings," she said, her voice rough with awe.

The bucks halted, then angled their magnificent heads to look behind them. Sura followed their gazes and gasped. Two does tripped lightly toward her, nodding their heads with each step. A fawn cavorted behind each of them, noses up and ears twitching.

The deer formed a semicircle around her, soft brown gazes roaming her face. Then, instead of speaking, they sang. Not in words, but notes with distinct characters, as if each deer were a separate instrument. The bucks sounded like bass fiddles, creating the undertones, while the does each played a different toned violin. The fawns leaped about, making cheery piping noises. They all tapped their feet to create a complex, infectious beat.

Sura laughed louder than she had in years, then began to dance. Though her body was unaccustomed to moving in rhythm, it shook and writhed and bounced along with the sounds of the deer herd. She made up words to accompany their tune, words that made sense in a way that would seem crazy tomorrow.

The deer joined her, dancing in pairs or alone or in small circles of flashing hooves and shining flanks. She laughed again. It didn't matter that she couldn't dance or sing. The deer didn't care. All they wanted was to give her this gift.

The song ended with a flourish, and Sura collapsed on the ground, panting. "Thank you." She wiped the sweat from her brow.

More suddenly then they had appeared, the deer were gone.

"No…" Sura scrambled to her feet and peered over the edge of the ridge, then inside the cave.

For a moment the loneliness threatened to tear open her heart, which felt as empty and shriveled now as it had been full to bursting a minute ago. She sank to her knees and covered her face with her arms.

Forcing herself to breathe, she grasped the memory of the dance and pulled it inside herself, storing it deep within where nothing, including time, could ever touch it. From her core it spread out to warm her, as if she had swallowed a tiny sun.

She sat back and hugged her knees, at peace once again.

10

Asermos

Rhia opened her eyes into a dim, gooey fog. A single square light shone above her, to her left. She blinked at it, then rolled on her side, gagging and retching.

"Keep it down over there," a woman snapped. The voice was familiar and carried with it a taste more sour than what Rhia's stomach was trying to expel.

"Mali?"

"In the flesh. What's left of it, anyway."

"Are we in prison?"

Her old nemesis sighed. "You're not as smart as they say you are. We're actually in a secret cave provided by my associates in the resistance, not far from where you were captured."

Rhia ran her hand along the cold stone beneath her. "We are?"

"Idiot. Of course we're in prison."

Rhia let her forehead drop to the floor. Its coolness eased her nausea and the overwhelming desire to throttle her brother's former mate.

She rubbed the back of her head, feeling for a lump or a sticky spot of blood that would indicate a hard blow, and found nothing. "They must have drugged me."

"I don't know why they thought they needed to. A runt like you should be easy to tuck under one's arm and place anywhere one wants. Like a basket of fruit."

"What happened to you?"

"Arrested, obviously. I didn't exactly stop in for tea."

"Where's Sura?"

Mali's voice lost its edge. "I sent her to Kalindos. You haven't heard from her?"

"No, but the weather's been bad for the homing pigeons."

The Wasp woman sighed. "Still no third-phase Hawk in Kalindos, I suppose."

Rhia pushed herself to a sitting position, her head reeling. Her vision slowly cleared so that she could see the bars now, and Mali's long, thin figure. She blinked hard. Her own cell had a bed, such as it was, and enough room to walk about. The Wasp's, on the other hand, wasn't even large enough to lie down in.

"Have they hurt you?"

Mali snorted. "They tried. They can't, not by beating me or peeling off my skin or hanging me by my heels, any of those tiresome methods. Once they figured that out, they tried other things, like this tiny cell. When they feed me, once a day, it's rancid meat, moldy bread—"

Rhia's stomach lurched. "Stop."

"It's not too bad. Maggots are nice and chewy when they're not overcooked."

Rhia gulped deep breaths to keep from vomiting. When the wooziness receded, she said, "If we're going to get out of here, we'll have to learn to get along."

Mali gave a harsh sigh. "You ran away when things got bad in Asermos."

"I had to protect my family. We've all been helping you from Tiros."

"I had a family. I could've run. But I stayed to protect our homeland." The Wasp sniffed. "You ran because you thought one of your children was the Raven baby. You thought that made you special."

"You'll be happy to know they've both been claimed by other Spirits."

Mali was silent for a moment. "What are they?" she asked in a muted voice.

"Nilik's a Wolverine."

"Like his uncle. What a plague. And Jula?"

"A Mockingbird."

Mali cackled. "I bet she makes you crazy."

"The last three years have been one long argument. I can't say anything without her contradicting or belittling me. It's exhausting."

"That's the way they are at that age."

"I was never that bad," Rhia said.

"Me, neither."

"You were horrible."

"To you. Not to my parents."

"Jula worships her father." Rhia swallowed the lump in her

throat at the thought of Marek. She hoped he would return to safety in Tiros rather than follow her to Asermos alone.

"Sounds familiar," Mali said. "Sura thinks her father's a god."

"Lycas, a god? That's because she's never known him."

Mali laughed. "I don't know how you lived with him all those years."

"Nilo was even worse, in a way, because his torment was stealthy. He'd plan elaborate tricks to scare me, then act completely innocent. There was no justice, because my brothers would punish me if I tattled."

"Brutes." Mali's tone indicated the word was a compliment. "I miss the way Lycas was before Nilo died."

Rhia uttered the next thought only because the bars protected her from the Wasp's wrath. "I think you'd like him the way he is now."

"Shut up," Mali growled. "He made his choice eighteen years ago, to leave me and Sura."

"He left to rescue my son and my husband."

"Which I eventually understood. He had to protect his family. But afterward, he went right back to Ilios to rescue a bunch of Kalindons he didn't even know."

"Most of whom were children," Rhia said.

"What about his own child? Didn't she deserve a father instead of a distant hero?"

"Are you proud of the way she turned out?"

"That's beside the point."

"Are you proud of Sura?"

Mali's voice crackled. "Yes. She's strong and smart and everything else I could have wished for."

"Lycas may not have been there to hear her first word, or see her first step. But everything he's done out there has shaped her."

"Shut up," Mali said again, more feebly.

A door opened at the end of the hall, letting in more light that pierced Rhia's throbbing temple. Two soldiers entered, each carrying a tray.

"Good, you're awake," the taller soldier said. "Breakfast time."

"Breakfast?" Mali said with a sneer. "It's past noon already."

"And how would you know that?" he said. "Give the new one that meal," he told the other soldier.

The other man slid a wooden tray through a small opening in the bottom of Rhia's cell door. She waited until he had backed away, then slid forward and grabbed it quickly. She lifted the lid, wrinkling her nose in anticipation of the rotting smell.

To her surprise, the meal wasn't spoiled. In fact, the baked chicken was steaming hot, its skin dotted with minced herbs. She squeezed the chunk of bread, which was soft instead of stale. The vegetables looked overboiled, but the water in her cup smelled fresh. Her stomach growled.

"Thank you," she said.

The taller soldier nodded. "And for you," he said, turning to Mali, "the usual." He shoved his tray through the hole in the door, then latched it shut.

Mali looked at Rhia's plate, then lifted her own lid. "Ugh!" She cursed and shoved the tray and its contents through the bars. Some of the meat fell just outside the cell, and Rhia swore she saw small things crawling over it. The shorter soldier bent to pick up the food.

"Leave it," his superior said. "She'll eat it later. She always does."

When the door shut, Rhia tore her chicken and bread in half. "Here, take some of mine."

"I don't want your pity," Mali snapped.

"They're trying to turn us against each other. That way we won't cooperate to escape." She placed a plate on Mali's side of the bars and put half her food on it. "Let's show them it won't work."

"I won't eat anything until they serve me something decent."

"They won't. They'll be happy to let you starve."

"Then I'll starve."

"Suit yourself." Rhia carried her tray to the bundled up lump of straw that passed for a bed. She began eating, not bothering to mute her smacking lips. "It's quite good."

Mali said nothing, just sat in her cell and stared out through the bars.

Rhia sighed and kept eating. She was determined to get out of this place. Alive.

11

Sangian Hills

Lycas loved the rain. It blurred the weak human vision of the Ilion soldiers and made the terrain too slick for their horses to gain footing. It obscured his fighters' footprints and made them impossible to track.

Rain had been all too rare this summer, but tonight, as his troupe neared the camp in the low hills outside Velekos, it drenched the land as if making up for lost time.

Soon the torches of the base camp appeared, visible only from the north, hidden from Velekos by high rock walls. His stomach grumbled at the thought of the meal awaiting him, and he smacked his lips in anticipation of the accompanying ale.

Just past the sentries, Damen was the first to greet them. Lycas was surprised to see Rhia's Crow-brother, as he usually stayed in Velekos unless there was urgent news. The lines on his face seemed deeper than ever, or maybe it was just the shadows cast by the sputtering torches.

"Glad to see you back," Damen said. "Any troubles?"

Lycas shrugged. "Another day, another platoon of dead Ilions. Nothing we couldn't handle, with Sirin's help. He's back at head-quarters now."

Damen nodded, giving a glance toward the north, where the guerrilla command center lay deep in the hills.

Lycas put a hand on his shoulder. "How's the family?"

Damen rubbed his forehead, ruffling short strands of gray hair that now outnumbered the black. "I'm a Crow. You'd think I'd know what to say after Lania's murder, how to make it better."

"Nothing will ever make it better."

"I know. But Nathas is my mate. I should be able to take his pain away. Diminish it somehow, heh? But I can't."

For lack of comforting sentiments, Lycas said, "We'll give those bastards justice. It won't bring Lania back, but…"

Lycas trailed off, out of words. He couldn't imagine what the girl's parents, Reni and Nathas, must be going through, not to mention Damen's son Corek, Lania's half brother. Long ago, Reni had agreed to bear Nathas and Damen a child each, partly so that they might progress to the second phase, but also because they all wanted children. The fact that the five of them created a lov-ing though unconventional family must have kept the Spirits from punishing them for becoming parents for the sake of power.

Lycas thought again of Sura, and wondered if she were alive. What had the world come to when a father couldn't take his own children's survival for granted?

His hand passed briefly over the sheath of his oldest blade, the one inside his coat, next to his heart. Deep within its hilt, wrapped around the base of the steel itself, lay a lock of hair from his infant daughter's head.

"You should have seen Lania's funeral." Damen walked with him toward the camp's main tent. "Hundreds of people. The Ilion police was out in full force to prevent rioting. No eulogies were allowed, because they feared it would rile up the crowd. I was only permitted the bare ritual, which had to be submitted and approved in advance." Damen shook his head. "Of course no calling of the crow, because that would be magic." In response to Lycas's sharp look, he said, "Don't worry, I called one later."

"Good." As they reached the tent's door, he heard the rustle of tired, familiar feet behind him, trotting to catch up. "Damen, I almost forgot. Nilik came with me."

The Crow man turned and broke into a smile, his dark eyes crinkling at the corners, accentuating the age lines. He moved forward to embrace the approaching Nilik, then suddenly stopped. His smile faded. "What are you doing here?"

Nilik blanched. "I came to fight." He took a step forward. "I'm sorry about Lania." His voice almost cracked speaking her name.

Damen shook his head slowly. "You shouldn't be here."

Lycas's chest turned oddly cold, his dread returning. "Rhia said he could come."

Damen gave him an incredulous look. "She couldn't have."

"Why not?" Nilik's voice was urgent.

The Crow wiped a hand over his face and blinked hard. "Nothing. It's just dangerous here for a newcomer. Be very, very careful." He came forward and put a hand on Nilik's arm. "Promise me. Your mother would have my head if anything happened to you."

Lycas scoffed. "She'd have mine first." He went inside the commander's tent, holding the flap open for them to follow. "Damen, tell me there's fresh meat left from dinner."

"I'll send over meals for both of you." Damen's voice came low, to Nilik. "Did you have your Bestowing?"

"Yes. I'm a Wolverine."

Lycas smiled at the pride he heard in Nilik's voice. Not a hint of whining for not being the Raven child. Lania's death had given his nephew a cause, a focus away from the prophecy's lifelong burden. Perhaps Wolverine had bestowed His Aspect on Nilik so he could avenge her death.

"Jula's a Mockingbird," Lycas added.

"Ah," Damen said. "Interesting."

"For once, I don't believe your stoicism." Lycas set his pack in the corner where he usually slept, noting that the tent floor had remained dry despite the rain. "Go on, say it. If one of Rhia's children isn't the Raven, it must be your son. The prophecy said it would be someone born of a Crow."

"In a hard and dangerous labor, I know, and Corek's birth certainly wasn't easy."

Lycas sat and tugged off his left boot, suppressing a groan of relief. "You should send him to Tiros for his Bestowing. It's not safe here anymore."

"I know that." Damen gritted his teeth around the words, and they all shared a moment of grieved silence for Lania's fate. Then the Crow said, "It's not worth the risk when he hasn't felt a calling. Getting in and out of the village now is treacherous. I thought for sure the Ilions would detain me this time, but they know I'm a Crow. My powers are no threat to them. They also know the Raven rumors about Corek."

"All the more reason to get him out of Velekos. Bring him here while you still can." Lycas pulled off his other boot. "I'll lend you a couple of my men to help sneak him out."

"His mother won't want to let him go, especially after—" He cut himself off and glanced at Nilik.

Lycas turned to his nephew. "Go find a spot in the barracks. I'll see you in the morning."

A brief shadow of disappointment crossed Nilik's face, then he straightened his posture. "Yes, sir. Good night, sir." He nodded to Damen on his way out.

Lycas peeled off his socks and frowned at the dampness around the toes. His boots were leaking. "I've discovered I like ordering family members around. I could get used to it."

Damen crossed to the opposite side of the tent, which could fit perhaps four or five standing men, and stood next to a small table for reading maps and writing letters. Lycas's tent wasn't nearly as elaborate as an Ilion field commander's, but he thought any sign of privilege distanced himself from the men and women he led.

"How are things in the Acrosia since Lania's funeral?" he asked Damen.

"The whole neighborhood's a tinderbox, especially with the Evius festival coming up. Every year it's worse, with them parading up and down our streets, shoving it in our faces that they own us now." He turned to Lycas. "The worst part is how many Velekons enjoy it. To them it's not a symbol of our oppression, it's a day off, a chance to drink free wine."

"Do the Ilions suspect our plans for the festival?"

"Hard to say. They've increased patrols, but so have we. It's only our Bears and Wolverines that keep their police from making illegal searches."

Lycas sighed. Velekos was so close, in so much danger, and yet if he entered, it would only put the people he cared about at risk—not to mention get him captured.

"Was there something you wanted to tell me?" he asked Damen. "Something you didn't want Nilik to hear?" He wondered if it had to do with Rhia's bizarre change of heart in letting her son come to Velekos.

"He'll hear it eventually." Damen stepped closer. "They've lowered the charges against Lania's killers. Manslaughter." His gaze fell. "Maximum sentence five years."

Lycas stood slowly, sure he'd heard the Crow wrong. "After what they did to her—"

"They're claiming self-defense."

"A sixteen-year-old girl against half a dozen armed soldiers?" He fought to keep from shouting. "How is that anything but murder?"

"She was breaking the law by doing magic, they say, so the soldiers were detaining a criminal, protecting the populace." Damen lowered his voice. "They fear us. No matter how many weapons they have, they still lack magic."

"That's their fault." Lycas paced the dirt floor of the tent, fists clenched. "Nilik will go mad. I think there was more between him and Lania than we guessed."

"She was in love with him." Damen crossed his arms over his chest. "She said they hoped to marry after their Bestowings. I think that's why she was so eager to go, despite the danger."

Dread filled Lycas's stomach. If Lania's killers faced leniency from the Ilion courts, Nilik would be more determined than ever to deliver his own justice.

At his age, with new Wolverine power coursing through his veins, such rage could get him killed.

Kalindos

Sura watched fire scorch the sky.

Dravek's torch still burned at sunset, but soon afterward a bright streak of light had caught her eye. The moon had set a few hours after the sun, leaving the sky dark and the stars close.

Now she lay on her back, watching meteors chase one another and counting the seconds between flashes. The balls of fire mesmerized her, so that when the thing from the previous night crept close again, hungrier, she did not shiver or even blink. It surrounded her like liquid, as cold as seawater but twice as thick, whispering of what it would steal if she did not give.

She gave. It didn't matter, she knew, staring into the sky. There were a million worlds out there that no one ever thought about. Perhaps on one of them, another young woman was lying on the ground gazing at Sura's sun, having her own self sucked out of her, drop by drop.

Her vision turned black at the edges, as though hundreds of gnats hovered around each eye. If this living void took away the sky, she would fight it.

But as the blackness closed in, shrinking her sight to a pinpoint of light, then nothing at all, she realized it was too late. The thing had her. Her soul pulsed out one heartbeat at a time, but still she felt no fear, only curiosity.

For inside her, the flame still burned.

Dravek waited for Sura to scream.

He had screamed, all night, when the living void had taken him at his own Bestowing. So had everyone else he knew. It had seemed worse than death, because it wasn't life being annihilated, but a soul, sucked out, chewed up, spit back inside a person in an unrecognizable form.

He understood why it had to happen. One had to be empty to receive the Spirit at the Bestowing. Fasting emptied the body, meditation emptied the mind. But nothing could empty the soul, nothing but that…thing.

He checked the stars' positions. Winter constellations were rising, which at this time of year meant the sun would be up soon, though no light grayed the eastern horizon.

By now it should have had her.

Unable to sit still any longer, he strapped on his pack. It wasn't heavy, since he'd brought no food for himself. He'd planned to spend these three days speaking with his Spirit, asking the questions that burned inside him. But She had remained elusive and silent.

Dravek slid the torch from its holder and started to cross the boulder field—a dangerous maneuver at night. One slip could leave him with a twisted or broken ankle. But Sura's silence drew him on. What if she were hurt or sick?

He told himself that his feelings for her were a product of their spiritual kinship. Kara often spoke of her "Wolf-brothers," and though he knew they all curled up together for warmth during weeklong winter hunts, it stirred no jealousy in him. Nothing like what he felt when Etarek or another former lover smiled at her.

He stopped short. As an experiment, he imagined Kara with someone else—another man's hands caressing her body, his lips closing over her nipple as she sighed and shuddered in his arms.

Nothing. He felt no jealousy, not even a spark of arousal.

He hurried forward onto the next rock. He would demand Snake's presence, demand answers.

Dravek had almost reached the other side of the field when a woman's laughter cut the predawn air. He looked up at the side of Mount Beros.

A breeze blew, rustling the needles of the surrounding pines and muffling the sounds of mirth. Dravek stepped onto the soil of the forest. He crammed the end of the torch into a gap between the two closest stones, then sat to wait.

As the sun rose, the wind died, and her voice came again, moaning and shrieking in what sounded like ecstasy. His body responded instantly, wanting to be the cause of those noises. He rubbed his face and groaned.

"What are You doing to her?" he whispered as he began to pace. "What are You doing to me?"

Snake wouldn't answer. Dravek turned to the torch and stared into the flame, usually the surest way to reach Her. He stared until he couldn't feel where he ended and the fire began. Then he sent out one last plea. Unanswered.

He sank to his knees, bent forward and grasped his head in his arms. His forehead pressed the damp soil. "Come to me," he pleaded. "Tell me what You want."

He repeated his Spirit's name, and Sura's, chanting into the ground near his lips. Here he would wait, no matter how long, until one of them appeared.

Then he would have his answer.

Sura had become fire.

The living void had left her empty, even as she laughed in its nonexistent face. Now she was filling again.

The rising sun shot through her body, burning her without pain. She cried out in welcome as its warmth flowed into her like the love of a man.

The clouds came. Rain soaked her for hours, but she didn't crawl inside the nearby cave. She lay on the ground, listening to the rhythm of the water on the rocks. Her fingers followed the trails of drops over her neck and shoulders and breasts.

As the dirt turned to mud, she sank into the earth. It oozed around her, cradling like a mother. She had come from the earth, as surely as she would return to it.

The sky darkened into evening, and she noticed a new faraway light, steadier than the meteors, brighter than the torch. It drifted closer, as if sailing on the breeze.

A bird filled her vision with feathers of every color, and she sat up quickly as she realized who it was.

Raven.

Sura scrambled to her feet, then fell to her knees and dipped her forehead to the mud, cursing her own boldness. How long had she lain there, lazily watching the Spirit of Spirits approach her as if it were an everyday occurrence?

"Forgive me," she whispered.

Raven landed without a sound on the edge of the ridge, casting a white light, warming and soothing Sura's outstretched fingers.

"Rise and behold," She said in a voice that shamed the wind.

Sura stood on shaky legs and gazed at the Mother of Creation, who towered twice her height. "I didn't know you would come."

"I come for everyone."

Sura quaked inside, not from fear, but from gratitude. She was truly a part of her people now, a privilege denied to her fellow Asermons.

Her fingers curled into fists. She would give her people this freedom to honor the Spirits, or she would die trying.

"Thank you," she whispered. "You have honored me."

"We need you all," the Spirit said, "as much as you need Us."

Sura stared into Raven's endless dark eyes. "What can we do?"

"Because of the acts of humans, some of Us will fall." Raven bent close to Sura's ear. "But what you asked the Eagle," She whispered. "Soon."

The Spirit folded Her wings against Her sides as all the feathers darkened to black. For a moment She looked exactly like a crow, and Sura took a startled step backward.

Then the bird's body lowered to the ground, lengthening, then twisting and curving into a familiar shape.

Snake.

Though the night was cloudy, the ridge was filled with a light like the moon's, glistening on the Spirit's ink-black scales. She lay coiled, golden eyes gleaming.

She raised Her head to Sura's height. "Greetings, my love."

Sura began to weep. "I knew it." Her lungs heaved into a sob, and she covered her face with her hands. "I was afraid you would come, and afraid you wouldn't." She should be grateful, but a part of her mourned the fact that she could never be with Dravek.

"Shame saps our power," Snake hissed. "I choose those few who are strong enough to do the right thing out of honor, not the fear of guilt."

"But how do we know what's the right thing?"

"It's not always obvious. It's not always popular. It's almost never easy."

Sura sniffled. "That doesn't much help."

"We can't give you all the answers. You'd just misinterpret them." Her tongue flitted out. "Besides, how else would you learn except through mistakes?"

"I've already made too many."

"There's no such thing as too many mistakes." Snake dipped Her head. "Let me show you something."

Inside the cave, a pool of water appeared. It glowed blue-white from within, and a faint veil of steam rose from its surface.

Sura's skin itched with mud and sweat. She took a step toward the pool, and it promptly vanished.

"Not for you," Snake said.

Sura spread her arms, displaying her muddy body. "But I'm filthy. I need to wash before my Bestowing."

"You have already been cleansed. By fire. Last year."

Sura's knees went weak at the memory. "That water could heal me. Bring it back."

"You are as healed as you will ever be. You're as clean as you will ever be. You're ready." Snake uncoiled Her long black body and glided toward her.

"No!" Sura backed up against the cave wall and tore open her shirt, revealing the scars that covered the left half of her back and chest. "Can't you see what happened to me?"

"I see more than you ever will." Snake slid forward, unblinking.

She pulled her shirt closed, clutching the edges as if to shield herself. "If I'm healed, why does it still hurt?"

"Sura, my love." Her name slithered off the Spirit's tongue. "Some things hurt forever."

Snake began to sway. Sura held Her gaze, mesmerized. She felt herself start to fall, and her fingers clutched the stone wall. She slid down, desperate to feel the earth beneath her.

Finally she lay on her belly, her head turned toward the Spirit.

Snake's eyes glowed, and Sura fell inside them.

She was naked, surrounded by fire but feeling no pain. It licked her skin, painting it in red splashes that glowed like embers.

Sura put her hand out, into the heart of the flame. It danced through her flesh, into her bones, daring her to join it. She moved her hips, her feet, her shoulders to its rhythm. It seemed as if her own heartbeat depended on it. Joy filled her as it had when she'd danced with the deer, but this was better, because it was for her alone. She spun and writhed with the fire, the only parent, lover, companion she'd ever need.

People appeared beyond the flames. Running, shrieking without sound, clutching at each other in terror. Her people.

She tried to reach them, but the fire held her back as if it were a solid wall. It wanted them, and unlike her, it could hurt them. It could kill them.

"No!" Sura breathed in hard, and the flames leaped into her mouth. She swallowed them, then reached for more. Only she could eat them, only she could save the screaming, burning people.

As she filled herself with the fire, it began to sear her throat and stomach. She looked down to see the flames pulsing through her skin, working their way out, desperate to join their cohorts in the frenzied feast of life. Sura ate faster, and the fire darted down her legs and arms, then pushed against her toes and fingertips.

"Please..." Her tears sizzled as they flowed, scalding her cheeks. If she kept the fire, it would consume her as she had consumed it. But if she released it, the others would die.

"Take me," Sura whispered.

Her eyes swelled in her skull, and just before they burst, she saw her people live.

Sura opened her eyes, closed them, then touched her lids to be sure they were still there. She sat up.

Snake lay coiled across the cave, just out of reach. The strange moonlight surrounded Her.

"I do not choose my servants lightly," She said. "Only the strongest enter my realm. If you can resist the temptation to misuse fire, I can trust you with a far more dangerous power."

Sura shivered at the thought of her second-phase Aspect, the ability to burn away memories with a mere gaze into another's eyes.

"Many mock your power. They fear you." The Spirit's tongue flicked out as She moved closer. "But this passion will save you. It may save us all."

She slid over Sura's legs, smooth and cool, around her back, finally curving around her waist in an embrace that felt as welcoming as an old friend.

This was it, Sura realized. The Bestowing. She prayed she would remember it always.

"Be mine," Snake whispered. "I accept you. I love you forever."

Sura's reverie was broken by an urgent thought. "What about—"

Snake squeezed Sura's breath from her lungs. She tried to finish the sentence, had to know if what she shared with Dravek was against the will of the Spirits. She had so many questions, but only one that truly mattered.

It was too late. Power surged through her, along with a peace that quenched every doubt.

Through his cloud of whispered chants, Dravek heard a voice speak his name. At last.

"Spirit, you've come." He lifted his head from the ground, then wavered with dizziness. It was morning.

He turned to see Snake standing near him in the form of a woman with long, tangled black hair, an earth-soaked face and eyes that glowed like stars.

Dravek blinked, and when his eyes reopened, he realized it was no vision. "Sura." He got to his feet, then swayed and stumbled. "Are you all right?" His voice was a bare rasp, his throat raw and dry.

"I'm wonderful, but you—what's wrong? How long have you been on your knees?"

He tried to shake the clouds from his head. "What day is it?"

"The third day is over. My Bestowing is finished. Look at you, you're shivering." She opened her pack and yanked out a blanket. "And so pale. Have you eaten?"

She stood on tiptoe to drape the blanket around his shoulders. Her body came close, radiating heat, making him shiver even more. He turned away to keep from trapping her in his arms.

"What are you?" he managed to choke out.

"A Snake, of course. What have you been doing all this time?"

He stared at the ground, his mind sinking into despair at her news. Had he really kneeled there for over a day?

"I was praying." *For all the good it did.* He tightened the blanket around his chest.

"I could see your fire every night," she said. "I wasn't afraid."

He turned to her. "I'm glad." He gazed at her mouth, chapped and red from her three-day ordeal. He licked his own lips, wanting to share what little moisture he had with her, cover her mouth with his own, heal its sunburn with his tongue.

Sura glanced past him, then broke into a sudden smile. "Look." She moved to crouch at the base of the closest boulder. He peered over her shoulder to see a pale, mottled snakeskin. It draped across her hands like a ribbon.

Dravek knelt beside her. "You should keep it, to remember your Bestowing."

"Don't be ridiculous. It was left here for you."

"I insist."

She pursed her lips. "We'll each take half."

"Don't break it."

"It's already in two pieces." She raised her hands to reveal the two halves. "Head or tail?" Before he could answer, she held out the head. "I've had enough staring for a while."

He took the skin from her carefully. It was still fresh and supple, a perfect mold of the animal it once contained. The skin's head featured two tooth holes and two transparent scales that had covered the snake's eyes. Sura was right; those vacant orbs seemed to be watching him.

He watched Sura wrap her half of the snakeskin around her tanned bare arm. "If it dries like that," he told her, "you won't be able to get it off without breaking it."

"Then I'll keep the pieces." She held out her arm and shone a smile that made his ribs ache. "What do you think?"

He gazed at her, covered in mud and sweat and snakeskin, and couldn't imagine anything more beautiful. "I'm getting married in three days."

She looked away and swallowed. "I know. Do you have time to train me?"

"I'll make time." Before he could say anything stupid, he stood and collected their packs. "You need to rest and recover. Day after tomorrow I'll show you some exercises to practice until I come back."

"You're not coming back."

"I will, once I'm in my second phase and I've had some training."

"I'll be gone. I have to save my mother." She took her pack from him. "Maybe I'll find my father, fight with his soldiers against the Descendants." A smile twisted her lips. "It'll be fun to burn them."

"Careful. Your hatred will devour you."

"And what would you know of hate?" Her eyes teased him, but there was a hardness behind them. "You've lived in peaceful, happy Kalindos your whole life."

"I was born in Ilios." He fought to keep the bitterness out of his voice. "I was conceived in Ilios."

"Oh." She put a hand to her throat. "Your mother—"

"She was captured in the invasion of Kalindos. Daria, too. Your father rescued them a year later, but she'd been a slave all that time. My father—whoever he is, there were several men who—" He stopped, sparing her the details. "Ilion noblemen." He ran his palm over his hair, grimy with three days' worth of dust and sweat. "Adrek told me that they wear their hair longer. It's a sign of their class, whatever that means."

"That's why you cut yours." Sura's dark eyes drooped at the corners. "I'm so sorry. I didn't know."

He attempted a shrug, but his shoulders were too tight. "At least we were rescued. Not everyone was so lucky."

"A friend of mine in Asermos is also…like you. And I know what it's like having a mother who was misused."

"Misused?" He tried not to scoff. "Your father might not be the world's greatest family man, but he's a hero."

She frowned. "He's killed a lot of Ilions, for whatever good that's done."

"If my father was one of those Ilions, it's done a lot of good." He kept his voice as smooth as ice. "I hope it was slow and painful, and his body was left out in the open, all alone. I hope that before he died, he felt the ravens eating his eyes and the vultures shredding his balls." He glanced away. "Sorry."

"I've heard my mother say worse." Her brows pinched, and she squinted up at him. "Where's your mother now?"

He swallowed hard. "They killed her."

Sura gasped. "But you said she returned from Ilios."

"She did. Adrek said she was never the same, though." He stepped away from Sura, to avoid the pity in her eyes. "One morning, when I was five, she threw herself off the porch, down onto the forest floor." He wiped his hand against the side of his shirt. "I don't think she knew I was watching."

Sura's hand went to her mouth. "Dravek…" She took a step toward him. "It wasn't your fault. Please don't be sorry to be alive."

He wondered why she would say that, how she could understand him so well when they'd known each other only a few days.

"I'd rather never have lived," he said, "if it would've spared my mother. But now that I'm here, I'm in no hurry to leave this world." He stared into her eyes, a moment too long, then turned for home. "Especially now."

13

Asermos

A shriek shattered Rhia's dream into a thousand pieces. She sat straight up into total darkness.

"Mali, what's happening?"

A grunt came from the next cell. "Why are you waking me?"

"I thought I heard someone scream."

It came again, longer and louder, from a room upstairs. A man, whose throat sounded like it would rip from the effort.

"Oh, that." Mali sniffed. "Torture."

"What are they doing to him?"

"Shh. Be quiet and I'll try to figure it out."

A sharp crack came, making Rhia jump, followed by another shriek.

"Sounds like a whip," Mali said, as though naming an ingredient in a stew she'd just sampled. "Go back to sleep."

"Are you crazy?" The last three days with Mali had answered that question for Rhia. "I can't sleep. We have to do something."

"One day I will. I'll wrap those whips around their necks, then hang them with weights on their feet, until the barbs chew through their throats."

"The whips have barbs?"

"To make us bleed. Well, not me, hardly at all, or a Wolverine. You'd likely pass out after one lash. Badgers usually last about ten, until the whip breaks through to muscle. Cougars, though—" she clucked her tongue "—not as tough as they pretend."

Rhia held back her horrified response, knowing it would have no audience with Mali. The room upstairs fell silent.

"Must have been a Cougar," Mali commented.

The silence was broken again, by a hacking, choking sound.

"Ah," Mali said, "they've switched him to the tub."

"Don't they have laws against torturing civilians?"

"Technically we're not civilians, we're 'suspected violents,' and the torture is to gather evidence for our trials. But no one's had a trial in years. At least not publicly."

Rhia shrank back on her bed, tight to the wall. She had to escape. Now.

"I'm surprised they haven't come for you yet," Mali said. "When they do, just remember one thing." Her voice came closer to the bars and lost its sarcastic edge. "The key to torture is to take away a person's hope. To beat it, you have to believe that you'll escape, that we'll win, that one day we'll have a victory parade by the waterfront with the Descendant scum pulling our carts on their hands and knees. Well, their knees and the stumps of their wrists."

Mali was so full of hate, Rhia feared the Ilions had already won.

The ceiling thudded with a heavy impact.

Mali gave a low whistle. "That didn't sound good."

A door slammed, then Rhia heard booted footsteps rattling down the stairs to their cells.

The outer door swung open with a clang. Rhia squinted against the light of a torch. Two men stalked toward her.

"Let's go," the heftier one said. "Now."

She shrank back harder against the wall, wishing she could cram herself into the tiny cracks where the rats lived. One of the guards unlocked her door, then the other lurched in and grabbed her arm.

"Don't make me carry you," he growled. Rhia stumbled, then recovered her footing so he didn't drag her.

"Remember what I told you." Mali stood and clutched the bars as they passed. "Picture the parade!"

Rhia's feet felt cold as they carried her up the stone stairs. At the top, a door opened, revealing a tall, nervous-looking officer near her own age.

"Bring her over to him," he told the guards.

They led Rhia forward. She blinked against the bright lantern light, momentarily blinded. But her nose smelled the blood.

A naked man lay faceup on a red-stained stone slab the height of a dining table.

"Tell us, will he die?" the officer barked as he paced.

She stared at him, confused. What kind of interrogation was this?

"You're some kind of Crow witch." He flapped his hand at the unconscious man. "You see these things."

Her shoulders ached from her restraints. "Let me get closer, and I'll tell you."

He hesitated, then nodded at the guards. They released her, and she stepped up to the table to examine the prisoner. His long dark hair was soaking wet, and his torso was covered in lengthy shallow cuts, as though he'd been carved with a dozen tiny knives.

She touched his bruised, wet face, then drew in a quick breath. It was Endrus the Cougar, one of her old friends from Kalindos. She'd heard he'd joined the Asermon resistance. Tears sprang to her eyes at the thought of the mischievous man she'd danced with at many a Kalindon feast. As far as she knew, he was still first phase, though they were the same age. He wasn't as strong as other Cougars in their late thirties. She gritted her teeth at the unfairness.

"Do you know him?" the officer asked.

Rhia shook her head. "I'm just upset because he looks so wretched." She closed her eyes and listened to the inner realm where Crow flew. No wings flapped to indicate the Spirit's approach. "But he'll live if he gets care immediately."

The three men let out harsh sighs. "Thank the gods," the officer said. "It would've been *us* tied to that pole tomorrow if he'd died. Take him back to his cell and call the healer."

"But, sir," one of the guards said, "how do we know she's not lying?"

"If he dies, we'll know, won't we? Now hurry up."

The guards hoisted Endrus into their arms and carried him out an exit on the opposite side of the room from where they'd entered. The men's prison must be on the other side, she figured. She looked around for more clues to the building's layout, but there were no windows. The outer wall was made of bricks— probably more than one layer, to keep in the sound. Not that they bothered with such insulation on the floor. They no doubt wanted the prisoners to hear each other scream.

"My name is Captain Addano." The officer pulled out a chair beside a desk. "Sit." When she didn't move, he patted the back of the chair. "I won't hurt you. I need your help."

"Why would I help you?"

"To serve your countrymen. To save lives." He gestured to a pole and chains on the other side of the room. "To avoid being thrashed into a quivering, vaguely woman-shaped block of meat."

She shivered, then cursed her own muscles for betraying her fear. Slowly she crossed the room and sat in the chair beside the desk. It smelled better over here, anyway.

Addano sat on the other end of the desk. "We might as well rest before our next interview." He opened the top drawer. "Would you care for some wine?"

She grimaced at the thought. The Ilions had brought their grapes north with them—in fact, it was one of the main motives for their invasion. The south-facing slopes near Asermos were well suited for the vintages that had been hit the hardest by pests and droughts back in Ilios. Her heart twisted at the thought of her family's farm used to grow the symbol of the occupation.

"Suit yourself." Addano poured himself a glass, then gulped it down as easily as water. She noticed that his dark hair was shorter than most Ilion officers, curling just below his ears instead of down to his shoulders. His tanned face and rough hands were etched with lines and spattered with freckles, as if he'd spent many years in the sun. Not a nobleman, she guessed.

"Ah, that's better." He set down the empty wineglass and smacked his lips. "It'll just be a minute."

She didn't want to ask what would happen in a minute. He'd said something about an interview. Why would he need her to—

Rhia's nape turned cold. Surely he didn't mean… "You want me to sit here and watch you torture my people? You want me to *help?*"

"Not help torture them. Help us not kill them. My boys are talented, but sometimes they get carried away." Addano looked down and noticed a spot of blood on the yellow part of his tunic. He sighed. "Not again. I should stand farther back, or wear a smock."

He crossed to a bucket and dipped a cloth inside. The water rattled with what sounded like ice. Rhia licked her lips.

Addano caught the gesture. "It's not for drinking." He dabbed the wet cloth against the bloodstain on his uniform.

"I won't help you," she said.

"Yes, you will. It's either that or face interrogation yourself. I'm sure there's some useful information in that mind of yours. Such as where to find your brother."

Her stomach tightened as she looked at the implements of torture on the side table. Would she be able to withstand it? As a Crow, she didn't fear death, but pain was another matter.

Heavy footsteps clopped up the far staircase. The captain looked up as he dried his hands.

"Ah." He smiled at Rhia. "You can give me your answer after we serve our next guest."

The door banged open, and a set of three guards dragged in a tall, hulking older man, whose head already bore a wound above the eye—no doubt delivered to subdue him in his cell. As they shackled him to the pole's crossbar, Rhia recognized him. It was Medus the Badger, once one of the fiercest men in Asermos. He'd been their chief of police when the Ilions had invaded, and for a time she'd thought him a collaborator. Clearly things had changed.

Medus swayed in his shackles, groggy, as they stripped him naked. She looked away, searching the room for anything she could use as a weapon, though she knew it was pointless.

"I hope you didn't hit him so hard he can't remember anything," Addano said. "It doesn't take much to knock out the brains of a beast." He turned and gave Rhia a little bow. "Present company excepted, of course." He shot her a mirthless grin before scooping a bowlful of ice water and tossing it in Medus's face.

The Badger woke with a defiant roar, which had no effect on the three Ilions. They conferred at the side table as to the most efficient means of extracting information. Their matter-of-fact tone curdled her blood. She put her face in her hands.

Rhia heard the clank of iron and the hiss of steam. As Addano turned to Medus, she crammed her hands over her ears just as she heard him say,

"Let's talk about Velekos."

Her breath caught in her throat. Why did the Ilion military in Asermos care about what happened in Velekos?

"Have you ever been to a neighborhood known as the Acrosia?" the captain asked Medus.

"All the time," Medus sneered. "Whenever I need your mother to suck my big Badger—auughgh!"

Rhia yelped at the sudden sizzle of burning flesh. She covered her face again so she wouldn't see Medus writhing and flailing in his shackles. Her mind fought to stay clear through the haze of fear and fury.

Mali had said to act as though escape were inevitable. Rhia had to cling to that hope, and if she ever did get out, she would take what she knew of the Ilions' suspicions straight to her brother. Lycas hadn't seemed to know the authorities were watching Damen's neighborhood. The interrogators' questions were a glimpse into the mind of the Ilion counterinsurgency, a glimpse that could save his life, and the life of the fledgling resistance. She couldn't walk away from such an opportunity, no matter how it rent her soul.

Keeping her gaze on the floor, she took her hands from her ears and listened.

14

Kalindos

Sura saw Dravek waiting in the boulder field, under a slate-gray afternoon sky, sitting cross-legged with his head slightly bowed. The closer of the two torches was lit, but not the other. She forbade her feet to run to him, despite the energy that had crackled through her all morning.

Her world had changed in the two days since the Bestowing. The damp forest filled her newly sensitive nose with the scents of decaying plants and living animals. Every bite of food held a thousand tastes, and her reflexes had turned frighteningly fast. Most of all, her skin felt as if a layer had been peeled back. She could feel each shift of her clothes, her blankets, even the air itself. When people approached her from behind, she felt the vibrations in the soles of her feet.

She had become a Snake.

Before her boot scraped the first boulder, Dravek looked up, no doubt catching her scent on the wind. The breeze blew the torch's flame in his direction, so that the heat waves in the air made his image blur and shudder.

She made her way across the field and joined him on the flat, dark red boulder. "Hello." Her voice, so loud in her head, was lost in the wide-open space and gathering breeze. Even the word felt shallow, too weak to express the feelings careening inside her. This would be their first and last day together as Snakes.

He looked up at her without quite meeting her eyes. "Have you recovered yet?"

She nodded. "I did nothing yesterday but sleep and eat. Sometimes I can't believe I survived."

"The Spirits take care of us during our Bestowing. No one's ever died, though we all think we will."

She sat beside him. "What do you mean?"

He gave her a sharp look. "The living void? The thing that feels like it's sucking out your soul? It comes to everyone the first two nights."

"Oh, that." She picked up a pebble the size of her fingernail and tossed it away. It disappeared into an abyss among the boulders. "How deep do these rocks go?"

"Sura."

She peered over the edge. "And what if you dropped something valuable? You'd never get it out."

"Sura." He waited to speak until she looked at him. "You laughed at the void, didn't you?"

She shrugged, feigning casualness. "It seemed to help."

He studied her face until she felt it flush. "You're not like anyone I've ever met," he said.

"You haven't met many Asermons."

"How did you get to be so brave?"

She looked away. If he could hear the speed of her pulse right now, he'd know her courage was failing. "The Ilions crave our fear. It keeps them in power. Every arrest they make, every home they steal—" *Or burn.* "They do it to make us feel helpless." She looked at her hands in her lap, twisted together like brawling cats. "One day I decided I wouldn't be afraid anymore."

He spoke with awe. "You can decide not to feel something and it goes away?"

Sura almost laughed. *If only.* "No, it wasn't that easy." The conversation was pressing in on her, and she decided to change the subject. "So how are the wedding preparations?"

He blinked, then shifted to face forward again. "Uh, everything's ready. Kara's still finishing her dress, she says, but I can't help her with that." He looked at her from the corner of his eye. "You'll be there?"

"Of course. The whole village is coming." Sura leaned on one hand and ran her finger along the sharp edge of the slab. "Etarek said he'd teach me to dance. He made me dinner last night."

"Ah. That's why the red flag was out on his porch." Dravek clenched his hands, making one of his knuckles crack.

"Was it? I hadn't noticed." She tried not to smile at the thought of Etarek signaling the world not to disturb them.

"Did he show you his stick collection?" Dravek said with a tight voice.

"For his drums? He played for me, but only a bit, since it was late and he didn't want to wake anyone."

Dravek rubbed his palms together. "How late?"

"Nothing happened. I was very tired from my Bestowing."

The muscles in his jaw relaxed. "Let's get started." He pointed at the flaming torch. "Snuff it, then bring it back."

Her hands went clammy at the thought of reigniting a fire, but she got to her knees, sank back on her heels and closed her eyes to concentrate. It was easy now to feel the flame. She snuffed it with a mere thought.

"Good," he murmured. "Keep going."

The heat spread inside her, searching for a way out. She could release it, make the torch spring back to life. But when she tried, she only saw the burning roof, heard the shrieks of children.

"I can't," she said through gritted teeth.

"Yes, you can. Try harder."

She opened her eyes and stared at the extinguished torch, at the black smoke wisping toward the sky.

"I can't do it."

"Why?" Dravek reached to touch her shoulder, then pulled his hand back. "You can trust me."

Still kneeling, she rubbed her hands hard against her legs to release some of the heat. Her mouth opened, but emitted no words.

"After tomorrow," he whispered, "you'll never see me again, so what does it matter?"

Her throat finally released the truth. "They burned him."

Dravek's eyes softened at the corners. "Who?"

"My mate." She sighed with the relief of finally saying it out loud. "We were out one night together." She felt her face twist as she remembered their last moments of intimacy. "Mathias was a Bear, so he smelled the smoke before I did. We ran to his house. The flames were worst at the doors and windows, because the Descendants didn't want anyone to get out, not even the children. We got inside and—" She wrapped her arms around herself and closed her eyes, remembering the pain, the choking smoke. "We dragged his little brother and sister out—they were on the first floor. By the time we got out, other people had arrived, including my mother. The roof was starting to cave. His parents were screaming."

She pressed the heels of her hands against her forehead. "He ran back in. I tried to follow, but Mother grabbed me. I called and called Mathias's name, but he never came back."

"Sura," Dravek whispered. "I'm so sorry." He touched her shoulder. "Was that when you decided to stop being afraid?"

She nodded and lowered her hands. "It was the day Snake claimed me. I'd never had any powers before, but after that day I could put out a fire."

He got to his knees in front of her and grasped her arms. "Don't you see? You *are* still afraid. They made you afraid of your only weapon." He took her face in his hands. "Use it before it's too late."

"Help me." Her throat ached, trying to hold back the words of longing. She touched his chest. "Help me forget."

Dravek's breath turned uneven as his dark gaze met hers. He slid his hands around her nape, up into her hair. She winced as her braid tugged her scalp. He leaned in close, and for a moment she thought he would kiss her. Panic streamed down her spine.

Instead Dravek reached behind her back and removed the binding on her hair. His breath came hot against her neck as he unwound the braid. She closed her eyes and inhaled the scent of the bare skin at his nape. It made her want to run her own hands over every part of him.

This is wrong, she thought. Even if these feelings let her use her power, they could lead to nothing but misery and disaster, and not just for her.

Dravek drew her hair in long black waves toward him, flowing over her shoulders and bare arms, making her skin tingle and spark.

"Just like when we met," he whispered. "I'll never forget the way you looked." His fingers tangled and twined in the black strands. "I'll remember it the day I die."

He leaned forward and buried his face in her hair, inhaling deeply. His mouth drew near her ear. "Make it burn, Sura." His hands crested her shoulders and slid down her back. "Do it now."

Her mind reached out through the haze of lust to sense the fire waiting, small and shivering, inside the extinguished torch. She offered it a fraction of the heat inside her. It sparked feebly, then fell back into coldness.

"More." Dravek's lips skirted the edge of her earlobe. "Give it all."

Sura drew a deep, shaky breath, full of his scent. She let out her heat, all at once.

The torch ignited.

Dravek looked past her at the flame as it reached for the sky. He let out a low whistle, then flashed a smile that banished the new chill inside her.

"I knew you could do it." He glanced down at the tiny space between them, then let go of her quickly and sat back on the boulder. "How do you feel now?"

She stared at the flame she had birthed, then up into Dravek's eyes. They reflected the torch behind her, glowing like those of Snake on the night of her Bestowing.

"Like they'll never touch me again."

* * *

Dravek gazed at Sura's determined face. Even if they never saw each other after today—the thought of which made his guts sink—he wanted her to have all the power and strength she deserved.

He cleared his throat and tried to shake the memory of his hands and face in her hair. "Back to the lesson. Let's spread the fire from one torch to the next."

"They're pretty far apart. Can you do that?"

"Almost. I was hoping we could try it together."

"It would be a good weapon." She scratched her neck as she thought. "How do we do it?"

His gaze adhered to the pale, puckered patch of skin she'd revealed as her hand shifted down from her neck. "Did you get that scar in the fire?"

Sura grabbed the front of her shirt and jerked it up over her collarbone.

Dravek reached forward. "No, don't cover it. Please."

She pushed his hand away, but lowered her own from her collar so that her shirt fell open at the neck.

"How far does it go?" he asked matter-of-factly, as if they were discussing a trail through the woods.

She cleared her throat. "In front, not far. To here." She placed her finger an inch above her heart. "It's bigger in the back. A piece of ceiling fell on me, and my clothes caught fire. Mathias's little brother got it worse, though. His face is still—" She twisted one of her black curls. "Luckily my hair was tied back, so it didn't catch."

He'd known the pain of many burns; the thought of Sura suffering like that made his fists clench.

Her gaze lowered to his hands, then flitted up to meet his eyes. "Do you want to see?"

Wonder replaced his anger. "Do you want to show me?"

She bit her lip and nodded. He fought to control his breath as he watched Sura unfasten three more buttons. She turned her back to him.

Slowly he tugged the collar of her shirt, exposing her left shoulder blade. She undid all but one button, just enough to keep her breasts covered.

The scar was both cratered and raised, in some places pale and shiny, in other places dark and ragged. He swept her hair aside to see better, laying it in front of her right shoulder. She shivered at his touch.

"Does it hurt?" he asked her.

"The healer said the skin died, so it doesn't feel much of anything." She swallowed. "So if you want to touch it…you don't have to, but if you did, it wouldn't hurt me."

He traced his finger along the edge of the scar on her shoulder blade, then caressed the center with his palm. His own skin suddenly seemed more alive than ever. "Can you feel that?"

"I sense your hand, but it's as if you're at a distance, through extra layers of skin. Like when your foot falls asleep and you rub it."

He wanted more than anything to follow the journey of his hand with his lips, to show Sura that these inches were as beautiful to him as the rest of her, if not more. He slid his fingers up her shoulder and just over the edge.

"Have you ever been burned?" she asked in a trembling voice.

"Several times, but never so bad. It helps having a third-phase Otter on hand."

"I couldn't get to a healer the night of the fire. Mother said I had to hide my connection to my mate." She turned her head so he could see the left side of her face. "He was high-profile in the resistance, and if they knew we were together, I'd be a target." Sura's lips pressed together. "I still feel like I have to hide it, even here."

"I won't tell anyone."

One side of her mouth ticked into a tight smile. "Anyway, Mother knew enough first aid to save my life, but by the time I saw an Otter, it was too late to stop the scarring."

"I'm sorry you suffered." His heartbeat quickened and skipped as his hand passed over the pale pink ridges on her back. "But this is the most magnificent thing I've ever seen."

She glared at him. "Don't mock me."

"You know I'm not." Sensing her discomfort, he pulled her shirt collar up to cover her. "It's a battle wound as much as any soldier's. You won it saving a life."

"It's still ugly."

"Nobody else has one just like it. It's exactly you, and that's what makes it magnificent." He drew his hand over it, through the soft fabric. "To me, anyway," he whispered, then immediately wished he could pull the words back into his mouth.

She buttoned her shirt with shaking fingers. Dravek shifted away, though his hands itched to touch her again. He knew he should fight this desire with every scrap of strength, but it felt like some larger force beyond their understanding was yanking them together.

Maybe Snake was testing them. If so, he could pass it. Only another day until the wedding, then two more days until he and Kara moved to Tiros. Three days of resisting the urge to kiss Sura, to touch her skin, to flatten her against the closest horizontal or vertical surface and fuck like wildcats.

He took a deep breath and wiped the sweat from under his eyes. No doubt he was failing the test just by imagining it.

Or maybe these feelings were a punishment, for him alone. Maybe Snake—maybe all the Spirits—hated him for his Descendant blood, for his evil, violent conception.

"It wasn't just me." Sura had finished buttoning her shirt and was now sitting with her arms around her knees, pulling them close to her chest. "Relighting that torch just now."

"It was you. I swear on my Spirit I didn't help."

"Not directly." She angled her head to look at him from the corner of her eye. "But when you touched me, I felt—" She stopped, then spoke slowly as if choosing her words with care. "It created heat. It gave me the fuel to light the fire."

He started to deny it, but realized he'd be a terrible mentor if he left out an important Snake fact. "When I've trained on my own, spreading fires or igniting them, I've found that it helps to think about sex."

She jerked her head to look at him, first his face, then lower, then back to his face. "Do you touch yourself?"

"No," he said quickly. "If anything, that makes the fire die." His heart slammed his chest as he searched for the best way to tell the truth. "It's the desire, not the satisfaction, that makes the heat."

"Oh." She looked away, then her gaze fixed on the cold torch. "Do you think we could—" She shut her mouth hard, clacking her teeth together. "Never mind."

Dravek turned away, fighting to slow his breath. They'd have to be crazy to try what she suggested. They were Spirit-siblings. They couldn't.

He looked up and realized the sun was descending already. Soon their time together would be over. He'd get married and leave Sura behind forever. This was their one chance. And if it worked…

He looked back at her. The wind blew her hair across her face, hiding her eyes. Black curls cascaded over the bare skin of her arm and neck, touching her the way he ached to do.

Dravek gave in and slid to sit beside her. He put his palm next to her arm without touching. Heat radiated between their skin like two coals.

"We could try," he whispered.

She turned her head and said, "It's wrong," even as she stared at his mouth.

"We won't touch." He leaned close to her face and inhaled her rich, sweet scent. He could smell her desire, almost taste it on his tongue. The heat rose inside him in a violent wave. "Spirits save me, I'd kill to kiss you right now."

She drew in a sharp breath, and he could tell it was only part shock. "Dravek, we can't."

"I know." His lips skirted the edge of her earlobe, so that only his breath would touch her. "But we want it. That's enough." He whispered against her neck. "Sura. Let's build a fire."

She sighed his name, and her hands loosened around her knees, opening her body to him. "Tell me how you'd kiss me."

He looked in her eyes and blinked slowly, hypnotizing her with his gaze. "Slow. Soft. When you close your eyes you won't know if it's me or just the breeze."

"Yes." She closed her eyes.

"You'll open your mouth, waiting for my tongue, but you won't get it yet." He breathed in her scent again. "I'll make you beg for it."

Her lips parted, as he said they would. "Please…"

"Not yet. You'll feel my teeth first, on your bottom lip. You'll imagine how wild it could be if we didn't hold back."

She smiled, an expression he'd rarely seen, and her beauty threatened to steal his words. He forced himself to keep speaking.

"Then just when you can't stand it anymore, you'll feel my tongue. Just one stroke, under your upper lip, but you'll feel it everywhere. On your nipples. Between your legs."

Sura gave a throaty moan, and he made a fist to keep himself from touching her.

"Go on." Her voice shook even on only two words.

"No," he said. "Now it's your turn."

She spoke, her eyes still closed. "You may be stingy with your tongue, but I'm not. I'll lick you everywhere. I'll suck your fingers, one by one."

He swallowed hard, his hands tingling. "Then what?"

Sura lay back on the rock. "Then I'll take you in my mouth."

He groaned. The heat was already surging from his core out to his limbs. He could almost release it now, set the torch aflame. But he didn't want to stop.

"I'll tease you," she said, "running the tip of my tongue up and around and under your entire length." Her fingers gripped the rock, kneading the unyielding surface as if it were skin and muscle. "Then I'll give you my whole mouth, where it's deep and wet and hot, and I'll give you my hand, and I'll stroke you until you're harder than you've ever been in your life."

Dravek collapsed beside her, the purpose of their exercise a distant memory. "I'll want to finish in your mouth, but I'll stop you just on the edge, and then—" He drew a shaky breath. "I'll lick the sweat from your neck, from your breasts, your belly, your thighs. I'll find places no one's ever kissed you. Behind your knees, between your toes. Anywhere you show me. Anywhere you let me." He paused, the blood swelling his veins, pounding in his temples. "Will you let me kiss you everywhere, Sura?"

She squirmed beside him as she exhaled. "Everywhere."

"When I finally taste you, you'll grind your hips against my mouth, dig your heels into my shoulders. You'll scream, but no one will hear. No one will know how much you love what I'm doing to you."

One of her fingers brushed his. "How much I need you inside me."

He paused, as if they really were about to cross that threshold instead of just pretending. "Are you ready for me?"

"Yes."

He couldn't stop himself. He touched her, just his palm, moving down her arm. He could feel her heat surge, and she cried out as if he'd just made her climax.

"I'll spread your legs wide," he said, "and I won't tease anymore." His hand reached hers, and she clutched it. "I'll slide deep inside you, pinning you to the ground." His thumb moved over her knuckles. "How will it feel?"

"Hot, and hard. I'll feel your bones grind against mine. I'll feel every inch of you filling me up. I'll clutch you tight inside, and you'll feel it against you when I come."

He gasped as reality started to blur. "I'll stroke you and move on you, again and again until you can't think. Until there's nothing in the world but our bodies."

"Dravek…" Her breath came hard and fast. "Are you ready?"

He moaned in anticipation, then realized she was talking about the torches. "Yes." He tightened his grip on her hand. "Give me the heat. I'll send it."

It shot up his arm, spreading throughout his body in the span of a breath. For a moment his mind was nothing but flame. Then he found his voice.

"I'll lift your legs over my shoulders and get deeper than ever."

"Yes," she cried, pouring more heat into him.

"I'll move faster, and faster, and I'll feel you come again, harder than ever, out of control, and then—"

He closed his eyes and let it go. The heat roared out of him, straight for the torch.

A sudden *whoosh* went up from their right. He rolled over on the boulder, and Sura sat up quickly.

The second torch was burning.

They scrambled to their feet, still clutching each other's hands.

"It worked." He turned to Sura, wondering if his face were as flushed as hers, his eyes as bright. "We did it!"

She yelped and threw her arms around his neck. He lifted her off her feet and turned in a circle, whooping, before putting her down. He grasped her face and moved to kiss her.

They froze just in time. The moment stretched out, and Dravek felt himself on the edge of the abyss, wanting to throw himself over.

They let go of each other at the same moment and stepped back. He wiped his face. "Sura, I'm so sorry."

"You're my Spirit-brother," she said.

"I know."

"And my mentor."

"I know."

"You're getting married tomorrow." She twisted the hem of her shirt. "Aren't you?"

He turned away, grasping his hair in both his trembling hands, then let out a howl of frustration. Despite the release of heat, his stomach felt sick, and a heavy ache tore at his groin.

"This is insane," he said.

"This is stupid."

"This is wrong."

They paused, silent except for the heave of their breath. Then together they slowly turned to look at the torch, the one that had been as cold as earth less than a minute ago.

Its flame danced and bobbed in the breeze, waves of invisible heat blurring the blue sky beyond. It couldn't comprehend what it meant, for Sura and Dravek, and for their people.

It just wanted to burn.

15

Asermos

Rhia stared at the floor and tried to hear Crow's wings beneath all the screaming. But it was true what Mali said; these men were good at what they did. The death Spirit was nowhere near.

"What do the blue flowers on the doors mean?" Captain Addano asked. "Wait, don't tell me yet. Think about it for a second or two."

The whip cracked, a man shrieked. From the corner of her eye, Rhia saw blood flick onto the floor as the guard drew back the lash again.

"Stop!" The man on the rack sobbed. She didn't know him; she felt like she'd never know anyone again. Years ago her mentor Coranna had told her she had to isolate herself from others' pain in order to be a good Crow. After only three days of this, Rhia had learned that lesson well.

"The flowers," the prisoner gasped. "Chicory. It's about not drinking wine."

"Why wouldn't they drink wine?" the captain asked. "To spite us?"

"Some drink too much." He fought to catch his breath. "Makes them crazy."

"They drink plenty of ale."

"Wine's stronger."

"True." Captain Addano came back to the desk and made a note. "But I don't think that's all. It's a symbol of something."

"Please, let me down." The man coughed.

The captain ignored him. "Blue is the only color that doesn't have red and yellow in it, the colors of the Ilion flag. Every day I see another house painted blue. Solidarity with the resistance."

The prisoner coughed again. "Please, some water, at least."

Rhia couldn't stand it anymore. She seized the cup and pitcher from the captain's desk, then strode over to the prisoner, taking care not to slip in the blood on the floor.

She didn't meet the wounded man's gaze, just tilted the cup to his lips and let him drink.

They'd shaved his head, roughly, and a trickle of blood from his scalp was about to run in his eye. She looked for a clean cloth. Seeing none, she pulled her sleeve down over her hand and reached out to wipe the blood.

The prisoner spat the mouthful of water at her. "Traitor."

She lurched back, too shocked to speak, then wiped her own face with her sleeve.

"Leave her alone," Addano said. "And now that you can talk, tell me what the Velekon resistance plans for the night of the Evius festival."

A door opened on her right, the one leading to the men's prison, and a young guard entered. "Sir, the Wolverine's ready."

Rhia's neck jerked. Captain Addano saw her reaction, then nodded to the young guard. "Thank you, Corporal. They'll be down in a moment to gather him." He gestured to the prisoner, speaking to the other two guards. "Take him down and tell them to clean him up, see to his wounds and give him as much food and water as he wants. He's been a moderately good boy today." He shrugged. "And some wine. Why not?"

Paralyzed with fear, Rhia watched them drag the prisoner out of the room. Which Wolverine was coming? Would she have to see her own brother tortured?

Addano stood and motioned between Rhia and the chair. "You'll want to sit down for this." He crossed the room and picked up the large wooden board that was propped up against the tub.

Rhia's legs felt weak, so she returned to her seat.

"Your constitution is admirable." He rested the board against the wall and opened the iron ankle and wrist rings. "Most men twice your size would need a bucket, if not smelling salts, after witnessing these scenes, yet you've not once even retched."

"I've seen worse on the battlefield." Her voice was hoarse with unshed tears.

"So unnecessary, all the fighting, all the bloodshed." He pulled open a drawer in the tall cabinet and withdrew a length of heavy chain. "You people are treated better than most colonies. You're not slaves. We give you fair wages to work in the vineyards and quarries, your farms yield more crops per acre than ever. Why must you resist progress?"

"It's our land." She shook her head. "It's the Spirits' land, we're just its stewards."

"I can understand why." He examined the inside of the tub. "They give you magic if you do what they want, it's a fair trade. But wouldn't you rather do what *you* want?"

Fury curled her fingers into fists. "Yes, I'd rather be on my way now, thank you."

Addano looked at her with bloodshot eyes. "Freedom has a price, I'm afraid."

"Yes," she whispered. "We know."

As a thumping sound came from the stairs, the captain held Rhia's gaze. "This one's different. We don't need you to tell us when he's dying." His lips formed a tight line. "We need you to tell us when he's dead."

Rhia shuddered and looked at the tub.

"He'll have to be drowned," the captain said quietly. "Second-phase Wolverines can't be decapitated. It would break the ax."

Something crumbled inside her. If the prisoner were her brother, they might as well strap her to the board with him. A tear crawled down her cheek, dwindling evidence that she could still feel.

The door opened, and the two guards stumbled in, dragging a large, dark-haired man, who appeared to be barely conscious. The captain came forward and grabbed the man's hair to help them lift him against the board on the wall.

Rhia let out a hard breath. It wasn't Lycas.

Guilt followed her relief. This man was undoubtedly *someone's* brother, and father and son.

They strapped his head to the board, and as the dark, matted hair fell back from his face, she recognized him.

Sirin.

"No…" she whispered.

"Your brother's executive officer," Addano said, "probably an old friend of the family." He stepped back and watched the others bind Sirin's wrists and ankles in the iron rings. "Public Enemy Number Two, and we're disposing of him in a back room like a common criminal."

She cleared her throat. "Why not a public execution?"

He gave her a sideways look, as if knowing she was trying to get information out of him. "The Ilion command has its reasons."

"Ready, sir." The guards stepped back to display Sirin bound and chained to the board. Even now they seemed frightened of his dormant strength and ferocity.

"Wait a moment." Addano turned to Rhia. "Is there a prayer or something you people like to use at this time? If you can do it quickly…" He flicked his hand toward Sirin.

"Thank you." Rhia swallowed, then approached the Wolverine on unsteady legs. A distant part of her mind realized that the captain had referred to them twice now as "people" instead of "beasts."

She touched Sirin's hand and stared into his glassy, pale blue eyes. Her heart twisted as she remembered the first time they'd met, after the battle of Asermos almost twenty years ago. He'd been a frightened boy, wounded by a Descendant sword, and she'd given him the happy news that he would live. Now she would finally feel Crow come for him.

She said a silent prayer to the Spirit to make his journey swift and peaceful. Sirin blinked, and his eyes seemed to shift her way through his drugged haze.

The captain cleared his throat. "Let's get on with it." He rubbed his face hard. "Put him in."

The two guards lifted the ends of the board and staggered over to the tub.

"Quickly," the captain said. "Don't prolong it."

They set the board in the wide tub with a crash and a splash. Addano let out a curse. "I knew it, not deep enough." He looked at the barrel of ice water. "We'll add this." The three men lifted the barrel and dumped it in the tub. The ice shifted and cracked, melting against Sirin's body. As the water closed over his head, he woke up and started to struggle. The guards drew their swords.

"He won't break free," the captain murmured as he walked slowly back to his desk.

The board shifted and banged against the interior of the tub. The guards' eyes went round and frightened. Their swords shook. Rhia moved forward to kneel beside the tub. *He should not be alone.*

Her ears filled with the sound of bursting bubbles as Sirin fought for breath. She pressed her hands to her eyes and began a prayer to Crow to ease his passage. But no words would come. Her tears flowed for Sirin, and for her people's fading hope of freedom.

A sudden snap came from the tub, and Rhia jumped back. Had he broken the board?

"It's probably a bone," Addano said. "They told me this might happen." He drew a hand through his already disheveled hair and shifted the papers on his desk.

Rhia sank to her knees again, rocking and sobbing. It was all she could do for Sirin now. At least he had someone to mourn his death. She and Mali might have no one.

The banging in the tub slowed and ceased, then the bubbles, until the only sound was Rhia's muffled cries. Still she did not hear Crow's approach.

"They say it takes Wolverines a while…" The captain made a paper-shuffling sound and cleared his throat. "You two, make sure you dry the chains thoroughly, or they'll rust."

"Yes, sir."

"Do it by hand, don't just hang them up and let them drip. I shouldn't have to tell you, but—" He took a few breaths. "It's too quiet. Talk about something. Anything."

"Yes, sir," the younger one said. "Uh…Sergeant Kiro, what are your, uh, plans for the Evius festival?"

"Oh! Yes," said the other guard, the one with the deeper voice. "I've been called to Velekos. My wife won't stop complaining about it. My first Evius away from the family, and I'll miss the games. They say our boy's a lock for the long jump. But it's not like I have a choice."

Rhia heard it then, the sound of beating wings. Crow was on His way at last.

"Why Velekos?" the first guard asked.

"They're shipping in more troops from Ilios the night before the festival. We'll meet them on the beach, help unload the horses, weapons, that sort of thing."

The wings came closer, then hovered. *Please,* she begged Crow, *take him now. End his suffering.*

The first guard snickered. "Whose boots did you piss in to earn that assignment?"

"It's an honor," Sergeant Kiro said. "The general will be on board."

"Shut up!"

Rhia lifted her head, though she could barely see or hear anything real in the face of Crow's presence.

Addano was standing behind the desk, pointing at her but

looking at his men. "Mind what you say around the woman, or we'll have to kill her, too. Then where will we be?"

"He's dead," she said, as much to distract them as to announce Sirin's demise.

"Get him out of there," the captain barked. "If she's lying, she's next."

"Feel his pulse if you don't believe me." She swiped the flood of tears from her cheeks and chin. "Before you take him, there's another prayer we do after death. If you please."

The captain nodded to the guard. "Hurry up."

They lifted Sirin, limp and dripping, from the tub. The captain felt his wrist and neck, then gave Rhia a long, hard stare. "Make it quick."

She approached the Wolverine's body. His right arm was bent at an unnatural angle. His face was contorted in agony. She closed his bulging eyes and murmured the prayer of passage, waiting for Crow to free Sirin's soul.

Still the Spirit hovered. She forced her face to remain straight and smooth. Finally she stepped back.

"Will you give him a proper burial?" she asked the captain.

"Of course."

His gaze shifted away from her face, and she knew he was lying. Sirin would be dumped in the river for the fish to eat. Forgotten, desecrated, alone.

16

Kalindos

Sura held her breath as Elora tied the ribbon on the back of her pale green dress. Her finger traced the neckline, ensuring that it didn't reveal her burns. She studied her figure in the mirror and tried not to wonder what Dravek would think when he saw her.

Elora looped Sura's braid atop her head and fastened it with several pins. "How's that?"

She turned to check the back of her neck. It felt good to have her hair up on such a sweltering evening, but…

"No one can see it," Elora said, "and no one would care, anyway. You're not the only one with scars in this village."

Sura touched her hair. "It's very pretty. Thank you. My mother never—" She clamped her lips shut, wishing she could bury the disloyal thought. With Mali in prison, now was no time for Sura to wish her mother had been more like Elora, to wish she'd taken time from saving the world to occasionally, perhaps, touch her own daughter.

"Your mother would be glad you're safe." Elora squeezed Sura's shoulders. "She'd want you to celebrate tonight."

Guilt pressed on her. It wasn't her mother's predicament that had left her pensive and distraught.

Elora touched Sura's cheek and looked at her in the mirror with a bittersweet gaze. Sura squeezed her soft, strong hand, remembering what Etarek had told her about Elora's own children. Her teenage sons had been captured during the Descendant invasion almost twenty years ago and had never been found. She'd only known one of them was alive when she came into her own third-phase powers several years ago.

They left the bedroom and headed for the front door of the healer's home, which was connected to the hospital and had a staircase outside instead of a ladder.

Tereus joined them at the door. He kissed Sura's cheek.

"You look beautiful," he said. "Did Elora tell you about Kalindon weddings?"

His wife winked at him. "Thought I'd leave that a surprise."

Sura was about to tell them she didn't like surprises, but the view from the hospital porch made her forget her words.

Dozens of people were gathering around a bonfire in a large clearing to her left. Kalindos had previously seemed tiny, but with all five hundred villagers in one place, it now appeared as large and lively as Asermos.

Long tables with benches sat among the trees, heaped with food and lined with mugs. Small torches flickered at the end of each table, spreading shimmering lights throughout the forest that reminded her of fireflies in the fields at home.

With Elora and Tereus, she moved to the clearing and joined the crowd. A three-man band was warming up on the opposite side of the clearing, one tuning a fiddle, another a pipe. Etarek was the drummer; he caught her eye and gave her a friendly wave, which she returned. He yanked his attention back to the band in time to start a quiet processional tune.

Elora tapped Sura softly on the shoulder. "Isn't she beautiful?"

She turned to see Kara approach from the right. Tawny curls cascaded over her wine-red, ankle-length robe. The Wolf woman smiled upon the crowd with full lips and laughing blue eyes.

A collective male cheer of appreciation rang out from the other side of the clearing. Dravek stood there, transfixed at the sight of his bride. Half a dozen young men gathered behind him, though he stood out by his greater height. His own wedding robe was a deep, dark green, the color of the forest in the dead of night.

Kara and Dravek each took a barefoot step forward into the circle. A young man and woman—their chief attendants, Sura assumed—stepped up behind them, reached around their waists, and untied the robes.

Underneath, they were naked.

Sura knew her mouth hung open but felt too paralyzed to close it. She looked between the bride and groom, positive the dancing torchlight was playing tricks on her eyes. She thanked every Spirit she could name that the shriek of horror was only in her head.

They were naked. *Naked!* In front of everyone—their parents, brothers, sisters, aunts, uncles, cousins, neighbors. In front of her.

The band silenced as Dravek and Kara met in the center of the clearing and joined hands. They were still naked. Sura wanted to cover her eyes, or at least lower her gaze to the ground to avoid looking at Dravek's—

Too late.

Her face burning, she tried to shrink back into the crowd, but people behind her strained forward to see. She stepped aside to let a shorter woman stand in front of her. Elora caught Sura's eye and batted her lashes in fake innocence. Tereus shook his head and sighed, looking like he couldn't wait until it was over.

Sura noticed several members of the crowd throwing not-so-subtle glances in her direction, surely enjoying her shock. She forced her face into stoicism, a skill learned from a decade of dealing with Descendant soldiers.

The attendants stepped forward, each with a pile of clothes. Slowly, ritually, Dravek and Kara dressed each other, taking turns, one garment at a time.

Elora leaned over and whispered to Sura, "It's to symbolize the journey from promiscuity to monogamy, and also shows that they have nothing to hide from each other or from us. A very old tradition, recently revived."

Sura had a sudden horrible thought. "Did you and Tereus—"

"No." Elora rolled her eyes. "This ritual's for native Kalindons only. We'd never foist this on an Asermon."

At last the bride and groom stood together, Kara in a soft violet gown and matching slippers, and Dravek in a new white shirt and black trousers, along with black boots so shiny they reflected the sparks from the bonfire.

A middle-aged woman stepped forward to address the crowd. Sura recognized her as Thera the Hawk, Etarek's mother.

"Welcome," she said in a strong, throaty voice. "A Kalindon wedding is a rare and sacred occasion. Among our animal counterparts, there are those who mate not just for an hour, a day or a season, but for life. The Wolf, for instance—" she extended a graceful hand toward Kara "—often remains with a mate until one of them dies. A Wolf person's strengths of loyalty, passion and devotion to family come to fruition in marriage."

Sura wondered how Thera would address Dravek's Spirit, since snakes in the wild typically didn't stay with a mate for more than a few minutes.

"Other people's Spirits have natural associates, who, in the interest of survival and propagation, spend their lives with several, if not dozens of mates."

Dravek's cheeks reddened, or maybe it was just the flames dancing over his face. A woman behind Sura whispered a bawdy comment to her friend that broke them into suppressed laughter.

Thera laid her hand on Dravek's shoulder—not an easy feat considering the difference in their heights—and raised her voice above the crowd's murmurs.

"Our groom proves that we are more than our Spirits. We cannot rely solely on instinct, or blame our Animal nature when we err. The ability to choose is what makes us human.

"As I have counseled this couple—and believe me, I counseled them very hard—" she let a small smile slip through in response to the crowd's laughter "—I can say with full confidence that Dravek and Kara are equally committed to making this marriage last a lifetime."

Sura saw the tightness around Dravek's eyes and mouth and wondered if these counseling sessions had taken place before her own arrival.

"Soon they will be bound together," Thera continued, "in body and soul. But first they will recite a set of vows whose power lies in their simplicity. Let us keep perfect silence so that we, the forest and the Spirits may all bear witness."

She stepped back and nodded to Kara. The Wolf woman gazed up at Dravek and took his hands. Her beaming smile disappeared as she stared solemnly into his eyes. Dravek began to blink rapidly, and Sura thought she saw a corner of his jaw twitch.

"Dravek," Kara's high-pitched voice rang clear. "In the name of Wolf, I promise to love you forever." The final word dropped as heavy as a stone.

Dravek let go of Kara suddenly. She looked down in surprise, but he drew up her chin to look at him. He clasped her face in both hands.

"Kara, in the name of Snake, I promise to love you." His jaw clenched, and a palpable tension spread through the crowd. "Forever," he choked out at last.

He moved to kiss her, but Thera cleared her throat. She held up a long, wide white ribbon. The firelight glinted off its silky smooth surface.

Dravek and Kara clasped each other's bare forearms near the elbow. Chanting, Thera wound the ribbon to bind them together on one side, Dravek's right arm to Kara's left. She let the ends drift and flutter in the breeze like flags.

Thera's apprentice handed her a red ribbon. She bound Dravek's left arm to Kara's right, in the same pattern as the white one but much more tightly, and she left no ends to dangle.

Sura gave Elora an inquiring glance. The Otter whispered, "White symbolizes joy and ease. The happy days awaiting them."

"And the red?" She was afraid to ask.

"Suffering. Conflict. It's tighter than the white one because these things bind us closer as husband and wife. You don't know how strong a love is until you've lost something together."

Thera came forth with a final ribbon, as black as a moonless sky. She tucked one end inside the loop of the red ribbon, then circled the couple, chanting with her apprentice. The black ribbon bound their bodies together, from shoulders to knees.

Elora leaned over. "Marriage should only be dissolved by death."

Sura nodded, fighting to keep her face serene and her eyes dry.

Thera finished the chant, then placed her hands on the couple's shoulders. "In the storms of life, may you take shelter in each other. You are wedded forever."

She nodded to Dravek, and he turned his fiery gaze on his wife. He kissed her hard, and Sura closed her eyes, ashamed of the way her own stomach plummeted. What had she expected? That he would cast aside the woman he loved for the sake of a lust that could never be consummated, much less honored?

When she opened her eyes, Dravek and Kara were still kissing, bodies melded together. The torch closest to the bride and groom began to flicker and flare, though there was no breeze. Sura looked around to see if anyone else had noticed.

Thera brought forth a knife with a long, thin blade. With several short, swift strokes, she sliced the black ribbon, which fell in shreds at their feet. They continued to kiss.

At a signal from the bride's parents, Etarek struck his sticks together to count off, and the music began. Kara broke the kiss and grinned up at her new husband. Bound at the arms, the couple danced a set of intricate steps, eyes locked on each other.

Upon the second verse, the crowd joined them in pairs, whereupon Sura was relieved to retreat.

In the first hour of the celebration, several men approached her to dance, but her body was too tight with apprehension to catch the rhythm. So she politely refused the men—less politely with each invitation—and stood watching on the outskirts, keeping her gaze away from Dravek and Kara.

Someone always seemed to be filling her mug. She diluted the meloxa with lots of honey water, but the sweetness only made her mind sing louder. The drink loosened her enough to tap her toes along with the infectious rhythm.

The song changed to a slower, writhing beat. Sura crossed her arm over her chest and hunched her shoulders to ward off invitations to that sort of dance. Two by two, the Kalindons pressed against each other, hips locked, hands roaming. The sight heated her temples until she thought she might pass out.

Sipping her meloxa, she watched Etarek pound the drum strapped around his neck. He used his hands instead of sticks for this song, lending it the low, primal sound of skin against skin. His hips and shoulders swayed to the throbbing rhythm.

The song built to a thrumming climax, with a flourish of fiddle and drums. On the last beat, Etarek shot a glance at her, catching her staring. He beamed, blue eyes glinting in the torchlight. She threw him a smile, trying to convince herself of her own confidence.

Etarek lifted the strap over his head, handed the drum to another man, then sauntered in her direction. He rubbed his thumbs over his palms as he approached her, and she could imagine the tingling sensation the drum would leave behind. His hands would be warm right now.

When Etarek reached her, he took her mug and examined the

emptiness inside. "Enjoying yourself, then." He handed it back to her. "What do you think of Kalindon weddings?"

"Stimulating." She looked around at the cavorting villagers. A dozen young men were dancing in a ragged line on one of the long tables. They stomped so hard, every unattended plate and mug tumbled off. She laughed, her head lightened by the meloxa and the music.

Etarek pulled her to the edge of the clearing. "Dance with me." He placed her arms around him and started to sway, but her clumsy feet tripped them.

"Relax and let me guide you," he murmured. "Watch my eyes, not my feet."

He began to move again. Her body fell into the rhythm, and somehow her feet figured out where to move—not gracefully, but at least in the right direction at the right time.

"See?" he said. "Much better."

She fumbled for something to say. "If you hear other people's feelings, isn't it hard for you to be in a crowd?"

"I can block it if I want, and I usually do. It gives people their privacy, and lets me focus on other things."

She let her mouth curve into a seductive smile. "What other things?"

"Music, for one." His arm tightened around her waist. "Try it. Feel the music, nothing else."

Sura eased her body against his. She tried to let the music flow through her and flatten the fears that the meloxa had heightened and distorted.

Something lay within Etarek's eyes that soothed and excited her at the same time. She thought back to the vision of the deer at her Bestowing, how happy and free it had made her feel.

It was right to want this man. Maybe later, he could make her forget what Dravek would be doing all night with the woman who had captured his body forever.

Someone small and giggling bumped into them. Sura looked down to see a young boy, maybe eight or nine, stumbling over his own feet. Kara grabbed his hands and gave Sura and Etarek an apologetic grin before whirling away with him.

"That's her little brother." Etarek smiled at them. "Must be the siblings' dance." He tilted his chin over Sura's shoulder. "Yes, there's Dravek and Daria, looking like they want to kill each other."

Sura didn't look. When Etarek turned back to her, she said, "You think Dravek and Kara will be happy? Their Animals are so different."

Etarek's eyes turned sad as he watched Kara whirl by with her little brother, the white ribbon fluttering from her right arm. "I can't say." Then his mouth twitched. "Tonight they'll be happy, at least. Did Elora tell you what they do with those ribbons on their wedding night?"

"No, but I can guess." Sura fought to steady her voice. "They tie each other to the bed?"

He looked impressed at her imagination. "You're right. One at a time."

"Who goes first?"

"That's a secret only they know. I've heard that the person who holds more power in the marriage is bound first."

She tried to sound casual. "And between Dravek and Kara—"

"Before tonight I would've said he did for sure. But when they took their vows, I heard a shadow of fear in his voice. From now on, I think she'll gain power and he'll lose it."

"Shouldn't a relationship be between equals?"

"It's not the people who aren't equal. It's their need. There's always one who can't live without the other just a little bit harder."

Sura thought of Mathias. Would he have wanted to claw out his own heart if she had been the one to perish in the fire instead of him? She doubted it.

"Let's not talk about them anymore." Etarek's gaze roamed her face, holding a hunger for more than a dance. It rekindled the longing born within her when she'd watched him play. It was time to put both Mathias and Dravek out of her mind. One was dead; the other might as well be.

She felt her heat flow into Etarek. Pressed against his hip, her body finally found the rhythm. Her shoulders loosened, swaying and tilting with his. The music seeped into her blood and made it pump and sing with a new urgency.

Just as she was about to suggest they take their dance to a more private, shadowy place, the song changed, into a fast rhythm that made her jaw drop.

Etarek let go of her. "Time to eat."

She followed him out of the dancing area as a half-dozen Cats tripped a complex series of steps, leaping, turning and flipping, connecting body parts in ways Sura would've thought impossible.

Daria bounced by them on the way to the clearing. She turned her head as she passed and curled her finger in Etarek's direction. He shook his head and turned away. Daria jutted out her jaw, then entered the dance circle with a flounce. Sura watched her move, wondering what else such a lithe body could do and what it had done with Etarek.

He gestured to the empty end of a long table. She sat on the bench with her back to the bonfire. Etarek rounded up two large, mostly clean plates and filled them with acorns, berries and strips of roasted meat.

He placed the plate in front of Sura and sat across the table from her. "Do you have a mate in Asermos?"

Her appetite fled. She pushed her plate away. "He was killed last year. Descendants, of course."

"Oh, I'm so sorry." Etarek set down his fork and sighed. "That makes this sound even more inappropriate than it already is."

She tilted her head, making it swim from the meloxa. "What?"

He blew out a tight breath. "May I sit next to you for this?"

She nodded to her bench. He came over and straddled it, facing her. Slowly his hand reached for hers, and she let him take it, hearing her pulse pound louder than the bonfire drums.

"This is going to sound very strange, considering we've only known each other eight days." He rubbed his thumb and forefinger over his lower lip, pinching it into a vertical crease. "Thing is, our people need my mother to—and for her to—I need to—"

"There you are, Etarek." Adrek approached with Kara's parents. "Everyone's asking for the Spirit Dance."

Etarek grimaced and looked up at them. "Give me a moment."

"Now," Kara's mother said, "or there'll be a riot." She winked at Sura, who smiled back, though she had no idea what they were talking about.

"Fine," Etarek said. "Next song." They moved away, and he stood up, heaving a harsh sigh. "We'll finish this in a few minutes. After you dance with Dravek."

Sura jolted. "I can't dance with Dravek."

"I'll make it a slow song so you can follow the steps."

She rubbed the back of her neck, which was heating at the thought. "But why do I have to?"

"No one can leave before the bride and groom, and they can't leave until they dance with their Spirit-siblings."

She looked around at the copious food and drink. "The party's almost over?"

"No, not for another two or three days. People just want to leave to go do…other things, and come back."

"What other things?"

"Sex." He cleared his throat and rested his hands on his hips. "But it's bad form to do it before the bride and groom. People are getting restless, so I have to go play the Spirits' song and you have to dance with Dravek. Then we can all get back to partying."

Her throat seemed to grow a lump. "Why not just skip it and let them go to bed?" *While I hide in the outhouse.*

He shook his head. "In Kalindos, common sense is no match for tradition." He turned to leave.

"Wait. What were you going to ask me?"

He started to speak, then bit his lip. "Later, when we're alone."

She watched him stride back toward the clearing and confer with the other drummer.

Kara ran past, dragging one of her Wolf-brothers, a lanky young blond man. "Spirit Dance!" She spotted Sura. "No excuses, get up there."

The crowd at the edge of the clearing parted, and Dravek came for her. Sura looked down into her empty meloxa mug, unable to meet his eyes.

His shadow blotted out the light from the closest torch. "Please do this for me," he said in a low voice.

She looked up at him. He bowed and offered his hand. His eyes were tinged with anticipation, as if this dance were one last gift the world had offered them.

Sura stood slowly, untangling her legs from the bench. She took his hand as casually as possible, and they walked back to the clearing together. The music's beat was slow, as Etarek had promised.

Dravek led her as far from the others as possible. "The dance could last a while. Kara has a lot of Wolf-brothers."

Sura breathed in deep as she laid a hand on his shoulder. He wrapped his arm around her waist.

The bonfire snapped and flared. She looked at it. "Did we do that?"

"Shh. Let's start before people get suspicious."

They began to move together, and Sura's mind turned from desire to embarrassment. "Sorry I'm a bad dancer."

"I'm glad. Now we have a reason to look awkward."

She glanced up at him and saw the corner of his mouth tug into a smile. She struggled for words to break the tension.

"Your wife is very nice."

Dravek threw back his head and laughed. The sound of it made her want to hug him. To others they must have looked like friends.

"What's so funny?"

"The tone of your voice when you said that. I don't have to have a Deer's powers to hear your real meaning."

"She *is* nice."

"Yes, Kara's wonderful. She's perfect. She's everything a man could want in a thousand lifetimes." He looked past Sura's face, his eyes going far away. "I've made a horrible mistake."

Her heart leaped. "No, you haven't. It's normal to have second thoughts."

"I'll never deserve her."

"Because of what we've done? It's in the past. You'll go away with her and forget about me, and in a few weeks you'll wonder why you ever felt this way."

He nodded, but didn't look convinced.

She regarded the red ribbon wound around his left arm and imagined it stretching over his skin later as his muscles strained and pulled against the binding in a frenzy of passion.

Her own skin tingled and burned. He drew in a hiss and loosened his grip on her hand. She looked up at him and saw that he had followed her gaze to the ribbon.

She knew she shouldn't ask. "Are you happy?"

He hesitated. "It's not important."

"It is to me."

His step faltered, and he let out a heavy sigh. "See these dark circles under my eyes? I've barely slept since I met you."

"Doubt you'll sleep tonight, either." She cursed her voice's bitter tinge.

"I almost broke the engagement."

Her breath caught. "Why didn't you?"

"And then what? Run away with you? Where would we go?"

"You tell me, if you've lost so much sleep over it."

"Tiros." He looked away, then back, into her eyes. "I thought we'd go to Tiros, to Vara. Explain it all to her. Maybe we're not the first Snakes to feel this way. Maybe she could help us."

"Maybe." Sura matched his gaze, while inside she begged her meloxa-weakened self-control to hold out until the end of the song.

"I had it all figured out," he whispered. "Until I thought how Kara would feel when I told her. I couldn't cause her pain. Maybe I'm a coward. But I'll sacrifice my happiness for hers."

Sura snorted, the spell of his eyes broken by the absurdity of his words. "You really believe you're being noble and selfless, don't you? You want to know what's going to happen? One day she'll realize you'll never be completely hers, and it'll hurt her that much more. If you'd given her up, she could've found someone who would really love her."

"I do love her," he hissed. "I had no doubts about marrying her until I met you. And we'll be happy once we leave Kalindos."

"I don't believe that. I think even before me, you wondered if you could be faithful forever." She cut off his protest. "I also think that in a few years, maybe sooner, you'll meet someone else you can't get out of your head. And maybe next time there'll be nowhere to run."

His dark eyes flashed with anger. "Why are you saying these things?"

"Because they're true."

"Because you're drunk."

"I'll miss you," she said, though she meant to say, "I hate you."

His glare slowly faded into a look of deep pain. "Sura, I just don't know," he said softly.

"You don't know what?"

"How I'll breathe without you."

The heat crept up from her toes, like the ground itself was on fire. She opened her mouth to speak, though she had no words.

"The song'll be over soon," Dravek said. "And there's nothing more to say, so let's just…"

She closed her eyes and focused on the touch of his palm against hers. Somehow she'd find a way to lock this moment away forever, so she could take it out and live in it again and again. It would sustain her like food.

The music pulsed through her veins, connecting her to Dravek. She heard the rhythm of his breath quicken even as the beat stayed slow. His hand on her waist remained perfectly still, showing the world not one indication of desire.

Then his thumb twitched against her lowest rib. Whether accidental or on purpose, the tiny motion set off a cascading reaction in her body. The images flooded back into her mind, the story of passion they'd created together, feeding off each other's desire. She opened her eyes and looked up at him. His gaze bored into hers.

She parted her lips, and the bonfire erupted.

17

Kalindos

Sura saw a streak of white flame shoot over their heads.

"Get down!" Dravek dragged her to the ground, covering her with his body. Around them, people screamed. Feet pounded away, and someone shouted for water.

Sura shoved Dravek's arm from her head. "We have to stop it." A shard of burning wood hit her cheek. She yelped and swiped it off.

"I am stopping it." He covered her face again. "Remember, you don't have to see the fire to control it. Concentrate."

She squeezed her eyes shut and felt for the base of the flame. It was angry, and hungry for freedom. She reached to smother it, forming a heavy, wet blanket with her mind.

The heat seared her as it flowed in like river rapids, soaking her core with flame. The breath she drew only fanned the fire. She held it in until she thought her lungs would burst.

The weight rolled off her, and she heard Dravek try to speak her name through his hacking cough. She reached out for him. Why was it so dark?

"Sura," he rasped. "It's over. Come back. Breathe."

She tried to force her lungs to release her breath, but they seized and spasmed. Her eyes wouldn't open.

"Help!" Dravek shouted. "Elora! Someone bring water!"

"Got it," said a voice Sura recognized as Etarek's. A trickle of cold water rolled over her cheek, then wet cloths pressed against her eyes and mouth.

"Where's Elora?" Dravek began to cough and hack again.

"She's coming," Etarek said. "Here, drink, or you'll be in as bad a shape as Sura."

Elora's voice came from above. "Is anyone burned?"

"Sura's not breathing."

The fear in Dravek's voice propelled her to try despite the pain. "Yes, I am," she croaked. "Rather not, though."

"Thank the Spirits." Dravek seized her hand, then hissed and dropped it. The heat had singed them both.

"Dravek?" called a voice behind him. "What happened? Are you all right?"

"Kara." Sura heard him turn and stand up. "Don't touch me," he said. "I'll hurt you."

Sura cracked open her dry eyes. Dravek's white shirt—what was left of it—was scorched black, and his face and chest were covered in soot. She put a hand to the front of her own dress, which seemed mostly intact. He had shielded her from the worst of it.

Etarek helped her sit up and put a cold mug to her lips. "It's just water. Drink."

Her dry lips pulled apart. As she swallowed, the burning began to ease, though her arms and legs tingled as if sparks were bouncing off the inside of her skin.

"Is everyone safe?" she asked Elora. She would never forgive herself if—

"No one was hurt, thanks to you and Dravek." The healer dabbed Sura's face with the cold cloth. "A few minor burns from flying embers, but nothing serious."

"Something was in that fire," Etarek said. "It's just not natural."

Sura gulped more water. Though it went into her mouth cold, it warmed as it traveled down her throat. Her stomach felt like she'd just drunk tea fresh off the stove.

Dravek sat beside her. "I have to go now, but I wanted to make sure you were all right."

Her eyes stung. "I'll be fine. But what about—" She regarded his hands, wrapped in wet cloths. "Will Kara be safe?" she whispered.

He looked at Etarek and Elora, who caught the hint and stood up.

"I'll go check on the others," Elora said.

"I better make sure the drums aren't damaged," Etarek added.

In a moment, Sura and Dravek were alone, though surrounded by people who were trying not to watch them.

"We did that," she told him. "We could have killed someone, maybe even destroyed the village."

"But we didn't. We made it go away. We saved everyone. That's all they know." He wiped one of his cloths over his face, which was pouring sweat. "We need to learn control. We just can't learn it together."

She shut her eyes, for the fire still pounded through her, wanting to join the heat radiating from his body. "Good night, Dravek."

She heard him sigh as he stood.

"Goodbye," he whispered, and turned away.

When his footsteps had faded, she opened her eyes to see Etarek approaching.

"Safe to touch you yet?" He offered a hand to help her up.

She grasped it and saw him wince, but he didn't let go. She stood with him, watching the crowd gather around Dravek and Kara, following them to their home with catcalls and hollers. Someone made a joke about the wisdom of lighting fires indoors.

Sura tugged Etarek's hand before the impulse could fade. "Let's go for a walk." She looked up at him through her lashes. "See what happens."

Etarek stared at her. "Are you talking about what I think you're talking about?"

"You know I am." She stepped backward, toward the dark edge of the clearing, dragging him along. "Let yourself hear what I'm feeling."

"Wait." He stopped.

"Is my hand burning you?"

"It feels good." He drew her closer and placed her palm against his chest. "Are you sure about this?"

"I'm sure I like you." She slid her other hand over his shoulder. "I'm sure I want you."

None of that was a lie, or he would hear it if he tried. The bonfire's flames had fanned her affection for him into something more urgent and needful.

Etarek's hands glided over her waist. Her body responded, and her mind tried to lock away the memory of dancing with Dravek.

She lifted her chin, craving a kiss, but his gaze darted behind her into the woods.

"We should go back to my house," he said.

"It'll take too long." She backed out of his embrace. "I want you now. On the ground." She slid her hand across her muddy neck, reveling in his gaze. "I want to get you as dirty as I am."

His eyes lit up, but he said, "We don't have a blanket."

"We'll use our clothes." She turned and ran. He would have to chase her now instead of talking. His footsteps followed close behind her.

Sura turned around a clump of undergrowth. Finding the space behind it empty, she reached back and untied her dress. By the time he joined her, she had it halfway over her head.

"Wait." He pulled her dress down to cover her. "I have something to tell you."

"Tell me later." She tugged at his trousers. "And don't worry, I've been taking wild carrot seed, so I can't get pregnant."

He gently removed her hands and held them in his own. "Perhaps you'd better sit."

The trepidation in his voice cooled her flame-fueled desire. She sat—a little more heavily than she'd planned, due to the meloxa in her head and the confines of the dress. Etarek didn't join her. She cursed herself for coming on too strong, though she hadn't thought it possible with a Kalindon man.

"Forgive me." Etarek paced in front of her. "I'd give anything to make love with you right now. But if I did, and then said this later, you'd think me a right bastard." He crouched in front of her so she could see his face, however faint, in the distant torchlight. "Would you have my baby?"

Her jaw plummeted. In the next breath, she barked a laugh so loud the rest of Kalindos must have heard her.

Etarek's face stayed solemn, which only made her laugh harder. She smacked his chest. "You *are* a right bastard." She wiped her mouth into sobriety and took a deep breath. "Yes, Etarek," she said in a low, serious voice. "I'd be honored to bear your child. In fact, why don't we have four or five, in case we need a few spares?"

"Sura, I'm not joking."

She kept laughing. "You must be, because if you weren't, then—" She stopped and looked at him. "Then I would have to hit you much harder."

He opened his arms. "Go ahead. Then think about what I asked."

Sura shook her fist under his nose. "What game is this?"

"It's not a game." He took her hand. "My mother needs to become third phase so she can communicate instantaneously with Galen in Tiros. Only then will we be able to coordinate an attack on Asermos."

Sura stared at him. "You're serious." She jerked her hand out of his. "Serious and insane."

He shook his head. "Unfortunately this is a rational decision. Too rational, if you ask me."

"The Council's ordering you to become a father? They can't do that."

"It's my decision. Sometimes we have to put aside our own desires to do what our people need."

Her mind boggled at the idea, and part of her still expected him to confess it was a joke. "It's your decision, but you won't be the one pregnant. You won't be the one raising a child in this horrible world."

"I know you don't want to end up like your mother, but I wouldn't abandon you the way your father did." His voice softened but maintained its urgency. "I'd do everything to help raise our son or daughter."

"If I stay here, you mean. What if I go home?"

"It's not safe to go home. It'll never be safe until our people throw out the Descendants. As a third-phase Hawk, my mother could help that happen. My father Ladek's a Bear—think what a warrior he'd be." He gestured in the general direction of Asermos. "And if your mother entered the third phase, she'd be invincible. They wouldn't be able to kill her with any weapon."

"Don't bring her into it," she snapped. "Besides, they'd just let her die of thirst. Invincibility isn't immortality."

"But with her new strength and fighting ability, she might be able to escape from prison."

Angry tears burned her eyes. "She wouldn't want me to have a baby just to get power. It goes against the Spirits' ways."

"Maybe the Spirits want different things from us. They want our power." He leaned closer so she could hear his whisper. "Without it, they'll die."

"But no pressure, right? Just the fate of the world resting on my womb. I won't do it." Sura turned her back on him but didn't get up. The meloxa had made her head too sloshy for sudden movements. "Why me? Why not some other woman?"

He sighed behind her. "They all said no. They're afraid their Spirits will punish them by perverting their second-phase powers."

"They're smart to have that fear. Why should I be any different?"

He moved in front of her and spoke in a low, calm voice. "Because you want to save Asermos. Maybe you want it enough to take the risk."

She bristled at his implication. "I'm not just thinking of the danger to myself. I'm not even trained in the first phase of my Aspect. In the second phase I could accidentally destroy someone's memory."

He was silent for several moments, and Sura was relieved she'd found an argument to shut him up.

Then he snapped his fingers. "We could go to Tiros for you to train with their Snake, just like Dravek and Kara."

Sura's gut twisted at the thought of traveling with the newly-weds. But then she wouldn't have to watch Dravek walk out of her life.

She put her face in her hands and dragged them over her scalp. She would *not* let her feelings for her Spirit-brother make her do something stupid.

"For that matter," Etarek continued, "Tiros has a second-phase Deer. I haven't had a mentor since mine died over a year ago."

"Then you should go. But not with me." She stood, focusing on her balance as she straightened. "I don't want a baby now. It's wrong for us and wrong for our Spirits."

His gaze fell to the ground, and he nodded. "I'm sorry I upset you." His hand moved as if to reach for hers, but then he dropped it before touching her. "Can I make it up to you with another dance?"

Sura thought about how being pressed against his body for several minutes might cloud her judgment. "No. I'm tired and drunk. I just want to go to sleep."

"I'll walk you home." To her suspicious glance, he replied, "Just to your door."

They skirted the bulk of the crowd and made their way down the main path toward the healer's home. Sura thought how the entire evening had been one surreal event after another—the naked wedding, the exploding bonfire and now this outrageous proposal. She longed to end it on something simple and real.

When they reached the porch, Sura stood on the lowest stair to bring herself eye-to-eye with Etarek.

"Thank you for understanding," she said. "You're not so bad, even if you are crazy."

"Thank you, I think." He placed a foot on the stair next to her. "Slap me if this sounds awful, but I'd like to see you again. Even without—"

She slapped him.

His eyes popped wide-open, and he put a hand to his cheek. "Never mind, then."

"No, I feel better now." Sura leaned forward and kissed him. He made a little noise in the back of his throat, and she pulled him into a deeper kiss, burying her hands in his long, soft hair. His arms slid around her back, slowly, almost cautiously, as if he were afraid she'd run away.

When the long, languid kiss was over, he smiled at her. "Good night." He gave a graceful bow, then walked back toward the pitiful remains of the bonfire.

Beyond him, in one of those trees, Dravek and Kara were consummating their marriage. Even the lingering sweetness of Etarek's kiss couldn't stop Sura from wondering whose wrists were bound to the bed.

Sura awoke to heavy pounding that echoed and amplified the throbbing in her temples. With a continuous groan, she rolled out of bed and tottered into the kitchen.

Growing up in Asermos, she'd drunk her share of ale, and even once tried that horrid Ilion wine the occupiers were always pushing on the citizens to sedate them. But neither had kicked her in the head like this Kalindon meloxa. The fermented crab-apple drink's hangover was as putrid as its taste.

Tereus sat at the kitchen table with a cup of tea. "You came home early last night, even for an Asermon. The party's still on if you want to join in."

She ran her dry, sticky tongue over the roof of her mouth. "I decline. Who was knocking?"

"Elora went to get it. Probably a patient." His expression when he saw her face made her wonder which shade of green it was. "Sit. I'll make you some tea."

Elora appeared at the kitchen door. "Tereus." Her voice was flat and frightened.

He stood immediately. "What's wrong?"

Thera the Hawk brushed past Elora to come to him. "I'm afraid I have bad news." She laid a hand on Tereus's arm. "Rhia's been captured."

The color drained from his face. "Captured? When? Where?"

"She and Marek were on their way to Velekos when the Descendants caught them. Marek was pushed into a ravine and fell unconscious. They left him for dead. When he came to, he saw them in the distance heading for Asermos with your daughter."

Sura watched as all strength seemed to leave her grandfather. His hand reached out, fumbling for the chair behind him. Elora helped him sit slowly, then turned to Sura.

"Water, please. And put some on for tea, as well. A lot of tea." She looked at Thera. "Bring the rest of the Council here. Now."

Sura scrambled into the pantry to fetch a fresh water skin.

When she came back, Tereus was holding his wife tightly. For the first time since she'd known him, he looked every one of his fifty-eight years.

He accepted the water with a nod of thanks, not letting go of Elora. Sura grabbed the largest pot she could find and went out the back door to the well.

Her hands shook as she pumped the water. For the first eight years of Sura's life, Aunt Rhia and Uncle Marek, along with Tereus, had paid her more attention than her own mother had. When they evacuated to Tiros, it was like losing her father all over again—worse, since she hadn't known Lycas enough to love him.

Her fingers slipped off the pump, and her hand went to her mouth. Rhia wasn't as tough as Mali. What if they tortured her into telling them where to find Lycas?

Her mind reddened and her fists balled so tight her knuckles cracked. She wouldn't let them take her whole family.

Sura shoved aside the pot and filled her hands with the cold running water, splashing it over her face until her head was clear. Then she put the pot back under the spout and pumped as she wiped her face with her other sleeve. By the time she was dry, her decision was made.

She went to the kitchen, brewed a large pot of sassafras tea and brought it to the front room. The other Council members had already arrived and started the meeting. A few appeared to have not yet gone to bed.

Etarek stood across the room behind his mother's chair, but when he saw Sura, he came to join her. For once, his eyes were serious.

Thera finished relating the Horse woman's message about

Rhia's capture, which had arrived by pigeon from Tiros that morning. Dismay lay upon the room like a shroud. Rhia had apparently earned considerable respect during her stay in Kalindos.

"We have to do something," Tereus said. "First Mali, now Rhia. They won't be expecting an attack to come from us. They'll be looking for Lycas."

Sura cradled her elbows in her palms at the sound of her father's name. From the corner of her eye, she saw Etarek look at her.

She stared at the wooden floor. If she couldn't have Dravek— and she *couldn't* have Dravek—then Etarek wouldn't be so bad. He was handsome and strong and funny, and she liked him. It should be that simple. Last night she was eager to take him in the damp, thorny woods.

His father, Ladek, spoke up. "We should make plans to attack on a determined day, then send a bird to the Tirons, demanding they join us."

"And what if they don't?" Adrek said. "We'll be slaughtered."

"Besides, we're out of pigeons." Thera turned to Sura to explain. "They can only fly one way, back to their home. The birds we have here all live here. If we let them go, they'll just return to Kalindos. We need to bring our pigeons to Tiros and exchange them for Tiron pigeons. Dravek and Kara will take them tomorrow when they go to Tiros for his Snake training."

Sura closed her eyes and took Etarek's hand. He gave it a firm, steady squeeze. She opened her eyes and said, "We'll go with them."

The rest of the Council turned to her with surprise. Tereus sank his face into his hand and shook his head slowly.

Thera rose from her chair. "Are you sure?"

"Kara knows the way," Etarek said. "She's been there before, and she can hunt for food."

"That's not what I'm asking," Thera said.

Sura stared into the Hawk's hazel eyes. "I know what you're asking." She paused, then looked at Etarek. His face showed understanding, and he nodded to his mother.

The room grew uncomfortably silent, as everyone studied the walls or the lines on the backs of their hands.

"No!" Tereus slammed his fist against the table. "I won't let you do this, not even for Rhia. The Spirits punish those who have children this way."

Elora spoke up. "But all signs show that They want us to find new ways to protect ourselves."

"Unless it's a test."

Everyone looked at Adrek. He folded his hands into a single fist on the table. "The Spirits have protected Kalindos for almost twenty years *because* we've stuck to the old ways."

"We know the risks," Thera said to him. "Punishments will be suffered by Sura and Etarek and myself and Ladek, *not* Kalindos as a whole. The Spirits wouldn't condemn the entire village for the actions of a few."

"We're all guilty if we stand by and let them do this." Tereus stood, scraping his chair against the floor. "It's a cold-blooded grab for power. Has anyone thought about the baby?"

"Of course I have." Etarek let go of Sura's hand and turned to him. "My son or daughter will be loved no less than any child borne from a bond of love."

He looked at Sura, and she nodded quickly, though the panic was rising inside. She had no idea how to take care of a baby and had to hope someone in Tiros would teach her. Her decision was feeling more and more like a step off a cliff.

Her grandfather stared at her. "Sura, is this what you want?"

"No," she said. "I want the Ilions never to have invaded. I want my mother and Aunt Rhia safe and free. I want a real father, not a war hero. I want everything to be the way it was before I was born, before the Descendants came."

They stared at her, and Sura closed her mouth for a moment, swallowing the bitterness. "But I'm not used to getting what I want, so I'll settle for this."

Tereus's face grew drawn, and he sank into his chair. Elora laid a hand on his shoulder and kissed the side of his head, whispering words Sura couldn't hear.

As the Council continued their meeting, discussing invasion and rescue tactics, Etarek tugged Sura's hand and tilted his head toward the door.

Outside, they sat on the porch together.

"Why now?" Etarek said. "Why wasn't it enough just to help your mother? Why does Rhia make a difference?"

"My mother's big and strong. Aunt Rhia is neither. She'd be easy to hurt." Sura twisted her hands. "I'm scared she'd give up my father. I can't let that happen. Or if it did, I could protect him by making him third phase, and he'd be harder to capture, almost impossible to kill."

Etarek rested his hands on his knees and slid his thumbs along the lengths of his forefingers. "Well, this will be a bit awkward."

She reached out a tentative hand to touch his arm. "Maybe not for long."

Sangian Hills

"Beautiful day for treason, heh?"

Lycas looked up, and then up some more, to see Feras strolling into his tent. The third-phase Bear, as the military leader of the Velekon resistance—not to mention outmatching Lycas by five years and fifty pounds—was the only person who dared to enter Lycas's quarters unannounced.

Lycas stood and offered his sole chair. "It's only treason for those who recognize the government's legitimacy. Which counts me out."

"Both of us." Feras grunted as he sat at Lycas's table, dwarfing it with his bulk.

Lycas picked up the stack of orders he was reviewing and laid it on his bedroll. "How are things in Velekos?"

"Settling down, unfortunately. Ten days after Lania's funeral, and most Velekons act as if nothing happened. Their capacity for self-denial is astonishing."

Lycas frowned. Unlike Asermos, Velekos had traded with the nation of Ilios for decades. Even now, many of the native Velekons profited from the closer ties the occupation provided. The villagers had let themselves be bought and tamed, trading their freedom, their identity and finally their magic for a few crusts of bread.

"Sometimes I don't blame them," Feras went on. "They want peace and stability."

"But they need war and chaos, and we're going to give it to them." Lycas tapped the parchment the Bear had brought. "What do you have for me?"

The Bear unrolled the long sheet onto the table, then set his water flask on one end to keep it flat.

"The Evius festival parade route." Feras's finger followed a red line along the streets. "The Ilions are avoiding the Acrosia neighborhood entirely this year. They claim the roads are too steep for their horses, which is complete tripe."

Lycas leaned on his knuckles and examined the map. The largest protests of Lania's murder had centered around her family's neighborhood, a hotbed of rebel activity long before her death.

He cursed. "That means our operation will have to leave the Acrosia to sabotage the festival. Are there enough sympathizers in the rest of the village to give cover?"

"Perhaps." Feras sat back with a sigh, the chair creaking under his weight, and pushed a mass of gray and black curls back from his face. "But the festival's only a few weeks away. It would take time to screen new safe houses."

"Too much risk for too little reward." Lycas scanned the map. "Ah." He jabbed his middle finger on a spot in the northeast. "Let's strike that instead."

Feras laughed. "The police station? Are you mad?"

"It's closer to the Acrosia than the parade will be. We can do a quick strike and go underground again in an instant. The place itself won't be well-guarded. Most of the officers will either be containing the festival crowds or getting their own selves drunk."

"But to what end are we attacking?"

Lycas squinted at him. "'What end'?"

"What do we hope to accomplish, other than putting the Ilions into a maniacal rage? There's no tactical advantage to be had. We'd never be able to hold the station."

"We don't need to hold it. We just need to get in long enough to steal weapons, release some prisoners and, if there's time, burn the place down." He picked up Feras's water flask and took a long gulp. "Wreaking havoc is an end in itself."

"That's guerrilla talk. This isn't the wilderness where there's no one to retaliate. If we anger the Ilions, they'll take it out on all of Velekos."

"And all of Velekos will finally wake up." Lycas's voice turned bitter. "Isn't that what you want? Or are you in the mood for a more leisurely revolution, in time for your great-great-grandson to die a free man?"

"I want it now." Feras pounded the table and pointed at him. "You don't know what it's like to live under their thumb. You may be the most pursued renegade in the entire colony, but you're free out here in the hills. You don't have children and grandchildren to think about."

Lycas held back a snarl. "Who do you think I'm doing this for? My daughter has spent the last decade in fear for her life in Asermos, a place that makes Velekos look like a festival by comparison. Asermos will never be free as long as Ilion troops are two days' march away in Velekos. Only when we bother them *here*—" he jammed his finger against the map of Velekos "—can we fight them *there*." He pointed east toward Asermos.

Feras sat silent, his arms crossed over his expansive chest. "The Velekon resistance agrees, but the rest of the village won't see why they should risk their lives for Asermos."

"It's not for Asermos, it's for all our people." Lycas formed a fist. "Remember, our goal is not compromise, it's not better conditions or more lenient laws under the occupation. Our goal is to send the Descendants back to Ilios."

"Liberation or death, heh?"

"No. Just liberation."

Footsteps approached the tent, and they turned their heads toward the door.

"It's probably our lunch," Feras said. "I asked one of your men to bring us food and drink. Damen tells me you're not eating enough."

Lycas snorted. "For a Crow, anything less than six meals a day counts as starvation."

Feras didn't smile. "You do look thinner than when I last saw you."

Lycas turned to the tent door, on the pretext of greeting his attaché, the young Bear whose footsteps he heard. More important, he didn't want Feras to see the worry on his face.

He'd been eating more than he'd eaten in the wilderness, but it wouldn't stave off his loss in bulk. The Otter healer said his health was fine, which left a more chilling explanation: his Spirit was weakening.

He saw it in his men, his Wolverine fighters. The youngest of them, like Nilik and the two other Tirons, didn't notice; they were busy reveling in their newfound powers. They didn't know how strong they *should* feel.

Lycas opened the flap before the Bear could announce himself. To his disappointment, the young man wasn't carrying food.

"Sir, the messenger from Tiros has arrived."

"Show him in."

The Bear motioned to Yorgas the Bat, who stood leaning against a nearby tree. He staggered forward, looking as if he could barely keep his feet.

"Bring him food and water," Lycas told his attaché, then waved for Yorgas to enter the tent. "What news comes from Tiros?"

"More than Tiros, I'm afraid, sir." Gulping for breath, the Bat wiped his sweaty, dark blond hair from his face. Then he glanced at Feras and closed his mouth.

"You can speak in front of him," Lycas said.

Yorgas gave a quick nod and attempted to straighten his posture against obvious exhaustion. "First, Mali's in prison."

Lycas's stomach turned cold, as if he'd just swallowed a bucket of ice. "Where's my daughter?"

"Safe in Kalindos. They sent a messenger pigeon the day she arrived."

He let out a long breath and was glad the other two men couldn't tell how weak his knees had turned. "Good. When did this happen?"

"Mali was arrested about two weeks ago, at her home in the middle of the night."

"Is she still alive?"

"No one knows. I'm sorry, sir."

Lycas turned over the events in his mind, trying to focus on the strategic implications and not on the image of his former mate in chains. She would feel little pain from their tortures, but they would find a way to make her suffer. The Ilions were imaginative, if nothing else.

Yorgas cleared his throat. "There's more."

Lycas stared at him, dread rising in his chest. "What more?"

"On my way here through the Sangian Hills, I came upon one of our platoons. They'd been ambushed by the Ilions, who apparently tricked our men into thinking there were about a tenth as many enemy fighters as there really were." His gaze tripped down to the floor, then up to meet Lycas's eyes again. "They got Sirin."

Lycas blinked at him. Sirin. His comrade. His friend. The closest thing he'd had to a brother since Nilo's death.

Feras filled the silence. "How many men were lost?"

"Three Cougars, two Wolverines and a Bear. The whole platoon, except for one Cougar who climbed to safety. He was the one I came upon, burying the others." Yorgas slipped his hands in and out of his pockets in a nervous gesture. "I went to headquarters first to let them know. I hope that's all right."

Lycas stared at him, then realized the Bat required an answer. "They'd need to deploy another squad to cover the territory of the one lost. Good thinking."

Yorgas nodded. "Thank you, sir."

"Is that all?" Lycas snapped, though he couldn't imagine what could be worse than the capture of Mali and Sirin. His own family was safe, at least.

The Bat spoke slowly, as if choosing his words with care. "A group of former Asermons have left Tiros to free Mali and the other political prisoners." He shifted his feet. "They asked that you stay here and not get involved. They said it would be too great a risk for you, and that they knew Asermos better now, anyway."

Lycas sighed through his teeth. They were probably right. But it took every bit of discipline not to jump on a horse and go barreling into Asermos to rescue Mali and Sirin.

Yorgas cleared his throat. "That's all, sir."

"Then go eat and rest. I'll send you back tomorrow with my answer."

When Yorgas was gone, Lycas began to pace. His fists clenched and unclenched as he walked the narrow space between the door and the table, muttering half to himself and half to Feras.

"I'll have to assign a new executive officer at the headquarters. There are a few men there I trust with my life. But who would take the job? Being second-in-command brings twice the work, half the glory."

"I'll let you get to that." Feras stood and rolled up the parchment. "We'll attack the police station as you suggested. Times are clearly desperate now. I'll be back in a week with a list of personnel, so we can start planning the attack."

"Thank you."

On his way out of the tent, Feras clasped Lycas's shoulder. "Don't worry. Sirin and Mali are two of the toughest people I've ever met. They'll survive this, and be tougher still."

When he was gone, Lycas left his tent and walked over to the training area, which consisted of a slope of woods that could be observed from above. The young Wolverines stalked from tree to tree, practicing stealth and speed, following the maneuvers shouted by their Bear leader. Lycas could see Nilik's face rigid with concentration.

They were fast and strong and quiet, but not as much as they should have been. At the end of the exercise, the Bear shouted his frustration and forced them to repeat it from the beginning.

Wolverines were weakening. It was the only explanation for Sirin's capture. The last time Ilions had come close to nabbing him, he'd killed eighteen men to keep his freedom, then laughed about it later. If they could get Sirin, they could get anyone, including Lycas.

He dwelled on this fact as long as he could, rather than think of Mali, and remember the way her sharp gaze used to stun him into speechlessness. It was probably just as well they had never fought on the same field; they would have either killed each other in a battle of wills, or he would have been too busy staring at her body to avoid his own annihilation.

She'd fooled him with her toughness. He thought she didn't need him, even after Sura was born. When he'd left for Ilios to rescue Marek and Nilik, she'd told him never to return. Like an idiot, he'd taken her at her word.

And Sura…at least she was safe. Next to Tiros, Kalindos was the farthest out of harm's way she could be. Neither village held much appeal to the Descendants. They lacked the rich soil of Asermos or the thick limestone deposits of Velekos.

But if he could, he'd bring Sura here, so he could see with his own eyes that she was alive, that the Descendant scum hadn't taken her soul and her hope.

And so that she could see that no matter what happened to her mother, she still had something left in the world, one person who would lay down his life for her.

19

Kirisian Mountains

Sura and the three Kalindons hiked in near-silence for the length of the first day. The trail was too rough for riding, and the Kalindons couldn't spare the horses, anyway, which was a relief to Sura. The trip to Tiros would be slower, but less painful, than the one she'd taken to Kalindos.

While Dravek had reacted with a stony sullenness to the news that she and Etarek would be accompanying them, Kara had welcomed their company.

"It's terrible what happened to your mother and your aunt," she said to Sura as they made their way uphill through the forest. "My father was taken in the invasion when I was four years old. Mother and I got away in time because she cloaked me with her Wolf invisibility. I can still feel her hand on my mouth, keeping me from crying as they led my father away." She sighed. "We found out later that he died in captivity."

"I'm sorry to hear that," Sura told her, resenting the Wolf less with every moment. "Sometimes I wonder if there's anyone in our two villages who hasn't been hurt by the Descendants."

They made camp when it became too dark for Sura and Dravek to see the trail. By the light of a small campfire, they set up their tents and made dinner.

As they ate, Kara snuggled in Dravek's lap and tried to feed him by hand. He played along at first, but his smile grew tighter. Finally, after she'd teased him several times by snatching back the food at the last instant, he picked her up and took her off his lap.

"Stop it," he said quietly. "It's silly."

"Oh, you're no fun."

"I'm tired. I just want to eat and go to bed."

"Bed." She clapped her hands. "Now *that's* fun."

He blanched and glanced at Sura, then Etarek. "I meant, go to sleep."

"Are you joking?" she said in a high-pitched voice. "We're newlyweds. There'll be no sleeping on this trip."

Sura looked down at her plate, wondering how she would fit the food past the lump at the top of her stomach.

"Dravek, don't mind us," Etarek said. "Pretend we're not here."

Sura snorted. "Good luck with that." She kept her gaze on her food, wondering how the comment had sounded to the others. Another two weeks of hiding her feelings would surely boil her insides.

Etarek and Kara began to discuss how much meloxa the four

of them could drink **per night** while leaving enough to make a decent gift for the Tirons. They seemed content with the result, until Dravek spoke up.

"You women can't drink if you're trying to get pregnant. Meloxa's not safe for babies."

Kara slapped her forehead. "You're right. How could I forget?"

"I don't know," he said. "It's all you talk about. Isn't that why we got married?"

She stared at Dravek. "It's not the only reason."

"Good," he said through a mouthful of dried venison. "But I still won't let you drink meloxa."

"*Let* me? Since when am I your child? I'm four years older than you." She glared at him. "If anything, I'm the one who has to take care of you."

He hunched his shoulders. "You don't have to do anything."

Sura squirmed on her log and gave Etarek a nervous glance. His eyes and posture reflected her discomfort.

They finished their dinners in silence, put out the campfire and retired to their tents. Sura and Etarek laid out their bedrolls beside each other, then sat face-to-face. Her heart was pounding, and she felt a little sick.

"You were right," she said. "This is awkward."

"We don't have to tonight. It's up to you."

"I need to show you something so it doesn't startle you in the middle of—" She touched the collar of her shirt.

"Your scars?"

"How did you know?"

"I saw a bit when we danced. I confess I was looking down your dress." He tilted his head. "What happened?"

She told him about the fire while he held her hand and

squeezed it at all the right moments. Then she turned and unbuttoned her shirt to show him the burns on her back.

Etarek made a tsking noise. "Sura, I'm so sorry."

She winced at the pity in his voice. "It doesn't hurt."

"Good." He passed his hand over her shoulder and down her back. "It doesn't matter." He turned her to face him. "I still think you're beautiful."

He kissed her, sweetly, and she tried not to compare his dismissive reaction to Dravek's, who had venerated her scars. Etarek was being kind in his own way.

She pulled back and gave him an uneasy smile. "Maybe we could wait until tomorrow?"

He nodded. "I know this is hard for you, after what happened to your mate. I'm here whenever you're ready."

She gave Etarek a quick, awkward kiss, then lay on her side facing away from him. It felt as if the entire Kalindon Council were watching them. Her body felt cold at the thought of bearing an unwanted baby.

It wouldn't stay unwanted, she knew, and that was what scared her most. The Descendants had killed or imprisoned nearly everyone she'd ever loved.

Somehow they'd find a way to take her child, too.

In Sura's dream, Dravek stood across the clearing from her, on the other side of the bonfire. Through the leaping, licking flames she could see he was naked. She touched her body to confirm that she, too, wore nothing. In the center of the fire stood a tall wooden stake that remained unburned.

Faceless people surrounded them, shrieking pleas in a language she couldn't understand. They pressed in, pushing her closer to the fire. Dravek held out his hands.

"Do you dare?" His voice was a whisper, but she heard his words clearly. "For me?"

She nodded and tried to step around the bonfire to join him.

"No, Sura. Inside."

Her blood ran cold. He meant for her to walk through the fire to meet him.

"Together," she said. "Count to three."

"One." His gaze bored into hers.

"Two." She moved to the edge of the flames and lifted her hands.

"Three," they spoke together as they moved in.

They screamed. It hurt worse than all the pain in Sura's life added together. She wanted to leap back out, but the agony in Dravek's eyes propelled her forward to take his hands.

The pain ceased. She breathed hard, gulping hot air that didn't sear her lungs but only filled her with power.

He moved forward and lifted her hands above her head, backing her up to pin her wrists against the wooden stake. She cried out at the feel of his hot flesh against hers.

The flames jumped higher as if in celebration. He brought his mouth to her neck, and Sura felt a moment of perfect happiness. She belonged here forever, in the fire, in his skin.

Something cool and smooth slid against her upraised hands and wrapped around her wrists. Dravek pulled his head away and looked up. She craned her neck to follow his gaze.

A long black snake was binding them to the stake. As it twisted around their upper arms, its tongue flicked over Sura's skin. Its gaze reflected the flames around it, but unlike the flat, glassy eyes of a real snake, these orbs sparked with wisdom and cunning.

"It's Her," Sura breathed.

The snake constricted, strapping them to the pole.

Dravek turned his head to Sura. "It's what She wants."

She smiled. He was hers. Their love would make them invincible.

Without arms to clutch him, it should have been awkward. But in the dream Sura's legs slid up easily to encircle his waist. He angled his hips to bring his hard length against her most sensitive spot. Every muscle in their bodies jerked with the sudden shock. Dravek dipped his head to hers.

His tongue flicked in and out of her mouth as he stroked against her, sending her into a frenzy. It was wild, blinding pleasure, but she needed him inside her. Her hips bucked and pitched in an attempt to reach him.

Finally he pulled back and paused, gazing down with eyes as dark as a moonless night.

"I love you," he whispered, then gave her everything, kissing her deep as he plunged inside her.

The world shattered.

The stake, the flames, the snake—all vanished. Sura and Dravek floated to the ground, locked in their embrace.

The dirt beneath them was cold, and the surrounding forest was gray and lifeless. Their skin no longer scorched like fire. But their bodies were still warm and alive.

"It doesn't matter," she whispered, holding him close. "This is all we need."

Sura's eyes jerked open into darkness. It took a moment to remember where she was, and who she was with. A tear slipped from her eye before she could stop it.

Etarek's voice rumbled beside her. "Was it a nightmare?"

No, she thought, staring at the ceiling of the dark tent. *This is the nightmare.*

His hand slipped over the blanket to touch hers. She drew it to cup her breast through her thin shirt.

Etarek sighed as if he'd been holding a breath for several minutes. "Are you sure?"

She couldn't respond in words, for no matter what she said, his Deer senses would hear nothing but sadness.

Instead of speaking, she pulled him to kiss her, as her mind and body tried to convince each other that he was the one she wanted.

20

Asermos

"Will I be needed tonight?" Rhia asked her guards as they made their last round before bedtime.

"Addano's off-duty," the oldest of the three soldiers said, "which means you're off-duty." He chuckled at his own joke. "So enjoy your vacation."

Relieved, she looked over at Mali, who frowned. They'd been using the information Rhia had gleaned from the interrogation sessions to figure out what the Ilions knew about the resistance, so Mali was no doubt disappointed Rhia had the night off. They'd given up trying to inflict pain on Mali herself and had resorted to keeping her in criminally horrid conditions. Neither method had gotten results. Now they were just keeping her as bait for Lycas. As soon as they caught him,

Captain Addano had told Rhia, they'd dispose of Mali like they did Sirin.

The door leading to the outside opened, and the captain's voice rang forth.

"Bring the women out to the yard. Now!"

The guards started and looked at each other. "What's he doing here?" said the one who'd spoken before. He called out to the captain. "Sir, are they being released?"

Addano gave an uncharacteristically harsh laugh. "In a sense. I have orders for their immediate execution."

Rhia's knees turned to water. Her hands slid along the rough walls of the cell, nails digging into the stone to keep her standing. "No…"

The guard shrugged. "Less work for us." He pointed at Mali. "You two get her. I'll take the little one."

Rhia couldn't see the expression on Mali's face, but the Wasp's posture remained straight and tall. Rhia shifted back her own shoulders and lifted her chin as the guard entered her cell. She moved forward at his gesture so that he wouldn't grab her. He pulled her arms behind her back, almost gently, then bound her wrists together with a thin rope.

They wouldn't see her cry or beg for her life. After all, she'd already died once. There was nothing to fear. Soon Crow would take her into His eternal realm of peace.

Then her mind showed her Marek's face, and those of her children, and she wanted to collapse on the floor, kick and scream and punch until they let her go. At that moment she felt like she'd tell the Descendants anything they wanted to know, just for one more glimpse of her family.

They were led out of their cells and turned right toward the iron door. Behind her, Mali walked without protest. "If you kill me," she stated, "you'll lose this war. When you're fleeing back to what's left of Ilios, you'll remember my words."

They opened the door, and the captain's voice came from around the corner. "Tie them to the blocks, then step back."

"We know what to do," Rhia's guard muttered under his breath as he tugged her out into the humid summer night.

In the torchlight she could see two large stone blocks sitting in the center of the exercise yard. Dark liquid stains covered the tops and sides. An ax rested against one of them.

Rhia's body trembled at the sight. Such a death might not be quick or painless. She closed her eyes and prayed out loud to Crow to have mercy on her and Mali.

Her guard shook her elbow. "Stop babbling. You'll wake the others." He led her to the block and pressed down hard atop her shoulder. In a moment she was on her knees, perversely grateful she no longer had to force herself to stand. As the guard bound her to the block, she squeezed her eyes shut and prayed for all those she'd left behind, all those she'd failed.

Then she thought of the only reason why she and Mali would be no further use to the Ilions: Lycas had been killed. Her tears flowed as she whispered his name.

The guards stepped back, and she waited to hear the heavy booted footsteps of the executioner.

A loud whistle came from both sides of the yard. The sound was followed by a *thup!* and muffled cries of the three guards.

An invisible hand grasped hers. "Rhia, it's me."

Marek.

"Hold still," he said. She heard the rough slide of a knife blade through rope, and in a moment she was free. She turned to see the guards on their knees, grasping at the arrows protruding from their chests. Their mouths opened and closed.

"Hurry!" Mali whispered, then fell back as her own bindings were cut. She rolled over and snatched the short sword from the sheath of the closest guard, who was groaning loudly. In three quick motions, she slashed their throats, and the yard was silent again.

Rhia looked for Addano, expecting him to appear any moment with reinforcements. Someone leaped from the shadows where his voice had originated.

Jula.

"Out. Now," she said in a hushed version of the captain's voice. Rhia followed her daughter to the corner of the yard, where she pulled aside a pile of brush to reveal a spot where the fence had been cut away at the bottom. Jula slipped through on her stomach.

Marek laid a hand on Rhia's waist. "You go first."

She slipped through, her back scraping on the bottom of the cut fence posts. On the other side, she got to her knees and soon drew her invisible husband into a tight embrace.

"You're alive," she whispered. "I knew it."

"Maybe it pays to be married to a Crow." He kissed her hard and quick as he reappeared, bow and all. "And part of a Wolf pack." He pointed to two trees, one on each end of the prison yard, where she assumed two other invisible archers sat.

Rhia turned back to the fence, looking for Mali, who wasn't coming. She pressed her eye to the gap between the slats. The Wasp was collecting weapons from the three soldiers.

"Mali, hurry!" she whispered as loudly as she dared.

"You go. I'll catch up if I can."

"What do you mean?"

She turned to Rhia, a sword in each hand. "They have twenty-four of our men. I'm going back for them." Her head suddenly jerked as if she heard someone coming, and the torchlight illuminated a grin of anticipation. "Run now. And, Rhia, if your brother's still alive…" Mali's smile widened. "Punch him in the gut for me."

Rhia shook her head. "I wouldn't want him to get sentimental."

For the first time in their lives, Mali laughed *with* her instead of *at* her.

Rhia hoped it wouldn't be with one of her last breaths.

By the time Rhia arrived at Bolan's door with Marek and Jula, her legs were screaming with exhaustion. Ten days of imprisonment had sapped what felt like a year's worth of strength.

Marek knocked and recited the coded message when Bolan responded. The Horse swung open the door and broke into a broad smile.

"Rhia!"

She gave him a hard hug, trying to hide her dismay at how the occupation had aged his formerly youthful, carefree demeanor.

He looked past her into the darkness. "Where's Mali?"

"She went back in to set more prisoners free," Rhia told him.

Bolan groaned. "Her courage will be the death of her. But hopefully not tonight. Come in, come in."

"The other two Wolves stayed behind to fight off any guards," Marek added. "They'll disperse and go home when they're done, and tell Mali to meet us here." He closed the door behind him. "At least, that's the plan."

"I hope you're right." Bolan grabbed a few things from the pantry, then led them through the dark, silent house, out the back door, and across a small clearing to the stable. The sight of it made her ache for her father's former horse farm nearby.

Inside the stable, Bolan divided the food among them. Rhia was too out-of-breath to eat, so she asked them how they'd managed to rescue her.

"Let me tell her, Father." Jula beamed with pride when Marek nodded. "First, Father and one of the second-phase Wolves spent the last two nights cutting those fence posts around the prison yard. One of them would saw while the other watched the guards to see if they were looking."

Marek tore another piece of bread from the loaf. "The Descendants still haven't figured out how to detect us Wolves. Even their guard dogs can only smell us, not hear us. They look in our direction but don't bark. It's like we're just another animal."

Rhia snorted. "To the Descendants, we *are* just another animal."

"Meanwhile," Jula continued, "I've been working with Panos, the other Wolf, riding on his back so he could cloak me with his invisibility. We got up close to the camp so I could hear one of the commanders' voices. Then we had to wait until he was off duty so I could take his place and order your guards to bring you out." Her brows pinched as she looked at Rhia. "Sorry I scared you with the execution."

Rhia shook her head. "There was no other way to get Mali and me out at the same time."

One of the horses began to stamp and whinny. Bolan held up a finger. "Someone's coming."

Bow in hand, Marek accompanied him to the barn door. Rhia

saw Bolan poke his head out to look toward the house, then wave to beckon someone over. She hurried toward the door, hoping to see Mali.

Instead Endrus and Medus appeared. They staggered toward the food but stopped when they saw Rhia.

"Traitor," Medus spat, and lunged for her. Jula screamed. The other three men barely caught the Badger in time to keep his hands from her throat.

"She sat there, in that prison, while they burned me," he said, "while they cut me. She sat there and watched!"

"I saved your life," Rhia said. "They would have killed you if I hadn't stopped them the last time."

"You should've let them," he growled. "I wanted to die."

"I'm sorry." She looked at Endrus. "But this was the best way to find out what the Descendants know about the resistance."

"While saving your own skin, no doubt." Medus gave her one last glare, then his shoulders sagged. "Which I can't really blame you for."

"It almost killed me to watch them hurt you." Rhia stepped forward, close enough to touch, and spoke to both men. "Please forgive me."

Endrus nodded slowly. "You were as much a victim as we were."

Medus stared at her with bloodshot eyes and finally assented. The others released him, and he shook his arms and straightened his back. Then the Badger and Cougar turned to the food and set upon it like starving dogs.

"Where's Mali?" Bolan asked.

Endrus spoke through a mouthful of bread. "Thought she was right behind me, but when I turned around, she was running back into the prison." He shook his head. "No one came out after that."

"You left her there?" Marek said.

"What were we supposed to do," Medus grumbled, "storm the place?" He glared at Rhia. "After what they did to us, we could barely walk."

"Do you think she's dead?" Rhia asked Endrus.

His mouth formed a grim line. "If not dead, recaptured."

Rhia sank onto the floor next to Jula and put her face in her hands. Surely the Ilions would kill Mali now, as a precaution against her future escape, or even as punishment for releasing Endrus and Medus. The Wasp's only hope was that they still considered her suitable bait for Lycas.

The question was, would her brother take it?

Sangian Hills

Nilik tried not to flinch as the Otter healer stitched the wound on his right hand.

"Third time this week," she said.

He put his other hand behind his back, as if that would undo its two cuts.

"Been doing a lot of these lately." She tied off the thread and cut it. "Not just you, Nilik. You all need to be more careful."

He flexed his fingers and examined the neat sutures on the base of his thumb. "Is it unusual to have so many injuries in training?"

"Unheard of. Next!" She pulled a clean needle and thread from her kit and beckoned to the Wolverine at the head of the line, one of Nilik's comrades from Tiros, who was holding a bloodstained bandage around his outer wrist.

Nilik shuffled back toward the men's barracks, which consisted of a long tent that held the bedrolls of twenty to thirty soldiers. There wasn't room to do anything in there but sleep, something he needed desperately. It was nearly dusk; he'd been up with the sun to train, and train, then train some more. His hand throbbed, and he cursed his own carelessness.

The older Wolverines, including his uncle Lycas, gave frequent lectures, complete with diagrams, on the safest and most efficient ways to kill the enemy. Instinct told Nilik to go straight for the heart, but the ribs and breastbone usually slowed the momentum, making his hand slip forward over the hilt onto the blade. Hence his injuries.

As his feet dragged him toward the barracks, Nilik recited the soft spots on a human body, especially places that would provide the most blood for the effort. Throat, upper arm, upper thigh, under the ribs on the left side. They'd practiced on fresh deer corpses provided by the Cougars and Wolves.

Then there was his first battle, the ambush in the northeast Sangian Hills.

He'd fended off two Descendants with his dagger and short sword. He hadn't struck a killing blow, but the rush of survival and victory were more than enough to satisfy him.

But not Lycas, who had saved him two Ilions to slaughter.

The first was the captain of the platoon, conscious but barely breathing, an arrow embedded in each lung.

"He can die fast or slow." Lycas lifted the soldier by his hair, making him groan with what little breath he had. "Your choice."

Nilik's hands shook as he grasped the captain's hair and placed his knife to his throat.

"Ear to ear," Lycas whispered.

"No." The Descendant started to struggle. "Not that way. Please."

Nilik held him still between his knees. "I'm sorry," he whispered, and made the cut.

Blood fountained from the man's throat. Nilik yelped and leaped back, shoving the captain to the ground.

Lycas put a hand on his shoulder. "Good. Next time, not so deep. Ideally you want to cut the vein but not the artery. But it's better than making the opposite mistake and cutting too shallow."

Nilik swallowed the bile in his throat as he watched the blood steam in the night air. The man stopped twitching.

"He's dead already, see?" Lycas steered Nilik to the left. "Let's try again."

"Now?"

Lycas squeezed his shoulder. "Everyone talks about their first kill, but the second is actually the hardest, because now you know what it's like. Best to get it over with so that next time you won't hesitate."

They stopped in front of a young soldier, no older than Nilik himself, who was bleeding from a sword wound to the stomach.

"The enlisted are tougher," Lycas said, "because they don't have enough hair to grab. Take him by the back of the collar."

Nilik hesitated, but not long enough to need prodding. He couldn't let his uncle see the fear that, as predicted, had increased since his first kill.

He lifted the man easily, his new Wolverine strength surprising him again. Barely conscious, this one didn't protest, but Nilik apologized anyway, and whispered one of his mother's Crow prayers as he put blade to skin, then sliced.

"Perfect." Lycas squatted and pointed to the soldier's throat, ignoring the young man's death spasms. "See how the blood cascades straight down, like rain over a sheer rock face. Hold him up a few more moments so his brain can drain. It ends it faster." He glanced up at Nilik. "There wouldn't be time during a battle, but it's a courteous gesture if you have the leisure." He stood up. "There, you can put him down."

Nilik gently lowered this one to the ground, laying him on his back. On an impulse, he placed the hilt of the soldier's fallen sword in his hand and rested it upon his chest.

"Another reason why the enlisted are harder to kill," Lycas said. "They're more like us. This boy might have been a farmer a few months ago, or an artist or a produce merchant on the streets of Leukos. The army takes them all, no matter their ability, because it's desperate. Ilios eats its young."

Nilik could only nod, afraid to open his mouth.

"You've done well," Lycas said. "Now go throw up."

"Thank you, sir." And he had, barely making it around the corner of the ravine before losing what felt like his dinner, lunch and breakfast from three days ago.

When his stomach stopped cramping and he could stand upright again, Nilik went to push back the hair that had fallen in his face.

He saw his hands. They'd been stained with blood before, but never a life's last drops. Cold and sticky, the fingers gummed together, and the lines on his palms glared up at him. These hands had brought death.

But they no longer shook.

Now Nilik shoved his hands inside his pockets as he made his way to the barracks. The rough material scraped the stitches, but he ignored the pain.

Someday soon, when he entered the Velekon garrison and grasped the throats of Lania's killers, he wouldn't apologize, wouldn't pray. He would laugh.

"Lycas!"

Nilik stopped when he heard the familiar female voice coming from the eastern edge of the camp. It couldn't be, not here.

Unless she'd followed him.

Nilik's stomach sank. His mother had arrived. Soon Lycas would know of Nilik's disobedience and deception. He'd be lucky to get home to Tiros on his feet instead of a stretcher.

For a moment he considered running in the opposite direction. But that would only put off the inevitable reprimand. He squared his shoulders and turned toward the voice.

Outside Lycas's tent, Nilik's entire family was gathered around the Wolverine. Lycas lifted Rhia in his arms, far off her feet, then set her down again.

"What are you doing here?" he said.

"Originally, to find my son and bring him home." She looked past Lycas and saw him. "There you are."

"Nilik!" Jula ran to him, slamming into his arms. "You're alive!"

"Of course I'm alive." He hugged her much as Lycas had embraced his own sister. "Why shouldn't I be?"

She clutched his hands. "We were so worried. It's all my fault."

Lycas's expression darkened as he looked at Nilik. "I thought you gave him the password," he said to Rhia.

"I gave it to him." Jula dipped her head. "I'm so sorry." Then her face brightened. "But then I helped Father break Mother out of prison."

"Prison?" Lycas held up a finger to Nilik. "You stay right there." He turned to Rhia. "Why were you in prison?"

"We were on our way to get Nilik." His mother gave him an imploring look, as though she wanted to embrace and smack him simultaneously. He stood his ground so she couldn't reach him to do either. "We came across the remnants of your ambush, and the Ilions found us."

Nilik felt sick. He had put his own parents in mortal danger. He stepped forward. "Mother, I'm so sorry. Please forgive me."

Lycas raised a hand to him. "Shut up until we tell you to speak." He looked at Marek. "Were you both taken?"

Nilik listened with a growing dread in his gut as his father told them the story of his fall and recovery, then his and Jula's harrowing rescue attempt.

"We tried to break out Mali, too," Marek said, "but she went back in to release the other prisoners."

"Endrus and Medus escaped," Rhia added, "thanks to her. They'll be here soon."

"They're good men, and valuable to the resistance." Lycas shook his head. "Mali was recaptured because she didn't run away with you?"

Marek sighed. "Brave to the end."

"We don't know if it's the end," Rhia said. "They might still keep her alive as bait for you, Lycas. Just like I was."

Nilik saw his uncle's brows lower in suspicion. "Wait a minute." Lycas looked at Marek. "That message from Tiros, the one about Mali, came on your orders, didn't it? Why didn't you tell me Rhia was in prison?"

Marek crossed his arms, undaunted. "I knew you'd try to rescue her and probably end up captured, because they were waiting for you. We couldn't take that risk. Besides, I had it under control." He gestured to Rhia. "Obviously."

"You lied to me." Lycas loomed over Marek. "You kept secret my own sister's imprisonment." He gave him a look of disgust. "What else could I expect from a Fox?"

Nilik stepped forward. "Don't speak to him that way. It's my fault Mother was captured, not his."

"Lycas, there's something else." Rhia put a hand on her brother's arm. "Sirin's dead."

Nilik caught his breath. Lycas stepped back, looking at Rhia as if she were a stranger.

"That's impossible. He's too valuable to execute."

"Maybe they couldn't risk his escape. Maybe orders came from higher up."

Lycas half turned away from her, swallowing hard. "Are you sure?"

"I saw him drown. His heart stopped."

"Did Crow take him?"

Rhia hesitated. "I don't know. When they took him away, Crow hadn't finished his journey."

He whirled on her. "So he could still be alive."

"They said they were going to bury him."

Lycas's face fell. "Then I pray he really was dead when they took him." He ran a hand over his scalp, pressing hard on the long black hair. "How do you know this? Was it a public execution?"

"No." She gave Nilik a long look, then turned her gaze back on Lycas. "They used me to make sure their interrogation wouldn't kill the prisoners, and then they used me to tell them when Sirin was finally dead." She shrank back as her brother's expression turned dark and menacing. "Please don't be angry with me."

Nilik's stomach churned. They'd as good as tortured his mother, shown her things a person should never see, and it was his fault.

Lycas's lip curled. "Not only did they execute my best friend, but they made my sister *watch*?"

"I'm not sorry I did it." She bit her lip. "It was horrible, but I learned a lot. I found out they know about the Acrosia, they know you're planning something for the first night of the Evius festival."

He cursed. "How can they know this? There must be a spy." He stalked back and forth, rubbing his face. "What else did you learn?"

"Ilion troops are landing the night before the festival. At the garrison. A general will be aboard one of the boats."

Lycas turned to her, a glint in his eye. "The garrison?"

Nilik's own skin tingled. The garrison was the only place he wanted to fight. Lania's killers waited for him there.

Lycas remained still for a long moment, eyes darting. Then he strode across the small clearing to his attaché. "Send for Feras, but don't tell him why."

As he came back over to them, Rhia asked him in a hushed voice, "You think Feras could be the source of the leak?"

"If he's not, he'll find out who is, or we call the whole thing off."

Nilik moved forward, heart pounding with hope. "Are we going to attack the garrison?"

Lycas's eyes narrowed at him. "If we are, whether I let you come along is still in question." He stroked the hilt of his throwing dagger. "Either way, that general will find himself facedown in the sand."

Rhia stepped between them and looked up at him. "Lycas, you can't have my son."

* * *

Nilik had never felt so small.

He stared at the floor of Lycas's tent, unable to meet his parents' eyes. "Mother, I'm sorry I disobeyed you."

"You're a man now," she said. "My wishes are to be respected, not obeyed."

"Then I disrespected you. It almost got both of you killed." He looked at them. "Don't blame Jula. She thought she was helping me fulfill my destiny."

His mother seemed to shudder. "Nilik," she said softly, "please come back to Tiros with us."

His jaw tightened. "I can't. I'm needed here in Velekos."

"You're needed more in Tiros. It's your home."

"How can you say that?" His face contorted with disbelief. "You taught me that we're all one people and we have to fight for each other. If we can beat them here, it'll be the beginning of the end of the occupation."

"They'll have to win without you. You're not ready."

"Lycas says I am, so does Feras. Why can't you just have faith in me?"

"It's not a matter of faith," Marek said. "We believe in your abilities." He stepped forward and dropped his tone into a non-negotiable territory. "But you're coming home with us."

"No, I'm not. How can you even ask me? I'm a Wolverine." He tapped his fist to his chest. "My Spirit is calling me to fight."

"Yes, but not here." Marek crossed his arms. "Come back and defend Tiros, or go north in the hills to the guerrilla command center." His jaw set. "Anywhere but here."

Nilik shook his head hard. "I don't understand. What's so bad about Velekos that I have to—"

His face froze as he suddenly understood. His mother was a Crow. She'd have only one reason for wanting so desperately to bring him home.

He looked at each of his parents while he tried to make his mouth and lungs work at the same time. His gaze finally settled on Rhia. "I'm going to die here, aren't I?"

She didn't look away or even blink. "I can't tell you."

"You don't need to." The agony in her eyes said it all.

Nilik's hand curled into an impotent fist, straining the new sutures. He wanted to rip them out with his teeth. No wounds mattered now, if he was about to die.

His gut ached, collapsing in on his last meal. What if it *were* his last meal? What if he'd already drunk his last ale, stalked his last prey, watched his last sunrise?

He placed his hand on Lycas's desk to steady himself. The connection to his uncle strengthened his resolve.

"I'm not leaving," he said finally. "If I'm meant to die here, that's what I'll do."

"Nilik, please…don't do this to us." His mother sounded as if she were choking on her words. Marek's face twisted and his eyes closed, but he said nothing.

Nilik took a deep breath and spoke slowly. "Crow takes us in His time. If I leave, I might still die the same day as I would here."

"You don't know that," she said.

"I'm not supposed to know when my life will end," he said bitterly, "so I can't make my choice that way. I have to ask myself, what would I do if I didn't know?"

His mother held her breath, as if expecting him to change his mind. He stared at the map of Velekos on the table. The Ilion garrison was marked in a ragged red rectangle. Lania's killers lived there, charged with manslaughter. In five years, they'd be home with their families, walking in the sunshine, enjoying the blood in their veins and the air in their lungs. She would still be dead.

He turned to his parents. "I'll stay and fight. It's what I do." He stared hard at Rhia. "Promise to be proud of me, not angry." His voice lowered to a whisper, despite the strength of his words. "I'll die to bring Lania justice."

Rhia squinted against the noontime sun reflecting off the white buildings below. From this vantage point on a high rock wall above Velekos it was easy to make out the Ilion settlers' houses—they tended to be painted white or pale yellow. Closer to the ridge was the Acrosia, the highest neighborhood in Velekos, where most of the rebels lived in homes painted a defiant blue.

She and Marek awaited two of them now. It had been two days since Lycas had "asked" Feras to find the Velekon spy or be tarred with the tag himself.

"Some days," Marek said, "I still can't believe the invasion happened. Remember when we used to visit Damen's family in Velekos every summer?"

Rhia managed a smile. "Nilik and Jula would eat fresh oysters until they were sick."

"They never learned." He put his arm around her. "Stop worrying. How can your vision come true, now that Lycas ordered Nilik to stay here during the garrison attack?"

She rubbed her arms, though the afternoon was warm. "Crow never alters His flight."

"How do you know?"

She remained silent, keeping her secret inside.

Marek turned her to face him. "Have you foreseen others' deaths beside Nilik?"

She nodded, reluctant to be specific. "When I first came into my powers, I had a vision." She shut her eyes against the image of a man writhing in the golden oak leaves, covered in blood. "It came true."

"Did you do anything to stop it? Did you tell that person?"

"No, it would have gone against my sacred duty as a Crow." Her gaze dropped to the ground. "And now I've violated it."

He pulled her close. "How could you not? Nilik's your son. Family comes before everything."

She smiled against his chest. He was talking like a Wolf, for whom devotion was the highest calling.

"Besides," he continued, "you haven't technically told anyone your vision. We inferred it on our own."

Her smile faded. Now he sounded like a Fox, muddying the rules to suit his own rationalizations. His wily side left him vulnerable to the temptations of deception and duplicity. She accepted the Fox in him, but it was the fierce, noble Wolf she'd fallen in love with.

He drew her away and looked into her eyes. "You saved our son."

"You saved him first."

"There was nothing else I could do."

She swallowed hard at the memory of Marek disappearing into the night after their kidnapped baby. He'd risked his life and sacrificed his freedom, following Nilik to the Ilion city of Leukos, where a noblewoman and senator had bought Nilik to raise as her own, and used Marek as a slave in her home.

And eventually, in her bed. His Wolf Spirit, weakened by the city, had left him in the care of Fox, who reminded him to do whatever it took to stay with Nilik. Rumor had it that his killing of the senator during his escape had prompted a backlash against their people and hastened the invasion of Velekos and Asermos.

The Eagle sentry gave a bobwhite whistle, the signal that a friendly party was approaching.

Marek pointed past Rhia and smiled. "Jula will be happy."

Rhia looked over the rock face to see her Crow-brother Damen and his young son Corek riding over the sandy soil toward the camp, followed by Feras.

She hurried down the ridge, Marek on her heels. By the time they reached the grassy slope on the outskirts of the camp, Damen had dismounted. She rushed forward to embrace him.

"I'm so sorry about Lania," she whispered. "How are her parents?"

He pulled back and nodded, his lips forming a tight, straight line.

She turned to Corek, who with his short mop of dark straight hair, looked like an eighteen-year-old version of his father. As he dismounted, she noticed he'd lost his usual sprightliness, inherited from his mother Reni. Grief weighed heavily upon all of them.

Corek hugged her without speaking. As she let him go, she said, "Jula's here."

His brows popped up briefly, then settled back into sadness. "I've missed her. That is, I've missed all of you." He turned and led his horse toward the camp, his steps lighter.

"Corek's staying here from now on," Damen told them. "It's getting too dangerous in town. The Ilions have declared martial law until the end of the festival."

She grimaced, then gave a brief wave to Feras as they made their way up the hill to the camp. He followed about fifty feet behind, still on horseback. Rhia didn't need to ask Damen why the Bear was so sullen.

They made their way along the wooded trail until they reached the clearing at the center of the camp, in front of Lycas's tent. Feras dismounted, then untied a long gray bag from the pack attached to his riding blanket. The bag held a large, round object.

Rhia's stomach tilted. "He didn't."

"Lycas gave him a loyalty test." Damen's lip curled. "How else to pass it?"

Lycas came out of his tent. "You have something for me?" he said to Feras.

The Bear tossed the bag toward him. It rolled until it hit Lycas's toes.

Rhia and Marek stepped closer as her brother knelt and untied the bag. He opened it, then looked inside without expression. "I don't recognize the face."

Feras shifted his lower jaw. "He was my brother."

Rhia clutched Marek's hand. Lycas just stared at the Bear.

Finally Feras added, "My stepbrother, to be exact, but I've known him all my life. Kalias runs—rather, he ran the Prasnos Tavern. The Velekon resistance has held many meetings in its back room." He clamped his mouth shut, his face twisted.

"Are you sure it was him?" Lycas said.

Damen stepped forward. "We used Nathas when we—asked Kalias about it."

Rhia wiped cold sweat from her forehead. As a second-phase Owl, Damen's mate Nathas could detect lies, but he'd no doubt never been used in such a brutal way. Her people were turning into the thing they despised most.

Lycas let out a long breath, then retied the bag. "How do we know there aren't more?"

"He gave us the names of three other collaborators," Feras said. "If we can find them, we'll deal with them. At least we know who to avoid when we make our new plans."

Lycas nodded. "I regret that this had to happen."

The five of them stood silent for several moments, then Lycas got to his feet. "Speaking of plans, I have a new one. A bigger one."

He opened the flap to his tent and beckoned them inside. As Feras passed, he snatched the bag out of Lycas's hand.

"You go on in," she said to Damen. "We already know the plan." Her chest felt leaden at the thought of it. Even though Nilik would not be taking part in the garrison attack, casualties would abound. She and Damen would be needed as Crows to perform triage for the Otter healers, telling them which soldiers could be saved and which needed nothing more than a peaceful passage to the Other Side.

Damen entered the tent, leaving Rhia and Marek alone.

"What are we becoming," Marek whispered, "when men turn on their own brothers? Treachery, then murder?"

Her stomach felt sick. "The Spirits won't let this stand."

His eyes narrowed. "This is what the Ilions have done to us. We'll never be the same. But what else can we do? We have to win this war." He looked at the sky. "Speaking of which, it's getting late, and I haven't made today's arrow-making quota. See you at dinner?"

She nodded. "I'd better go help cook." Regardless of their culinary skills, Crows were expected to assist with meals, to help make up for the amount they ate. But right now, she felt as if she'd never look at food again.

She watched Marek trot off, then made her way alone to the mess tent. On the way there, she stopped when she saw one of the sentries accompanying a pale, hulking man with a mass of dark curls and a grubby beard. They drew closer, and Rhia stopped in her tracks.

"Sirin."

He halted, too, staring at her without expression.

"You're alive," she whispered.

"No thanks to you." He advanced on her. "Did they set you free after you did their bidding?"

The hairs rose on the back of her neck. "I had no choice."

"There's always a choice."

"What was I supposed to do, overpower three soldiers, bite through your chains and set you free?"

"You could have refused to stand by and *watch* your own people tortured and murdered." He glared at her. "But it's no surprise—you always were a coward."

She put her hands on her hips. "It wasn't out of fear." *Not entirely,* she thought. "I did it to learn what they knew about the resistance. It worked. Lycas has changed his plans to attack Velekos." She gestured behind her toward Lycas's tent. "He'll be happy to have your assistance. Not to mention see his best friend alive again."

Sirin pulled in a deep breath through his nose, then let it out. He nodded to the sentry. "Let's go."

As they passed her, she asked Sirin, "How did you survive?"

"The water was ice cold," Sirin said while continuing to walk away. "It must have slowed my pulse."

"Did they bury you alive?"

Sirin snorted and turned to her. "As if they would give me that respect. They dumped me in the river. That woke me up, and I managed to get the stones off me and swim downstream underwater." For a moment, his eyes flashed amusement. "A pretty little huntress found me washed up on the bank. She fed me, set my broken arm, which is nicely healed now." He gave her another dark look. "Again, no thanks to you."

When he turned away again, she continued toward the mess tent. She hoped that one day Sirin would realize she'd actually saved his life, by announcing his death too soon.

Until then, she would watch her back.

22

Kirisian Mountains

Sura and the three Kalindons traveled for another week without incident. The dry weather let them make good time, but water was scarce for drinking and nonexistent for bathing.

She and Etarek were fast becoming friends. His sunny nature complemented her dark, dry outlook. After the first tentative encounter, their nights of passion grew long and adventurous, turning a burden into a gift. Yet despite their mutual enjoyment, she couldn't forget that their union held a purpose beyond their own pleasure.

Their compatibility contrasted with Kara and Dravek's disharmony. One moment the Wolf displayed an ingratiating sweetness toward her husband; the next her barbs turned as sharp as her arrows. But Sura couldn't feel too sorry for Dravek; he'd built an emotional wall of ice that deflected his wife's insults and affection. One day Sura realized she couldn't dredge up a memory of his smile.

As they came within a week's walk of Tiros, the terrain grew rockier and the trees sparser and stubbier. The few flat places for camping lay along the cliffs now. After weeks in Kalindos and its heavily forested surroundings, it felt strange to come out of their tents in the morning and see the sky.

One evening during dinner, Kara seemed unusually quiet and inward-looking.

"Can't wait to sleep in a real bed again." Etarek screwed the top onto the meloxa flask and winged it across the campsite.

Dravek deftly snatched it from the air. "And have a long bath," he said before taking a swig.

Etarek shook his head. "Not in Tiros. I hear they barely have enough water for drinking. Right, Kara?"

The Wolf gave a guarded glance at their surroundings, apparently ignoring the conversation.

"Why would anyone live where there's no river?" Dravek tossed the flask back to Etarek. "How do they survive?"

"They have wells," Sura said. "My mother told me there's a reservoir that fills in the springtime. And the Tiron River is only a few hours' walk away."

Kara stood suddenly, spilling her uneaten food to the ground. Dravek leaped to take her hand.

"What's wrong?" He followed her gaze to the west. "Someone coming?"

She shook him off and walked to the edge of the ridge. The Wolf stared at the sun as it touched the flat horizon of the Tiron Plain. Flaming red, it seemed to bulge and shimmer.

Kara gasped, then took several sharp, quick breaths.

Dravek hurried to her side. "What is it?"

"No, don't touch—" She dropped to her haunches, holding out a hand to ward him off. Her head tilted to the side as if she were listening to a faraway voice. Then she lifted her face to the setting sun. The red rays reflected off her dark golden hair and in the depths of her blue eyes.

She disappeared.

Dravek stepped back and whispered his wife's name. She shimmered into view again.

"Did you see that?" Her eyes overflowed with tears. "Invisible. Second phase. Dravek, I'm pregnant."

He whooped and swept her into his arms. They spun in a circle, Kara's legs kicking the air. Etarek applauded, and Sura followed his lead, even as her gut twisted so sharply she almost doubled over in pain.

Dravek put Kara down and kissed her with a passion equal to that of their wedding. Kara beamed up at him, and whispered, "We're going to have a baby."

He gazed down into her eyes. "He'll be as beautiful as you." He pulled her close again. "I'm sorry we've been fighting. I've been so rotten."

"No, I'm sorry. I was scared and took it out on you." She pulled back and smiled. "But that's all gone now."

Sura focused on the remains of her meal. They looked as if the last eight days of bickering had never occurred. How could a baby make things simpler instead of more complicated?

Kara stared at her hands. "Let's see if I can do it on purpose." Her outline shimmered, then dissipated as she vanished. "I did it!" A short silence fell, then her voice came from the other side of the ridge. "And my stealth is better, too. I can't wait to hunt tomorrow morning."

"You're not hunting when you're pregnant," Dravek said. "You could fall."

"When do I ever fall?" Her voice was teasing but held an uneasy edge.

"Yesterday."

"That was just a skid. Barely scratched my knees."

Sura looked between Dravek and nothing. Here was the defensive tone she had come to expect from them.

"You're not used to this terrain," Dravek told Kara. "You should try out your new powers somewhere safer."

"If I don't hunt, what'll we eat?"

"There's plenty of roots and berries in our packs."

Etarek spoke up. "Only a few days to Tiros. We can go without meat that long."

"Stay out of it, Etarek." Kara reappeared and advanced on her husband. "Why can't you be happy for me? Why do you have to ruin everything?" Her eyes brimmed with tears.

His face fell. "Kara, I'm just worried about the baby."

"And I'm not?" she shrilled. "I'm such a horrible mother that I won't take care of myself?"

"I didn't say that. Look, just forget I said anything." He turned away, clenching his fists. "Do what you want. I trust you."

"No, you don't." She followed him to the campfire. "You have no faith in me."

"I do. I'm sorry for what I said." Sura saw his eyes flash as he passed her, but he had his back to Kara so she couldn't see his pained expression. "I take it back."

"You can't take it back this time." She caught up to him, but he didn't turn around. "I'm tired of you bossing me."

His mouth twisted. "*Me* bossing *you?*" he muttered. "Now she's delusional."

"*What did you say?*"

"Nothing." He rubbed his face hard with his knuckles. "Just forget it." He tried to move away again.

"No." She grabbed his arm. "Look at me when you speak."

"Stop it." He jerked out of her grasp. "I'm not a child."

"Then don't act like one. You always do this, say mean things and then squirm out of the conversation."

Sura put her plate aside, her stomach too tight to take anymore. Though her father had left before she was too young to make memories, she imagined her parents having fights like this every night.

"This isn't a conversation." Dravek moved away from Kara again, this time toward the edge of the cliff. "This is you haranguing me. Again." His teeth gritted around the last word.

Etarek cleared his throat. "Uh, maybe we should—"

"It's the only kind of conversation we have," Kara told Dravek, "so that's what I'm calling it."

"Please stop it." Dravek uttered the plea to the sky, as if Raven Herself would swoop down and rescue him.

Kara stalked over to him, hands on her hips. He made a move to avoid her, and his feet came close to the cliff's edge. Sura stood up.

"Be careful," she said, but her words were overrun by Kara's voice.

"You can't run away from me, Dravek. I'm your wife."

She reached for his arm, and he turned on her.

"I said, stop!"

Her head jerked back as if he'd struck her. Then her eyes went blank and her jaw slack. She stared past Dravek at the orange horizon.

In the shocked silence, Sura realized that the excitement of Kara's invisibility had made them forget one important fact: Dravek now had second-phase powers, too. He could erase a person's memory.

"Kara?" he whispered. "Kara, look at me."

She squinted at his face as if she were trying to recall his name. Finally her eyes sparked with recognition. "Dravek."

"Yes. Yes, it's me, love." He went to embrace her, and she stepped back.

"What are you doing?"

He lowered his arms. "You know me, right?"

"Of course. You're Daria's little brother." She took another step back, eyes darting. Her face lit up when she saw Etarek, then clouded again as she examined their surroundings. "We're near Tiros. Why?"

Sura's heart froze.

"Oh, no," Etarek whispered.

"So I can train with Vara." Dravek's voice shook. "So we can deliver the Kalindon pigeons. You don't remember?"

"I delivered pigeons before. With Daria and her father."

"Yes, last year. You remember, that's good. What else do you—"

"Hello," Kara said to Sura with a tentative smile. She turned to Dravek. "Who's she?"

Carefully he grasped her shoulders. She gave his hands a curious look but didn't shrug them off.

"Listen to me," he said, "and know that I'm not lying or playing a joke." His gaze bored into hers. "I'm your husband."

"My husband?" She broke away from him and gave a nervous laugh. "Why would I marry you?" Her hands flew to her mouth as soon as the words were out. "Oh, no, that sounded awful. It's not that I don't like you. But you're not exactly the marrying type. I can't imagine anyone—" She stopped and twisted her hands together. "This is a joke." She looked at Etarek. "Right?"

"No..." Dravek clutched his hair. "Spirits, no. Kara, I'm so sorry." He reached out for her. "Let me explain."

"No." She backed away, then turned to Etarek. "You tell me."

He looked at Dravek, who nodded. Etarek motioned for her to sit beside him. As he explained what had happened, Dravek paced the edge of the ridge.

Sura dreaded her own entry into the second phase. Would she herself someday cause the same harm in a moment of anger? If only they'd reached Vara a few days sooner, Dravek could have learned to control this treacherous power.

"I'm *pregnant?*" Kara's eyes filled with tears, and she clutched Etarek's wrist. "Am I sure it's his?"

"That's why you're in this state," Etarek said. "He entered his second phase the same time you did. You argued, and he—" His glance shifted to Dravek, then back again. "I'm sure it was an accident."

Sura wondered if Etarek had heard something in Dravek's voice that cast doubt on that statement.

"We'll get your memory back when we get to Tiros," she told Kara. "Vara will help us."

Kara looked at her. "Who *are* you?"

"This is Sura," Dravek said, "my Spirit-sister."

Etarek kept his voice level. "Her mother Mali is in prison for leading the Asermon resistance."

"Oh." Kara's eyes went soft and round as she looked at Sura. "I'm sorry."

Dravek took her hand. "Let's go talk this over, just the two of us."

"The two of us?" She yanked her hand out of his grip. "You stole months of life from my mind, and now you expect to cuddle up? Make love?"

"No, I just want to talk. Maybe I can help you remember."

She scoffed. "Think your famous tongue can bring back my memories? Or maybe just make new ones?" She turned away from him again. "We'll talk tomorrow, Dravek."

He stood slowly, his face twisted with dread. "I'll get my things and sleep with Etarek. We'll switch tents tonight."

"I can't sleep with her." Kara looked at Sura. "I don't even know her."

"Then I'll sleep outside." Dravek went to his tent and yanked out a blanket. "You can be alone."

"I'm a Wolf. I can't sleep if I'm alone." Kara turned to Etarek. "Can I share your tent?"

Etarek shook his head. "I'm with Sura."

"It's only a few nights. We're almost to Tiros."

Sura took a step toward them. "You can't sleep with my mate."

Kara clucked her tongue. "We won't do anything. And this way, Dravek won't have to sleep outside."

"You want me to sleep with your husband?"

"I don't care what you do with him." She met Dravek's eyes, which filled with pain, then softened her voice. "You're his Spirit-sister. I sleep with my Wolf-brothers on long hunts. To keep warm, plus it bonds us."

Sura gritted her teeth. The last thing she and Dravek needed was more bonding.

"I'll sleep outside." Dravek threw the blanket over his shoulder and stalked up a narrow trail.

Sura turned to the others, intending to stake her territory. Kara looked up at her, and behind the Wolf's defiant bluster, Sura saw confusion and despair.

"We'll take turns sleeping alone," Sura said. "I'll go first tonight. You stay with Etarek."

Kara's shoulders relaxed. "Thank you. That's very kind." She rubbed her arms. "I'm sorry for being unreasonable."

Sura bent to pick up the dirty dishes. "I'm sorry you lost your memory. It must be terrible."

"It feels like I woke up from a long, cloudy dream. The worst part is, everyone sees a different me than I do. And I'm the one who's wrong." She chewed her fingernail and looked at the place where Dravek had disappeared. "Am I in love with him?"

Sura wondered. "Enough to marry him."

She looked at Etarek. "It must have happened fast."

"You've been together about six months," he said. "And since then you haven't been seen with another man."

Surprise crossed her face. "Not even you?"

Sura blinked. "Were you and Etarek mates?"

He gave Sura a warm smile. "A long time ago."

Kara made a *hmph* noise, then turned toward the west and the sky's fading light. She lifted her hands before her face and scrunched up her forehead. She shimmered from view, then reappeared.

She breathed a sigh of wonder. "It's true, then." She cupped her hands over her belly and gave a sad smile. "Was I happy when I found out?"

"Very happy." Sura went to the Wolf but stopped short of touching her. "So was Dravek."

Kara sighed with her lower lip out, blowing her hair from her face. "I wish I could have that moment back." Her brows pinched together. "But what if I can't? What if my feelings are tied to that time and place?"

"You were destined to love him," Etarek said. "How else can you explain something so unlikely?"

Kara shook her head sadly. "Love is an accident, not destiny. You'll understand when you're my age," she added, as if she were fifty-two instead of twenty-two. "I probably did love Dravek, though it doesn't seem very easy."

Sura gazed into the campfire's dying flames, and wished that were true.

Dravek lay on his back, watching clouds obscure the stars. It reminded him of how the light had disappeared from Kara's face as the memories slipped away from her. She'd looked so vacant. Lost. Alone.

But nothing in her mind changed the fact of the child in her womb. Whether she ever wanted him in her bed again, he would stay in her life.

Then there was Sura, who occupied his thoughts, especially as he lay awake at night, hearing how thoroughly Etarek pleased her. She sounded so happy, and yet on the rare occasions when Dravek met her eyes, he saw an unendurable sadness lurking within. He wanted to take that pain away, though he knew he would make it worse. Destruction seemed to be his only skill.

Dravek turned on his side on the hard rock just as a rumble of thunder rolled across the sky. Moments later, he heard the rain make its way across the rocky cliffs until it pelted his face and hands like a thousand wet pebbles. He drew the blanket over his head, but soon it was drenched.

Something nudged his foot. He pulled down the blanket to see a cloaked figure standing over him.

"Are you crazy or just stupid?" Sura hissed. "Come inside."

"I can't."

"Then you're crazy *and* stupid." She yanked the blanket off him. The rain drove into his face so hard he couldn't see. To avoid drowning, he stood and followed her down the trail and into the tent.

"The right side's leaking." She tossed him his pack. "Get changed over there where you won't drip on the dry part. Good night."

Dravek heard her lie down on the far side with a grunt. He peeled off his wet clothes, shivering even in the warm night air. As he rubbed himself dry, he glanced over his shoulder at Sura, though he couldn't see her in the near-total darkness.

Her scent mingled with his own and Kara's, and the blanket wrapped around her smelled like Etarek. To his nose, even more sensitive in his second phase, it was as if all four of them were in the tent.

Without meaning to, he cleared his throat.

"I've already seen you naked," she said. "I was at your wedding, remember?"

Her sardonic tone eased his tension. "Then what's the harm in looking now?"

He heard her feet fidget under the blanket. "It's too dark."

"And I'm already dressed, anyway."

She laughed. "You are not."

"Outwitted me again." He grabbed a dry set of clothes from his pack.

"A salamander could outwit you."

He said nothing as he dressed, then stretched out on his back beside her. Water seeped over the left half of his shirt, so he scooted closer to Sura.

"I told you it was wet." She inched forward against the tent wall to give him more room.

He lay on his side facing away from her. Her back pressed against him, and her heat radiated through the blanket and their thin layers of clothes. He sighed and draped an arm over his face, as if that would fight off the images of skin and sweat. The rain pounded on the tent roof.

"What did it feel like," she said, "when you made her forget?"

He didn't want to remember that moment. "It felt like fire."

"I know you'd never hurt her on purpose." She drew in another breath, as if to utter another sentence that began with, "But…"

He couldn't bear the silence of her doubt. "I'd do anything to take it back."

"I had a friend who lost her memory falling out of a tree. One of the Otters treated her concussion, and she was fine a few days later."

"Kara's memories are burned. I don't think they can be recovered, any more than a log can be rebuilt from its ashes." He covered his face with his hands. "I can't believe I did that to her. I don't deserve her love."

"But loving you is part of who she is."

His throat tightened. "Not anymore. Now I'm back to being her best friend's obnoxious little brother."

"If that was how she saw you, how'd she fall in love with you in the first place? Snake seduction magic?"

He hesitated. It was hard to explain without dishonoring Kara.

"No magic, just meloxa," he said. "And no, I didn't try to get her drunk. There was a party midwinter—celebrating a birth, I think. We shared a few dances, then she took me to bed. I think she wanted to prove she could resist me a second time."

"Despite your famous tongue."

From her voice he could almost see the mocking smile curve Sura's lips. He wiped his cheek as it heated with embarrassment.

"Anyway, her plan didn't work. She became despondent or furious when I'd so much as look at another woman." He frowned. "She didn't mind the men, I suppose because they couldn't give me children—they couldn't trap me the way she wanted to. That was her word, *trap*." His voice hardened. "Like I was another wild animal for her to hunt."

"Why would you agree to be trapped?"

"I loved her. I hated seeing her unhappy." He gathered the courage to admit the full truth. "And I loved the way she craved me. I grew addicted to the need in her eyes, even as it diminished her. One night in the middle of making love, she gave me an ultimatum—marry her or she'd leave me that moment."

"That's not fair. And I bet she was bluffing."

"I almost said no. There was a moment when I saw it all so clearly. That what we both needed most was to get away from each other."

Sura turned to face him. "What stopped you?"

He hesitated, wondering if she could understand. "I imagined the look on Kara's face if I said, 'yes,' and how she would look if

I said, 'no.' Seeing her smile, knowing I was the cause, made me feel like less of a monster."

"Why would you think you're a monster?"

He shifted onto his back and turned his face toward her. "My father raped my mother." His mouth twitched after he said it, as if it wanted to take back the words. "I was made from violence and pain, from the power of several men over one woman. She almost died giving birth to me, and then took her own life because I was a constant reminder of what had happened to her."

"None of that is your fault." She lifted her hand as if to touch him, then pulled it back.

"Are you afraid of me now?" he whispered.

"No."

Her voice trembled, but he didn't smell fear, and her hands were as warm as ever, lying on the blanket between them, an inch from his chest. His heightened Snake senses threatened to drown him in his awareness of her heat.

"Sura…"

Her breath caught, and he felt her skin chill. The passion in his voice had made her afraid—and not of his forgetting powers.

"Yes?"

He brushed his warm hand against her cold one. "I've never wanted to not hurt someone as much as I want to not hurt you."

It was as close as he could come to a declaration of love. He could never have her, no matter what she felt, no matter what happened to his marriage. They were Snake and always would be.

Sura wove her fingers around his, and the heat under their skin flared. "What do we do?" She was whispering now as the rain turned to a drizzle.

"I don't know." Holding his breath, he lifted her hand to kiss her palm.

She let out a choked cry, then seized the front of his shirt and pressed her forehead to his. "I can't do this," she whispered, "be with you and not be with you. It makes me hate myself."

"No." His throat tried to cut off the words. "Hate me instead." He brushed his lips over her cheek, feeling her jaw move as her mouth opened. He wanted to cover it with his own, but resisted, moving to kiss her fluttering lashes, then her forehead.

Sura stroked her smooth cheek against his stubbled one, breathing him in. The warm, rich scent of her desire drenched his mind, and his hands shook with the effort not to caress her body.

The rain strengthened into a roar, and he pulled Sura into a tight embrace. They clutched at each other, and for a moment he felt relief flow through him like a cold drink of water. Then the press of her against him became agony, and he nearly bit his tongue in half to suppress a groan of longing.

"I wish I could make us forget who we are," he said. "Then we could find a place where there's nothing between us."

She pulled back to look at him, her nose almost touching his.

"Could we do that?" Her eyes turned sad. "Run away and leave everything and everyone we know? Everyone who needs us?"

He didn't want to think about all the others, not now when they were so close and she smelled so good. "I need you."

He lifted her chin to take her mouth, taste her tongue, fill himself with her wetness. Already he could feel her lips swollen with the heat of desire.

The rain stopped. Sura and Dravek froze, their breath mingling in each other's mouths, which held their place a fraction of an inch apart.

"We can't do this," she whispered.

He forced himself to let her go, and Sura eased herself out of his embrace. His body mourned the loss of her, as if she were the sole source of warmth in the world. She turned away.

He drew the blanket up to cover her shoulders, trying not to notice that they were trembling, like his hands. "I'll sleep outside now that the rain's stopped."

"The ground is wet."

"And cold. It'll help."

She didn't reply, only curled her knees to her chest as if doubled in pain.

Once outside, he lay on the damp ground and let it steal his body's unbearable heat. It seemed as if his desire for Sura could set the sea on fire.

Though he ached to release himself, he vowed to store this feeling deep inside. One day, as his power grew, it would rain fury on his father's people like hail.

He would burn them all.

23

Tiros

Sura shivered in the shadow of the Tiron watchtower, where Cougars stood ready to shoot arrows into her and her traveling companions. It reminded her of the Descendant garrison near Asermos.

Between the watchtowers stood four powerfully built, solemn-faced young men with swords and knives unsheathed. Kara stopped and bowed in greeting. They nodded in return, each of them watching one of the visitors. The center guards—the two with the swords—wore bear claws on leather cords around their necks. The outer two wore long, thin carved wooden claws—Wolverine, Sura guessed. She tried not to stare at the fetishes, a sight she hadn't seen in years; Kalindons didn't wear them, and Asermons weren't allowed.

"State your name, Animal, home and business," the taller and older of the Bears said. "Now."

Kara introduced them, then added, "We're here to see Vara, and to deliver pigeons."

"And meloxa," Dravek said.

The four men jerked their heads to look his way. "How much meloxa?" said the Bear who had spoken before.

"Enough to go around." Etarek unfastened a flask from the mule's pack and tossed it to him. The Bear caught it deftly in one large hand, then unscrewed the cap and took a cautious whiff. He smiled.

"I'm Krios. Go on in." He nodded at the younger Bear. "Take the Snakes to Vara, then show the others where they can get tents."

"Wait." Sura looked at Krios. "Has there been any word from Asermos about Rhia and Mali?"

"Rhia escaped. She's not here, though." He shook his head. "Last we heard, Mali was still in prison."

Etarek touched her shoulder. "I'm sorry."

She tried to give him a grateful smile, but her feelings were tied in a knot. At least Rhia had broken free, which meant Lycas was safer. But her heart twisted at the thought of her mother in chains, and she resolved to continue her quest to reach the second phase. With a mentor here in Tiros to guide her in her new magic, she would pose less of a danger to others than Dravek had. Or so she hoped.

They entered the village between the watchtowers. Sura forced her gaze to remain forward and resisted the temptation to look up. In Asermos, the soldiers preferred it that way.

They passed rows of tents and poorly constructed shanties on the outskirts of town. Refugees, no doubt. She kept her breath shallow to minimize the smell of squalor. At least they have their freedom, she reminded herself.

They came to a small white stone house near the center of town. The curtains in the sole window were drawn, though the sun hadn't set.

"Vara's house." The Bear pointed to the wooden door. "Wait until I leave before you go in." He hurried off, beckoning Kara and Etarek to follow him.

Dravek and Sura stepped onto the narrow porch stairs. He knocked on the door, and when he lowered his arm, their knuckles bumped. Her pulse leaped at the brief touch. One of his fingers reached out and brushed her palm.

The door opened, and a tall woman stared down at them. Her long blond braid was spliced with gray strands, but her face was young and striking, with full lips and blazing dark eyes. When Sura opened her mouth to introduce herself, the woman held up a hand to silence her.

She examined them for a long moment, lingering on the space between their bodies.

"You are Snakes?" the woman whispered. They nodded. Her gaze went blank and distant for a long moment. Then deep frown lines creased her forehead. "Oh." She closed her eyes and pinched the bridge of her nose. "This is awful. Please come in. I am Vara."

They shared a look of trepidation, then stepped over the threshold. Vara reached quickly behind them to shut the door.

The dim front room appeared to be a kitchen, but Vara led them to another door without offering so much as a drink, which Sura's dry tongue and throat resented.

Beyond the door was total blackness. Sura strained to adjust her eyes to the windowless room. Goose bumps rose on her arms at the rush of cool, clammy air.

"Hurry." Vara bustled past them, disappearing. She patted a wooden surface, which Sura assumed was a table.

After banging her knee on the chair, Sura sat next to Dravek. In the dark, she felt acutely aware of his presence.

"How do you see in here?" he asked Vara.

"It's my home," she said in a low voice. "I know every inch. And I see better without light since I entered the third phase." She sank into a chair across the table. "Sura, I've been expecting you. The Kalindon message about your mother mentioned you were a Snake. And, Dravek, what's taken you so long to come to me? Have you been training on your own?"

"With Snake's guidance, yes."

"Look where it's gotten you." She sighed. "Touch each other again."

Sura put her hands in her lap. "Why?"

"Take his hand. Now, please."

Sura heard his skin slide across the surface of the table. Dreading the result, she moved her palm over his. Their fingers intertwined.

Vara let out a heavy breath. "As I feared. There is tremendous heat between you."

They yanked their hands apart.

"So?" Dravek's voice shook. "It's warm out, and we've been walking all day."

"Your bodies generate more heat than others, so I guessed you were Snakes even outside. In here I see more clearly, because my home is dark and cold."

"See what?" Dravek asked her.

"Heat, as shades of gray light. The closer to white, the hotter. It's a Snake's third-phase power. You two didn't know that?" When they didn't reply, she gave a harsh snort. "This Descendant occupation keeps our young so ignorant. When I was your age, we worked with our mentors from the day after our Bestowing, no matter how far we had to travel."

"What did you mean about what was between us?" Sura asked.

"I see emotional heat, as well as physical. It's how I wipe memories without destroying the personality of their carrier. My mind makes an emotional map of sorts. I try to maintain the integrity of that map." Her voice angled toward Dravek. "I'll teach you how to do this before you hurt someone."

Sura squirmed in her seat. *Too late.*

"As I was about to say." The Snake woman's voice softened and sobered. "The heat dances between you, flaring white when you touch."

"Is that not normal for Snakes?" Sura asked her.

"With Snakes, there's no such thing as normal." A smile seemed to curve her words. "However—" her voice came stern again "—the pattern I see between you is that of new lovers."

"No!" they said simultaneously.

"Unrequited lovers, then."

Shame flooded Sura, and she couldn't speak.

"Hmm." Vara rapped her fingernails on the table. "I see from your blushes that I'm correct. I'm relieved you haven't given into this temptation."

"I'm married," Dravek said.

"And I have a mate, of sorts," Sura added. "Besides, it's forbidden for Spirit-siblings to be together that way. It's taboo to even think about it."

"Why?" Vara asked calmly.

Sura recited the rationale. "So we can work together without distraction. So our desire doesn't twist the wisdom of our Aspect and pervert our magic."

"Dravek, what happens when you and Sura work together?"

He shifted in his seat. "We start fires."

"You mean, you reignite fires."

He cleared his throat. "We *start* them. There was a cold torch—"

"You're sure it was cold?" Vara's voice shot from across the table.

"I'm sure," he said in a hard voice. "It just happened."

"Sura, do you know why it happened?"

Dravek spoke up again. "It wasn't her fault—"

"I. Asked. Her."

Sura rubbed her hands together in her lap. If they wanted help, they had to tell the truth.

"We were—" She drew in a deep breath, then let it out. "We were discussing our feelings." No, that wasn't the *entire* truth. Another deep breath. "We described what it would be like to make love."

"To each other."

"Yes." Sura averted her gaze from Vara, though she couldn't see her.

"Don't be embarrassed. A Snake should always speak frankly in matters of sex. Our Spirit's power resides in it." Her voice flattened. "Though usually we stoke our desire without fantasizing about our Spirit-siblings."

"Should we be separated?" Sura asked.

Vara spoke urgently. "It's too late. Your longing would only increase. You'd be more dangerous than ever."

"Have we done something wrong?" Dravek asked her.

"Feelings aren't right or wrong. Only you know in your hearts whether your actions have been just."

"I wiped out almost a year of my wife's memory," Dravek snapped. "I'll hazard a crazy guess that that was wrong."

She was silent for a moment. "Did you do it on purpose?"

"No." He gave an abrasive sigh. "But I was angry with her. I've been lashing out since we got married last month." He took a couple of short, uneven breaths. "I hated her for not being Sura."

A dizzy heat rushed over Sura's scalp, as if her head had been doused in hot water.

Vara spoke calmly. "Your wife no longer remembers your vows."

"She doesn't even remember falling in love. She has nothing but disgust for me."

"So." Vara made a self-satisfied noise in her throat. "You feel guilty for getting what you want."

"It's not what I want!" Dravek said. "I never meant to hurt her." Pain shot through his voice. "I stole a year of her life. I can never make that up to her."

"You can start by letting her go."

He hissed in a breath. "She's pregnant."

"I know. I feel the heat of your second-phase power."

Sura realized she could feel it, too. She'd thought it was only the increase in their desire for each other that had sparked a larger flame.

"What's the point of this power," Dravek asked, "if all it does is hurt people?"

"After a great trauma," Vara replied, "forgetting can save one's sanity."

"I know how memories can hurt." His voice took on an edge, and Sura knew he was thinking of his mother. "But they're part of who we are."

"I'd forget if I could." Sura cleared her throat and forced her voice to steady. "I'd forget the way pieces of Mathias's charred flesh stuck to his bones when we took him out of his house. I'd forget the way his skeleton crumbled when we wrapped him in the burial shroud. Most of all, I'd forget the smell."

No one spoke for several moments. Finally Vara said, "I can help with that if you want."

She closed her eyes. "More than anything."

"But back to the matter of you two," Vara said. "Have you had dreams or visions about each other? Sura?"

Sura knew from Vara's tone that her own cheeks were flushed. She was glad the room was dark so she wouldn't have to watch Dravek's reaction.

She closed her eyes as she began. She told them the dream of the flames, the one she'd had the first night of their trip, right before she'd made love with Etarek. She described her and Dravek's naked bodies pressed against the pole, their wrists bound by the black snake. Her voice threatened to break when she reached the part where it all vanished upon their love's consummation.

"What does that mean?" Dravek asked Vara in a whisper.

She drummed her nails on the table in a way Sura was already tiring of. "I won't deny it troubles me. I'll consult with a Swan to be sure about the interpretation, but my feeling is that if you give in to your lust, you'll lose the fire. You may even cause Snake to leave you both for breaking the taboo."

"Forever?" Sura said.

"I don't know. But for the sake of your power, for the sake of all the good it can do for our people, you can never succumb to this temptation."

Dravek spoke in a hostile tone. "So Snake gave us these desires so we could burn our enemies, but She'll punish us for acting on them?"

"I'm sorry." Vara's voice softened. "I know the force of a Snake's passion. It rips us apart sometimes."

"All the time," Sura whispered.

"If you choose to separate to ease your pain, I'll train you individually." She reached across the table and took their hands. "But if you accept this challenge and hone your powers together, you could give our people new hope."

Sura felt part of her crumble inside, and she wanted to pull away. She'd already been asked to bear a child so that her parents and Etarek's could gain power. Now she was expected to put herself through the agony of routinely touching a man she loved but could never have. *It's not fair.*

But this was the path that had been laid for her. For others, the path led to death in battle or years of imprisonment. She shouldn't complain.

She let go of Vara's hand. "We'll give you our decision tomorrow."

24

Velekos

Lycas skulked along the edge of the courtyard separating the two
sides of the garrison, his clothes soaked in the blood of dozens.

With martial law about to be declared in Velekos, half the
garrison's troops had left before sunset for the village, to thwart
the rumored disruption to tomorrow's Evius festival. Reinforcements would arrive at high tide before midnight. Until then, the
fort was undermanned.

So Lycas had struck.

A small force of Wolverines and Badgers had approached the
front gate disguised as Ilion soldiers. Silent as snakes, they
slashed the throats of the guards, then opened the other gates to
let in the remaining guerillas. Soon the garrison was crawling
with rebels, as hidden as spiders beneath a rug.

The young Bear commander of the second platoon had been killed, along with three of his men. Lycas now commanded the fallen soldier's platoon, which he'd redivided into two squads down from three, to fill in the holes. Somewhere on the other side of the garrison, Sirin was leading his own company. Spirits willing, they would meet at the top and watch their archers shoot the incoming Ilion troops.

None of the blood on Lycas's clothes belonged to him. No knife could cut him, no sword could slash him. Only an arrow could kill him, and all the arrows were on his side.

Such as those in the quivers of the four Wolves who flanked him now. The wide stone courtyard was empty, except for four guards facing the open archways out to the sea, their red-and-yellow uniforms glowing in the torchlight.

Lycas gave the signal, and the Wolves vanished. They crossed the courtyard, silent and invisible.

One of them shouted, "Now!"

Four arrows flew out of nowhere, each striking a guard in the back of his neck. The Ilions staggered and stumbled. The Wolves ran forward and jerked them away from the archways before they could fall out.

Lycas signaled to his three first-phase Wolverines to follow him. They sprinted to join the now-visible Wolves.

The nearest Wolf planted his foot on the back of the writhing Ilion, then wrenched the arrow from his neck. Lycas knelt and sliced the Descendant's throat. The soldier twitched once before dying.

"They're coming," whispered the Wolf.

Lycas looked through the archway out onto the bay. Three small ships bobbed toward the shore, lanterns at their bows and sterns.

"Let's move out."

The squads regrouped, and the platoon moved as one from the courtyard toward the south tower. Twelve sword-wielding Bears raced in front, followed by ten Wolverines, with a half dozen Wolves and Cougars bringing up the rear.

The tower's heavy wooden doors swung open. Dozens of Ilions streamed out, swords raised.

Open battle was upon them.

Lycas grabbed the closest Wolf. "Get first and third platoons here, now!"

Then he turned toward the oncoming Ilions, drew his longest daggers and bellowed the Wolverine war cry. The call came from deep in his gut, where his rage and sorrow boiled.

His fighters joined in, even the Bears and Wolves and Cougars. The hairs on his arms and the back of his neck stood straight, and every muscle clenched.

The Descendants slowed, boots skidding on the stone floor and eyes sparking with fear. The walls themselves seemed to quake at the sound.

Lycas charged.

Two soldiers converged on him. Their swords slashed at his sides, but he felt no more pain than if they'd slapped him with wooden sticks. Before they could raise their weapons again, Lycas plunged his daggers into their guts. Hot blood streamed over his hands. He twisted his wrists as he yanked the blades from the soldiers' flesh. The men collapsed, groaning with their last full breaths.

Roaring the Wolverine cry, he led his fighters to form a bent line. They charged again, closing the line like a door, forcing the Ilions away from the right wall and the short stairway to the upper level.

The other two platoons arrived, and Lycas ordered them into position. He signaled the archers and several Bears and Wolverines to follow him up the stairs.

At the top, he opened the door. As his men streamed through, he turned to evaluate the battle in the cramped room below. Limbs and bodies littered the floor, and soldiers fought atop their comrades' writhing forms. He longed to hurl himself into the center of the melee, wade ankle-deep in Ilion blood, but he yanked his mind back to the mission.

The stairs led to a narrow hall, where more Ilions waited. With no time to deliver killing blows, he fought merely to debilitate, with kicks and parries and quick slashes. Lycas and his Bears and Wolverines pressed on, guarding the archers.

He reached the end of the hallway and launched up the stairs, leaving behind another contingent of fighters to prevent the Ilions' pursuit. He brought the archers, along with the two Tiron Wolverines and two Bears.

Lycas charged through the final door, into the rainy night.

The tower was teeming with fighters locked in combat. The stone surface was slick with rain and blood. Clearly the men in Sirin's company had already arrived.

Lycas stationed the Wolves and Cougars at the edge of the wall, then grabbed the young Bear commanding the first platoon. "Have them fire on the arriving troops after they've landed on the sand, not a moment before."

The Bear nodded and turned to his task. Lycas surveyed the situation atop the tower. The heaviest fighting was taking place on the far end, opposite the entrance.

A cluster of Ilion soldiers had barricaded themselves into one corner. Two of them were using their swords to swing and hack at something at their feet. Lycas beckoned the Tiron Wolverines to follow him over.

"Hold him down!" a Descendent in the corner shouted. Lycas heard the snap of a breaking bone, and one of the attackers shrieked in pain.

As Lycas approached, six Ilions held up their swords. Though they were outnumbered two-to-one, Lycas had no doubt he and his comrades could overcome these scared little men.

When they were within twenty paces, one of the soldiers in the middle of the pack shouted with triumph and held aloft a round object with long, thick, matted hair. Blood dripped from it, mixing with the sheets of rain.

The head of Sirin.

The other soldiers laughed at Lycas. "You're next, beast!"

Lycas stared, uncomprehending, at the rugged face of his best friend. A distant corner of his mind wondered how a second-phase Wolverine could suffer such an injury. Had their Spirit weakened that much?

His mind struggled to form words within the sea of red fury.

"You take the far left one," he said quietly to one Wolverine. "And you the far right," he said to the other. He unsheathed two daggers—a long one for stabbing, and the sharpest one, for slicing. "Give me the rest."

The Ilion soldiers stepped forward, and Lycas charged.

He drove his shoulder into the first one's stomach before the man could slash with his sword. The elegant but now useless weapon clattered to the ground as they rolled together, tripping the next soldier. Lycas slashed the throats of both while they were off balance, then sprang to his feet to face the onslaught.

Six of them surrounded him, including the one who had held

Sirin's head aloft. From the corner of his eye, he saw the Tiron Wolverines holding their own with their opponents.

Lycas slashed and stabbed, and when all his daggers were embedded in soldiers, he seized the dead ones' swords and kept fighting. He kicked and punched, gouging eyes and cutting throats, crushing rib cages with an elbow or foot.

When they were all on their knees or writhing on their backs, he dispatched them, one by one. No mercy, no quarter, not after what they'd done.

He stared at the last one as the enemy's life poured out in a pool across the stones, diluted by the giant drops of rain. The man gazed back until the light faded from his eyes.

The twang of two dozen bows shattered Lycas's reverie. He almost smiled; the Ilion reinforcements arriving by sea would find the garrison less friendly than expected.

He looked across the top of the tower to see that the fighting was over, and his men had the staircase well-guarded.

As his two Tiron comrades watched, Lycas knelt beside the remains of Sirin's body. Bitter tears stung his eyes, but he would not let them fall.

"Go with Crow, my friend," he whispered, "and don't look back this time. Our people will remember you in song." He laid Sirin's dagger atop his chest, tucking its hilt inside the leather chain of his Wolverine fetish. "I'll make sure it's a drinking song."

Half-numb, he collected his weapons and his two Wolverines, then made his way toward the edge of the tower, where the archers were raining arrows upon the Ilion troops landing from the ships.

"We'll move out as soon as those ships turn back," he told the Wolverines. They already knew the plan, but it calmed his mind to review it out loud. "We'll get our wounded, steal as many Descendant weapons and horses as we can, then head for the hills before more Ilions arrive by road."

One of his Bears approached, marching a young Ilion soldier before him at sword point.

"Sir, this one surrendered. What should we do with him?"

Lycas looked down at the blood-smeared face of the soldier, who stared up at him with contempt. "Where's the garrison prison?" he asked the Bear.

"One floor down, sir. We passed the entrance on the way up."

"Let's take him there. I need to check the situation below." He turned the young Ilion toward the stairs. "In you go."

On the next floor, they entered the narrow corridor. The prisoner's hands shook as he held them above his head.

"Are you Lycas the Wolverine?" he asked.

"Maybe. Why?"

"You killed my father."

Lycas scanned the hallway ahead of them for threats. "Personally?"

"Yes. In Ilios fifteen years ago. I was three."

"Did you join the army for vengeance?"

"I joined the army for a job. I came to Velekos for vengeance."

"Then I should probably kill you out of respect." Lycas stopped at an arched doorway that had been knocked off its hinges. "This looks like the prison."

At the other end of the hall two Bears were sifting through the dead Ilions, collecting weapons. He called to them to join him.

When the Bears arrived, he shoved the young soldier through the doorway, never letting go of the uniform's red collar.

A desk sat in the anteroom outside the cells, but no guards

were posted. They'd probably left to help defend the garrison, or save their own skins.

Without speaking, he gestured for the Bears to precede him into the cell block. Swords drawn, the three men slid with their backs to the wall, through the doorway and into the main row.

He saw their stricken faces as they took in the sight. They lowered their swords slowly. The stench of blood slammed his nostrils.

The tallest Bear turned his head to look at Lycas. "No one's alive, sir. We can smell it."

Lycas entered the block. The floor between the cells ran thick with blood, flickering black in the torchlight at either end of the row of cells.

The first cell was empty, so he shoved the young Ilion soldier inside and closed the door. "Watch him," he told the Bear who had spoken.

Six cells stood open. In front of each, a man lay dead, stabbed, beaten, his throat slit.

The Bear to his left shouted. "Someone's alive!" He sheathed his sword and ran toward the other end of the corridor. Lycas followed.

A man lay facedown near the far wall, dressed neither in prison drab nor an Ilion uniform. A pool of blood spread around him. As Lycas came closer, he saw the man's left hand twitch, clutching the hilt of a short sword.

The Bear pressed his fingers to the pulse of the injured man's neck, then sighed as he sat back on his heels. "Not alive for long."

"I wonder who—"

Lycas stopped, the breath freezing in his lungs.

He knew this soldier's scent. It was more like his own than any living man.

Nilik.

* * *

Rhia watched the incoming Ilion troops fall bleeding onto the sand, their agonized faces lit by the swinging lanterns on the landing ship's bow. Her Crow instincts begged her to help them, but she and the healers had to stay hidden in the bayside cave or the Ilions would kill them—or worse, hold them hostage.

The few soldiers who broke through and managed to storm up the beach toward the garrison were cut down by Marek and several other second-phase Wolves who stood invisible at the bottom of the hill.

She moved back into the shelter of the cave, closed her eyes and prayed her husband would not suffer nightmares. He was a hunter, not a warrior, and each death caused him to die a little inside.

Someone touched her shoulder, and she yelped.

"Sorry," Damen whispered. "It's unnerving to be so close to them, heh?"

"I'll be glad when it's over and we can head back to the hills." She let out a sigh. "I'm just glad Nilik's at the camp, safe and sullen."

"He won't stop trying to avenge Lania's death."

"Maybe her murderers have already been killed in the battle."

Damen shook his head. "Our soldiers wouldn't bother fighting caged men, when there are bigger threats."

The corners of her mouth trembled. "You saw the vision as clearly as I did. You know he dies young. It'll be soon no matter what."

"But not tonight." He took her hand and threaded her arm through the crook of his elbow. "You've done all you could."

"What kind of mother would I be if I didn't try?" She leaned against him and wiped a rebellious tear from her cheek. "It feels like I swallowed a brick."

"This'll be worth all the worry," Damen whispered. "The weapons in that garrison could supply an entire regiment."

"A lot of men are dying in that garrison. After this, Ilios will squeeze Velekos so hard, you won't be able to breathe."

"Eh. It's impossible to squeeze a flea."

She huffed a semilaugh. "You pay too much attention to my brother."

"It won't be painless. I don't know if any of us will live to see the liberation, no matter how old we grow." He touched his wrinkled cheek. "Those of you who aren't already old."

"They're retreating!" someone shouted. "The Ilions are going back out to sea!"

Rhia dared to peer around the corner of the cave. It was hard to see in the darkness through the driving rain, but the lanterns on the ships seemed to be moving out into the bay.

"Thank the Spirits." She turned to one of the healers. "Light the torches. The wounded will be arriving soon."

They hurried to set up lights within the rudimentary hospital they'd constructed inside the cave. It wouldn't fit many people, so some would have to be treated in the rain.

Rhia carried a small torch outside to look for a level, sheltered spot where they could treat patients.

From a distance, her brother roared her name.

Her heart froze. Without turning, she knew what he held in his arms. Nothing else could put that pain in his voice.

"No…" She lifted her gaze to the bay's black horizon. The waves rolled in, relentless. Crow's wings smothered it all.

She turned to see Lycas dashing toward her over the sand.

About twenty paces away, he stumbled, almost falling to his knees. He lurched to regain his balance, then tumbled in the sand, the body in his arms rolling forward.

It was as she'd seen it at the moment of Nilik's birth—her son facedown in the sand, bleeding, a sword near his outstretched hand.

Crow would not be cheated.

"Nilik!" Her scream tore her throat as she dropped to her knees beside him. She grasped his shoulder and turned him on his back, her own cry echoing in her mind, mixing with the sound of Crow's wings.

Nilik's shirt was torn to rags. His hair was loose and tangled, its light brown strands streaked with blood. His face was bruised and swollen, almost unrecognizable. She touched his jaw, cheeks, eyebrows, seeing him with her hands, for her eyes blurred with a flood of tears and rainwater. This wasn't happening.

To her right, Lycas coughed and choked, struggling to rise to his hands and knees. "He came." His arms gave way, and his face hit the sand. An arrow protruded from his back.

"Somebody help my brother!" she screamed into the wind, but Damen was already at his side with a third-phase Otter healer.

A young Otter woman dashed toward Rhia and Nilik, carrying a roll of bandages.

Rhia held up her hands. "It's too late."

The girl stopped and stared, as if uncomprehending. Rhia wanted to scream at her, shove her away, make her stop looking.

She turned back to her son. As if in a trance, she opened his shirt and examined his body. The rain splattered on his chest, washing the stains to reveal three wounds—one large to the chest and two smaller ones to the abdomen. The smallest wound of all gushed the most blood.

"Nilik," she whispered, though she knew he couldn't hear her.

He opened his eyes, just to slits. "Mama."

Her chest felt like it would cave in. He hadn't called her that since the day he learned to walk.

His breath heaved and gurgled. "Mama...don't let Him take me." Blood dribbled from his mouth, and his hand flailed until it found hers. "Don't let me go."

"You'll be all right," she choked out. "He'll take good care of you. You're my son."

"No!"

Rhia's face crumpled at the sound of Marek's approaching cry. He sank to his knees at Nilik's feet and released a soul-rending howl to the sky.

Rhia touched Nilik's cheek and held his blue-gray gaze until it shifted past her. "I love you," she whispered. "Go now."

The fear faded from Nilik's eyes, then a moment later, life itself. The cries around her peaked to crescendos, but they were swamped by the sound of Crow's wings.

Every organ inside her body seemed to twist in on itself, and she doubled over, emitting a soundless shriek of grief. She closed her eyes and formed two useless fists in front of her face.

"Why?" Rhia rocked forward and back, again and again, each time coming closer to Nilik's body. Finally she pressed her forehead against his shoulder, still warm with the life that had left him.

"*Why?*" she screamed into the sand. Her fists opened beneath her, forming claws that would tear the skin from her own neck, mix her blood with that of her firstborn. "Nilik, why?"

Marek crawled up to collapse beside her. He uttered an incoherent prayer, his voice soaked in tears. She slid her hand into his and squeezed, as if she could hold him in this world.

Rhia sobbed out the words with her halting breath. "Had. To be. A hero." Tears soaked her face and stung her dry lips. "What kind of hero breaks his mother's heart?" She let go of Nilik and clutched Marek's arms instead, lest she start shaking their son and asking him if he finally understood that there were more important things than vengeance.

But to a Wolverine, even a dead one, that was a lie.

For the first time in decades, Lycas felt a cold fear that gripped his heart like a fist. He couldn't breathe.

His fingers dug into the wet sand as someone touched his back, examining the arrow wound and murmuring the phrases *punctured lung* and *we can't move him.*

Why had he been shot? Had the Ilions regained the tower? Had one of his own archers turned traitor?

He heard his sister's wails and knew that he'd been too late to save Nilik. His breath wanted to come hard and fast in grief, but the effort brought only agony.

"We'll have to move him soon," Damen said. "More Ilions will be here within the hour."

A female voice answered, ragged with age. "He won't survive the trip to the hills. He needs surgery, somewhere with good light and clean conditions."

"For Spirits' sake, you have to do *something.*" Lycas had never heard Damen so angry.

"I can sedate him. He'll do less damage to himself that way."

Lycas tried to protest, but the silver light of a painkilling spell surrounded him. His eyes drifted shut.

In the gray haze of semiconsciousness, he felt a presence, one of long claws, sharp teeth and unforgiving temper.

Wolverine.

"Am I dying?" he asked his Spirit.

"Yes." Wolverine moved closer, a hulking, dark shape in the mist. "And no. Death is the path the arrow put you on. But another force blocks the way of My brother Crow."

"I don't understand."

"Soon you will come into the fullness of your third-phase powers." He paused. "Hopefully before it's too late."

Lycas tried to comprehend the first statement. "Third phase? I'm a grandfather?"

"As of today."

Sura was pregnant. His fear spiked, for her life and Mali's life. "Where is she? Is she safe?"

"I don't keep track of people who aren't Mine." Wolverine came closer, breaking through the mist, His lithe, brown body hunched like a bear. "I'm the one who's dying."

Lycas stared at Him. "That's impossible."

"It happened before."

"The Collapse?"

"I almost died then for the same reasons I'm dying now."

Lycas felt a strange desire to protect this fierce creature, though he was sure if he tried to touch Him, he'd find himself with one fewer arm.

"The Descendants are killing the land. The rivers are dying. The wildest Spirits are losing power here, just like in the cities of Ilios."

Lycas remembered. When he'd gone to Leukos to rescue Marek and Nilik, his powers had fallen to almost nothing. He hadn't been the only one.

"What about Cougar? Wolf?"

"Also in decline, though not as quickly as I. That arrow in your back was an accident. It wouldn't have happened if Cougar were at full strength."

So Lycas had been shot by one of his own fighters, but not a traitor.

"How can we save you?" he asked the Spirit.

"Drive out these invaders."

"I'm trying," he said through gritted teeth. "I've piled Ilion corpses at Your feet, by the thousands."

"So you have. It's the other reason why I'm dying."

A tearing sensation traveled down Lycas's chest, as if a giant dagger or claw were coming out of the earth, opening him up. Shrieks of agony tore his mind, but no sound came from his throat.

"Bear My mark," Wolverine rumbled. "May it remind you of My new wish."

The pain crested over him in wave after wave. "Anything," he gasped.

"Have mercy on your enemy. Your tactics are effective, but taken to an extreme, they beget misery and retribution. One day your brutality will bring disaster to your people."

Lycas bristled at the reprimand. "Everything I do is for You, and all the Spirits."

The claw dug deeper, and he spasmed in pain.

"Liar," Wolverine hissed. "You kill for yourself, and for your brother. But Nilo's death has been avenged a hundredfold."

Lycas fought to clear his mind, roiling in anguish that was far more than physical. He had no choice but to surrender to his Spirit's wish.

"You have given me life and strength," he said. "I give You my obedience."

Wolverine seemed to find it sufficient. "You will find your greatest strength when you face your greatest weakness."

Lycas had no idea what that meant, but he nodded. Anything to stop the pain.

"Now." The invisible claw traveled up Lycas's abdomen and chest, this time tracing and healing the gash. "Find something to live for besides death."

Lycas drew in a sharp breath that in his head sounded as loud as the waves. His body gave a sudden jerk.

Power surged through him, greater than before. The third phase.

He opened his eyes to see that he'd been turned on his side, and that the rain had stopped. The clouds drew away from the horizon's stars. The waves of the bay shuffled against the sand.

"Uh-oh." A young female voice called out. "He's waking up already."

"Impossible." The old woman he'd heard earlier approached. "I sedated him enough to last a…"

Her voice faded as Lycas pushed himself to his hands and knees. Though he could still feel the arrow in his back, the pain was gone. He could breathe.

"Pull out the arrow," he said.

"Absolutely not," the old Otter said. "Your lung will collapse and you could bleed out internally."

"I promise that won't happen." His guts felt as hard as iron. "Take it out while you still can."

"I won't. Now lie down right now before you go into shock."

"Lycas?" said a hoarse voice.

He raised his head to see Rhia staring at him. She knelt next to Marek beside Nilik's body. Her face was soaked in what must have been tears, now that the rain had stopped.

Lycas heaved himself to his feet, prompting a gasp from the Otter and a squeak from her young assistant. He staggered over to his sister, who gaped up at him.

"What happened to you?" she said.

He looked down at his torn shirt to see the mark of Wolverine traveling from his throat to his navel, one long, jagged claw mark.

"I'm third phase." He stared at Nilik's broken, battered body. "Not soon enough. Maybe if I'd run faster—"

"He couldn't be saved." Her voice broke. "Why was he here?"

"He must have escaped his guards at the camp and come to the garrison to avenge Lania's death. Tonight was his only chance, and he knew it."

"Did he kill her murderers?" Marek asked in a hard voice.

Lycas nodded. "All six. Let them out of their cells one by one, as far as I could see, even gave each of them a sword."

"Message for Lycas!" shouted a man behind him.

The crowd cleared a path for a young Bear, who ran up to Lycas and stood panting before him.

"Sir. The Eagle says—" The messenger stopped and gaped at the arrow coming out of Lycas's back.

"I almost forgot." Lycas turned around. "Pull it out."

"Sir? I don't know if—"

"That's an order."

The Bear grasped the arrow in trembling hands. "Are you sure?"

"Hurry!"

The young man yanked hard, but the arrow wouldn't give. He

tried again and again. Lycas's flesh had closed upon the arrow, forming steel-hard scar tissue.

Lycas cursed. "Just break it off."

The Bear snapped the arrow, then handed the rest of it to Lycas. He frowned at it—at least a two-inch portion, including the sharp head, was now a part of his body.

He tossed it onto the sand. "What's the message?"

"First of all, the Ilion general has been injured but not killed."

"Good. Bring him with us."

"Yes, sir. Also, the Eagle sees the Ilion troops landing south along the coast. They could be here in as little as an hour. What are your orders?"

"We retreat to the hills like we planned," he told the young man, "with all of us gone in half an hour. Get as many weapons as we can carry. Use the Ilions' supplies and horses to transport the wounded." He looked at Rhia and forced out the last order. "Leave the dead."

A fresh flood of tears slid from her eyes, and she turned away.

"Yes, sir." The Bear ran for the garrison.

Lycas looked at his sister. As Marek cut several locks of Nilik's hair, Rhia knelt at the boy's feet, unlacing his boots.

"They're almost new." She wiped her sleeve across her face. "Someone else can use them."

Damen approached Lycas. "I'll make sure he and the others get a proper burial."

"You're staying?"

"Rhia can't, she's an escaped prisoner." He pointed down the bay to the lights of Velekos. "I'll head halfway to the village, then turn around and come back, pretend I've just arrived, that I'm here to perform my duties to the dead."

Lycas gave him a narrow look. "They'll suspect you. You'll be arrested—soon, if not tonight."

"I can't leave." Damen looked at the bodies strewn on the beach. "I stay for the dead. I stay for Velekos."

Lycas watched him turn and head for the village. Damen had taken only a few steps before he stopped and sat beside a nearby soldier, one who was clearly nearing his last breath.

Lycas knelt beside his sister. "I'm sorry," he whispered.

"You tried." Rhia tied the laces of Nilik's boots together. "Some things must happen." The bitterness in her voice chilled his blood. "Only Crow knows why." She dropped the boots and covered her face. "I'll never understand."

He slipped his arm around her shoulder. She leaned into him and sobbed, her body quaking.

Lycas stared at Nilik and for the first time, did not think of his own twin brother. Instead he imagined Sura lying dead at his feet, her life stolen by a Descendant sword.

Wolverine's edict faded in Lycas's mind, as his rage burned on.

25

Tiros

"Dinner's ready." Sura stuck her head inside the tent to see Etarek sitting in the dark, hands over his ears. "It's almost midnight. We should eat and get some sleep."

He shook his head. She crawled inside and gently pried his hands from his ears.

"What's wrong?"

"The voices—everywhere." His hands shook in her grip. "Feels like they're trying to get inside my head." He pulled away and rubbed his scalp.

She sat beside him. "You're not used to being surrounded by so many strangers. But if you come out, you can meet our neighbors and see they're not so bad. The couple next door used to be friends of my mother before they escaped Asermos."

"It's not that I don't know them." He seemed to be trying to steady his breath. "It's that they're there."

"You feel their moods when they talk?"

"They're not as content as they pretend to be. Those so-called friends of your mother's, they're glad she's in prison."

Sura's curiosity overcame the momentary hurt. "How do you know?"

"It's in their voices." Etarek turned to her suddenly. "Do you feel different?"

"Different than what?"

He rubbed his eyebrows. "Different than you did yesterday."

"I'm in a new village. Of course I feel different." *I wish I'd never come here.*

He squinted and cocked his head. "What did you just say?"

"I said, 'I'm in a new village. Of course I feel different.'" She wondered if he were going deaf or just not paying attention.

"I'm not deaf, and I always pay attention to you."

She gaped at him. He stared back.

She pointed at her head, which was starting to swim. "Did I just— Did you—"

"I heard your thoughts, not just your feelings." Slowly he turned and took her shoulders. "I'm in my second phase. You're pregnant."

Her jaw dropped. "You're joking." Sura's thoughts formed a wordless storm of panic.

"You can't tell?"

She closed her eyes and furrowed her brow. "No." Was something wrong with her? Was someone else having his child?

"We've been in the wilderness. Where would I have found someone else?"

Her eyes popped open. "You hear *exactly* what I'm thinking? In words?"

Etarek winced and nodded. "But only when you speak. It's like an echo to the words I hear out loud." He put a hand to his head. "That's a Deer's second-phase power, but I'm supposed to be able to control it. I can't. I hear everything."

She clamped her lips together.

"Don't worry," he added, "if you say exactly what you think, I won't hear anything. At least that's what the Deer woman here in Tiros said would happen."

Her gaze darted around the tent, then alighted on the door. She moved out of his grasp to leave.

"Wait," he said.

She turned back to him.

He opened his arms. "We're going to have a baby."

She attempted a shaky smile, then moved forward and hugged him. Her pulse pounded in her temple as her head rested on his shoulder. Then she pulled back, pointed her thumb at the door and made eating motions, afraid to speak.

Sura found Dravek and Kara sitting on opposite sides of the campfire, sharing a silent dinner. She grabbed two plates and began to fill them with food, wondering how to broach the topic.

"Dravek," she said in a low voice so Etarek wouldn't hear. "When you turned second phase, did you feel different?"

"My senses of smell and touch sharpened, but not all of a sudden. I didn't notice my new skill until I accidentally used it." He gave Kara a guilty glance. She glared at him with contempt. He turned back to Sura. "Why do you ask?"

She stood up straight. "Why do you think I ask?"

His plate slid off his lap to the ground. "You're pregnant?"

"How wonderful," Kara said without expression. She scowled at the meat in her hand. "This chicken is greasy."

"It's supposed to be that way," Sura told her. "They don't fly, so they have more fat than wild birds."

"They sit around their whole lives waiting to be eaten?"

"At least most chickens get to grow up. They don't have to search for food, they don't have to watch out for predators."

"Sounds like the life of a plant."

"Excuse me," Dravek said. "Are you really talking about chickens when you just told us you're pregnant?"

Sura turned to him. "Etarek hears all our thoughts when we speak. He can't block them."

Horror crept over his face, and he shut his mouth.

"His Spirit is punishing him." Kara glared at Sura. "You weren't meant to have this baby."

She stepped back and touched her belly, already feeling protective. "It's too late now."

"Poor Etarek." Kara shook her head. "I probably knew this would happen."

"We all knew," Sura snapped. "We accepted the consequences." Which had seemed much less frightening in the abstract.

"You should get back to your mate," Kara said, her voice flat with sarcasm. "Celebrate."

Without another glance at Dravek, Sura returned to the tent. Etarek was sitting with elbows on his knees, hands over his ears again.

He looked up when she entered. "You'll all avoid me now."

She shook her head but said nothing.

"Well, I wanted silence, and now I've got it." He took the plate. "What's this?"

She focused her thoughts on the food. "Chicken." She realized how abrupt that sounded. "It's a domestic bird. Mostly they're used for eggs, but when they get old and unproductive—"

"I've heard of chicken," he said gently. "I just didn't recognize it." He took a bite, chewed slowly, then swallowed. "Tastes like pigeon."

They ate in silence. Sura noticed that with every bite, the meal tasted stronger, its scents richer, just like Dravek had said would happen.

She tried to get beyond her trepidation over their new powers and focus on the baby itself—herself, himself, whatever. It seemed impossible that this time next year she'd be lugging around an infant. What if she stole its memory? Would it have to learn to love her all over again?

She thought of her parents. Though Lycas and Mali weren't Spirit-siblings, their Aspects could be considered counterparts. They were each called by a Spirit who aligned itself with only one sex; Wolverine called male warriors, while Wasp called the female ones. Lycas and Mali shared the same realm, which should have prevented them from falling in love.

But it hadn't, and they'd been miserable.

She put her plate down suddenly, her throat too tight to swallow.

"What's wrong?" Etarek said.

She tried a breath, but it jerked in a sob. He put his arm around her shoulders, and her face twisted, her eyes and nose filling with water.

"I don't know—" she hiccupped "—if my mother will ever see her grandchild. And my father—"

"They will." Etarek pulled her closer. "They're practically invincible now. So's my father, as a Bear. You did that for them."

"The Descendants could starve her to death, or give him a disease. They can drown."

"Don't think of it." He kissed her temple. "Think of this. My mother's third-phase now. She can speak directly to Galen here in Tiros. In the morning we'll go see him, have him reach for her, if she hasn't called to him already." He handed her a plate of food. "Tonight, just eat, then sleep."

She stared down at the plate of pale meat and summer squash. "What is this?"

"You just told me it was chicken."

She scrunched up her face with the effort to remember. Something wasn't right.

"A lot of the houses here have chickens," he said. "Your cousin's place had a nice garden. Too bad they're in Velekos or we could've stayed there."

She thought about her day, trying to fill in the missing blank spot. She and Dravek had met Vara, then the four of them had visited Rhia's house and found it empty. Then tonight she and Etarek had realized they were having a baby.

Then what? How did she get this plate of food?

She set it aside untouched. Etarek finished his portion, then ate what was on her plate when she offered it to him, wordlessly.

"You must be tired," he said. "I'll clean up."

She nodded. When he was gone, she slipped under the blanket, which smelled strongly of their mingled scents. It provoked an unbidden desire deep within her, for the one thing that would obliterate her confusion.

Etarek came back momentarily. "Kara and Dravek said they'd clean up, on account of our good news."

She gave him a tentative smile, which he misread as politeness.

"Good night, then." He lay beside her and turned onto his side, facing away.

She touched his back, trailing her fingers along his spine. He let out a deep exhale, then turned to face her.

"You still want me?" His whisper filled with awe.

She answered him with a kiss, so deep it made him groan.

"I never dared hope." He drew her body close against him. "I want to be with you, Sura. I know everything's backward, but maybe we can make it work."

The conviction in his voice gave her hope. Maybe they could find their way to love one day, despite their odd beginning. Maybe one day it would give their child the security it needed, and their Spirits would no longer punish them. Maybe this was what Snake had meant when She said Sura's passion could save them all.

"You don't have to speak." He tore off his shirt and placed her hand on his chest. "Just touch me. Make the voices go away."

Sura pushed away her doubts and immersed herself in their passion, its patterns grown precious and familiar over the weeks. She'd thought it would feel empty and pointless after she became pregnant, for they weren't in love. But she loved what he did to her body, and loved pleasing him back, to see the bliss on his face and hear his cries.

In the onrush of pleasure, she struggled to keep her own voice silent so that Etarek wouldn't hear her thoughts. His rhythm never wavered, and soon she was climbing a peak as surely as the wind crested the mountains around them.

Unable to hold back completely, she gave a low moan as she climaxed, ending in one word, "Etarek…"

He stopped. She opened her eyes to see him staring down at her.

"What's wrong?" she whispered, even as the ice in her veins told her it was over.

"You said his name."

"I said your name."

"Not in your mind." He clutched her hair, and fear flashed through her. "Inside you said—"

"No…" She reached for him. "Let me explain."

He pulled away from her. "I knew there was someone else there when we made love." He put his head in his hands. "I thought it was your mate. I thought you were mourning a dead man. Instead you were thinking of your Spirit-brother."

She turned her burning face away. "I never meant to hurt you."

"*Hurt?*" His harsh whisper shook. "You were with me out of duty. Why should I expect you to want me for myself? You had to think of *him* to make it bearable."

"That's not true." She scrambled for an argument, though she knew each word condemned her. "Haven't you ever thought of one person when you were with another? A flash of comparison, or remembering what pleased them?"

"Stop it." He covered his ears. "Your mind tells me it wasn't a flash."

"What else does it say?" She pulled his arms down. "Does it say I've been with him? Does it say I've ever betrayed you?"

He lowered his gaze. "Not with your body." He tugged his wrists out of her grip.

"I'm sorry." She wanted to touch him but knew he'd shirk her off. "I can't help the way I feel."

He reached for his trousers. "Put your clothes on. I can't talk to you when you're naked. Not anymore."

She picked up her shirt with trembling hands. Tears threatened to squeeze from her eyes again, but she'd cried enough for one night.

When they were dressed, they sat in silence, listening to the crackling fire outside.

Finally Etarek spoke. "Does he feel the same way?"

She nodded.

"How do you know?"

"He told me."

Etarek paused with his head cocked, in that posture she already dreaded, hearing the echo of her thoughts. "He showed you. He touched you." His fingers clenched. "I thought he was my friend."

"He is."

"It all makes sense now, why he's been so sullen. He was jealous. And he and Kara—" Etarek suddenly looked at the door. "Kara." He leaped to his feet and opened the flap.

"Wait!" Sura grabbed his calf. "Leave them alone. Etarek—"

"Don't!" He seized her hand and took it off him. "Never speak my name again."

Etarek strode outside. Sura scrambled to her feet and followed.

Dravek and Kara were already standing when they got outside. "What's going on?" she said. "Why are you yelling?"

Etarek stalked over to Dravek. "Why did you make Kara forget she loved you?"

Dravek held his ground and said nothing, just glared down at the Deer.

"Tell me." He grabbed the front of Dravek's shirt. "Tell me, or I'll pound you into the ground."

"It was an accident," Dravek said, enunciating each word in a hiss. "And don't forget what I could do to you if you threaten me."

Etarek let go and stepped back. Without turning, he pointed back at Sura. "Say her name."

"Keep your voice down." Kara glanced around. "People will think we're a bunch of crazy Kalindons."

"Say it." Etarek's finger shook in Sura's direction. "I want to hear your thoughts when you speak the name of your Spirit-sister."

Dravek's gaze tripped past him to land on Sura. He stood straighter as they stared at each other. She took a step forward, shaking her head. Her lips pleaded his name without sound.

He came to her, brushing past Etarek. Dravek stopped in front of Sura and caressed her cheek with a warm hand. Behind him the campfire flared.

When he spoke, she didn't need a Deer's ears to hear his thoughts.

"Sura."

END OF PART ONE

PART TWO—
ONE YEAR LATER

01

Tiros

A baby cried.

Sura straightened up from the hen's nest, so suddenly she almost crushed the egg in her hand. She waited to hear if anyone would call out that they were attending to the child. She couldn't remember who was home besides herself.

Hearing nothing, she left the chicken coop and trudged toward the narrow house, a small brown terrier trotting at her heels.

The baby wailed again.

"Coming!" Sura shoved the back door, which didn't budge. She grabbed the handle and tugged it open.

"Pull, not push," she muttered to herself as she entered the house through a kitchen, then turned left to the bedroom, following the squeals.

She picked up the little girl and cooed to her as she checked her diaper. Dry. Could she be hungry? When had she last nursed?

A large sign was nailed to the wall over the crib, written in red charcoal.

Check Lists At Front Door.

Sura carried the baby into the kitchen and found several sheets of parchment on the wall near the entrance. The top one simply displayed the word *Malia.*

"That must be your name," she said. Sura herself had been named after her grandmother, so she must have named her daughter after her own mother, Mali.

On one sheet, three tick marks lay under the words *Feedings Since Sunrise.* Sura brushed aside the window's thick curtain and squinted into the piercing Tiron sunlight. Small shadows tilting left meant early afternoon. If Malia had nursed three times since sunrise, she wasn't ready to eat again. Or was she?

"Hello?" she called toward the stairs. Where was everyone?

For no reason Sura could discern, her daughter's cries quieted, then ceased. She stared down at the infinite mystery in her arms. Malia's hair was thick and red like her father's, but her deep black eyes were her mother's alone.

"Have I told you lately that you're the most beautiful girl in the world?"

The baby blinked.

"I probably have."

A knock came. She peered through the window to see Etarek, so she unbolted the locks and opened the door.

"Sorry I'm late." His smile broadened at the sight of Malia. "There's my girl." He looked past them into the house. "You alone?"

"I think so." She moved out of the doorway so Etarek could enter. He had knocked, so obviously he didn't live in this house, though his faint scent lingered in the corners, as if he had been here recently.

"Did you heat water?" he asked.

"For what?"

He brushed past her and planted his finger on one of Malia's sheets next to the door. "It's written right here."

Sura read the words. "Bath, Etarek, afternoon."

Etarek picked up the pail. "I'll go get water. Maybe you could light the stove."

"I will."

He walked out and shut the door behind him. Sura turned to the stove, but then Malia began to cry.

"Are you hungry?" Sura retreated to the other room and sat on the bed. She unbuttoned her shirt, offering Malia a chance to nurse. The baby averted her face and flapped her hand. Something felt wrong.

A stack of papers with crumpled edges lay on Sura's nightstand. The top sheet read:

Me: can't make new memories, because of Malia. Started when pregnant, got worse after birth. Write everything down. Bring this everywhere. Read it often!!!

She thumbed through the sheets until she found the one labeled *Etarek.*

Lives alone. Hears everyone's thoughts when they speak, because of Malia.

She frowned. Deer and Snake had perverted Etarek and Sura's second-phase powers, because they'd purposely conceived a child they didn't want. Sura remembered this fact because it had been arranged before she got pregnant, before she apparently started losing her memory.

She flipped through the pages to see what had changed.

Thera: can't stop hearing Galen's thoughts. Communication spotty.

So Sura and Etarek weren't the only ones to suffer for their misdeeds. She wondered about her own parents, and turned the pages to see. Her mother's page had one entry:

Mali: still in prison?

Her father's page contained several entries, on various dates.

Lycas: not dead.

Not dead.

Not dead.

Not dead.

Not dead.

The front door opened, and Etarek walked in with a pail. Its sloshing sound told her it was full of water.

He looked toward the stove and sighed. "You forgot already?"

Her stomach dropped. "Forgot what?"

"Never mind. I'll do it." He regarded her with a pained expression. "Malia doesn't nurse."

"What do you mean?"

"She's bottle-fed. You have trouble remembering to feed her, so everyone takes turns. The Turtle woman made up a formula that gives Malia everything she needs."

"Oh." Sura pulled her shirt closed, feeling foolish. "I knew that."

"No, you didn't," he said softly. "I'm sorry." He moved toward the stove, disappearing from view.

Sura wished she could forget how much she'd hurt Etarek, forget the disgust and bewilderment on his face when she'd thought of Dravek as he made love to her. But her memory was not so merciful, and since the last year had been a blur, the pain of that night remained fresh in her mind.

Sura rocked her daughter in a way that seemed to soothe the child. She couldn't remember having done it before, but she had to trust her instincts.

Etarek appeared in the bedroom doorway. "Is she ready?"

She almost asked, "For what?" but knew it would upset him, so she just smiled and nodded, though she had no idea what she was answering.

He approached her and gently eased Malia out of her arms. The baby looked tinier held in her father's hands. He brought her to his face and kissed her nose, then nuzzled her eyebrows. She gave a wet gurgle, emitting a trail of drool.

"I've got her," he said. "Take a nap."

"I think I was doing something before all this."

"There's an egg on the table. Were you in the henhouse?"

She snapped her fingers. "That's it," she said, though she had no recollection of it whatsoever.

"You need sleep more than the family needs eggs." Etarek touched her shoulder. "That's why I'm here, so you can rest."

Her eyes felt heavy and thick, so Sura didn't argue. She curled up on her side and watched Etarek tug the curtain shut, dowsing the room in darkness. She wondered if she would remember any of this later.

Sura woke to the sounds of arguing in the kitchen. She recognized Dravek's voice through the closed bedroom door.

"Jonek needs two parents," he said. "You love Kara, why not live with her?"

"She hasn't invited me," Etarek replied. "Besides, I can't live around anyone in my current state."

Sura craned her neck to see a baby sleeping in a crib a few feet away. Her own child?

"Maybe if you stop feeling sorry for yourself and show you can be a responsible father," Dravek said, "Deer will give you control of your second-phase powers."

"Show I'm a responsible father by taking care of your child?"

"I take care of yours here, while Kara and my son are living alone. It's wrong."

"Then you move in with her," Etarek replied.

"She won't have me."

"You're her husband."

"Not in her mind."

"Convenient. Frees up time for all the Tiron women chasing after you."

Sura slid out of bed and crept toward the door.

Dravek's voice came low and threatening. "I haven't touched one of them. I've been faithful to Kara."

A sudden crash made Sura jump. It sounded as if a chair had fallen over.

"I hear the truth." Etarek's voice came louder now. "You're not faithful to *Kara,* you're faithful to *Sura.*"

"What difference does it make? And stay out of my mind."

"I would if I could. It's a miserable place to be."

Sura opened the bedroom door, making it creak. Standing at opposite ends of the table, the two men blanched when they saw her.

"Sorry I woke you," Etarek said. "Is Malia still sleeping?"

She nodded, assuming that was the baby's name.

Dravek came to her side, his movements slow but not cautious. "Can I get you anything? Is there something you need to know?"

"I just woke up." She tried to smile. Though her mind was cloudy, she knew she was glad to see him. "Your hair grew."

He touched the end of his hair, which now fell in black waves to his shoulders. "It does that." Dravek pointed to the nightstand. "Check your lists and let me know if you have any questions. Meantime, can I bring you something to eat?"

She held up a finger and returned to sit on the bed. She flipped the pages until she found:

Dravek: Lives here. Son Jonek lives with Kara.

"So they had a boy," she murmured.

Her eyes widened at the sight of *Check this box if I still love him.* The charcoal mark looked as if it had been erased and re-traced many times.

Sura was dismayed to see in large letters at the bottom of Dravek's page:

DON'T TOUCH

She was about to ask him why when the front door opened. A young woman with shoulder-length brown hair breezed through.

"Hello, Jula." Dravek sent Sura a significant glance. She recognized the name from her childhood as her cousin. She found Jula's page right away:

Mockingbird. Loves apples and someone named Corek. This is her family's house. Brother died at the Battle of Velekos.

"Nilik…" Sura's gut sank as she whispered her cousin's name. How many times had she learned this terrible news?

She forced herself to get up and enter the kitchen. "Jula, it's wonderful to see you." She left off the phrase *after all these years.* "How's Corek?"

Her cousin gave her an indulgent smile. "I wish I knew. It's been weeks since a letter's come from the Sangian Hills." Jula held up a piece of parchment. "But Damen sent the latest news from Velekos. Come read it with me."

Sura sat next to her cousin with the letter on the table between them. The men looked over their shoulders. As far as she could remember, they couldn't read, but maybe they had learned in the past year. All she knew was that Dravek's proximity still made her skin sing.

Jula chuckled. "Damen says the Ilions have finished their 'dispersal,' relocating all the people from the Acrosia into other parts of Velekos."

"Why is that funny?" Etarek asked.

"He says it spreads the rebellion that much faster. The tactic has completely backfired." She rested her cheek on her fist. "Everything does eventually."

Sura tried to concentrate on Damen's letter, but she knew she would forget everything it said. Instead her mind clung to the memories it could hold, whether it wanted to or not.

She remembered the day it all changed in Asermos. She was ten years old.

Jula groaned. "The Ilions say their temple to Evius will be unveiled in time for this year's festival in Velekos."

"It's an insult to the Spirits," Dravek growled. "I'd like to tear it down with my own hands."

"Don't they already have one in Asermos?" Etarek asked. "Sura?"

She heard him speak her name, but didn't answer. In retrospect, the temple had probably been a bad place to hold a rally.

"Sura, are you listening?" Jula whispered.

"It doesn't matter," Etarek said. "She won't remember it in an hour."

"She's remembering," Dravek said softly, "but not what we tell her. When the present's too much, she thinks about the past."

Sura's mother had led a march through Asermos to protest the working conditions in the quarries. Or maybe it was to protest the erection of another Ilion temple, or the outlawing of public magic. Each week brought a new cause.

Mali had let Sura march that day, at the front of the parade. It was meant to be a peaceful demonstration, safe for children. No rioting allowed, no burning of the Ilion flag, a red sun on a yellow field. Its waving rays had always made Sura think of a bloodshot eye.

By sunset, two little girls lay dead in the streets of Asermos. The Descendants later claimed that the children had been crushed by "the mob," but Sura remembered how the military ambushed the parade with a line of sword-wielding horsemen, how they shouted about 'teaching these sorry beasts a lesson.' She remembered the hoofprints on the girls' dresses.

Two nights later, Mali left the house after putting Sura to bed. When she returned hours later, Sura crept out of bed and inched open the door to the kitchen. Her mother was kneeling naked next to a bucket of water, washing blood out of her own clothes for the first time. But not the last.

"Where's my father?" she asked Jula, interrupting the news report.

Her cousin pursed her lips. "He's in the Kirisian Mountains building a new battalion. He sends messages, but he hasn't come to Tiros since—" Her fingers twisted around the wooden pen. "Since we lost Nilik."

"I'm sorry about your brother."

Jula gave her a tight smile. "I know. You tell me every day, sometimes more than once."

Sura's face heated. She knew she should shut up, but another question nagged her. "Does my father know I'm here?"

"No. It's too dangerous to tell him in a message. If the Ilions intercepted it, they'd come after you. Most of the people in Tiros don't know who you really are."

Sura bit her lip. "Did you already tell me this?" Jula nodded. Sura pushed back her chair. "I'd better write it down."

She hurried into the bedroom, repeating the new information to herself as she crossed to her nightstand.

Malia stirred and burbled, transfixing Sura with a dark-eyed gaze.

"You're wet, aren't you? I can smell."

As she scanned the room for fresh diapers, Dravek appeared in the doorway, hands propped on the frame.

"Don't tell me," she said. "I can find them." She spotted the basket in the corner. "Got it!"

He came to stand beside the crib. "Want some help?"

"No. The things I can do, I like to do myself." She picked up the squirming Malia. "Don't I?"

"Yes, you're a very good mother."

She snorted. "How? I don't even know her."

"She knows you, and that's what matters. Did you write it down?"

Sura laid Malia on a clean towel atop the dresser. "Write what down?"

"The note about your father."

She gasped. "My father? What happened to him?"

"Nothing. Here, let me change Malia and tell you what to write."

"Thank you." Sura sat on the bed and picked up the parchment sheets along with a sharpened piece of charcoal.

As she searched for her father's sheet, she passed Dravek's. She gazed at him as he tended to her daughter. He glanced over and caught her watching him. His smile was pure affection, untinged by pity.

"Ready?" he asked her.

"In a moment." She hid her own smile as she marked a certain box on Dravek's page.

Asermon Valley

"What in the name of all the Spirits is *that* supposed to be?"

Rhia had no answer for Marek as they peered south from a wooded ridge in the Asermon hill country. "The Ilions have been working on it for weeks." She turned to Sani, the Eagle lookout who had brought them here. "What can you make out?"

Sani shaded her eyes from the morning sun. "I see a lot of buildings."

"Right." Rhia reined in her impatience, knowing the third-phase Eagle couldn't remember what it was like to see out of normal eyes. "But how many? What type?"

She scrunched up her face and counted off on her fingers. "Approximately three hundred, based on the number of rows and the number of buildings in each row. That's twice as many as the last time I was here, about two weeks ago."

"Are they all homes?" Marek asked.

"No. Some of them have signs outside, which tells me they're probably businesses. But from what I've seen, no one's living there yet other than the builders."

"So it's like a brand-new village," Rhia said. "But why here? It must be ten miles from Asermos. And for who?"

"Ilion settlers?" Marek suggested. "Maybe they don't want to live around our people. Or maybe it's a temporary camp for the vineyard workers during the harvest. It's a four-hour ride from Asermos to the farthest field. This would be roughly in the center of all of them."

Rhia frowned at the distant wooden buildings. From here they all blurred together in a brown mass. "I want to get closer." She moved toward the trail at the edge of the ridge.

"Uh-uh." Marek caught her elbow. "It's not safe. We can ask at the meeting if anyone has more information."

She halted, knowing he was right. Tonight, like many nights in the last several months, she and Marek would meet at a local farm with a small group of sympathizers—mostly people who lived on the outskirts of Asermos, though a few brave souls ventured out from the village itself. They would share intelligence, arrange for supply shipments and speak to potential recruits, each of whom had to be vouched for by three people whom Rhia trusted.

Their message was spreading, counteracting the Ilions' propaganda and assuaging the concerns of the fearful and the weary. By recruiting not just warriors, but also cooks, scribes, stretcher bearers, makers of bows and arrows or paper and ink, they gave each person a purpose—and with it, hope.

It also kept her and Marek away from Tiros, a place made bitter by memories of their son. Countless mornings this past year, she'd catch herself ready to call Nilik down for breakfast. The reality would slam her gut so hard, she'd have to sit until her legs could support her again. The food would get cold, but no one complained.

"Wait," Sani said. "Looks like they're building a high fence."

"Probably to keep people like us out," Marek said. "People like Lycas and his troops."

In the last year, Rhia's brother had expanded his military operations from the Sangian Hills—where Feras had taken command of Sirin's former battalion—to the even more rugged Kirisian Mountains north of Asermos. From there Lycas struck targets closer to their home village.

Or so she had heard. She hadn't spoken to him directly since she and Marek and Jula had returned to Tiros almost a year ago.

"Maybe you're right," Rhia told Marek, "but what if the fence isn't to keep people out, but to keep them in?"

Sani cried out behind her. Rhia turned to the Eagle, who was pinching the bridge of her nose, eyes squeezed shut.

"A vision. It has to do with that thing." Sani flapped her hand in the direction of the makeshift village, then whimpered. "It hurts when I seek them on purpose." Her face suddenly flushed, then paled, and she sank to sit on the ground, with Rhia's arm to steady her.

Finally the Eagle opened her eyes, blinking rapidly. "As usual, it makes no sense."

"What did you see?" Marek said.

"A black circle in the dust, maybe ten feet wide, lit by a white light. Not sunlight." She steadied her breath. "More like moonlight, but much brighter."

"You didn't have to seek the vision." Rhia brushed the strands of graying brown hair out of Sani's eyes. "But thank you. Maybe it'll mean something to the people at the meeting tonight. Maybe it's a map or an Ilion religious symbol."

"It was just a plain circle." Sani rubbed her arms. "I know I shouldn't add my own emotions to it, but it made me sad and angry and afraid—and hopeful, all at the same time." She looked up at them. "See? I told you it didn't make sense."

Marek helped the Eagle to her feet. "I'm sure someday it will."

Rhia stared out at the distant mystery and hoped that "someday" wouldn't be too late.

Captain Addano sat at the dinner table in silence. His wife and children also did not speak, because they knew better.

He didn't look at his meat as he ate it, but focused on the grain of the table's wood and the seams of the cloth place mats. The sinews of the roasted mutton reminded him of the flesh of his prisoners. Many years ago he'd enjoyed meat cooked rare; now Nisa either cooked it well done or found herself scraping it off the wall.

As the meal came to a close, she cleared her throat. Addano shut his eyes to avoid sending her a withering glare.

"A letter came from Ilios today," she said softly. "From your mother."

His hand tightened on his knife, and he heard his young son and daughter suck in their breaths. He laid it down beside his plate, picked it up again, then stretched forward to set it in the middle of the table, out of easy reach.

The letters never held good news.

"Give it to me," he said.

"Now?"

He bit his tongue to avoid the easy sarcastic remark. "Yes. Now."

She withdrew the folded parchment from her apron pocket and laid it next to his plate, her hands shaking. He could remember when she'd tremble at his touch out of desire instead of fear. Before they'd come to Asermos.

He broke the seal and unfolded the letter. Nisa shifted the lantern closer so he could read.

My Dearest Dimitris,

Thank you for your letter. It will probably be the last I receive, as my address has become in doubt. Your sister and her children and I are living in Salindis with their grandmother, but by the time you get this, I may have moved on.

It's happened, son. They've finally taken our farm, like all the others. The government gave it to a Leukon nobleman. He's never been here; I don't think he even knows where the Saldos region is. They say we didn't pay our taxes, but we did, I have the records. They keep raising them without telling us and blame it all on the wars. They won't even let us work on the farm because it's cheaper to have slaves bring in the crops.

I'll try to remain in the area so you can find me when you come home. They say Asermos is beautiful and bountiful. I hope it's worth all this money and all these lives. The fact that the names of your father and brother are etched on a slab of rock in Leukos is pitiful consolation.

Give a long hug to your wife and children for me. You are truly blessed to be where you are, together.

All my love, Mother

He folded the letter, then creased and recreased the page until the edge was as sharp as a razor.

"What does it say?" Nisa whispered.

Addano slid it across the table. "Read it." He shoved back his chair and stood up. "Read it out loud to the children. Let them know the latest escapades of the glorious Ilion nation." He shot a glare at each of the ten-year-old twins. "Maybe then they'll stop whining to go home." He grabbed the bottle and stalked toward the door. "I'm taking a walk."

"Dimitris."

He heard her footsteps follow him, and he turned in time to see her flinch.

She rubbed the back of her left hand. "I wish you wouldn't walk around at night drinking by yourself." She met his gaze, for just a moment. "I worry about you."

He reached out and touched her cheek, cold beneath his fingertips. "Nisa, don't you understand?" he said softly. "I walk, and I drink, every night, to keep these hands from your throat."

She shuddered, and he tucked a golden curl behind her ear, letting his fingers trail over her neck. He turned away before he could see her tears.

Addano walked the twilit streets of Asermos, unfettered and unmolested. A pair of soldiers stood on every corner, ready to enforce the civilian curfew, should need arise, which it hadn't for several weeks. Either the Asermons had been cowed by the mass arrests, or they were waiting for something to happen, something the prisoners would not reveal under any amount of persuasion.

He came to the old hospital, where he leaned against the outer fence and tilted the wine bottle to his lips. He studied the front yard, wondering on which spot his brother had fallen when they'd shot him in the back twenty years ago. Had his killer aimed and fired from the thatched roof, or from that maple, where the leaves now glowed bloodred in the torchlight? An injured and unarmed prisoner-of-war, his only crime was wanting to go home.

Because of his brother, Addano had asked to come to Asermos. The army had granted his request because he could connect with people, make them want to share their deepest secrets. Force was only necessary in desperate situations.

These days, Ilios was always desperate.

His head felt heavy, and he let it tip forward to tap the cold lip of the bottle. Below him, the toes of his boots protruded under the wooden fence. A wily detective once stalked in them; now they were filled by the stumbling feet of a common thug.

Ironic, since he'd joined the army at nineteen to escape a life of crime. He'd become an officer by working his way up through the enlisted ranks, instead of having his commission handed to him straight out of basic training like those effete young noblemen. Now they'd taken his family's land...

"Dimitris."

Out of the corner of his eyes, Addano saw his wife approach with another bottle of wine. The one in his hand was almost empty.

"You know me too well." He traded bottles with her.

"I know a little wine makes you dangerous, but a lot of wine makes you safe." She shifted to stand out of reach, her hands resting against the fence. "I figured I'd find you here."

"I come for inspiration."

"For your job."

"Yes."

"Does it work?"

He took another slug of wine. "It used to."

Until last year, he could console himself with the fact that no matter how his prisoners suffered, at least he'd never taken the life of a defenseless man. He was better than the cowards who'd killed his brother.

But Sirin had dispelled that delusion, Sirin and the dozens of other corpses Addano had created on orders from his superiors. He might as well be a priest of Xenia, the death goddess, for all the time he spent in her temple, offering payment for their souls' easy passage.

His superiors called them "extrajudicial executions." Since torturing civilians was against Ilion law, once prisoners had been abused, they couldn't go back into the court system, and they certainly couldn't be released.

"We could take a walk by the river," Nisa said, "like we did every evening when we first came here, remember?"

"I don't go to the river anymore."

He had people do that for him, take the bodies and weigh them down with stones. Always downstream from Asermos, he ordered, so that no recognizable pieces, half-eaten by fish, could wash up for the neighbors to see.

"Your mother's letter," she said, "it made me think, perhaps, we should go back to Ilios. Help her and your sister and your nephews find a new home."

"You know I can't leave my post."

She cleared her throat and took another step away from him. "When I say, 'we,' I don't mean you and I. I mean, the children and I."

His hand clenched the fence post, and he heard her take in a sharp breath.

"With your blessing, of course," she added.

"Blessing?" He turned to her. "Blessing of what? The gods? The Spirits? A blessing from me would turn to dust in my mouth." He advanced on her, and marveled that for once she didn't recoil.

"Dimitris—"

"Nisa," he pleaded in a whisper, "the occupation won't last much longer. Ilios is breaking, I can feel it."

"Shh." She cast a nervous glance over her shoulder. "You shouldn't be telling me this."

"I'm trying to make you stay, just for a while." He drew his hand up her arm, ordering his fingers not to squeeze and twist until she begged for mercy. "Soon we can all go home together."

The dismay in her eyes made her words unnecessary, and he wanted to clamp her mouth shut so she wouldn't utter them.

"I can't live with you anymore." Her lower lip trembled. "Please let us go before you kill us."

"Before?" He yanked the empty wine bottle out of her hands. "*Before?*" He lifted the bottle by the neck as though to bash out her brains. Nisa didn't cringe, just stared straight ahead, resigned.

Addano slammed the bottle against the fence. It shattered, the glass clattering on the stones of the road.

"It's too late." He flung the broken bottle neck at her feet. "I've already killed you."

He turned away from her, clutching the half-empty bottle of wine.

He'd never come back to the hospital, he vowed, never again stand by this fence and mourn what had been taken from him.

Tonight, he would go to the river.

Tiros

"Can I tell you something odd?"

Dravek marked his place on the reading lesson and looked at Sura sitting beside him at the table. Leaning her head on her hand, she blinked at him.

"Go ahead," he told her.

The lantern light cast shimmering shadows of her long, dark lashes. "The back of my neck and shoulders are tingling, like I'm wrapped in a blanket. Did you put something in the tea?"

"No." He broke into a warm smile. "You've mentioned it before when you're teaching me to read."

"What do you think it is?"

"Contentment."

"You've felt it?"

"Not since I was young."

She chortled. "Since you were young? Are you so ancient at nineteen?" Her smile faded. "You're still only nineteen, right?"

He nodded. "Like you."

"I remember being eighteen, and I know it was last year. But I don't remember my birthday."

Dravek felt a pang in his chest at the lostness on her face. "Your uncle Marek caught a pheasant and roasted it for dinner."

She brightened. "I must have loved that." She glanced at the stairs behind them. "Is he here now?"

"He's outside of Asermos with your aunt Rhia. It's just us, your daughter Malia and your cousin Jula. She's out delivering the news from Velekos." He focused on his reading lesson. "This one's confusing. When this letter is here, it sounds different than when it's at the end of the word?"

"I'll show you." She reached across to point to the text. Her skin brushed his, and he jerked his arm away. "What's wrong?"

He explained for the hundredth painful time. "We're not allowed to touch outside of training."

"Why?"

"Vara says it intensifies our powers."

"Oh. Does it?"

"Yes." A gross understatement. Having her so close but untouchable created a constant, consuming fire inside him. They could now start a deliberate blaze just by touching hands. Fortunately Vara had taught them how to channel it into a precise, controlled force, with no more accidents like his wedding's bonfire.

Sura chewed the inside of her cheek. "You've had to tell me all this before, haven't you?"

"You remember?"

"No, but it seems like something that would've come up."

"It's probably on your sheet. But yes, it comes up a lot."

"Does Jula know?"

"She knows it's Vara's orders. She knows she's the one who helps with anything that involves touching you. But she doesn't know why." He wondered how much he should confess, how much longer he could hold back the words he wanted her to remember. "The worst was when you were pregnant and your back ached so bad." He tucked his hands under his arms at the thought of stroking her long, strong muscles. "I could've rubbed the pain away, but…"

"I would've liked that," she whispered. Then she cleared her throat and pointed to the parchment. "Anyway, when this letter comes at the end of a word—"

"My marriage is over."

"Oh." Sura was silent a moment. "Is this the first time I've heard this?"

He nodded. "As of tomorrow, Kara and I will be separated a year. Under Tiron law, we can divorce." He traced unsteady lines within the corner of the parchment. "She wants to marry Etarek."

"That's good, right?"

"For them." Dravek rapped the end of the wooden pen hard against the table. "I feel like I failed. If I hadn't made her forget, we'd still be together."

"But would you be happy?"

He twisted the pen in his hands. "I'd get to live with my son."

"Stop before you break that." She took the pen from him and set it aside. "From what I remember last year, you didn't get along, and you felt trapped into marrying her."

"But at least she—" He cut himself off.

At least Kara wasn't forbidden. Marrying her had felt like the right thing to do, even more so after Sura came along. Now he could no longer use Kara to avoid his feelings for his Spirit-sister.

Dravek's feet tingled as the floor vibrated in the direction of the front door.

A knock came, then the shouted code word, "Sparrow!"

Dravek grimaced as he pushed back his chair. "It's your aunt Rhia. She's been away for two months, since right after Malia was born." He called out the coded response, then unlocked the door and opened it wide.

Rhia staggered through, dripping wet. "What a ride. We could barely see the road for all the mud. Marek's stabling the horses. They're a mess." She gave Dravek a perfunctory hug, then turned to Sura, who was standing behind the chair, gripping its back. "It's wonderful to see you." To Rhia's credit, she didn't advance on Sura with an embrace, understanding that to her niece she was a near stranger.

Sura, however, came forward and took her hands. "I remember you." She studied Rhia's face. "You've aged."

Rhia's eyes widened, then she laughed. "Oh, you mean in the last ten years. Yes, I'm afraid I have."

A whimper from the other room turned into a wail.

"Sorry," Rhia whispered. "Guess I was too loud."

"It's all right." Sura started to walk toward the bedroom. "It might be feeding time, anyway." She gave Dravek a questioning look, and he resisted the urge to answer. He made a subtle gesture with his thumb, at the schedule tacked to the wall.

"Oh!" Sura examined the parchment. "Looks like she fed an hour ago. Maybe she needs changing." She passed into the bedroom. The door swung shut behind her, as it always did when it wasn't propped open.

"How is she?" Rhia asked Dravek in a hushed voice as she set down two packs at the bottom of the stairs.

"Same as before. Malia's healthy as ever, though, so Sura's memory isn't keeping her from being a good mother."

"She has a lot of help from you."

Dravek wasn't sure how to take the comment. While Jula remained ignorant, perhaps willfully so, of his feelings for Sura, the signs had not escaped Rhia's notice—nor her judgment.

"Jula helps even more." He pointed to the array of notes on the wall.

"Thank the Spirits Sura knows how to read." Rhia wrung out her sleeves and wiped the wet hair out of her face. "At least the Descendants have given us one useful tool."

"But if not for them, Sura wouldn't have been pressured to have a baby in the first place, and she wouldn't need to read all the things she forgets." Dravek heard his voice curdle with hatred.

"The Ilions aren't hopeless," Rhia said. "They have Guardian Spirits, they're just not connected to them."

"How do you know?"

"I've spoken with the dead," she told him, "those who linger in the Gray Valley out of bitterness. Many of them hold a piece of another person's soul. It looks like an animal." Rhia grabbed a mug and the pitcher of water. "I once saw a man I knew who'd been slaughtered by a Descendant soldier. The dead man tormented a snake, twisting it, dangling it by the tail, stepping on its head. The soldier who murdered him must have been a Snake."

Dravek turned away, troubled at her confession and at the fact that she used a Snake as an example of a Descendant Spirit.

She cleared her throat. "There's a meeting in an hour at Galen's. Marek's joining me there. You should come."

He knew that the source of her invitation wasn't only generosity, but also the desire to keep him away from Sura. He looked at the bedroom door just as it opened.

Sura stopped short when she saw Rhia. "Hello."

Dravek's heart sank at the sight of her surprise. "It's your aunt Rhia."

Sura blinked hard, then scanned the room. When her gaze rested on the travel packs next to the stairs, she said, "Did you just arrive?"

"Yes." Rhia set down her mug. "Dravek and I are going out for a few hours, but we'll leave you instructions. I saw your cousin Jula just down the street—she'll be home soon if you need anything."

Sura's eyes grew distant and thoughtful. Dravek remained silent, aware she was reviewing what she knew about her cousin and aunt from long ago. She saw the notes pinned around the door and went to read them. He stepped aside, but she reached out and touched his arm, as if to steady herself.

Dravek knew he should pull away, but he was the only thing in the room she recognized. After a few moments, he slid his hand over hers, then gently removed it from his arm.

She stared up at him. "Your hair's long."

"Do you like it?"

She shrugged. "It looked better short."

"Then I'll cut it."

"No. It reminds me it's not now anymore. Or rather, it's not the same 'now' my mind lives inside."

From the corner of his eye, Dravek saw Rhia watching them,

with the same disapproval the rest of the world would lay upon them. He dared to hope that somehow, someday, he and Sura could be together.

Without that hope, he'd have one fewer reason to live.

Sura sang Malia to sleep, reciting a song from her childhood as she circled the kitchen table. She thought it funny that she knew all six verses from fifteen years ago, but apparently couldn't remember her daughter's name from day to day.

A knock sounded at the door. Malia cried, lurching back from the precipice of sleep. Sura wanted to echo her wails. If she didn't rest soon herself, her face would become well acquainted with the floorboards.

She shuffled to the door. Tacked to it was a large sign bearing what seemed to be a password.

"Sparrow!"

The deep male voice made her jump.

Sura tucked Malia into the crook of her left arm, quickly undid the two locks, then cracked open the door.

She looked up, up into the shrouded face of an enormous man. Rain dripped in rivers off his hood, creating a glistening waterfall over his eyes, which were nearly invisible.

"Let me in," he said.

"Do I know you?"

"I know the password." He pressed his palm against the door. "You have to let me in."

He brushed past her, slammed the door behind him, then hurried to lock it. He took a quick look into the bedroom, then paused to listen at the bottom of the stairs. Satisfied, he nodded and headed for the bread basket on the table.

Malia quieted in her arms, as if sharing Sura's speechless surprise.

"Where's Rhia and Marek?" he asked her.

"They're not here."

"Jula?"

"Not here."

He stuffed a huge piece of loaf into his mouth, then glanced around the kitchen. "Ale?"

She pointed to one of the cabinets. He withdrew the large tankard and started to lift it to his lips.

"Mugs are on the counter."

He lowered the tankard. "Forgot my manners." He poured himself a mug. "So where is she?"

"Rhia or Jula?"

"Either. Both."

She checked the notes on the table while he downed the entire mug in one long swallow. "Rhia and Marek are at Galen's." Galen—another name she recognized from her childhood.

"Good. I was on my way there, anyway."

Sura found another scrap of paper. "And Jula's delivering the news." Shoulders aching, she adjusted her grip on Malia. "Who are you?"

He set down the mug and pulled back his hood. "I'm Lycas."

Sura's jaw dropped. She was face-to-face with her father for the first time in nineteen years. Nothing about him was familiar—not the piercing black eyes or the thick black hair that curved around his neck in a long ponytail. Certainly not the scruffy beard, which held several visible strands of gray.

A crooked smile scrawled across his face. "See, I'm just a human after all, despite what the Descendants say." He poured another mug of ale. "So what's your name?"

She couldn't speak, couldn't even remember where her tongue was.

"On second thought," he said, "don't tell me. If I'm ever captured alive, they'll want to know who helped me in Tiros. I can't give them your name if I don't know it." He downed the ale, then slammed the mug on the counter and let out a loud belch. "Pardon me." He wiped his mouth with a filthy sleeve. "I'll go find Rhia now."

He flipped up his hood, pocketed another piece of bread, and tramped toward the door. When his hand touched the knob, he stopped. She struggled to find her voice, to speak the name she'd never called anyone.

Lycas examined her face, then lowered his dark gaze to Malia, who had finally fallen asleep.

"Cute baby," he said. "A lot quieter than mine was at that age." He swung open the door and disappeared into the rain.

"Wait," she whispered, but he had already slipped into the darkness. "Father…"

Sura walked into the bedroom as smoothly as her aching feet and swimming head would allow. She placed Malia in her crib. The child stretched, but continued to sleep.

Sura stared at her daughter, already wondering if it had really happened. All her life she'd wished Lycas would walk through the door. Now that he had, he didn't know her. Why should he? He'd spent his life doing more important things than learning the contours of her face.

She touched it now, cupping her palm around her jaw, wondering if it were as strong as her father's. Everyone used to say her cheekbones were her mother's, but what about her nose? She ran her finger over the bridge as she made her way back to the kitchen. No, it curved up instead of down.

As she was crossing her eyes to study it, she noticed that his boots had left muddy prints all over the floor. She retrieved the broom from the corner and started to sweep. The boards were damp from the rain, and her efforts only smeared the dirt. Still she swept, turning the images into ragged lines.

Sura left one print intact, a left foot, the one next to the stove, where he had drunk the ale. She stood toe-to-toe with the print, her own right foot dwarfed by the huge outline.

She put the broom away. If she forgot this incident later, the footprint would remind her. Just in case, she hurried back to the bedroom and scribbled a note on Lycas's page.

He's here.

04

Tiros

"The Spirits are weakening," Rhia told the small group assembled around Galen's table, "at least according to my contacts. The Asermons are struggling to reach Them, especially the wilder Spirits. It's exactly as Wolverine told Lycas when he progressed to the third phase." She kept her voice steadier than she felt inside. "If we don't liberate these lands soon, we'll lose our one advantage—our magic."

"And then what?" Dravek looked at Rhia, then at Vara sitting next to him. "We won't surrender, will we?"

Marek scoffed. "Never. As long as we breathe, we fight."

"Exactly." Krios the Bear raised his mug to Marek, then looked at Rhia. "Your brother would say the same. Even without magic, we'd still push them out. Ilions can't win our kind of war, and we won't fight their kind of war."

"As long as we have the support of the people," Marek said, "it's just a matter of time."

Galen sighed. "But without magic, without the Spirits, why would the people support a revolution? There's been no peace in Asermos for eleven years. They're weary of war."

"All the more reason we need to end it." Rhia pushed her chair back, then stood and paced in Galen's kitchen. "I think we're getting close. With Lycas and Feras controlling most of the territory outside the two occupied villages, they're almost ready to move into the final phase." She swallowed her ever-present dread. "But these last two months, I can't even confirm Lycas is alive."

"He must be," Vara said. "If he'd been captured or killed, the Ilions would have told the world."

"They didn't tell anyone when they captured Sirin," Rhia pointed out. "If they want to avoid making a martyr out of Lycas, they'd put him in a cell and let him die of thirst. Or poison him or—" She stopped and rubbed her temples. No sense darkening the conversation further.

"Wait a moment." Galen lifted his hand.

Rhia held her breath at the sight of his faraway look. He was no doubt receiving a message from Thera, the third-phase Kalindon Hawk whose powers fluctuated nearly as much as her son Etarek's. Sometimes her communications were clear, but usually Galen deciphered her meaning from disjointed words and feelings.

Several seconds went by, then a faint smile curved the deep lines of Galen's face. "It's Berilla," he whispered. "My old apprentice in Asermos. She must have entered the third phase." He covered his ears and stared at the intricate pattern on the woven cloth at the table's center, the one he used to clear and focus his mind.

Galen's eyes popped wide. He moved his lips, but no sound came out, as he spoke to Berilla over many miles. Breath quickening, he listened intently, gray-streaked brows pinching together.

Rhia's own face hurt from clenching its muscles. She sat next to Marek and massaged her forehead to ease the tension. Staring at Galen wouldn't make the message come through any faster.

"No!"

Rhia jumped at the sound of Galen's voice. His eyes were squeezed shut, and his hands clutched the edge of the table.

"Wait—Berilla!" He drew in a deep, sharp breath. His eyes opened slowly.

"What happened?" Rhia whispered.

Galen drew his hands down over his paling face. "Orders came from Ilios today. The Descendants plan a full-scale invasion of Tiros and Kalindos."

Dravek sprang to his feet. "What?"

"Why?" Krios said. "We have nothing they want."

"We're aiding the guerrillas and the resistance in Asermos and Velekos." Galen's hands shook as they filled his cup with water. "And the Ilions are tired of fighting battles they can't win. They think they can win here."

"Of course they can," Krios said, "if they bring a whole battalion. Invading a village with a population that can't run away—that's their kind of war."

"When will this happen?" Rhia asked.

"I don't know," Galen whispered.

"Can you ask Berilla?"

"No." His hands sank to the table, rattling the cup. "We were cut off. She may be unconscious." He closed his eyes. "I fear she's dead."

Lycas caught up with Corek at the Tiron stable, where he was still haggling a boarding price with the stablemaster. Together they hurried through the driving rain to the home of Galen the Hawk.

Lycas rapped three times on the door and shouted, "Sparrow!"

Excited voices rose inside. The door opened, and Rhia dragged him across the threshold.

"You're alive!"

He eased out of her embrace. "I wish you wouldn't sound so surprised."

"And Corek!" Rhia hugged the soaking young man hard enough to wring a puddle of water out of his cloak. "What are you doing here?"

"Lycas said I should see Galen." Corek pulled back his hood. "For help with my Bestowing."

A gasp filled the room, as Lycas had predicted. Corek was the last remaining Crow progeny without a Spirit, his generation's last chance to fulfill the twenty-year-old Raven prophecy.

"We're pleased to hear that," Galen said finally. The old Hawk got up from his chair, his posture more hunched and rigid than Lycas remembered. They bowed to each other, then Lycas greeted Krios the Bear and Vara the Snake.

A young man sitting next to Vara stared at him with unabashed awe, then came forward, tripping on the table leg in his haste.

"You saved my life," he said to Lycas.

"This is Dravek," Rhia said. "He was one of the infants in the convoy we rescued all those years ago in Ilios."

"Ah, yes. You've changed a bit since then." He turned to Vara. "Just the woman I wanted to see."

Rhia pulled out two chairs. "Lycas, we have news. The Ilions are launching a full-scale invasion of Tiros and Kalindos."

He stared at his sister, who had just uttered his worst fear. "That's impossible. How do you know?"

"Berilla, Galen's old apprentice, just became third phase."

"When will they strike?"

"We don't know," Galen said. "Berilla was cut off. She may even be dead."

Lycas's fingers curled into fists. "They're killing third-phase people now?"

"Possibly." Galen sighed. "Neither village can hold off a regiment or even a battalion. What are we going to do?"

"We can't defend both villages. Send a message to Thera. Tell her to evacuate Kalindos, have them come here." Lycas took off his wet coat and tossed it over the back of a chair. "As for Tiros, I need a map." He slapped the table as he sat. "And some ale."

Both were placed in front of him. Dravek leaned over his shoulder to study the map. Lycas gave him a dark look, and he backed off.

"Asermos is a three-day march from here," Lycas murmured, "but we'd know if troops were being mobilized." Ilions had no flair for skulking. "It'll be at least a week before they move out."

"What are they waiting for?" Marek asked.

"Reinforcements from Ilios, or redeployed soldiers from

Velekos." He looked at his brother-in-law. "A big army is a slow army. Why do you think I keep my troops split into small units?"

Rhia leaned on the table across from him, studying the map upside down. "If we can't defend Tiros from that many soldiers, can we keep them from getting here in the first place?"

"I like the way you think, little sister." He pointed on the map to the bridge over the Tiron River. "This is the only passage for a hundred miles in either direction. The banks of that gorge are too steep for horses to cross."

"So we take out the bridge?" Krios said.

Lycas nodded. "I've been considering it for a while, as a last resort. It not only keeps more troops from moving in, it cuts off the northwest garrison from the rest of the army." He tapped his finger against a square symbol west of the Tiron River. "Which means Feras can take it as soon as the bridge is out. He's got enough men now to hold it."

"But without that bridge," Dravek said, "Tiros will be isolated, too. No one will be able to get from here to Asermos and back."

"It'll be harder, but not impossible. Our people can cross upstream in the mountains or downstream in the hills where the banks are lower." Lycas drew his finger down the rough surface of the map. "We control those areas."

Dravek gave him an admiring smile. "Sounds like you have it all figured out."

Lycas chuckled. "Yes, until about two hours from now when a new disaster changes everything." He studied the map and felt a surge of excitement at the thought of turning this last Ilion gasp of aggression to his own advantage. "A garrison would be a real base of operations. It would change everything."

It would also give his men a safe place to keep Ilion prisoners, showing mercy as Wolverine had dictated. Over the last year, Lycas had tried to mind his Spirit's edict. In the Sangian Hills and Kirisian Mountains, he'd ordered his men to avoid battle when possible, if it didn't mean giving up territory.

But when the battles came, his first duty was to protect his own people. Giving quarter to even one Descendant soldier would put the whole camp at risk, and cause more deaths in the end. So they slaughtered all who dared to fight them.

He consoled himself with the fact that the Ilions would rather die in battle than be prisoners of "beasts."

He noticed the carved wooden snake fetish dangling from Dravek's neck. "I'll need your and Vara's fire talents for a different mission."

The young man's eyes sparked. "Speaking of fire, have you seen Sura yet?"

Lycas tilted his head. "My daughter, Sura?" He looked at Rhia. "Isn't she in Kalindos?"

"She's at my house," Rhia replied.

His stomach went cold. "Sura—is at your house?"

She nodded. "And your granddaughter, too."

His mouth twitched with a sudden panic. "Why didn't you tell me? You could've sent a message."

"And have it intercepted? The Descendants would come for her in a moment. I didn't want her to end up like her mother."

From the corner of his eyes, Lycas saw Dravek squirm and cross his arms.

Rhia squeezed Lycas's forearm and smiled. "We'll go home so you can finally meet her."

He put his face in his hands, feeling like an idiot. "I already did."

* * *

Sura sat at the kitchen table, rereading the note she'd left for herself.

Lycas was here. Now at Galen's house with Rhia. Dark hair, deep voice, big. Scary. Rather rude.

She wondered if she'd written the note earlier tonight. She'd found it here after putting Malia to bed.

What if he left town without coming back? She couldn't remember his face. What if she never saw it again?

A knock came at the door, and she scrambled to open it. Too late, she saw the sign telling her to wait for the code word.

She recognized Dravek and Vara, and the small woman in front of them looked like an older version of the Rhia she remembered from her childhood.

The large man must be—

"Sura…" he said. "I'm—" He let out a gust of air. "Forgive me. You must think I'm a complete bastard."

She met his gaze and lifted her chin. "Technically you are a bastard. As am I."

In the corner of her eye she saw Dravek's jaw drop. Lycas, however, merely smiled.

"Do you remember me coming here earlier?" he asked her.

She shoved her note at him, then gripped the edge of the door to hide her shaking hands.

He read it and laughed. "Scary, heh? Good to know." He glanced at the sky. "It's raining."

She backed up and pushed the door wide. He let the others precede him, then crossed the threshold, still swaggering a little, despite his words of contrition.

"Lycas, this is your daughter, Sura," Rhia said pointedly.

"Yes, thank you," he replied through gritted teeth. He shoved a mass of wet black hair out of his face and looked at Sura. "I'm afraid I made a bad impression before."

"Apparently so."

"You deserve better."

He lifted his arms halfway, then dropped them to his sides. She hugged her elbows and rounded her shoulders to signal she did not want to be embraced.

The room fell silent. Everyone seemed to be fascinated with a different corner of the house.

Sura shifted her feet. "I guess you want to meet Malia," she said to Lycas.

"Who?"

She stared at him. "My daughter."

"Oh." He rubbed his face. "Sorry. I didn't know her name." He glared at his sister.

"You never asked." Rhia yanked off her rain cloak and hung it on a peg. "Try not to scare her, too."

Sura picked up the lantern, opened the bedroom door and tiptoed to the crib. Her father appeared suddenly beside her, and she wondered if he always walked with such stealth.

Malia was sleeping with her head turned to the side and one arm stretched in the same direction, as if she had fallen asleep in the middle of reaching for an elusive object.

"Don't wake her for me," Lycas said softly. "I know how fragile sleep can be at that age."

Sura's hand tightened on the top rung of the crib. "How do you know that? Do you have another child somewhere?"

"No, I—"

"Are you sure?"

"As sure as I can be, and you're right, I don't know how babies are at that age." He held out his palm, cupped. "When I left you, I could hold you in one hand."

"I was two weeks old." Her whisper faded. "Two weeks."

"I know. I'm sorry." His hand moved toward hers along the crib rail, then slid back. "I take it she gets that red hair from her father. Is he a good man?"

"From what I remember." Guilt twinged her chest again, for the pain she'd caused her former mate. "He's a Deer."

"He must be a good father, then. He'd always hear the reason why a baby was crying. I could never figure that out."

Sura wondered if she'd cried more before or after he walked out of her life.

"Look," he said, "I know what you and Etarek did, having this baby to help our people. And of course, I can never repay you for saving my life."

"Saving your life?"

"I would've died at Velekos if I hadn't entered the third phase."

"Oh." Her head seemed to spin. She would definitely have to write *that* down. "How are your powers?"

"Fine. Nothing strange, like Thera. Probably because I knew nothing of your plan to have this child."

"That's fair. It wasn't your fault."

He tapped his fingertips on the crib rail. "I changed my mind. I'd like to hold her, even if it wakes her up."

Sura swallowed the lump in her throat. "Go ahead."

Lycas put his hands halfway into the crib, then withdrew them, put them back in, then drew them out again. "Maybe you'd better—"

"I'll get her." She set the lantern on the dresser, then leaned past him to pick up Malia. The child stirred without opening her eyes. Her mouth worked as though she were nursing, and one foot kicked out as she was lifted from the crib.

Lycas crooked his arms to let Sura place Malia in them. She carefully slid her own hands out from under the child so he was holding her alone.

The harsh lines of Lycas's face didn't soften, but for a few moments, his breath came quick and rough. Sura turned away, then straightened the bedcovers, which were already straight, and wiped off the nightstand, which was already clean.

"I don't know what to say," he whispered.

"You could start with 'congratulations.'"

"That seems insufficient. And inappropriate, considering the circumstances."

"I'm happy to have her." She fought to keep the edge out of her voice. "In spite of everything."

"Congratulations, then." He said it with finality, which seemed to indicate he was ready to set Malia down.

"You can put her back if you want."

"Oh. All right." He sounded relieved. She didn't begrudge him his lack of grandparental instinct. No doubt he was more accustomed to holding an enemy's broken head than a fragile infant.

Malia woke fully when he put her down. She started to cry in great gasping wails. Sura watched Lycas's face to see if he would wince at the sound, but he didn't.

"Sorry," he said.

She picked Malia up and rubbed tiny circles on her back, not knowing exactly why. "Let's bring her out there. My notes tell me she likes having lots of people around. She loves Dravek especially."

"Maybe he reminds **her of you**." He retrieved the lantern and held open the door. **Sura kept** her expression neutral as she passed him to enter the kitchen, where Vara and Dravek sat at the table.

Rhia set a mug of ale and a cup of water in front of the two empty chairs, then reached for Malia. "I'll get her back down. The four of you need to talk in peace."

Sura reluctantly let her aunt take the child, then sat next to Dravek. His hand drifted over the back of her chair as he gave her a comforting smile. The need to touch him made her ache inside.

Lycas sat across from her and rested his hands on the table. "Sura…" He stopped, as if the word felt strange in his mouth. "All of you. I need you for a special operation. We've stolen weapons, sabotaged roads, invaded garrisons. But there's one thing even more precious to the Descendants."

He reached in his pocket and withdrew a shiny maroon sphere, which he rolled to the center of the table. Sura's stomach curdled.

"What's that?" Dravek said.

"It's a grape," Sura replied. "They make wine out of it. They send the best of it back home and use the rest to sedate the Asermons."

"And Velekons," Lycas added. "The Ilions depend on this crop more than wheat or barley or any vegetable. Their own vineyards in Ilios were nearly wiped out by a pestilence fifteen years ago, when I lived there. It's one of the main reasons why they invaded our lands." He jutted his thumb over his shoulder. "Many of those vines are maturing this year, and from what I'm told, the hot, dry weather this season has been ideal." He popped the grape in his mouth. "The harvest begins in two weeks."

Sura's heart raced as she realized his intentions. "You want to burn the vineyards."

He raised his eyebrows at her. "How did you guess?"

"When I lived there, it was all I could think about."

He leveled a solemn gaze at her, as if just now realizing all she had suffered under the occupation.

"We'll burn one," he said, "and hold the rest hostage. The ransom will be the release of all political prisoners." He looked at Sura. "Including your mother."

She drew in a quick breath. What if it worked? With the resistance members free, surely they all could expel the Ilions from Asermos.

"Won't they just put troops to defend the vineyards?" she asked Lycas.

"Then that's a different kind of success," he said. "Forcing them to redeploy from other areas, which will be weakened as a result. Either way, we keep them on the defensive." A corner of his mouth twitched into a smile. "Besides, placing a soldier out in the open, in view of our archers, is one step away from building his casket."

"I'll go," Vara said. "I want to kick the Ilions out of Asermos, the way they kicked me out. I want to meet my grandchildren."

"Thank you." Lycas nodded to her, making water drip from his hair onto the table. "Your third-phase heat vision will help with night operations." He examined Dravek and Sura. "Vara told me that together, you two can control fires and even start them from nothing."

"She told you—?" Sura glanced quickly at Dravek. He blinked and tilted his head in a subtle gesture that said her father didn't know the source of their power. Sura sat back in her chair. Maybe their training had grown tamer in the last year.

Vara cleared her throat. "I explained to Lycas how well you and Dravek have learned the maneuvers I've taught you."

"I'll go." Dravek's hands clenched. "I want to destroy these monsters and everything they love." He turned to Sura. "I know you do, too."

Sura's desire for revenge surged, but was quickly swept aside by a wave of guilt. "What about Malia?" she asked Dravek.

"Etarek and Kara could care for her until you get back. She needs more time with her father, anyway. But it has to be your choice."

"Yes," Lycas said. "I won't ask you to leave your daughter."

She looked him in the eye and spoke in a low voice. "No, I expect you wouldn't."

The edges of his mouth tightened. "I regret the pain I caused you and your mother." He leaned forward, and she felt the weight of his stare. "But let's get something straight. I don't regret leaving to go to Ilios. Everything I did was for my family and my people, especially you. I sacrificed everything to make sure you lived in a land of freedom."

"You failed."

He shook his head slightly. "Not yet."

Sura ran her thumb over the nicks on the rim of her cup. Could she do to Malia what Lycas had done to her? Did she have a choice?

Of course she had a choice, but not one she could live with.

"I'd like to speak with Dravek alone," she said.

"I understand." Lycas stood, scraping his chair against the wooden floor. He met Vara at the door. "I'll stay at your mentor's house tonight," he told them. "We leave in the morning."

Sura's throat was too thick to let her reply. She couldn't watch him walk out her door. Though she'd been only a few weeks old the first time he'd done it, her mind had recreated the moment.

She'd lain in her crib in the corner, crying. Her mother sat at the table, as Sura was now, refusing to cry.

The door closed behind them. Dravek got up to lock it, then sat down again, this time across the table instead of next to her. In the other room, Malia began to cry again, and Rhia's low voice responded in soothing tones.

"Don't you have a son?" Sura asked Dravek. When he nodded, she said, "How can you just leave him?"

"How can I ask others to leave their children and fight in my place? I want Jonek to have no memory of what it was like to live under oppression. I want to end this, now." He jabbed his finger against the table. "The sooner those prisoners are free, the sooner it'll all be over."

"What if they don't let them go?"

"Then we burn every vineyard."

She closed her eyes, imagining the green hills of her home turned black and scarred. "All that beautiful farmland."

"It's only fire. Kalindos burned to the ground ten years before I was born. Now you can hardly tell anything happened."

She remembered tall, healthy trees covering his home village, and felt a sudden longing to return. To be anywhere but Tiros, where she couldn't remember one day to the next.

Her memory was an even bigger issue. "What if I forget the battle plan and get someone killed?"

"Vara and I would be with you." He leaned forward, dark gaze intense on her face. "And you're brilliant with fire in our training."

"How? Don't I forget what I've learned from the day before?"

"No. Somewhere in your mind or your body, the memory sticks." He gestured to her bedroom. "Before Malia, you didn't know how to change a diaper, but now you do. It's the same with our training. You can still learn, Sura. You just don't remember learning."

She felt more confused than ever. "I don't remember anything at all."

"Trust me, when the time comes, you'll know what to do." He started to reach across the table, then pulled his hand back. "Part of me wants you to stay here, where I know you'll be safe."

"Nowhere is safe in this world. We need to change that." She took a deep breath, then blew it out. "I should feel sad at leaving Malia, but I barely know her." She put her face in her hands. "Will I ever be a real mother to her?" Her throat tightened her voice so that it pitched up. "Why does Snake hate me so much?"

She heard Dravek leave his chair and come to her side. He slid his arms around her.

"Don't." She tried to get her elbows inside their embrace so she could push him away, but he held her too tightly. So she surrendered, curling her arms around his neck and clutching his back.

If she concentrated with all her strength, perhaps she could nail this memory to the wall of her mind, so that it would never fall through a hole into eternal nothingness.

Tiros

Rhia was up before dawn. It was getting harder to sleep in this house, the air so heavy with memories of Nilik. On this day, the anniversary of his death, she thought she would choke on it.

She fed the chickens and collected the eggs from the hen-house, then stumbled in the darkness through the small yard back to her home, which no longer felt like her home.

Marek was sitting alone at the end of the table when she returned. His elbows were propped on the surface, his hands folded in front of his face. He stared at the front door as if waiting for someone to walk through it.

"Good morning," she said, in a whisper that in the utter stillness, sounded as loud as a roaring wind.

He turned his head and didn't speak at first. She set the lantern atop the stove and started to put the eggs away.

"Rhia," he whispered. "Come here."

She sat beside him, and he took her hand. His face, shadowed by the lantern light, looked drawn and weary.

"We should meet the evacuating Kalindons in the mountains," he said in a hoarse voice, "help them find their way to Tiros."

She cocked her head at him. "But several of them have already been here. They know the way."

He hesitated, staring at their joined hands. "They might run out of supplies."

"I'm sure they have enough. There's no reason to leave anything behind."

He fell silent and let go of her hand. His gray gaze settled on the door again. Dark circles rimmed his eyes.

"Marek, what's this really about?" she whispered.

"Maybe they don't need us." He looked at her, and her heart twisted at the sight of his sadness. "But I need them. I know you know what day it is, why neither of us slept last night. I can't stay here in Tiros. It feels...dead."

"I know." She brushed a lock of pale brown hair behind his ear, wishing she could take his pain and make it hers alone. Maybe seeing his people, reconnecting to Kalindos in its time of need, would bring some life back into his eyes.

"We'll go as soon as Corek gets back from his Bestowing," she said. "It's just a few days. Maybe he'll—" She stopped herself, not daring to voice the hope that Damen's son would be Raven.

"Thank you." Marek leaned forward and kissed her, softly. "Thank you," he said again.

A voice came from the top of the stairs. "This time I'm going with you." Jula crept down the steps and stopped halfway, eyes glittering in the lamplight. "No arguments."

Rhia looked at Marek. "I forget. Which of us are the parents?"

He smiled at their daughter. "Of course you can come. But only if you find someone to take care of the animals."

She sat on the step and put her chin in her hands. "What if we let Etarek and Kara and Jonek stay here? That way Malia won't have to move. She'll miss her mother as it is."

"Good idea. They can move into Sura's room as soon as she leaves today." Rhia looked at the lightening sky outside the window. "Which won't be long. I should wake her."

As she headed for the door of the ground-floor bedroom, she heard Jula whisper to Marek, "Can Corek come with us, too?"

Rhia knocked softly on Sura's door, then entered. It was tricky, introducing her to a strange new world every morning. Today she would let Sura wake up, meet her daughter for the seventieth "first time," and eat breakfast before hearing the news that she would be leaving Tiros and Malia with her father. If she still wanted to go, that is.

Rhia sat on the edge of the bed. "Do you know me?"

Sura nodded. "Aunt Rhia." She rubbed her eyes, then glanced at the window. "It's early."

"It's a big day. I'll explain in a while." She set the lantern on the nightstand. "For now, just read your notes."

Sura blinked and yawned. She seemed unusually calm, but maybe the early hour had dulled her ability to panic.

Rhia tiptoed to the crib. Malia was still sleeping and didn't smell like she needed changing.

"Your daughter's fine for now. Breakfast will be ready soon."

Sura sat up in bed and gave another sleepy nod.

It pained Rhia to think of how much her niece was suffering so that a few people might progress in power. Though it had saved Lycas's life, she doubted the justice of the process. The simple act of reproduction was certainly no guarantee of maturity. She thought of Endrus the Cougar, and others her age, who would have been just as strong as their peers, but for lack of children. The whole system seemed to cause untold misery, on top of what her people already suffered.

Rhia went back to the kitchen, where Marek was already cooking breakfast. His posture seemed straighter now, as if he'd shed a burden. It would never completely leave him, or Rhia. But every moment in this house added to its weight, and the thought of leaving Tiros gave her a strange sense of hope.

She sliced the bread, then turned away so she could pretend not to see Marek toss a piece to Hector. The dog reared on his hind legs to snatch it from the air, then trotted beneath the table.

From Sura's room she heard the sliding of a dresser drawer. A few moments later, another, then a third, opened and shut.

"She's up now." Rhia put a hand on Marek's back. "Save some bread for the humans?"

He gave an innocent shrug. "I don't know what you're talking about."

She knocked on Sura's door and entered when beckoned. Fully clothed, her niece turned from the dresser with an empty travel pack. She set it open on the bed, where a pair of pants, a shirt and several pairs of socks lay arranged.

Rhia stared at the bag. "You're packing."

Sura froze, clutching the straps. "Shouldn't I be?"

"Where are you going?"

Her face crumpled. "Then it *was* a dream. My father didn't really come, did he?"

Rhia stepped forward carefully, as if the moment could break if she trod too hard. "How do you know he came?"

"Because I was there." Her brow furrowed. "Wasn't I?"

Rhia took in a deep breath. "You remember. Oh, Sura." Unable to contain herself, she lunged forward and hugged her niece.

"Wait." Sura wriggled out of her embrace. "What was wrong with my memory?"

"You couldn't make new ones. You'd leave the room and come back not knowing why you were there."

"I did?" She put a hand to her head. "When?"

"Since before Malia was born. Do you remember?"

"No." She squinted at the floor. "I remember last night, when Lycas came."

"The first or the second time?" When Sura hesitated, Rhia added, "Was he alone?"

"No, you and Vara and Dravek were there. He asked us to help him burn the vineyards."

"What about before that?"

Sura's eyes scanned the walls, as if the answer were painted there. "Nothing."

"Sura, I think your punishment is over." She wanted to hug her again, but didn't dare. "As of last night, you stopped forgetting."

Sura didn't seem to share Rhia's happiness. She just looked confused. "Why now? I'm not being a good parent. I'm leaving my child."

Rhia took her hands. "You're leaving to protect her world. Maybe it's a sign you're doing the right thing."

"How?"

Rhia sat on the bed with her. "When Marek was your age, he couldn't control his Wolf powers. He had no choice but to turn invisible at night, because he'd become a father before he was ready."

"You mean with Nilik?"

Rhia breathed deep, letting the pain of her son's name pass through her chest. "No. He had a mate in Kalindos, two years before he met me. She and the boy died in childbirth."

Sura's eyes widened. "How terrible."

"But when Marek came to the aid of Asermos in its first battle with the Descendants, Wolf gave him his powers back."

"I don't understand."

"He was ready to take responsibility for someone other than himself." She glanced toward the kitchen, remembering how Marek had looked when he came to Asermos that night, her first glimpse of him in the moonlight.

"Then my father was right to leave me," Sura said in a flat voice. "I guess it's what the Spirits wanted him to do."

"That didn't make it easier on you and your mother. War makes everything simpler and more complicated at the same time."

Sura gazed at the crib. "I barely know Malia, but she knows me so well."

Rhia slid her arm around her niece's waist. "She'll know you the rest of your life."

Sura's mouth tightened, then she whispered, "I'm afraid she already has."

Sura tried not to look as miserable as she felt.

It wasn't the steady rain seeping through her coat or the wind that made its hood a useless barrier against the water. It was the absence of Malia that made her feel empty and heavy.

Her body seemed to have a better memory of the child than her mind did—she only remembered meeting Malia last night, but when she'd picked her up "for the first time," her arms knew just how to hold her and rock her.

That bodily memory now made her want to curl up into a ball and cry. But her father was watching her, discreetly, from the other side of the campfire as he tossed a rope over a high tree branch to secure their food from bears. She was careful not to sit too close to Dravek on the tree stump they shared.

She focused on the fruit and bread Rhia had packed for the troop. They had traveled quickly today, far up into the northern hills where they would avoid Descendant detection, and had had no time to hunt. But one of the rebel fighters, a first-phase Kalindon Cougar named Endrus—apparently a close friend of Dravek's stepfather—had met them at this campsite with two freshly killed rabbits.

Faint thunder rolled across the sky, and rain sizzled on the campfire. Lycas looked up as he fastened one end of the rope to their food pack.

"One more day of rain," he said, "and the vineyards will be hard to burn."

"Naw," said Endrus. Lounging on his side, the Cougar picked a piece of dinner from between his teeth. "Such a dry year, a little rain won't make a difference. Those vines are as brittle as an old man's bones, I tell you."

"They'd better be." Lycas grabbed an apple from the food pack, then tied it shut. "The faster it burns, the sooner we can get out. Fewer casualties." He hoisted the pack high above their heads and tied the end of the rope to a stub of a branch on the tree's trunk.

"Speaking of casualties," Sura said to her father, "is it true you have the archers maim the Descendants, shoot them in the legs, so you can slit their throats?"

"It's the most humane way to kill a man." He sat on the ground without a grunt. "It's fast, and with a sharp enough dagger, almost painless."

"But that's not why you do it, is it? You do it because that's how livestock are killed, and it humiliates the Ilions to be slaughtered like animals."

"Does it?" He peeled the apple and gave Vara a sly look. "I hadn't heard that."

"Sura," Endrus said, "there's a reason behind every tactic. First of all, we can't let any of them live. They'd run to their superiors and give away our position."

"And except when we were at the garrison, taking prisoners slows us down," Lycas pointed out. "We survive by staying mobile."

"I understand all that." She tugged her cloak tighter around her neck. "But why slit their throats?"

Endrus answered her. "If the Ilions worry they'll be killed in a dishonorable way, they won't want to come out to the hills to fight us. It's the only way a few hundred fighters can scare an entire army." He tapped his temple. "We get into their heads."

"They want us in open combat." Lycas tossed his apple peel to Endrus. "We won't give it to them."

"Until we're good and ready." Endrus gnawed the peel. "So, Dravek, how are things in Kalindos? When I left ten years ago, they were starting to get weird."

"Weird how?"

"Going back to the old ways. More rituals and prayers. Longer feasts. There was even talk of bringing back naked weddings."

Sura surprised herself with a laugh. She could have sworn Dravek was blushing, but it might have just been the campfire glow.

"Uh, well." Dravek scratched his chin with one hand and jabbed her in the ribs with his other elbow. She laughed harder. "I haven't seen many weddings. Usually people just show up for the reception."

"I saw one last year." Sura smirked at Dravek. "It was magnificent."

"Didn't you get married last year?" Vara asked him.

He rubbed his face again. "Yes. I did."

"And were you naked?"

He pulled back his shoulders and lifted his chin. "Gloriously so."

The others laughed long and hard, and Endrus nearly choked on his apple peel. Sura felt her spirit begin to lighten.

Vara finally yawned. "Who's first watch tonight? Someone other than me, please."

"I'll do it." Lycas wiped his utility knife on a clean rag and slipped it back into one of his many pockets. "Sura, you'll join me."

She shoved the last piece of bread in her mouth. With a last glance back at Dravek, who attempted an encouraging smile, she followed her father into the dark.

She hurried to keep up, slipping on the wet leaves, but he had disappeared. "Where are you?"

"Over here," came a voice to her left, followed by the crunch of teeth into an apple. She stepped out in that direction and promptly tripped over a root. She cursed and kept going, with a slight limp from a sore toe.

A hand grabbed her elbow. "Stop, before you fall into the ravine." Lycas led her a few steps to the right. "There's a rock behind you. Sit until your eyes adjust."

Sura obeyed. The pines' thick canopy blocked the cloudy sky's stingy light.

"I apologize," he said. "I forget sometimes that others don't share my night vision."

"I'm not much of a sentry."

"That's not why I asked you out here."

"Ah, well, if you were hoping for a cozy little father-daughter chat—" she stood and brushed off her trousers "—I think sleep would be a more productive use of—"

"Sit."

She sat. It was as if he'd yanked the strength from her knees. She glared at him.

"You think I can't see the look on your face?" he said. "Stop it. You won't get special treatment because you're my daughter."

"Not even a nice word at my funeral if I died?"

"Sura." His voice came low and soft. "If you died, I'd destroy the world."

Her breath caught, then she cleared her throat. "Really, there's no need. A haircut and a month of mourning will do."

"Shut up and let me speak."

She shrugged. "Since you ask so nicely—"

"Now."

She closed her mouth, turning her lips under her teeth to remind herself to keep it that way.

"All who follow me believe in the cause with every last speck of their souls. The cause is not peace, not reconciliation, not better treatment under Ilion law. The cause is nothing less than liberation. We won't stop until we drive the Descendants from this land forever. Do you support that?"

"I do." She felt it in her bones.

"Would you give your life for it?"

She hesitated, thinking of Malia. But all this was for her, anyway. "Yes. I'd die for the revolution."

"That's not what I asked." He came closer to her. "There's no such thing as a glorious death. The days of martyrdom are over."

Her stomach clenched as she thought of Mathias, burned alive in his own home.

"In a war like this," Lycas said, "survival itself is a victory. When we live, we live to fight another day. Our mission is to make them get sick of the war before we do." He put his hand on her shoulder. "So when I ask if you'll give your life, I mean your *life*, not your death."

She nodded, trying not to squirm under his touch. "My life. All of it."

"Good." He squeezed her shoulder and let go. "Now if—"

"And my death," she said, "if necessary."

"It won't be." He took another bite of apple as he stepped away. "You'll have adequate protection."

"You've never taken fire into your body and given it out again. Soldiers and archers can't protect me from that."

"Your training and judgment will protect you. I trust you, and you have to trust me as your commander." He paused, chewing. "Do you?"

"Yes. As my commander," she added under her breath.

"Thank you. Go get Dravek so I can speak to him."

She stared at Lycas, whose outline she could now see in the dark.

That was it? A philosophical pep talk from the father she hadn't seen since she was two weeks old?

She got up and started to walk away, then stopped.

"Anything else?" he asked.

"What happens when they set my mother free?"

"*If*, not *when*." He made a noncommittal noise in his throat. "It's up to her whether to join us."

"Do you miss her?"

He snorted. "That has nothing to do with anything. The revolution needs her."

"What about you?"

"What *about* me?" His voice turned harsh. "Sura, if you're on this mission because you hope your parents will miraculously reunite—"

"Don't insult me. I just wondered if you still care about her."

"It was nineteen years ago."

"So the answer is no?"

"The answer is irrelevant. Now send me your Spirit-brother and go to bed."

She stumbled back to the site, cursing every rock she tripped over and pretending her father was on the other end of her foot and her words.

Dravek lay asleep in his bedroll. She knelt beside him and tugged his sleeve.

"I'm awake," he murmured.

"Lycas wants you."

He sat up alert and reached for his shoes. She noticed a tiny white shirt lying atop his pack, which he was using as a pillow. "What's that?" she whispered.

"Oh." He gave an embarrassed smile and picked up the shirt. "It's Jonek's. I figured for a day or two it would still smell like him." He took a quick whiff, then dropped it back on his pillow. "More or less."

Sura untied her own pack, then pulled out one of Malia's baby blankets.

They started laughing. "A couple of brave warriors, aren't we?" he said.

"Keep it down over there, you two," Vara growled.

They glanced over at her, then Dravek dipped his head to whisper in Sura's ear. "I'm glad you came with us, or I'd have had to pack one of your shirts, too." He sprang to his feet and disappeared into the darkness.

Sura laid out her bedroll next to Vara, then quickly changed her clothes. Before repacking her bag, she tiptoed over to Dravek's bedroll and stuffed it with the shirt she'd worn all day. She smiled as she returned to bed.

All in the name of the mission.

06

Tiros

Rhia lurched out of bed at the knock on the door. It wasn't concern for who it might be that made her hurry down in total darkness, avoiding the fifth stair's creaky left side. It was the fear that Malia would wake and start to cry again. Since Sura had left, the child seemed to do little else.

She reached the door and spoke through it in a low voice. "Password?"

"Sparrow."

She jerked open the door. Corek stood on the porch, the lantern in his hand casting an orange glow onto his stubbled, sunburned face. She checked the dark street behind him. "Are you alone?"

"Yes. I came home before sunrise to avoid the crowds."

Her breath caught. Raven had come for him? Or not?

He glanced past her, and she waved him inside, though she briefly considered making him tell her what his Spirit was first. As he passed, she realized he'd grown taller and thinner in the last year since they'd been in Velekos.

Corek set the lantern on the table and looked around the dark kitchen. "This house is the same as I remembered it from years ago."

"That makes one of us."

He cast her a sympathetic gaze. "Nilik avenged my sister's death. I can never repay him, or you, for his sacrifice."

"It's not as if you asked him to do it." Her hands fidgeted with each other as she waited for the news. Corek was so like his father Damen, mysterious and taciturn. Compared to Jula's constant chattering, she found his reticence refreshing, despite her own momentary edginess.

"You must be hungry after your fast," she prompted, hoping it would spark discussion about his Bestowing.

"I ate the food Galen left me." Corek turned to the wall next to the front door, where the family's fetishes hung on pegs—a black feather for Rhia, a gray and white one for Jula, pieces of wolf tail for Marek and Kara (and a fox tail for Marek), and a spoke of deer antler for Etarek.

Corek stepped over to the row of fetishes, then reached up slowly and ran his finger along the quill of the black feather.

Rhia's gut plummeted. Not Corek. Spirits knew his generation needed a Crow. But not him.

"I never thought I would be Raven," he said. "Not even after I failed my first Bestowing." He put his hands in his pockets as he turned to her. "Did my father ever tell you? I tried about two years ago, before Lania. My parents made me, though I didn't feel called." He scratched the back of his neck, ruffling his shoulder-length black hair. "Nothing happened. No Spirits came."

"He never told me." Her throat thickened, and she fought to keep the sorrow from her voice. "It wasn't your fault, Corek. You just weren't ready." She stepped closer to him so she could maintain a whisper. "I have an extra fetish upstairs that you can have until you find your own feather."

"Thank you." He blew out a breath and looked at the window. "I've let everyone down."

"No." She touched his arm. "The Spirits provide what our people need."

"Our people need a Raven."

"And Crows. You're the first new Crow since I was called twenty years ago. Your father and I won't live forever."

"My father." His jaw tightened, accentuating sharp cheekbones. "He'll be disappointed."

"Damen will be proud, and happy to be your mentor."

"I'd rather train with you." He glanced at her. "If you'll have me."

She had to admit, the idea of an apprentice pleased her. Perhaps it would help fill the void left by Nilik. "We can start right away, if you're willing to travel with us. Marek and Jula and I are leaving to meet the Kalindons as they evacuate."

"Jula's going?" His eyes glinted with life for the first time since he'd entered. "I think I'll come along."

She gave him a teasing smile. "She might not like you anymore once she finds out you're a Crow like her mother."

Someone stirred in the room above the kitchen, and Rhia heard Jula's soft feet hit the floor.

"Go on up," she said. "We'll leave tomorrow, after you've rested from your Bestowing."

Corek put his foot on the first stair, then turned to her, his face taut with tension. "My father told me about the ritual you and he had to endure after you became Crows."

Rhia shivered to think of it, to this day. In order for her to face others' death without fear, she had to die herself and be brought back to life by her mentor, Coranna. She found out afterward that every moment of her life since then had cost a moment in another person's life, as Crow's ransom.

"Let's not worry about that now, since your father and I can't resurrect you until we become third phase."

His shoulders relaxed, then one eyebrow popped up. "Er, if Jula and I ever get married, don't expect grandchildren for a long time, heh?" Without waiting for her reaction, he bounded up the stairs.

Rhia watched him go and wondered how long before he realized the terrible burden of being Crow. This war kept the death Spirit's servants busy. Before it ended, Rhia feared she would watch many more souls pass forever to the Other Side.

Asermos

As Dravek examined the vineyard from their hilltop vista, he thought he could see the grapes glisten in the sunset. Just above the horizon, heavy blue clouds formed a solid mass that extended over most of the sky, making the last yellow rays cast long, lurid shadows over the landscape.

The vineyard would be bright soon enough. He licked his lips.

"Ready?" asked a soft voice behind him, a voice that warmed the back of his neck.

He looked over his shoulder to see Sura approach. "It looks just like the map Endrus made. He said this vineyard is isolated, so it's not well-guarded against thieves. The others won't be so easy."

"I hope there won't be any others." Sura stood next to him as they watched the last sliver of sun slip beyond the horizon. It was the first time they'd been alone together since the night her father came.

"Why is it blue?" she asked Dravek. "That spot of sunlight left on your eyes after you look away."

He blinked and watched the sun's afterimage float over his vision. "I never noticed that before."

They waited, silent, for several more minutes.

"What was I like?" she said finally. "Back when I couldn't make memories."

He shifted his feet, wanting to take her hand. "You were happy."

"How could I be happy like that?"

"Maybe because you kept meeting Malia." He didn't mention the way Sura's eyes would spark whenever she saw him.

"Rhia said you took care of me and my daughter."

"We all did." *It was a privilege,* he thought.

"Someday you'll have to tell me everything. What Malia looked like when she was born. What I was like when I was pregnant." She fell silent. "I hope we start soon. It smells like rain."

"Look." He pointed down to their right. "I think it's Endrus."

A torch borne by one of the rebels bobbed to the northwest corner of the vineyard. Another passed it to go to the southwest corner, nearest to the house.

"That must be Bolan," she said. "He'll calm the guard dog."

Sure enough, a sharp bark came from outside the vintner's house. Bolan tossed his flame into the vineyard before dashing toward the animal. As a third-phase Horse, his powers of animal communication could soothe the dog into silence.

Two more burners streamed from the eastern end, then three ran straight south through the middle.

It had begun.

Vara would keep the flames from reaching the house—Lycas's orders were to harm only property, not civilians. The Wolverine himself, along with a pair of young Bears, would detain the vintner and give him demands to deliver to the Ilion authorities. As an extra precaution, Vara would gaze into the man's eyes and make him forget what they looked like.

"It'll get smoky," Dravek told Sura, "but remember, you don't have to see the fire to control it."

"I know." He could tell she was fighting to keep her voice steady.

"Pull in the heat and give it to me. Just like we practiced yesterday."

Her posture eased a bit. When they'd left Tiros, Sura had had no faith in her own abilities because she couldn't remember their year of training. Yesterday Vara had put them through one more practice maneuver, using a rocky clearing and a series of woodpiles. Sura had astonished herself with her own skill.

The vineyard began to burn, orange flames spotting the corners and then the middle. The torches raced and dipped to light more vines, their bearers hidden by the smoke and darkness.

"We've never done one this big," she said. "Never this strong."

"We can do it." He took her hand. "Just give me the heat."

She drew a deep breath, and through her skin he felt her pulse steady.

The wind shifted, bearing the unmistakable chill of an approaching rainstorm. Billows of smoke headed up the ridge, straight toward them.

Sura tugged his arm. "Let's move!"

They skirted the ridge, hand in hand, but soon the smoke arrived, obscuring the ground in front of them. It smelled acrid yet sweet, like burned honey.

Sura shrieked, and his arm jerked backward.

Together they tumbled down the slope of the ridge. Dozens of small rocks bit through the fabric of Dravek's clothes. Sura yelped in pain.

They slid to a stop at the bottom. He crawled to her. "Are you all right?"

She nodded, coughing and hacking. "Scraped half my skin off, but nothing broken. You?"

"Fine." Heavy smoke poured over the vineyard, obscuring their view. "We'll have to do it by feel."

"I can't," she shouted above the roar of the flames. "Too many fires close together."

The wind changed again, but this time in temperature, not direction.

Rain was coming, any minute.

"We need higher ground," Sura said. "We need to see."

The land's slope was steady, with no undulations that would give them height, other than the ridge they'd just tumbled from. Finding a safe trail back up would cost too much time.

Sura pointed past him. "There!"

A white wooden barn sat at one end of the vineyard. Dravek saw a large, hinged window on its upper level.

They took off for the barn, chased by the smoke and the crackle and snap of burning branches.

Inside, mules and oxen kicked the sides of their stalls in fear. Sura and Dravek dashed through the barn and climbed the ladder into the loft. She ran to the window, slipping on the hay. She slid back the bolt, and together they pushed open the twin doors.

The entire vineyard was burning, lines of orange stretching toward each other, yearning for union.

"It's beautiful," she whispered.

"But it's not over." He pointed to several isolated, sputtering blazes. "The torch bearers can't go back in to relight. The smoke would kill them." He looked at Sura. "It's up to us."

They knelt beside the window, facing each other. Dravek looked past her shoulder.

"There." He indicated the lower right corner. Two of the vines were burning, but slowly, and they were too far from the others. "First let's strengthen the blaze, then move it to the next row."

She slipped her palm against his, and he let the feeling burn into every corner of his body. He lived for these moments, when he could lose himself inside his thoughts of Sura and how much he wanted her, needed her. Loved her.

Desire flared between them. He sent the heat.

The blaze brightened on its vine, but didn't spread.

"It's not working." Her lips tightened. "What are we doing wrong?"

"Nothing." He touched her cheek, his thumb tracing the corner of her mouth. "We just need more."

She met his gaze, holding it until he felt like he was falling into her eyes. They had done nothing more than touch hands in their training sessions with Vara. It had always been enough.

"Do you want to kiss me?" she whispered.

His palms tingled, and the sensation spread up his arms to his shoulders, then his nape. "I want to kiss you." Dravek grasped her chin and brought his mouth toward hers. Her lips parted, beckoning.

He stopped a hairsbreadth away. He could almost taste her. He needed to taste her.

His tongue slipped out, too far, and brushed the underside of her top lip.

The grapevines exploded in a shower of sparks, which fell upon the adjoining plants and ignited.

Sura gasped, her face close to his. "We did it."

"Yes." He drew back to gaze into her dark eyes. "We can burn the world with this."

She stared up at him, the left half of her face in shadow from the brilliant blaze. "Dravek…" she whispered. "Touch me."

He grazed his fingertips over her neck, through the back of her hair, then followed the line of her scar beneath her shirt. He longed to kiss every inch of it, whether she could feel his lips or not beneath the dead, battered skin. He would make her feel them, someday.

Her breath came faster, and she let go of his other hand to unfasten the top two buttons of her shirt. He slid the collar down to expose her left shoulder, to show her he preferred this burned, imperfect side. He leaned in, placing his lips near her skin without touching it, following the edge of her scar.

Beneath the pulse pounding in his ears, he heard a hiss from outside. It grew louder, closer. He struggled to draw away from the intoxicating scent of her skin.

"No," Sura said.

Dravek jerked his head up and looked outside.

Rain, pouring in sheets from an angry sky.

He gave a harsh sigh. "Now what?"

"More." She stroked his chest hard through his shirt. "We can do anything that doesn't give us release."

He would follow her instincts. He lunged to kiss her mouth, at last.

"No." She turned her head aside. "I want that so much, I think I'd come the moment I had it. Then we'd lose the power."

His hands slid down her back, greedy for her flesh. "But anything else, right?"

"Yes." She pressed her mouth to his neck and bit hard. His body seized. In the vineyard another grapevine burned brighter, defying the rain.

Dravek sank back against the hay bale and pulled her to straddle him. The pressure of her warm softness nearly drove him over the edge. She ground against him, and he groaned deep in his chest. She froze.

"We'd better take this slow," she murmured, "or the rain will win."

He nodded, his face wet with sweat against her neck. She eased herself away an inch or two from him, then rose and fell, stroking him through their clothes. His muscles clenched, and his toes cramped inside his boots.

"Stop." He trailed his fingers down into the neckline of her shirt. "Can I see you?"

Her lips parted, and the corners of her eyes flickered with doubt. Then she glanced toward the sizzling, smoldering vineyard. "Yes," she whispered. "Now."

He unbuttoned her shirt, drawing his fingertips against her skin with every new exposed inch. She closed her eyes and held her breath.

When he reached the last button, he parted her shirt to expose her full, round breasts. For a moment he only gazed at them. Then he leaned forward and put his mouth near her nipple, so she could feel the warmth of his breath. She trembled, her whole body vibrating against him.

The fire outside spread further, despite the strengthening rain. They would overcome this. They would win.

He drew her nipple between his lips, caressing it with his tongue, then the edge of his lower teeth. Sura stiffened and cried out, her back arching. She tried to grind her hips again, but he held them still. It had been so long, and his ache for her was so hard.

Dravek dug his fingers into her thighs as he suckled her. She moaned again. Between the sound of her passion and the feel of her muscles straining under his touch, his control was capsizing. He focused on the fire outside, on channeling the heat between their bodies into the vineyard.

But something was shifting. No matter how hard and fast he sent the fire out, it bounced back, stealing his breath and scorching his skin from the inside out, heightening the ferocity of his desire.

He pulled away and looked up at her flushed face and red, swollen lips. "Sura, make me stop. I need you so much, I can't hold back. Tell me to stop."

"Don't stop," she murmured, her fingers gliding through the hair at the back of his neck. "Send it out. All the heat I give you."

"It's coming back." He spread his palms over her breasts, and the heat under his skin spiked again. "We're not just feeding the fire anymore. It's feeding us."

"Can't stop. Rain'll kill the fire." Her voice slurred, as if from delirium. "Dravek, I need you." She slid her hand between them, down to where he wanted it most. "I can't stop touching you."

He meant to shove her away, to break the spell the fire had woven, awakening a force that could surely kill them. But when he pushed, their bodies refused to part. She tumbled backward in the hay, and he fell on top of her.

For a moment they remained motionless, pressed together. Dravek stared down into her dark eyes and saw his own desire reflected there.

Her hands glided down his back, and lower still. "It would be just like this." Her legs tightened around his thighs. "Think what it would be like inside me."

He could think of nothing else. The fire was ripping him in half. He needed to come, was on the edge, just a few more strokes. It felt like he would die if he didn't.

But if he did, it would end everything. A war as fierce as the one outside raged in his mind.

He dared to get closer, though he knew he couldn't trust his control. He slid against her, feeling the heat and moisture beneath her clothes. She cried out at the pressure and lifted her hips

Through his closed eyelids Dravek saw the vineyard flare and burst as the flames spread, hungry and insistent. A moment later the heat seared him, inside and out, driving him on.

He moaned and clutched her body. "I can't stop." His hips jerked against her. "It's too much."

Her body froze as she finally seemed to realize the danger. "No." She shoved at his chest. "Dravek, stop."

"Can't," he gasped. He pushed her shirt open and filled his hand with her breast as his orgasm began to crest. "I need you. Sura—"

Something seized him by the neck and yanked him upward. The world spun and pitched, and a searing pain ripped his spine and limbs.

Dravek found himself dangling in the open air above the barnyard. His feet kicked, desperate for solid ground.

Huge fingers tightened on his neck, and he heard a roar louder than the flames.

"What are you doing to my daughter?"

"Lycas, no!" Sura leaped to her feet, pulling her shirt closed. "Don't hurt him!"

"Why?" Her father's eyes blazed with the reflection of the fire. "Give me one good reason why I shouldn't bash this rapist's brains against the ground."

"It's not what it seems." She stared at Dravek, flailing at the end of Lycas's outstretched arm. "It's how we build our power," she told her father. "With our desire. Ask Vara."

Rage shadowed his face. "She told you to do this?"

"Not touching, not like this." Her words tumbled over one another. "Please don't be angry with her." Her fingers clenched, as if she could hold Dravek up by will alone. "Don't hurt him."

"You're both Snakes." He shook Dravek, and Sura whimpered, fearing he would break his neck. "She's your Spirit-sister," he said. "It's disgusting. It's wrong."

"It's not wrong." Dravek ceased his struggle and turned his eyes to Sura. "I love her."

A warm wave swept through her body, even as her stomach curdled with fear.

Lycas slowly turned his head to stare at Dravek. "You *what?*"

"I had to say it before you murdered me." He kept his gaze on her. "I wanted her to know."

She took a step forward. "Dravek, I—"

"Don't. You. Dare." Lycas held out a hand. "No daughter of mine—"

"Please." She sank to her knees. "You don't understand."

"I understand perversity." His arm muscles bulged as he tightened his grip on the back of Dravek's neck.

"No!" She crawled to the edge of the hayloft. "If you kill him, I'll jump."

Her father's hand flew out as if to grab her, but she was out of reach.

"Sura, don't do this," Dravek said with what sounded like diminishing breath. "Please."

She stood and spread her arms, ready for a headfirst, backward dive onto the barn floor. "You need us," she said to Lycas in a strong, steady voice.

The three of them stared at each other for a long moment.

Vara called from the vineyard. "Lycas, we're finished, let's move out!"

He gave Dravek one last glare, then hurled him facedown on the floor at Sura's feet. She knelt to help him up.

"Don't touch him," Lycas said. "That's an order."

Dravek held out his hand to stop her. "Do what he says, Sura." Slowly he got to his feet, then wiped away the hay stuck to his face. "I'm all right."

"Only because I can't afford to kill you," Lycas growled.

They left the barn and rendezvoused with Vara and Endrus, who gave them looks of trepidation before joining them in the retreat up the ridge. Bolan and the others departed in another direction, eventually to return to Asermos.

After half an hour of running uphill, Sura's chest felt like it would crush her lungs flat. She took heaving breaths and forced her legs to keep moving up through the forest, all the way back to the new campsite, farther east than the one they'd left earlier.

The moment they stopped running, Sura collapsed on the

ground. Her face and lungs felt seared with smoke, and her legs threatened to cramp. But the physical pain couldn't dim the triumph in her mind.

They had won the battle, and Dravek loved her.

While Endrus, Sura and Dravek set up a rudimentary camp in the damp woods, Lycas took Vara aside, out of the other Snakes' earshot. He made no effort to mask his disgust as he told her what he'd seen in the hayloft. The memory made him want to crush someone's head between his bare hands.

Vara examined the frayed edge of her rain cloak as he spoke. "What they did was outside the bounds of training." She gave him a calm gaze from under her dripping hood. "But it worked. Isn't that what matters?"

He ignored her logic. "Why didn't you tell me that was the source of their power?"

She uttered a low laugh. "When I told you that together they could start and spread fires better than any Snake I've ever heard of, you didn't ask where that power came from. If you'd stopped to think, rather than being greedy for a new weapon, you would've realized that it didn't exactly come from butterflies and fluffy clouds." She shifted closer and softened her tone. "You know Snake's domain."

"Fire."

"And sex." She dropped her hand to brush his palm with her fingertips. "Remember?"

"Not really," he said, though their encounters were impossible to forget, even half a lifetime later. "It was a long time ago."

"If you want, I'd be happy to—" her glance flicked down, then up again "—spark your memory."

He hesitated, breathing in the scent of her sweat, heightened by the rain and the long run to the camp. He could almost remember how she tasted.

"Not interested." Lycas stepped back so she couldn't feel his skin cool with the lie. "I'm sure Endrus would meet your needs."

She glared at him as she crossed her arms. "I always preferred your brother, Nilo, anyway. He was much kinder."

"No, he wasn't." Lycas turned away. "He was just better at hiding his meanness."

He strode back to the camp, where he found Endrus, Sura and Dravek tying a sleeping tarp between three trees.

"Dravek, come here."

"Yes, sir." Without hesitating, the young Snake dropped the rope and crossed the campsite—a brave feat, considering he'd almost been throttled.

He took Dravek's shoulder and steered him away from the camp, out of Sura's hearing range. Despite his tight grip, he could smell no fear on the boy. "What you did out there tonight—"

"Sir, I regret you found us in that…position."

"Shut up and let me finish." He couldn't look at the little bastard's face after what he'd done. "You're more experienced with your magic than Sura, correct?"

"I suppose."

"And Vara has trained you thoroughly."

He nodded. "And I taught myself, with Snake's guidance, before I came to Tiros." He paused. "Why do you ask?"

"If the Ilions don't respond to our demands, I'll have Sura and Vara burn more vineyards. With the right weather conditions, we can do two at a time. Sura will stay in my squad, and Vara will go with the rest of the platoon to another location." He paused to let the Snake grow nervous.

To his credit, Dravek waited for him to continue instead of asking about his own assignment. Either he was thoroughly cowed or defiantly confident.

"For you," Lycas said finally, "I have a special mission."

He knew he shouldn't relish his latest idea so much. But not only would it strike a deciding blow against the Ilions, it would put distance between Sura and this depraved young man.

It might even get him killed.

Kalindos

"I can't believe you had the gall to come back," snarled a familiar voice above Dravek's head.

He stopped, just in sight of the Kalindon fire wall. Other than the Ilions, his sister Daria was the last person he wanted to see.

She dropped to the ground beside the trail and glared at Dravek. She glanced at Endrus beside him, and her eyes widened.

"Uncle Endrus!" She launched herself into his arms. When he set her down, she held up her bow. "Guess what? I became a Cougar just like you and Father."

"Congratulations." Endrus stepped back and gestured to Dravek. "Your brother and I are—"

"He's not my brother anymore."

Dravek's stomach froze. "What do you mean?"

"We heard what you did to Kara, wiping her memory."

"It was an accident, I swear on my Spirit."

"Right." She put her hands on her hips. "Everyone knew you'd cheat on her, but with your own Spirit-sister? I never thought even you'd be that sick."

"Wait. How did you know—"

"Etarek sent a message. Later he tried to take it back and say he was just imagining things, but that must have been after he realized he'd gotten the better woman out of the whole sordid affair."

Dravek's fist clenched. "Don't you dare speak that way about Sura. You don't even know her."

"Not half as well as you, apparently." Her smirk faded. "If you had to have your perverted trysts with that little Snake, why not just break it off with Kara? Why'd you have to take away a year of her life?"

Endrus held up a hand. "I don't have time for this. You got Lycas's second message?"

"Galen sent it to Thera's mind two days ago." She looked at him, the corners of her eyes drooping. "Is this plan the only way to save Kalindos?"

"Unless you think a few dozen archers can defend the village from an entire battalion. As I recall, it didn't work so well the last time."

Daria hunched her shoulders, and Dravek wondered if she remembered her capture as a two-year-old, despite her perpetual denials.

She jerked her chin in the direction of the village. "Go on, they're expecting you."

As they moved away, Dravek took a last look back at his sister. She was watching him with sad, round eyes.

He and Endrus trudged on toward the fire ring. Its door was open, the boards scattered in random piles. Dravek's fingers twitched at the sight of the mess. It would take all day to repair the wall.

A lanky figure with long dark blond hair pushed a wheelbarrow full of rocks through the opening. Dravek stopped at the sight of his stepfather.

"Adrek?" Endrus gasped.

Adrek dropped the handles of the wheelbarrow. It tipped, spilling the stones, but he was already at their side.

"Endrus!" He threw his arms around his fellow Cougar and pounded him on the back. Then he pulled away and ran his thumb over the scar on his friend's cheek. "Spirits, what did those Descendants put you through?"

"About a million adventures, each of which will require one mug of meloxa to tell."

Adrek laughed, then gave Dravek a cold glance before wrapping his arm around Endrus's shoulders. "We'll have a welcome-home party like Kalindos has never seen. Come on, I'll take you in to see everyone."

Endrus gestured to Dravek. "What about your son?"

Adrek didn't even look back. "That Snake's not my son."

Dravek's lip curled. "Coward."

Adrek stopped, then slowly turned, his green eyes full of rancor. "Do you have any idea what you've done to me?" He advanced on Dravek. "I can't even look Kara's parents in the face after the way you hurt her."

"It's none of their business, or yours."

"You're lucky they didn't drag you back from Tiros and throw you in jail." He scowled up at him. "Times like this, I wish I never brought your whining, worthless self back from Ilios."

Dravek breathed deep in a failing attempt to control his temper.

Endrus cleared his throat. "I could really use a drink. Maybe we should—"

"Stay out of it, Endrus." Adrek narrowed an unflinching glare on Dravek. "I should've known, with your Descendant blood, that you'd bring us nothing but shame and sorrow. Instead I raised you as my son, for your mother's sake." He raised a finger to Dravek's face. "If it weren't for you, she'd still be alive."

Dravek's fist shot out. Adrek's hand swept it aside before it could connect with his jaw. With an almost offhand gesture, he twisted Dravek's arm behind his back and forced him to his knees.

Dravek's eyes blurred from the pain. "Don't talk about my mother," he choked out.

"You should be glad she can't see what's become of you." Adrek released Dravek's arm with a shove. "I hope you burn with the rest of them."

Dravek sprang to his feet, shaking out his throbbing arm. "Don't you dare threaten me."

"You plan to use your powers on us?" Adrek sneered. "Make us forget what a little rat snake you are? It won't work if we don't look at you. And everyone knows it."

He beckoned Endrus to follow him. Instead Endrus waited for Dravek and walked beside him through the fire-ring opening. On the other side, people loaded rocks into wheelbarrows and carts, moving the stony trench to the outside of the fire ring.

Someone shouted, and in a few moments a small crowd was running to greet them—or more precisely, to greet their long-lost friend Endrus, who'd been in Asermos working with the resistance for over ten years.

No one gave Dravek more than a glance. He turned and walked into the village alone.

"I'm so sorry." Tereus opened the door of the healer's home for Dravek. "It's unconscionable how they're treating you. Please sit. I'll bring you some water."

Dravek looked around at the warm confines of the building, where Elora the Otter had treated many of his accidental burns. "Got any meloxa?"

"It's not even noon," Tereus said, "but then again, you probably need it." He led him into the kitchen and set a flask, a water pitcher and a mug on the table.

Ignoring the water, Dravek poured the contents of the flask into the mug. The meloxa was sharp and sour on his tongue, and seemed to burn a hole in his throat going down. He barely repressed a cough. "Thank you," he said hoarsely.

Tereus slid into a chair across from him. "So tell me all about my great-granddaughter."

Dravek noticed that Tereus considered Lycas his son, though they weren't blood relations. By contrast, Adrek hadn't asked Dravek about his new son Jonek, Adrek's own step-grandson.

Still, the thought of Malia made him smile. "She's beautiful. And sweet, too. She lets anyone hold her." He shifted the mug on the table. "She feels like a daughter to me, maybe because I see her more than I see my own son."

"Or maybe because you're in love with her mother."

Dravek's face heated. Instead of replying, he took another swallow of meloxa.

"I've known you since you were a boy," Tereus said. "You wouldn't hurt Kara on purpose."

Dravek shook his head emphatically, though he would always wonder if erasing her memory had been nothing but an accident. "She got hurt just the same. I should be glad I'm not in jail."

"There are more urgent matters facing the village right now. Speaking of which, we need to call everyone together so you and Endrus can give instructions."

"Kalindos seems so empty already," Dravek said.

"The sick and the pregnant and the ones with small children have already left for Tiros. We're grateful Thera's powers have stopped fluctuating, and that she got Galen's thought-message so we could evacuate in time." He folded his roughened hands on the table. "I didn't agree with Sura and Etarek's decision to have a child for this reason, but their actions may have saved innocent lives."

Dravek tried not to think about the not-so-innocent lives that would meet their end soon.

"Are we doing the right thing?" he asked. "I don't mean the evacuation, but—the other part. What does the dream world tell you?"

Tereus steepled his fingers and pressed their tips against his mouth. "Swan has rarely been so clear in Her messages. This plan will end in disaster."

Dravek's mouth went dry, and he took a gulp of water. "We should call it off, then."

"She's equally adamant about what will happen if we don't do it. There's no escape from the Descendants." He rubbed his thumb over the palm of his other hand. "It's easy for me to say it's wrong. I didn't live through the first invasion of Kalindos. Both of Elora's sons were stolen that night."

Dravek nodded. Nearly all Kalindon families had been decimated by the attack, but Elora had lost everything. Her children had never been found, alive or dead. "What does she think about this?"

Tereus looked him in the eye. "She says it's time for Kalindos to stand up."

Dravek took the last sip of meloxa and wondered at her choice of words. Kalindos would stand up indeed. But by doing so, their homes, their lives, everything they'd ever known, would fall to ashes.

Asermos

Captain Addano entered the officers' mess and was dismayed to find it less than empty.

General Lino hailed him. "Addano, get over here and listen to this."

Addano nodded and crossed the otherwise empty dining room toward the general's table, which also held three majors, the general's staff officers.

As he sat down, they gave him looks of undisguised contempt. His job offended their sense of Ilion honor, even as they ordered him to continue it.

He hated them in return, but they were the only reliable sources of information. He hoped tonight's news would be better than last week's, when he'd heard about the takeover of the Tiron garrison and the destruction of the bridge. Sometimes he felt like he was the only one who noticed the occupation wasn't going well. Or maybe they all knew it, but no one wanted to voice the reality.

General Lino poured him a half a glass of wine, then set the carafe at the other end of the table. "I've ordered wine to be rationed until we can get a shipment in from Ilios, if they can spare it."

"This is fine." Addano tilted his glass. "Thank you, sir."

The vineyard fires had stolen one of the few bearable aspects of living in Asermos: cheap wine. The Ilion command had rebuffed the ransom demands of the rebels, provoking six more arsons in the last three days.

Luckily Addano had about fifty bottles in his home, a stockpile that should last him five or six weeks.

"I thought you should know," the general said. "We're going to fill the hamlet this fall instead of waiting until spring. All the native Asermons from the outlying farms—about a thousand head."

"Why now?" he asked. "I heard it wasn't even finished."

"With so few vineyards left, we don't need so many beasts for the harvest anymore. Better to contain them."

"Contain them from what?"

Lino scoffed, then slowed his voice as if he were speaking to a child. "The bandits, of course."

Addano blinked. Even now that the guerrillas occupied more territory than the Ilion army and controlled one of their garrisons, the senior officers still insisted on calling them "bandits."

The general poured himself another glass of wine—a full one, Addano noticed. "I wouldn't normally share such strategic intelligence with a junior officer, but I'll need some of your men to help with the relocation. I could have Major Strato here make the assignments, but your operations are so…specialized—" he raised an eyebrow "—I thought you should recommend which men can be spared."

"Thank you, sir," he said, ignoring the frowns of repugnance on the majors' faces. "How many do you need?"

"The question is, how many do *you* need to maintain your work?" He waved his hand toward the major. "You two figure it out. I don't want your mission undermined. It's too valuable."

Addano said nothing as the overboiled green beans slithered down his throat. He tried to forget how the fresh ones from his father's farm had tasted, lightly steamed and coated in butter.

He also tried to forget how the information he'd gathered from the prisoners had steered the Ilion military in the wrong direction five or six times. The harder he pressed them, the worse intelligence they offered. His superiors thought the mistakes meant he wasn't pressing hard enough.

So he'd killed the ones who'd lied to him, and now they all said nothing. Why he hadn't been relieved from duty for incompetence was beyond him. His superiors seemed to think the prisoners' suffering was an end in itself.

Addano cleared his throat. "Sir, if I may—"

They all looked at him at once, the general with an indulgent smile.

He shut his mouth, then wiped it with his napkin before continuing. "I'm curious. Does this order come from Ilios or is it a local decision?"

The general stopped smiling. "It's my decision."

Addano looked away and nodded. "Yes, sir. I'll check my

roster and get Major Strato a list of personnel to help with the relocation. I can do that right now, if you like."

Lino fell back into his easy manner. "Now, that's not necessary. Stay, eat, enjoy our company."

His mouth suddenly dry, Addano lifted his wineglass and saw that it was empty. He let out a sudden cough to hide his panic, then went back to eating.

The general returned to the topic at hand. "The sooner we get those farm people into that hamlet, the sooner I'll sleep at night. The bandits are pressing in on Asermos from all sides."

One of the majors chuckled. "Once they see what we do to Kalindos, they'll come around."

Addano swallowed his bite of unrecognizable meat. "What are we doing to Kalindos?"

General Lino raised his eyebrows. "Completing a very old mission."

Captain Addano searched his memory for Kalindon missions and could only come up with one—the invasion twenty years ago, the one that had left a blot on the entire nation of Ilios. *Kalindos* had become synonymous with *dishonor.*

He put his fork on his plate. "If I may be dismissed, I'll get to work on those rosters now."

Lino waved him off. "I wish you'd take more leisure, but I admire your dedication. It's good to see in a young officer."

The others laughed, and Addano's face flushed. At thirty-eight, he was older than all of them besides the general, and was several years from his next promotion, which he knew he'd never see even if he lived to be a hundred.

He left the dining room, forcing his gaze away from the half-full carafe of wine.

Downstairs in his "office," an Ilion woman was scrubbing the blood off the floor near the whipping post, her shoulder-length blond braid bouncing with each grating stroke.

"Evening, Captain Addano." Rilana's voice was chipper, considering her task. Any civilians who could gain the security clearance to work in the prison were too patriotic to question what went on in here. In their minds, Addano's work kept them safe from the "beasts."

He sat at his desk, wishing Rilana would leave. He wanted to take a draught from the bottle of wine hidden in the back of his bottom drawer without feeling obliged to share it with her.

She scrubbed on. Addano's heels tapped the floor in a nervous rhythm as he debated whether to pull out the bottle. Instead he reached into the opposite drawer and withdrew his staff roster.

The names blurred and swam before his eyes, which he rubbed with fingers that trembled. When had he last slept a full night or day? Since long before Nisa left. Since before the nightmares.

The ghastly dreams hadn't surprised him, considering the way he spent his waking hours. It bothered him more when they stopped, because it meant there was no part of him left to horrify.

Rilana hummed a familiar tune, keeping time with the scrape of her horsehair brush against the wooden floor. Lulled by the rhythm, he closed his eyes, grasping for a few moments' sleep.

Suddenly she gasped. "My apologies, sir."

He started awake. "Hmm?"

"I hope my singing didn't bother you. I get off in my own world sometimes."

"No, please continue. It reminds me of home."

"You're from the south, too?"

"From Saldos. The countryside." Ilios had only annexed this area two generations ago. Many people there still identified more closely with the region than with the Ilion nation itself.

"I'm from Salindis." She wiped stray hairs from her forehead with her wrist. "A town girl my whole life."

"My mother lives there now." He looked at her. "How did you get here?"

"By boat."

"No, I mean, what made you decide to come all this way?"

"They said there'd be jobs." She gestured to the blood-stained floor. "There are jobs." She glanced at the clock. "If you don't mind, sir, I have to get home to my children for dinner. The littlest one's been losing weight."

"Of course." He tried to blot out the image of his own children, the way they used to look around corners as they moved through the house, to see if he were coming. "Go right ahead."

Rilana finished quickly, then wished Addano good-night. She left with her bucket of water that was no doubt as red as the sun on the Ilion flag.

The moment the door closed behind her, Addano pulled out his bottle of wine, uncorked it and took a deep gulp. He set it down, the thick glass bottom slamming the wooden table.

His mind clear at last, he set the staff roster aside, then unlocked the center drawer of his desk. He withdrew his work log, the one detailing what they'd done to every prisoner, the questions asked and answered, the dates and methods of execution.

From a side drawer he extracted a sheaf of blank paper, then methodically cut sixty sheets. He refilled his inkwell, sharpened the nib of his pen and set to work.

By midnight he'd copied the entire work log. He set this aside and began again. Long before sunrise he finished, returning the original log to the locked drawer.

Addano addressed two large brown envelopes, one to his mother—he hoped she still resided at his sister's mother-in-law's house—and another to the Salindis newspaper.

At last he returned to the staff roster, poring over the list of names. He chose the men with no wives and children, as well as the men he didn't like, the ones who reported late for duty or ridiculed his accent behind his back. These he put on the list for Major Strato to reassign to the hamlet relocation project.

The others, the family men or the ones who'd been loyal colleagues, he left in his own service.

He would at least give them the honor of looking their betrayer in the eye.

Kalindos

Dravek paced around the small campfire in the center of his empty village, waiting to burn.

A decade of fire suppression within Kalindos had made it a tinderbox. Thick underbrush grew beneath heavy-crowned trees. He'd planned to do controlled burns in late winter when the ground was damp, but there would no longer be a need.

A messenger had come from Asermos three days ago with news that Ilion troops were making their way up the Velekon River to Kalindos. Each night since then, the few remaining Kalindons had stayed up, anticipating an attack. The waiting had turned Dravek's stomach into one huge knot.

He hoped it would be tonight, and not just to end the agony of delay. The weather was warm for this part of autumn, and the brisk winds would stir the flames. It was as if the air itself wished their success.

Few Kalindons remained in the village; few were needed. Most of the archers—Cougars and Wolves—and a half dozen Bears and Wolverines were all that remained, along with a pair of Otters who would meet them at the rendezvous point on the trail to Tiros, to treat injuries. Though this strange 'defense' of Kalindos had been Lycas's idea, Dravek had engineered the details here with Ladek and Drenis, the third-phase Bear and second-phase Wolverine.

"You should get some sleep."

Adrek appeared out of the darkness, probably thinking he'd startled Dravek, who had smelled him coming and hoped he would change his path. It was the first time his stepfather had spoken to him since their fight.

Dravek resisted the urge to jam his unlit torch down Adrek's throat. "I'll sleep tomorrow morning."

"What if they attack tomorrow morning?"

"They'll come at night. Even though most of you see better in the dark than they do, it still provides them with more cover than daylight. Ladek agrees."

The Cougar paced around the circle once more in silence, then sat on the ground several feet away. "I didn't mean what I said about your mother."

"Everyone thinks it, including me." He turned the torch over in his hands. "How could she ever get over what they did to her, with me reminding her every day, just by existing?"

"It wasn't like that." Adrek drew his palm over his stubbled jaw. "If anything, you gave her something to live for."

"She had Daria. She had you."

Adrek grunted. "Me, with my own nightmares of Ilios. I couldn't help her." He slid a finger along the curve of the bow. "Maybe no one could."

Dravek stared into the flames. "I didn't eat breakfast."

"Sorry?"

"The morning she died. I wanted a quail egg, like the day before, but she said we didn't have any, we only had fish. So I wouldn't eat." He closed his eyes, remembering the last time he saw her face, sunken in despair. "For years, I thought that was why she jumped." He looked at Adrek. "Crazy, isn't it?"

"That explains why you always ate whatever I put in front of you. Not like Daria, who was so finicky." Adrek's face was shadowed by the fire. "Will you accept my apology, son?"

"I'm not your son." He walked to Adrek's side and held out his hand. "But I'll accept your apology—"

"Thank you."

"—as soon as I hear it."

The Cougar took his hand and let Dravek help him up. "I'm sorry." His green eyes didn't blink as they looked up at him. "Your mother loved you."

"I know." Dravek let go of him. "But that never solves anything."

Adrek was about to reply, when he suddenly lifted his chin. "What was that?" He listened for a moment, then frowned. "I keep imagining I hear the scout, but it's just wishful thinking. I want this to be over."

"Think we're doing the right thing?" he asked Adrek, telling himself he didn't care about his stepfather's opinion.

"This is war. There is no right thing."

"But our people are safely evacuated. We could just leave. Let the Descendants come and find it empty."

"They'll follow until they catch us." Adrek stared past him toward the western end of town. "We came home the morning after they took your mother and sister. Found the Kalindon elders, every third-phase man and woman, strung up on the paddock posts." He pointed with his bow into the distance. "Old men and women, throats slashed or heads bashed in. Your mother's father. My father."

"I know," Dravek said quietly. "But it wasn't these soldiers."

"These soldiers would do it if they could. They'd kill us both and take Daria back to Ilios." His lips curled. "Do you know, if we hadn't rescued her, she would've been working in a brothel by the time she was twelve?"

"But a whole battalion." Dravek looked into the village that would soon become a graveyard. "I'll be a mass murderer."

"You'll be a hero."

Dravek was about to retort when he saw Adrek's face go taut again.

"That time I definitely heard something."

The ground vibrated beneath Dravek's feet just before Daria shot out of the darkness.

"They're coming, by the river." She panted, patting her chest. "The scout said half an hour, no more."

Dravek picked up a handful of torches and lit them all at once from the campfire. They snapped and sparked in the wind. "Take these to the others. When they're finished, they should snuff them out and get into position outside the ring."

"Dravek, I—" She stamped her foot and blew out a breath. "I hope you don't die."

"Thanks." He gave her the torches and dared half a smile. "You, too."

When she scampered off, he picked up the last two torches and lit them, then handed one to Adrek. "See you on the other side."

Dravek ran to the base of one of the nearby ladders. Using a ring attached to a pulley, he drew the torch up to the bridge, then climbed the ladder.

He opened the door on his old home, the one where Kara had proposed to him, where they'd once shared a marriage bed. It was empty now except for the fuse.

Here and in several other houses, a stovepipe had been stuffed tight with pitch-soaked ropes and suspended a few feet from the ceiling. The ropes protruded from each end of the pipe, and at the bottom end, a pile of dry brush lay on the floor, leaves and pine needles and kindling.

He checked the windows—which here in Kalindos were just square holes cut in the wall—to make sure they were shut tight. Then he took a deep breath and stretched to light the top of the fuse.

"Forgive me," he whispered.

The fuse lit, forming a double glow with the torch upon the walls of his old home. He backed out and shut the door quickly.

A long, thin cloth lay on the porch. Dravek stuffed the cloth under the door—tight enough to seal it but not too tight to keep it from opening. In less than an hour, the Descendants would come to this house, ready to yank out its inhabitants. By then the fuse would have burned down to the brush pile and smoldered from lack of air. The moment the soldiers opened the door, the back-draft would swallow them whole and engulf the tree in flames.

Theoretically, at least. He'd tested the timing of the fuses, but there was no safe rehearsal for the rest.

He lowered the torch, scrambled down the ladder for the last time, then took off for the fire ring, where he was met by several other Kalindons. Endrus carried Dravek's torch over the top of the ring while the rest of them slipped through a tiny hole cut far from the entrance. Everyone dashed across the wide, moonlit firebreak to the trees beyond.

Dravek hid with Endrus behind a thick arrowwood bush, where he could see the trail if he peered through a small gap in the leaves. He carefully snuffed his own torch, ensuring that enough heat lay within its core to resurrect it.

The Descendants came, a dozen soldiers slinking on the trail from the river. They hacked at his fire ring with hatchets to create a hole wide enough for three or four men to walk abreast.

Dravek saw Daria standing behind a thick-trunked hickory. She gripped her bow as she watched the Descendants begin their invasion. He knew she was dying to let arrows fly into their flesh. But not a single Kalindon moved. Though the Ilion soldiers scanned the forest for lookouts, they saw no one. Dravek hoped it didn't make them suspicious, but rather confirmed their belief that Kalindos was a village of lazy, foolhardy drunkards.

Once the hole was complete, the Ilions advanced in full force, with no war cry, but trampling the soil so hard that the ground seemed to quake beneath Dravek's feet. Instead of their usual red-and-yellow uniforms, they wore dark brown shirts and trousers with no insignia or buttons, and their swords were sheathed at their sides. No part of them reflected the moonlight shining across the barren firebreak.

The troops kept coming, running in step. Dravek stopped counting the rows of four after he reached two hundred.

They would all die here.

Finally the entire battalion had passed into Kalindos. Ladek and Drenis were the first out of their hiding places. They uncovered one of several large wooden pieces of wall that had been buried under leaves around the fire ring. They carried it across the firebreak and heaved it vertical to block the opening. As they held it in place, four other Kalindons tied it, sealing the ring.

The Descendants were trapped.

With a silent prayer to Snake, Dravek reignited his torch. It seemed as bright as the sun in the darkness. Instinctively he wanted to shield it from the eyes of the Ilions, but the Kalindons had thickened the fire ring so that no one could see through it.

Six Wolves gathered around him. They lit their torches from his, then took off, three in each direction. Their speed and stamina would place them around the circle in less than five minutes, and their stealthy footsteps would raise no alarm.

Dravek began to count under his breath, knowing the torch-bearing Wolves were doing the same. When they reached three hundred, they all would light the ring.

One hundred.

Ladek had predicted that when the order came to retreat, the soldiers would head in the direction from which they'd come, toward the river and their ships, rather than take off on an unfamiliar path. So most of the archers had been positioned here, near the Descendants' original entrance.

Two hundred.

Adrek ran up with his longbow. Dravek lit his extra torch and handed it to the Cougar. "Burn it all."

Adrek sprinted to the deer blind perched in a hemlock tree just outside the firebreak. A cache of arrows waited for him there, their tips soaked in flammable pine pitch.

Three hundred.

Dravek stepped across the rocky trench and lowered his torch to the wall. The dry wood sparked and smoked, and just as he'd hoped, the wind blew generously. The ring was ablaze.

He jammed the unlit end of the torch between two of the rocks in the trench, then moved back into the firebreak, where he could feel it all.

Dravek closed his eyes. For the first time in over a year, he stoked a fire with something other than lust. He wouldn't use thoughts of Sura to vaporize and kill.

Instead he thought of how they'd murdered her mate and his parents, set the windows and doors ablaze so even the children couldn't escape, how they'd left Sura with scars inside and out.

Rage made his blood pulse hot through his veins. He turned its rhythm into fire.

His inner vision showed him the arc of Adrek's first arrow. It stopped midtrajectory, caught in a treetop. Dravek pushed it, and the tree burst as if it had been struck by lightning.

Kalindos was burning. He took a deep breath to counter the crushing feeling in his chest. Better that their home disappear, better it rise in sparks and ashes than fall into the hands of tyrants.

"You'll never take us," he whispered.

He stretched out his hands, feeling each separate blaze around the circle, drawing them together into one strong beast. He had only to feed it.

Within the ring, soldiers yelled to one another, their voices charged with fear and anger. But not pain. Not yet.

A house exploded. Dravek put his hands to his face, slippery with sweat. By now someone had died because of him, maybe several people. He was no better than his father.

The fire stretched into the distance, curving as the Wolves ran around the circle, lighting more sections of the ring. The shouts of the Descendants came closer.

Dravek finally opened his eyes. Kalindos burned like a nighttime sun. The wind howled hot and hard, stoking the flames into a massive, roaring conflagration.

Now the soldiers screamed. Dravek covered his ears and backed away across the firebreak. Some had reached the ring, seeking the entrance that no longer existed. A few tried to climb over in panic. One made it as far as the top of the wall before Endrus shot him in the neck.

The Descendants spread out, searching for a safe place to climb. A group of them shouted ahead to his left. He cursed as he realized the ring in that section was burning too fast. Soon it would crumble and leave a gap, and they would all pour through.

The wind shifted, wafting the smoke his way. Even if the archers could hear him over the roaring flames, they could no longer see their targets. It was up to him.

Dravek knelt in the dirt, closed his eyes and fired.

The flames streamed from the wall and enveloped the soldiers. They ran and fell, burning. He shrieked with them.

There would be more. They would find another hole.

Get up, a voice inside him ordered.

He rose and staggered around the burning circle, firing again and again as the desperate soldiers tried to break through.

They raped your mother, the voice reminded him. *They killed your grandfather. Now they're killing you.*

If he survived this night, he'd be dead inside. He could feel his soul crumble to ashes like the wall in front of him.

A pain spiked his chest, and he realized how short and rapid his breath had become. The fire was devouring the air and replacing it with soot.

He turned to warn the others, but his knees gave way and he found himself on the ground. The air here was cooler, sweeter, and he wanted to curl up on the dirt and go to sleep, where he'd never hear the screams again.

A hand seized the back of his shirt collar. "Let's go!" Daria yelled. "Ladek gave the retreat order."

"Not yet." He gave a deep, hacking cough. "Some might escape."

"No one's getting out of there unless they learn to fly. Now get up!"

He placed a foot under himself but couldn't rise. "Where's the rest of our squad?"

"Endrus has my father right behind you. We need to get to the rendezvous point together." Daria knelt beside him, her face smeared in soot, blurring in his vision. "Hold still and don't fight me."

She jerked him to his feet, then bent and grabbed him around the hips. Then she stood, lifting him over her shoulder. The world tipped, and he yelped. She secured his arm around her neck and began to run. He saw nothing but Daria's boot heels and the ground passing beneath him as he slipped into a semiconscious fog.

When Daria finally set him down, he opened his eyes to see they were at the rendezvous point, on the forested trail to Tiros. He sat up, head throbbing. The night filled with the sounds of coughing, groaning and vomiting. Through the trees, more than a mile away, Kalindos burned.

Elora sponged his face with cool water. "Can you speak?"

He choked out a hoarse "Yes," then asked her, "Did we all get out safe?"

"So far." She put a hand on his shoulder. "Adrek's in bad shape, but I think he'll make it. Endrus, I can't say. If I'd been beside them at the fire, I could've stopped it, but the heat and smoke—"

"Where are they?"

Elora helped him stand and led him over to where Adrek and Endrus lay side by side on stretchers. Daria knelt between them, holding one hand of each. Dravek collapsed to sit beside her.

"We did it," she whispered to the Cougar men. "We got every one." She kissed her father's hand. "They'll never hurt us again."

Adrek's gaze wandered to meet hers. He opened his mouth.

Elora touched the side of his head. "Don't try to speak."

Endrus stared up at the night sky, chest heaving in short, liquidy breaths, face contorted in agony. Elora knelt beside him and chanted, filling his torso with a white light. It was only a painkilling spell, Dravek knew. He couldn't be healed.

The Cougar's face relaxed in response to Elora's touch, but as the minutes went by, his breaths became shallower, and Dravek found himself holding each of his own breaths until the next time Endrus's chest rose and fell.

Finally Endrus breathed no more. Daria let out a long, choking sob. Dravek touched her shoulder, knowing she might lash out. Instead she wrapped her arms around his neck as she cried.

"No…" Adrek groaned in grief for his friend, his own breath harsh and ragged.

One by one, the other Kalindons came and knelt by Endrus's head, laying their hands on his hair or his shoulders as they whispered prayers.

Finally Elora tugged Endrus's blanket to cover his face. "We'll take him with us and have his funeral when we reach the others in the mountains."

When they made camp that night, Daria came to Dravek as he stood guard near Endrus's body.

"Father's doing better," she said.

"Thanks to Endrus. Didn't you say he carried Adrek out of the fire?"

She nodded. "Elora said Endrus died because he was first phase. His body just couldn't handle it."

"You're only first phase."

"I didn't take nearly as much smoke as they did." She put her hands in her pockets. "Why should we have to have children to make us strong? It's not fair."

He shook his head. He'd given up trying to fathom the Spirits' ways.

"Thank you for saving my life," he told his sister.

"Oh, good, you didn't forget." She sat beside him, her boots shifting the dry leaves. "Are you going back to Asermos?"

"After Endrus's funeral. I have to find Lycas." *And Sura*, he didn't add out loud.

"I'm going with you."

"Lycas can always use more archers." He paused. "Did you kill anyone in that battle?"

"Wasn't much of a battle." She hunched her shoulders. "We roasted them like pheasants. The ones I shot were already on fire, so it's hard to say what killed them."

He wiped his nose, where the acrid scent of burning flesh seemed to linger. "I wonder what the Ilions will do now."

"I don't know," she said, "but whatever it is, they'll have a thousand fewer men to do it with."

11

Kirisian Mountains

In the hour before sunrise, Lycas sat inside his tent at the guerrilla headquarters, examining the Asermon map in the lantern light. Only two vineyards remained unburned, but they were closest to the village itself and therefore the most dangerous to attack.

Lycas heard the heavy, uneven footsteps of Medus approaching his tent. Though at fifty-five, the Badger man was as strong and fierce as ever, his time in the Ilion prison had left him with a noticeable limp.

"Come in," he said, before Medus announced himself.

"Morning." The brawny man swept aside the flap. "You asked to see me?"

Medus's position as Asermon police chief and his years in the village's resistance—not to mention the time he spent working with the Ilions when they first arrived—gave Lycas insights he'd be hard-pressed to find elsewhere. He'd made the Badger his executive officer over the Kirisian Mountain troops, which now numbered in the hundreds. Each company of a hundred men was authorized to independently carry out attacks on Asermon targets of opportunity. Little by little, they were pressing in on his home village.

Without preliminaries, Lycas announced, "I'm gathering the Kirisian battalion for an all-out assault on the hamlet."

"Hmm." Medus rubbed his considerable growth of gray-and-blond stubble. "It's awfully close to Asermos. They could send reinforcements from the garrison."

"Not if Feras distracts them with an attack of his own." He held up a sealed parchment. "As I'm ordering him to do."

The Badger's eyes gleamed in the lantern light. "Sounds like we're entering the final phase at last."

"My hand is being forced." Lycas crossed the tent to the wall that held the map of Asermos, on which the hamlet was outlined in red. "My scouts tell me they're moving our people inside. Our sympathizers from the outlying farms, the ones who've given us food and supplies all these years. The Descendants are putting them in the hamlet, then giving their properties to Ilion settlers."

"They're stealing our farms out from under us?" Medus's hand crept over the thick club on his belt. "It's an outrage."

"It's genius." Lycas paced in front of the map. "They've taken our lifeline. We still have the moral support of the population, but they can't give us logistical support when they're penned up in the hamlet. We'll have to start raiding farms to feed our troops, which hurts our reputation as friends of the people."

"Can these Asermons leave the hamlet if they want?"

"No." Lycas picked up the latest intelligence briefing from the scouts. "Reports indicate that the relocation is meant to be permanent. The hamlet is basically a small, fenced-in village. The residents have adequate food, decent housing—even jobs. They have everything but their homes and their freedom."

"For how long?" Medus asked.

"Until the Ilions have beaten us."

Medus scoffed. "They're delusional. We're on the verge of winning."

"Maybe." He folded his arms and stared at the mark of the hamlet on the map. "But with a thousand hostages, the Ilions can demand our surrender."

"So when do we attack?" Medus asked.

"Within the week. One of my scouts should arrive soon with better plans of the hamlet—the layout, what time they change the guards, that sort of thing." He handed a stack of sealed orders to Medus. "See that these are sent right away. We need our battalion here, and Feras at the Asermon garrison, before it's too late."

"Yes, sir." Medus snatched the orders and walked out, his hurried pace nearly disguising his injury.

After a few silent moments, footsteps crunched outside, on the ridge overlooking the distant Asermon hill country below. Lycas recognized his daughter's slow, sullen gait, her boots scraping the rocky dust. She was no doubt pining over Dravek again. He'd barely been able to look at her since the incident in the hayloft, and when he had, her eyes had held no shame.

Vara spoke outside, near Sura.

"They say that war is ten percent terror and ninety percent boredom."

Sura harrumphed. "This is both at the same time."

The two women were conversing in what they must have thought were low voices, but he could hear them clearly.

"Dravek will be fine," Vara said. "His training over the last year has taught him control."

Lycas almost snorted. Dravek didn't look very controlled when he was tearing off Sura's clothes last week. Lycas's temples pounded at the memory.

"We're in love," Sura said. "I don't care who knows it." The volume of her voice rose, as if she knew Lycas were listening.

"I suspect I'm in a tiny minority, but I don't judge you." Vara sighed. "This world grants us so little joy, we should take it wherever we can get it, and in however small a dose."

Lycas rubbed away the tight spot in his chest. He couldn't remember the last time he'd shared joy of any kind with anyone.

"So you think we can be together?" Sura asked Vara.

"Not if you both want to keep your Spirit."

"What if that's just a silly superstition?"

"Maybe it's silly for the more common Animals. But the rare ones like us should spread our talents across the lands. After your apprenticeships, you and Dravek owe it to our people to move to different places that need Snakes. There's a practical reason behind all of the Spirits' decrees."

"I don't care about the practical reasons."

"Of course you don't. You're young and in love. But that doesn't change the fact that if you give in to your feelings, Snake could take back Her Aspect. Perhaps another Spirit would claim you."

Lycas shook his head. How could anyone consider changing Spirits? He would be nothing without Wolverine.

"What would you be," Sura said to Vara, "if you couldn't be a Snake?"

"Insane." Vara gave a laugh, which Sura echoed bitterly. "In any case," the older Snake said, "it's not a decision to make until after the war."

Sura snorted. "I've heard that phrase, 'after the war,' for ten years now. It's become nonsense, like saying, 'on top of the sky.'"

Lycas's gaze fell to the bottom of his tent's door, under which the first scarlet light of morning now shone. *I'm trying,* he thought. *I'll end this war, if I have to swamp the Asermon Valley with Ilion blood.*

"Look!" Sura cried.

Lycas heard Vara suck in a slow, horrified breath. "They did it. They really did it."

He shoved aside the door and stalked to the edge of the ridge, where the women stood, transfixed by a sight in the east.

A dark veil covered the horizon, shimmering brown and purple into the morning sky. The haze turned the sun's first rays to bright pink, and Lycas could look straight at the orb without squinting.

Kalindos burned.

Throughout the camp, others left their tents to gawk at the distant cloud. Two of Lycas's best Wolverines, Kalindon natives themselves, dropped to their knees and prayed silently together, faces contorted.

Lycas had expected to feel elation at this moment, knowing the enemy had been vanquished on a larger scale than ever, knowing that Ilios had begotten its own fate.

But dread slithered under his skin. Kalindos had just defeated itself. He had ordered it.

All at once his strength flowed from him. He stared at his hands, flexing his fingers as the power left their tips, coursed hot down his wrists and up into his shoulders, then down his body, all the way to his feet. As the power slunk away from his body, it left behind a cold, limp sensation he barely recognized.

Weakness.

Lycas raised his gaze to the sooty eastern sky. "No…"

"What's happening?" shouted one of the Kalindon Wolverines. "I can't feel my fingers."

Lycas saw them stare at their hands in bewilderment, as he had done a moment ago. Past them, another Wolverine staggered out of his tent, clutching at his chest.

Vara's voice came from behind him. "Lycas, what's wrong with the men?"

He tried to speak, to reassure everyone that it was just a momentary disturbance.

But the sudden void sucked out his breath, and he fell to his knees, unable to utter the terrible, world-ending truth.

Wolverine was dead.

For the first time in over a year, Rhia entered the Gray Valley. It looked as lifeless as she'd remembered it. The landscape had no color of its own, but was only a monochromatic reflection of the light shone upon it—now an unseen red sun.

The dead tree loomed as black and menacing as ever. She could swear it had grown.

She glanced behind her at the fog that led back to her world. She would never admit it out loud to Crow, but she harbored a secret fear of being trapped in the Gray Valley.

Rhia waited several moments for someone to appear, then

turned right and began to walk. She didn't like to travel to the left, toward the cave of the never-born. Crow had taught her that He'd reserved that place as a womblike haven for those who died before their birth. She understood that for them it continued the comforting presence of their mothers' bodies. But it still made her skin crawl.

"Nilik!" she called as she walked, her voice and steps echoing against the cliffs on either side. She searched the rocky facade for movement along the ridges, where disconsolate souls often lurked.

"I know you're not here," she whispered. Nilik had gone to his death willingly and for a purpose that meant the world to him.

But Marek had insisted she look. He'd slept little on their journey into the Kirisian Mountains to meet his fellow Kalindons. The impending attack on his village, coupled with the anniversary of their son's death, had turned his thoughts dark and obsessive. The newest Descendant atrocity had opened Marek's old wounds, memories of the things he'd done to keep Nilik alive.

Footsteps rattled the rocky soil behind her. Rhia stopped and closed her eyes. *Please don't let me be wrong. Please don't let it be my son.*

She turned. Sirin stood on the trail, looming over her, his skin and hair absorbing the dull red light around them. Only his pale blue eyes seemed alive.

He was almost close enough to touch—not that Rhia would try. She knew better.

She stepped back, away from his glowering face that held no forgiveness.

"Traitor," he whispered. "You put me here."

She kept her voice steady. "You died in battle, not because of what happened in that Asermon prison."

"One thing leads to another," he hissed. "The arm I broke in that tub cost me my life in the fight."

"You said it had healed."

"It shattered at the impact of the first sword." He held up his arm, which stretched whole and straight in this world. "I'd broken limbs before and had full use of them in less time than that."

"Lycas said Wolverine is weakening. Maybe that's why—"

"Weakening?" Sirin's eyes flashed. "You don't know the half of it." He grabbed her arm.

She bit back a scream at his touch. Cold snaked through her body as if her blood had turned to ice water.

Sirin dragged her down the trail, away from the dead tree and the fog. She focused on the sound of Corek's steady drumming, using it as an anchor to the real world.

They reached the top of a low ridge, where she could see into the distance. Sirin pointed to a remote, flat section of the Gray Valley.

"Do you see it?"

Rhia widened her eyes to take in the invisible sun's dim red light.

Stumbling across the wasteland was a low, hulking animal, one she'd never seen before. Its muzzle drooped and swayed as it moved. It lurched to a stop and lifted its head to peer around.

The creature had small round ears and a long furry tail. Light brown fur streaked its dark flanks. By its shape, it almost looked like a small bear.

She drew in a sharp breath. "Wolverine."

"He's dead." Sirin took her shoulders and turned her to the right. "He's not the only one."

Rhia's jaw dropped slowly, until she could feel the stale breeze curl down her throat.

In the other world, Corek's drum skipped a beat, then two beats. Then it pounded faster, calling her back.

She slipped out of Sirin's grip and ran.

Marek was screaming.

Rhia sat straight up, ears ringing from her husband's cry. Her head swam from the time in the Gray Valley and the heady scent of the thanapras herb they had to burn to get her there.

Jula's arms draped around Marek's shoulders as he rocked and keened. Corek set the drum aside and stared at Rhia, eyes round with fear.

Rhia crawled over to Marek in the darkness of the tent and found his hands, cold and trembling.

Marek's teeth chattered. "He's gone," he whispered. "Wolf's dead."

"I know." She slid her arm around Marek's shoulders. "I just saw Him. Wolverine and Cougar and Bear, too."

His head jerked. "Why?"

"I don't know." She swallowed hard, fighting a sense of doom. "I thought it was impossible. Spirits can't die."

"Do you believe now?" He spoke through gritted teeth. "They were weak before, during the last Collapse." Then he murmured to himself, "But They didn't die before the last Reawakening. How would They come back?"

She turned his chin to face her. "They can't die. They're eternal. There must be another explanation." What could kill a Spirit? And which Spirit was next?

Corek slid quietly out of the tent, Jula following with a sorrowful look back at her father. They left the tent flap open, letting in the early-morning light.

Rhia saw Corek grab Jula's arm. "Look at that," he said.

Jula let out a yelp.

Rhia and Marek scrambled out of the tent to see a rust-colored haze spread across the sky in front of the sunrise.

"Smoke," Marek whispered. "It's coming from Kalindos." His voice broke. "The Descendants came back." He turned to the tent and yanked the nearest peg out of the ground. "If we skip breakfast and don't stop to rest, we'll reach my people by midday. They'll need us." His hands shook as he folded the tent's fabric, slapping it together and finally rolling it into a sloppy bundle.

She kept her voice soft. "They're our people."

He was right about the needing, though. Once they met the Kalindons, she and Corek would no doubt preside over at least one funeral.

That morning, the sun passed in and out of shadow as Rhia and her family hiked along the trail. The distant cloud of smoke changed color and thickness as the wind shifted.

As Marek had hoped, they reached the Kalindons shortly after noon. Rhia found the strength in her exhausted limbs to dash the last few yards into her father's arms. It had been ten months since she'd seen him, when he'd traveled to Tiros for Nilik's memorial.

Tereus hugged her close. "I've missed you so much." He embraced Jula, then drew a deep sigh as he let her go. "You won't believe what's happened."

"We know," Rhia said. "The Ilions invaded Kalindos. From the smoke cloud, it looks like they burned it."

"I burned it," came a scratchy voice behind Tereus.

Dravek appeared, paler than Rhia had ever seen him, his hair cropped short again. He stepped closer, as if realizing they could barely hear him above the wind in the trees.

"Lycas ordered me to do it," he said, "but I was the one who lit the fires."

"You burned Kalindos?" Marek lunged at Dravek and seized the front of his shirt. "You burned my home?"

"It was my home, too." Dravek struggled to untwist Marek's hands from his collar. "I'm sorry."

"I'll make you sorry." He pulled back his fist.

"Marek, stop." Rhia grabbed his arm. "It's my brother's fault. Dravek was only following orders."

Marek shoved the Snake away, following him with a blood-shot glare. Rhia realized that the last time Kalindos had burned, thirty years ago, Marek's parents had perished.

"I don't understand," she said to Dravek. "Did you burn it to keep the Ilions from getting in?"

"No." He held her gaze. "We burned it to keep them from getting out."

Her knees felt weak, and she had to blink hard to keep her head from swimming. "You killed them?"

"A thousand men." He finally looked down. "It's why the Spirits died, the ones who were there with me."

"Did Snake die, too?" Jula asked him.

"No. Maybe She has lower standards for honorable warfare." Dravek scoffed and wiped his forehead. "But I think it was some-thing else. Drenis said—" He interrupted himself and addressed

Jula and Corek. "That's our second-phase Kalindon Wolverine." He glanced at the rest of them. "He said his Spirit had been weakening for a long time."

Rhia nodded. "Lycas mentioned it after the battle last year. He was accidentally shot because a Cougar or a Wolf missed their target. I thought it had gotten better since then."

"Because he'd reined in his bloodthirst," Marek said bitterly. "But Lycas couldn't resist the idea of so many Descendants in one place." He drew a heavy hand through his hair. "Wolf was already weakened by the occupation. The burning of Kalindos killed Him."

Tereus shook his head sadly. "Come, let's find you a space to sit and get you some food."

As Rhia passed Dravek, she saw his eyes turn dim and dispirited. No doubt the smoke inhalation had injured him, but she recognized that haunted look. Marek had worn it after the first time he'd taken a life. Some men weren't born to kill.

Up ahead, in a rocky clearing next to the mountain face, a funeral pyre had already been laid out. Rhia forced her legs to carry her forward.

Endrus lay upon the pyre. She clutched the wood, inhaling the oil that had been sprinkled upon it, and fought back tears.

Corek came to stand at her elbow. "Did you know him?"

"I last saw him when I was in prison in Asermos. He almost died there." She thought of her sister Alanka. Endrus had been one of her closest friends and even a mate for a short time. It would break her heart to hear he'd perished with her home village.

They held the funeral that afternoon, setting Endrus's pyre ablaze. Dravek used his remaining strength to stoke the fire when it sputtered from insufficient oil. Rhia chanted the prayers, then called the crows, and Corek followed her lead. Adrek wept the hardest, until his eyes were bright red from smoke and tears.

Rhia held in her own grief until after the crows departed. When she heard their calls fade into the distance, echoing off the mountainside, she turned away from the crowd and heaved great sobs for what her people had lost. Not just Endrus, or Nilik or the trees and homes that made up Kalindos.

They had lost themselves.

That night, during a restless sleep, Rhia dreamed of a box of fire.

She woke to discover she wasn't the only one.

12

Kirisian Mountains

Sura watched her father prepare to hide.

For three days he and his platoon had tried to retrain themselves to fight without magic. The stabs of the Bear and Wolverine weapons looked tentative, and the arrows of the Cougars and Wolves flew awry as often as they hit their targets. But even without magic, their skill and experience could give them victory against an equal number of Descendants.

Unfortunately they were always outnumbered.

So this morning, Lycas had sent messages ordering the entire battalion to retreat farther up into the hills. Sura hated the thought of sitting in the dry, barren mountains when Asermos was so close, and so close to liberation.

Dusk was creeping over the headquarters as the platoon

packed up everything but their tents and bedrolls. No one spoke above a whisper—exhaustion and defeat had stolen their spirits.

Sura stalked to her father's tent and swept aside the door, though she knew she was being insubordinate by walking in unannounced.

Lycas faced away from her as he stared at the Asermon map still pinned to his tent wall. He held his hands behind his back, his shoulders sunk into a slumped posture she'd never seen before.

"What?" he said.

The words stuck in her throat—or more precisely, in her brain, because she'd lost them.

"Uh…"

He turned quickly and scowled. "I thought you were Medus."

She sounded and smelled nothing like the Badger. But Lycas could no longer pick up her scent or recognize the distinctive fall of her steps.

"What do you want?" he asked her. "I'm busy packing. You should be, too."

She steeled her courage and stepped forward. "This is your answer to the loss of your Spirit? Run away and hide?"

"Until conditions improve."

"They won't." Her lips tightened for a moment before she could speak again. "Wolverine's not coming back."

"He left because I fought too hard. If we stop fighting—"

"He didn't leave, Lycas. He died."

His jaw muscles tensed. "When are you going to start calling me 'Father'?"

"When you start acting like one. When you can look at me without contempt."

"I didn't make you tear open your shirt for your Spirit-brother."

She gasped, as hard as if he'd slapped her.

"I know," he said. "You love him. As if that makes it right. As if that solves anything in this world."

He sounded bitter, petulant, nothing like the Lycas she knew. "Can you even hear yourself?"

"Not over the sound of your voice."

"You're acting like you're twelve."

He stopped, his scowl fading. "That's how old I was when Wolverine first spoke to me." He drew a dagger from his belt, a blade she recognized as one of his oldest. "He came to me first, in a dream. It was another year before my twin brother had the same vision. I don't know why He waited to call Nilo." He sighed. "Maybe Wolverine knew we'd never be happy apart."

It was true. Two decades after her uncle's death, her father still carried that void inside him.

He rubbed the left side of his chest, just under his heart. She thought she saw him wince.

"Are you all right?" Stupid question, she realized.

"I don't know." Lycas spoke more softly than she'd ever heard him. "I don't know what I am anymore." He let out a long breath and sat on his bed. "Except tired. You should get to sleep early tonight, too. We have a hard journey ahead of us tomorrow."

He set his elbows on his knees and ran his hands over his head. She heard him draw a breath between his teeth, as if in pain. Without Wolverine's inhuman strength, she realized, Lycas was feeling every ache of his forty-three years.

"We can't let Mother down," she said.

He stared at the floor. "She's survived this long. There were no Wasps at Kalindos, so she probably still has her powers. She'll think of something. Or someone else will think of something." He closed his eyes. "I'm all out of thoughts."

She felt her own eyes grow hot watching her father shrink into himself. How could she blame him for his despair? He'd spent half a lifetime fighting the Ilions, having nothing of his own but his Spirit, and now even that was gone.

The sound of a horse's hooves reached her ears. "It sounds like the messenger."

Lycas said nothing. A few moments later, Vara shouted his name from outside the tent. Still, he didn't move.

"In here," Sura called to her.

Her mentor swept through the tent door. "You need to read this," she said to Lycas. "It's urgent, from the Ilions."

"Read it to me." He rubbed his eyes. "I can't see so well anymore."

"Lycas—" Vara opened her mouth to say what Sura knew was a string of harsh words.

"Here." Sura brought the lantern over to her.

"Thank you." Vara drew in a quaking breath and began. "Dear Lycas. We know you're weakened. One of our prisoners, a second-phase Bear, died tonight from a beating he should have shaken off. We've tested the fortitude of our other prisoners and realized that your warrior Animals have lost their powers."

Sura gasped and looked at her father. His face frozen, he stared at Vara as she continued.

"If those who have taken up arms against us surrender now, we will spare the civilians of Asermos, Velekos, Tiros and Kalindos. Refuse our offer, and we will hunt down your people wherever they flee. Without magic, you'll be powerless to protect them. We will kill your men, then ship your women and children to Ilios."

Sura held back a groan of dismay. She tried to read the parchment over Vara's shoulder, but the Snake's hands were shaking so hard, the words blurred.

"As a token of our sincerity—" Vara stopped and swallowed hard "—tonight we shall have our vengeance for the massacre at Kalindos, and tomorrow at dawn we shall execute the mother of your child, Mali the Wasp."

Sura's feet went numb, and she forgot how to breathe.

Lycas sprang to their side so swiftly, Sura jumped back in surprise. He snatched the message out of Vara's hand and scanned it, eyes flashing from side to side.

"Death by drowning," he whispered. "In public."

Sura put her face in her hands, stifling a sob. It would work, even on a third-phase Wasp, even if it took hours. The grapeheads would crowd around to gawk at the bloated corpse of Sura's once-invincible mother.

She wanted to plead with her father not to let it happen, to ride in and fight to the death to release Mali and all the other prisoners. But he would have done it long ago if it weren't a suicide mission.

Lycas began to pace, and her heart lifted at his reborn energy, however frenetic.

"They'll call it all off—the execution and the retribution—if we surrender tonight." He glanced at them. "By 'we,' they mean the three of us, and the others who helped burn the vineyards." He let out a harsh curse and crumpled the letter in his fist. "This is what I get for not killing the soldiers guarding those farms.

Now they can identify us." He stopped and looked at Sura. "I'd surrender myself if it was the only way to stop this. But as long as I'm alive, I won't let them take you."

Her eyes softened as she looked up at him. "What do they mean by vengeance for Kalindos?"

Lycas studied the parchment again, rubbing the back of his neck. "Maybe they mean to burn Asermos or Velekos or Tiros. But those villages are far too big to surround. Kalindos had a built-in trap with that fire ring."

Sura looked at the map of Asermos on her father's otherwise empty wall. The town was far too sprawling to burn. The Ilions might choose a neighborhood, but even then, they had no way to trap the civilians inside.

Her gaze shifted to the outlying areas, to the two remaining vineyards they hadn't yet burned due to their proximity to the village. The largest was within sight of the hamlet the Ilions had built to house her people.

Her hands suddenly turned cold, the sensation spreading into her spine and down her legs.

She forced out the terrible truth.

"They're going to burn the hamlet."

Less than an hour later, just before sunset, Sura and the rest of the platoon were ready to go.

She waited next to her horse as Lycas inspected the troops. The soldiers and archers remained unusually quiet. Sura could smell the sour tang of fear on their breath.

Beside her, Vara grumbled as she adjusted the strap of her riding blanket. "It's a trap. The Ilions knew we'd figure it out and come riding in to save our people, undermanned. They'll have at least a hundred soldiers guarding that hamlet, ready to capture us the moment we arrive."

"What else would you suggest we do?" Sura said. "Run away?"

Vara frowned. "I didn't say we shouldn't attack. I'm only telling you what to expect."

Sura wished Dravek had returned in time to join them. On the other hand, she was glad he was missing what was surely a suicide mission.

She would have liked to say goodbye, though, and kiss him just once before she left this world.

Lycas mounted his horse, and the rest followed suit.

Sura's horse shifted beneath her, stepping to the side, no doubt feeding off the anxiety of his rider. She took a deep breath to calm them both. She'd never galloped into battle, but she'd galloped *away* from enough vineyards in the last two weeks to feel more confident of her ability to stay astride.

Lycas rode down the line on his favorite dark bay mare, the one with the white stripe on her face. His own face was smeared with dark green Wolverine war paint, and his long black hair flowed loose over his shoulders. Even without his powers, he was ten times as fearsome as most men.

He examined the line of thirty men and women—eight Wolverines, eight Bears, four Badgers, five Wolves, two Cougars, one Bat and Sura and Vara. When he got to the end, he rode back to the center and stopped.

After a long, silent moment, he said, "You feel alone inside yourselves. I know. I've felt the same way since Wolverine left."

Sura's chest tightened at the sadness in her father's voice.

He cleared his throat. "My brother died at the beginning of this war. I'll probably die before the end of it."

The platoon members murmured weak protests. Sura bit her lip and blinked to keep from crying. As much as she wanted them all to have a normal life, she couldn't imagine her father dwelling happily in peacetime. His wounds ran too deep.

Lycas continued. "We've all lost someone. A few of us have lost everyone." He nudged his horse to walk along the line. "But we are not alone." His voice strengthened. "Our Spirits have not abandoned us, any more than our fallen brothers and sisters have abandoned us. Crow can never take them away, as long as we remember them."

Sura's breath came faster as hope dared to spark within her. She looked at the rest of the platoon. Their backs straightened, and their hands curled around their weapons.

Lycas's voice boomed forth.

"Tonight we ride to Asermos, but we fight for Kalindos, for Tiros, for Velekos and all the lands in between. We are not four peoples but one." He stopped his horse in the center of the line. "We are the Reawakened."

The entire platoon shared a collective gasp. The back of Sura's neck tingled at the sound of the word. *Reawakened.*

"We are *not* the Reawakened because we have magic," Lycas said. "Magic didn't make us great warriors. We made each other great, through years of training and discipline. Nothing can take that from us. Nothing can take our will to fight for our people." He struck his fist against his chest. "The Spirits chose us, and when we stand as one, They live inside us."

Lycas urged the horse into a trot, up and down the line. His black hair mirrored the horse's flowing mane and tail as they moved.

"Dead or alive," he shouted, "the Spirits ride with us tonight.

They fight with us. And we fight for Them." He drew his longest dagger. "We fight for Wolf!"

"For Wolf!" the Wolves called.

"For Cougar!" He stabbed the dagger into the air.

"For Cougar!"

"For Bear!" he roared.

"For Bear!"

"For Wolverine!" Lycas stretched the end of the word into a war cry that held as much power as ever. The other Wolverines joined him, and every muscle in Sura's body trembled. For a moment, she doubted the Spirit had died at all.

She joined in, with everyone else, regardless of Animal, until the hills themselves seemed to quake. She cried out until her throat ached and her lungs felt like they would burst.

"To Asermos!" Lycas roared through the noise, and they rode as one.

Rhia groaned in dismay as she and the hundred-plus Kalindons approached Lycas's empty headquarters just after sunset. It looked as if it had been abandoned in haste—the tents stood open, and the campfires had been covered only enough to douse them, not conceal them.

"Maybe they've left for the hamlet," Tereus said as he dismounted with a sharp exhale. "Perhaps they had the dreams, too, or they found out about the burning some other way."

"They haven't been gone long," Dravek said. "I can still smell their horses."

Marek rode to the edge of the ridge and looked down into the valley. "You're right. The dust isn't even settled yet on the lower part of the trail. We can't be too far behind them."

Rhia bit her lip hard. If only they'd skipped one more meal, or gotten up an hour earlier that morning. After the entire camp of Kalindons had dreamed of the box of fire, Tereus had used his Swan powers of dream-speak to understand their meaning. The hamlet would burn, full of people.

Rhia and every other able-bodied Kalindon had ridden as fast as they could, to warn Lycas and save the hamlet. The terrain had been rough, and from here on in it would be easier traveling, except for the darkness.

"Let's light another torch," she said. "And keep riding."

Asermos

"To the water that delivers us from all vermin!"

Captain Addano held his wine goblet high to the hurrahs of the six guards. He took a tiny sip and smiled as they drank deeply of his offering.

Sergeant Kiro swallowed, then let out a gasp. "Sir, this is the best wine I've tasted all year."

"A special vintage for a special occasion." He held up the empty bottles, one in each hand. "Tonight we celebrate the end of the plague known as Mali the Wasp. As a token of my appreciation to our friend the drowning tub, I offer it the rest of my glass." With a dramatic flourish, he poured the red liquid into the empty tub.

The guards hooted and applauded. "I would've finished it for you," said one, laughing. "As a favor, of course."

"A gracious offer, but I want Mali's last watery breath to be tinged with the gift of Evius." He bowed to the cheers, his head already floating. "Now hurry and finish. If General Lino finds out I've let you drink on duty, I'll be next in line for execution."

As they quaffed the contents of their goblets, he went to sit at his desk so that he could finish his letter, and so that none of them would fall on him when they collapsed.

It took less than ten seconds for all six to topple. The last one, Sergeant Kiro, gave Addano a bewildered gaze as he realized what had happened.

"Sir…why?" he choked before the drug stole his consciousness and perhaps his life.

"It's all in the letter." Addano started to sign the bottom of the parchment. The letters of his rank and first name appeared ragged, clearly written by a trembling hand. He took a deep breath and let it out slowly. Then he spent his last shred of concentration on smoothing the signature of his last name. He wanted to leave no doubt as to his certitude.

He put down his pen, then placed the letter in the center of his desk. As an afterthought, he set stone paperweights at two of the corners so it wouldn't blow away. He noticed how slow and deliberate his movements had become—an effect of the narcotic in his small sip of wine. Perfect.

Humming the Ilion national anthem, Addano pulled a pair of women's boots from his bottom drawer. He lifted the keys from his desk, made his way through the maze of unconscious guards, and went downstairs to the women's prison.

"Put these on." He tossed the boots to Mali as he entered the cell block.

"A bit early, isn't it?" She sprang to her feet as if she were going to a party. "What about all my admirers? You're not snuffing me in secret like you did Sirin, are you?" She clucked her tongue. "And after I sent written invitations."

He lifted the keys on the ring hooked to his belt. "See these? They're yours."

"Mmm-hmm. And which part of you do I have to suck before you tell me it's a joke?"

"It's not a joke, and I wouldn't put anything in your mouth that I wanted to remain attached to my body."

She glanced into the next cell, where Berilla the Hawk lay drugged and silent, as always.

"You're setting me up, aren't you?" Her gaze flicked past him. "Where are the guards?"

"Upstairs asleep, possibly forever." He pulled the bag of opium powder from his vest pocket and shook it next to his head. "I drugged their wine."

She gave him a sideways look, still skeptical. "Looks like you had a few sips yourself."

"I did, just one." He tossed the bag over his shoulder. "That way it won't hurt so much when you kill me."

Mali's face froze. "What do you mean?"

"If you escape, it'll be my fault, whether they know it's on purpose or not. But if you kill me, I can keep some small scrap of honor. Besides—" He looked at the ceiling. "Maybe when I'm dead, I won't see their faces anymore."

"You mean the guards?"

"Or hear their screams."

"Oh. You mean us." Without looking away from him, she crouched down and slid the boots through the bars.

"Take the other prisoners and go," he said. "You can still save your people."

"What people? Where?" She stuffed her feet into the boots.

"They're burning the hamlet tonight with a thousand Asermon natives inside."

She jerked the bootlaces to tighten them. "Where is it?"

"Take the road toward Tiros about fifteen miles, then look to the east. And hurry." He held out the key ring and stepped closer to the bars so she could see. "This small one is for the weapons closet on the first floor, and the ones with the—"

"Thank you." Her hands flashed between the bars. One snatched the keys while the other grabbed the back of Addano's head.

Steel slammed his forehead. A sharp pain exploded through his skull. His knees gave way, and he collapsed. Red and yellow splashed across his vision, then all turned to black.

Addano felt his leg twitch and kick, like that of his boyhood dog when its back was scratched. His fingers spasmed, nails scraping the stone floor. Something hard and cold pushed against him. His body was rolled over like a sack of flour.

The pain faded. He waited for Xenia to gather him up in Her dark robes and carry him to the afterlife.

She came, in the form of a giant black bird whose eyes glowed like the stars in winter.

You're not what I expected, he thought to the bird, just before it enveloped him in violet light.

Asermon Valley

The arrow was coming loose.

As Lycas rode through the night toward the Asermon Valley, he pretended he didn't feel the two-inch piece of wood embedded in his chest, chafing the scar tissue that had held it in place and protected him for the last year. Jolts of pain jabbed his core with every slam of his horse's hooves, but his face and posture showed no hint. If his troops knew that every twitch of muscle brought their leader closer to death, it would destroy their morale. Right now, their morale was all they had.

He tried not to obsess over it, tried to focus on the tactics they would use to attack the hamlet, tried to envision the elements of the different scenarios they might face—the number of enemy combatants, the situation of the civilians, the size of the blaze.

But his mind shifted relentlessly, to the night he'd received the wound, at the Battle of Velekos, from an accidental shot of his own archer. He should have pulled it out right away, before his body became too hard and solid to extract it without risky surgery. He'd known that Wolverine could die, that one day his own flesh could turn as soft as the day he was born.

But denial and determination had kept him going this long. Why stop now?

They were skirting one of the last two remaining vineyards when Vara shouted his name. He slowed his horse so she could ride up beside him.

"They've set the fire, I can feel it." Her voice was taut with tension.

"How far away?"

"A mile or two. We should see it just over the next hill."

He signaled for the troops to increase their speed from a trot to a slow canter. He wanted to rush in at a full gallop, but riding in the dark was treacherous, especially since the Cougars could no longer lead with their night vision. A horse could step in a hole and break a leg, throwing its rider and bringing down the whole line.

They reached the top of the hill and came to a halt. The distant fire leaped out of the darkness like a thousand meteors falling at once.

Yorgas the Bat joined Lycas. "Sir, the people are screaming. I hear women and children."

Lycas's pulse raged in his temple. He didn't want to believe the Ilions would roast a thousand civilians, but the ears of a Bat never lied.

Vara rode up and stopped on the other side of him. "I have an idea to help us overcome the odds." She gestured to Sura behind them. "Let her handle the fire. I'll make the soldiers forget why they're there."

He furrowed his brow. "Wipe their memories? Doesn't that take time?"

"Not when I don't bother with finesse." She leaned in and lowered her voice. "I can burn all their memories in a moment. They won't remember who they are, much less what they're fighting for."

He turned on his riding blanket to look straight at Sura. "It'll be the biggest fire you've ever controlled. You can do this alone?"

"I won't just control it." Sura's strong, steady gaze held his. "I'll extinguish it."

"How?"

"Let me worry about that."

He saw his own despair and determination reflected in her ink-black eyes. Like him, she didn't plan to survive.

He shook his head. "Sura, I can't let you—"

"I'll help her," Vara told him, "as soon as the troops have been subdued." She held up her palm to Sura. "Wait until I get there before you take the fire inside you."

"Sir," Yorgas said suddenly. "I hear fighting."

Had one of Lycas's other platoons already arrived? Impossible—there hadn't been time for them to receive the news, prepare to fight and then travel to the hamlet.

Lycas didn't care. No matter who rose to assist or oppose him, it would be his last battle. "Let's get closer."

When they were less than a quarter-mile from the hamlet, Lycas saw that the fire was contained within the fence, which remained intact. Cries of panic and shrieks of pain came from the other side. From here he could see no gate, no way out.

About a hundred Ilion soldiers, some on horseback, were

clustered outside the eastern end of the hamlet. As Yorgas had heard, they were struggling with another group of fighters, near a gate that appeared locked and barred. The Descendant soldiers outnumbered their opponents at least four-to-one.

But no longer.

He signaled his troupe to halt, and turned to face them. "We circle around to approach them from the east, drawing them away from the hamlet." He handed his torch to Medus. "Stay here with Sura. When the soldiers move away, take her to the gate. Defend her with your life."

"Yes, sir."

Lycas looked at his daughter one last time. "Good luck."

"You, too." They stared at each other for a long moment, then she closed her mouth.

He took a deep breath, pain piercing his chest, and began the Wolverine war cry. The others joined in, until the ground seemed to shake beneath their horses' hooves. Then they rode, streaming down the hill.

The Ilions turned his way, their red-and-yellow uniforms illuminated by the flames that now reached higher than the hamlet fence.

"Remember Kalindos!" the Ilions shouted as one, and rushed at Lycas's troops.

Instead of meeting them head-on, Lycas and his fighters rode to the left, down the grassy slope away from the hamlet. Most of the Ilion soldiers followed, no doubt eager to vanquish their prime enemy now that he was weak.

A tall Descendant on horseback charged Lycas, who twisted his body and barely avoided the slash of sword. Lycas's horse reared in panic, unaccustomed to the chaos of battle.

Another Ilion came at him, and Lycas rolled off his mount to escape.

His body slammed the ground. The arrow stabbed him from within.

Lycas wanted to scream in pain, but he had no breath to make a noise. He struggled to get his feet under him.

A heavy weight tackled him from behind, driving his face into the mud. A hand grabbed his hair and jerked back his head. A low voice growled in his ear.

"It's your turn, beast." A blade touched his throat.

Roaring in pain and rage, Lycas shoved his arms and knees against the ground. He flipped over on his back, crushing his attacker beneath him. The man's breath whooshed from his lungs.

Lycas grabbed the gloved hand that held the knife. He squeezed, but no bones shattered in his grip. The blade came closer to his neck.

"He's mine!" An Ilion swordsman rushed them, pointing his weapon at Lycas's gut. Lycas arched his back and launched a desperate kick. The toe of his boot landed in the groin of the oncoming soldier. The man screeched and doubled over, still holding his sword.

"Lycas, close your eyes."

The commanding voice belonged to Vara. He obeyed.

Suddenly the soldier holding him loosened his grasp. Lycas rolled to his feet. He seized the soldier he'd kicked, then twisted their bodies around so that he had him in a headlock facing Vara. Lycas averted his eyes.

The Snake woman stepped closer. Lycas's would-be attacker went limp in his arms.

He dropped him and wrenched the sword from his hand. The

Ilion stared up at him with bewilderment. Lycas resisted the urge to end the man's confusion with a jab to the heart.

"Behind you!" Vara shrieked.

Lycas spun, lifting the sword. It met another blade arcing down toward his head. The steel-on-steel clash reverberated throughout his body. The Descendant bore down hard, stronger than any Lycas had ever fought. But he knew that his opponents hadn't gained strength; he had lost it.

In one desperate motion, he shoved the Descendant back and made a flailing slash with his sword. A red ribbon opened across the front of the man's neck, just above his leather chest armor. He put his hands to his wound. The blood oozed through his fingers, and he collapsed.

Lycas stopped, panting, and whipped his gaze around, looking for more attackers. His fighters had formed a circle around him and Vara. Without it, he realized, the Ilions would have swarmed him, and he would already be dead.

Amid the melee, Ilion soldiers wandered, either unarmed or with their weapons hanging loose at their sides. They jerked their heads back and forth, eyes wide with panic and confusion. Vara's victims.

A Descendant broke through and rushed at Lycas, roaring and raising his sword. Lycas tried to lift his own sword, but a blinding pain pierced his chest. He dropped the weapon and ducked into a lunging tackle. He knocked the man off his feet and landed on top of him. As they hit the ground, the arrow stabbed Lycas's flesh again, stealing his breath.

"Hold him," Vara said.

Unable to raise his left arm, Lycas jammed his right one against the soldier's throat. The man's eyes bulged, then lit up, reflecting the golden glow of Vara's gaze. Lycas felt him slump beneath him.

Cold sweat covered Lycas's body, and he knew the end was approaching. He struggled to his feet, where he swayed, light-headed.

Vara gave a gurgling cry. He spun to see her standing rigid, eyes wide.

"No."

There was a sucking sound, of steel exiting flesh, as an Ilion yanked his sword out of Vara's back. She fell to the earth and landed on her side. Her dark gaze met Lycas's before turning blank.

"Vara!" Lycas drew a dagger and leaped upon the soldier, roaring in grief and rage. They wrestled each other to the ground, weapons flying from their grips. The soldier rolled on top and wound his fingers around Lycas's neck.

Black spots filled his vision. Instinct told him to fight off his attacker, but experience reminded him it wouldn't work. He forced his hands down, feeling for a vulnerable spot. The soldier's chest armor had ridden up, leaving the bottom of his torso exposed. As his sight dimmed, Lycas's right hand slid to his dagger belt and unclasped the sheath of his longest blade. With a desperate lurch of his hips, he shifted the Descendant's weight so he could withdraw the knife. Then he shoved it deep inside the man's abdomen.

The soldier jerked and spasmed, his grip on Lycas's neck tightening, then releasing. He coughed, and a spurt of blood shot from his mouth, drenching Lycas's face with hot, coppery-tasting liquid.

Breath rushed into Lycas's right lung, the only one that still worked. His strength at an end, he struggled to toss off the soldier's deadweight. Suddenly the man disappeared, yanked backward by an unseen hand.

Above him, a woman spoke Lycas's name in a voice that would burn glass.

Mali.

He choked a breath in and out.

She held out a hand. "For Spirits' sake, get up."

Though he would've thought it impossible a few moments ago, he rolled onto his hands and knees, and finally his feet. The pain inhabited every inch of his body, but he couldn't accept her offer of help.

He wiped the blood from his face with his right arm and spat the remnants from his mouth. "How'd you get out of prison?"

"Killed someone." She glanced past him. "Look out."

Lycas pivoted in time to duck a blow from an approaching Ilion. He drew another dagger from his belt and plunged it into the man's gut, up under the rib cage until he felt the tip pierce the heart.

In his death throes, the soldier slammed Lycas's left side with the hilt of his sword.

The arrow inside him jarred loose at last. As he let the dying soldier drop, he doubled over from the spike of pain.

Beside him, someone gave a gurgling grunt. He looked to see another Ilion, sword raised, poised to slice Lycas in half. Or he would have been, had Mali not jammed her own short sword into his neck.

Lycas stepped back from the gush of blood. "Thank you."

"Hah." She glared at him. "You owe me."

More than you could ever know, he thought as they turned as one toward the next onslaught of Ilions.

For the first time in their lives, Mali and Lycas fought side by side, and here in his final battle, he felt as if he'd come home.

Sura was born for this moment.

She strode toward the gate, torch in hand. Though Medus the Badger fended off attackers beside her, and injured Ilions and Asermons crawled over her path, she was alone with the fire. If she and the flames devoured each other, as in her Bestowing vision, then so be it.

The fence was still intact—no doubt it had been left unburned by the Ilions to trap the people. When she reached the gate, she could hear their cries, hear them banging on the wooden surface, hear the thuds of those who tried to leap over the fence. It was too high even for a third-phase Squirrel, and slanted inward at the top.

"Stand back now!" she called through the tiny gap between the fence and the gate. "This is Mali's daughter, Sura, from Asermos. I'm trying to let you out."

She retreated several paces, the mud under her feet slick with blood. Then she held up the torch, closed her eyes and hurled its heat at the lock.

The wood around the latch exploded into thousands of sparks, and the door swung open. She leaped aside just in time to avoid being trampled. Her ears stung from the sound of the screams, and the air was pungent with sweat, blood and fear.

A middle-aged man holding a small boy passed her. She grabbed his arm. "Are people still trapped in the buildings?"

"Yes." He panted and coughed. "Hundreds, maybe."

She saw a carved wooden otter around his neck. "Take this." She handed him her torch. "Find the other Otters and set up a healer's area."

When he was gone, she stood beside the fence opening, arms over her head to keep the sparks from her face, waiting for the flood of fleeing people to pause so she could enter. All she needed was one moment, one person to hesitate.

From the corner of her eye, she saw the remains of a skirmish near the gate, with maybe a dozen fighters. Her father had led most of the Ilion soldiers down the hill. She hoped he lived to bury whatever was left of her after tonight.

Inside the gate, a woman bent down to pick up her child. Sura squeezed through, leaping over the woman's outstretched arms and into the hamlet.

Her lungs ached as she ran past the burning homes and shops, but she let the rhythm of her steps and the rush of hot wind lull her into a trance. Nothing stood between her and the fire. Nothing ever would.

She reached the hamlet's central square. Here, she could feel the blaze as one great creature.

The fire rose around her, feasting on wood and flesh and hair. She wanted to take it in but remembered Vara's command to wait for her.

Children screamed in a house to her left. Sura took one last look over her shoulder for her mentor, then shut her eyes to the orange and yellow glow. She could wait no longer.

Sura called upon Snake and breathed in the flames.

The house stopped burning, hissing as though it had been doused in cold water. Smoke wisped from one corner of the roof, but she staunched that last bit of heat, as well.

"I will devour you," she said, and breathed in again.

A house across the street fell to instant smolder, fading from brightest white to darkest black in Sura's inner vision.

"You will not have us."

The flames slid into her as easily as air, filling her belly with pulsing, rising, swirling heat. She wanted to laugh. This was her gift; this was her destiny.

The next breath came hotter, and slower. She began to feel full, as if the fire would burst out of her if she took too much.

No. If she let it loose, it would kill again. She swallowed hard, and a searing pain shot through her body. There was nowhere to put this heat—no lakes or rivers nearby, and the surrounding land was too dry and held too much fuel for her to shove it into the soil.

"Take me," she said. "Become me."

She raised her palms and drew the heat through her finger-tips, through the pulse of her wrists.

Around her, flames turned to cinders. Cinders turned to ashes. The world cooled as she sucked in the fire through every pore.

Until this moment, she hadn't understood the full reach of her powers. The child she'd borne had given her strength, and now she would give it back the only way she could. After this defeat, the Ilions would retreat in shame, and Malia would grow up in a land of freedom. She would never have to lower her gaze as she walked down the street, never see the people she loved beaten and burned.

Malia would never have to do anything like this.

Sura took one last deep breath, and felt herself turn to flame.

Rhia scrambled through the gate with Dravek, Elora and Marek as the straggling residents limped and crawled from the burning hamlet. The fire's fumes and the stench of charred flesh stung her nose. She pressed a vinegar-soaked cloth to her face and made her way through the flaming wreckage, searching for survivors.

"Sura!" Dravek shouted. He scanned the hamlet, but Rhia saw few people stirring. She feared that everyone who could escape already had.

In the distance, a woman screamed. Without looking back, Dravek dashed toward the center of the hamlet.

"My baby…" a woman cried from Rhia's left. "No…"

Marek ran toward the voice. Rhia and Elora followed as fast as they could.

A woman knelt, wailing and keening, at the end of the walkway of a burning house, rocking a small child whose arms were draped around her neck.

But as Rhia came closer, the little girl stirred and looked up at them, her eyes wet and tinged with red. "Mama, someone's here."

Elora rushed to kneel beside the woman. "It's all right. See, your baby's fine."

"In there!" The mother pointed to the house, then grabbed Marek's arm. "My boy's upstairs."

Rhia looked up at the second floor, which was half in flames, then at Marek. He couldn't be thinking of…

He was already gone. Before she could shout to bring him back, Marek was through the front door, which now hung by a single hinge.

"Marek, no!" She lurched forward, but Elora grabbed her arm in a strong grip.

Rhia stared at the house, watching the wooden walls shift and burn. Inside, a child screamed, and the woman at Rhia's feet shuddered and moaned.

She counted the moments. When she reached two minutes since Marek had entered, she forced herself to turn away. People needed her, and she could do nothing for Marek until he returned. If he returned.

Crow's wings slammed her mind from every direction, and she blinked back the smoke- and grief-induced tears. How had it come to this, Ilions burning innocent civilians? They would claim it revenge for Kalindos, but women and children had not died there; only soldiers who would have captured and sold them.

She put her face in her hands. The earth itself seemed to cry out for peace at any cost.

But perhaps peace still had a higher price than victory. After tonight, no Asermon would submit to Ilion rule. They would fight on until the last Descendant died or sailed for home.

A great ripping noise came from the house behind her. She whirled to see the top floor caving in, the roof collapsing under its own weight.

It teetered, burning, ready to fall.

On Marek.

Sura burned. Her clothes dropped from her body in charred scraps that tumbled away in the wind.

The flames licked her skin from the inside out. They wanted their freedom. They couldn't have it.

"You're mine," she murmured.

Her skin cracked and peeled, and she screamed in agony, feeling her resolve weaken. Any moment she would release the blaze back into the village, and they would all die.

"Sura!"

She opened her eyes to see Dravek staring down at her. Her vision blurred with tears that turned to steam.

"You came." She smiled through her pain, which seemed to fade under his gaze.

She took another breath to speak. The heat rushed in again, searing every inch of her. She screamed again and wondered if there could be a more excruciating way to die.

Dravek stepped close to her, and she saw her own flame reflected in his black eyes.

"Don't touch me!" she pleaded, though she wanted more than anything to feel his hands on her once more.

"Give me the heat. Like we practiced, remember?"

"It's too much." She tried to move away, but her legs shrieked at the slightest twitch of muscle. "I'll kill you."

"I don't care." He came close enough to touch. "I'd die for you, Sura."

"Please go." Another breath, and she would burst. She felt her eyes begin to swell.

Dravek lowered his head to hers. "Give me the heat."

He kissed her. The fire flared from her body to his, which seized as he groaned in pain.

Sura pushed against him, trying to break away. She wouldn't take him to the Other Side with her. He had to live to see his son grow up, live to see the end of this war.

Then she felt the heat rush out of him as quickly as it had left her. It was going somewhere else, somewhere safe.

She yielded then, melding her body to his and letting him take it all. Dravek pulled her close, kissing her harder. Her body shuddered again and again, cooling, pulling her back from the brink of death.

Sura captured more flames from the hamlet, starting with the homes near the gate. She pulled in all the heat, giving it to Dravek with her kiss, her hands and her body. His fingers tangled in the loose strands of hair flying around her face, then his touch traveled over her shoulder and down her back, caressing the scars from a distant memory.

Unlike that fire, this one would not wound her. This fire was at their command, and they would devour it.

A great roar came from behind Rhia, like a thousand angry cougars. She spun toward the gate to see the blaze rushing her way.

"Get down!" She pulled Elora to the ground just as the flames passed in a red-orange curtain.

She looked up from the pile of ashes she'd landed in. The fire was streaming from the other end of the town, as well, as if sucked out of the houses by an enormous breath.

The flames converged in the center of the hamlet, transforming into a giant white spark like a bolt of lightning. It expanded, pulsing and glowing.

Rhia shaded her eyes and held her breath. The white pillar seemed to want to explode and fill the sky, envelop every thing, living and dead. She wanted to run but could only stare, even as it blinded her.

The light shimmered, sparked once more, then shrank to a tiny point. It flickered out.

"What was that?" said the woman with the child.

"Sura." Rhia's heart twisted. Her niece had taken the heat of the entire hamlet into herself. If Dravek had reached her in time, he had been consumed, as well.

Rhia sat up, her body heavy with grief. She shifted to look at the house Marek had entered. Though no longer burning, the roof still teetered.

She screamed his name as the roof collapsed.

Locked in the desperate kiss, Sura squeezed her eyes shut and searched for flames, even the smallest smoldering flickers that could reignite and consume a room, a house, a child.

Nothing. They had won.

Dravek eased his mouth back an inch from hers. They gazed at each other for a long moment, eyes burning, breath coming hard.

Then he kissed her again, and again, and she let the heat build within her, for its source was no longer death but life itself.

He bent down and lifted her into his arms.

"What are you doing?" she said.

"You're naked. Can't let the neighbors see you like that. This isn't Kalindos."

She laughed, then ducked her head as he carried her into one of the closest houses, one the flames hadn't reached yet.

"Hello?" Dravek called out, but no one answered. He set Sura on her feet. "Hopefully someone your size lived here before they evacuated. Let's find you some clothes." He opened the nearest door, tripping over the threshold. "I think this is a bedroom. Maybe there's a dresser— Ow!" he said, after a sound like bone smacking against wood.

Sura crept forward, her hands outstretched, eyes straining for light. Her hip hit something soft, and she reached out to touch a mattress.

Dravek bumped against her in the darkness. "Sorry," he said, and put out a hand to steady her. His fingers brushed her waist.

She held his hand against her skin, where it was meant to be. "Are you?"

He drew in a breath. "Am I what?"

"Sorry."

He shifted his hand so that his thumb curled up to graze her breast. "Not for anything, Sura. Never again." He slid his other hand around her waist and turned her to face him. "I love you."

"I love you, too." She brushed her lips over his neck as a familiar hunger rose within her. "I want you." Her voice came low, insistent, predatory. "I want you now."

To her ecstatic relief, her eternal gratitude, he didn't protest or even hesitate.

Instead, he took off his clothes.

The moment the house stopped crumbling, Rhia ran for the wreckage, slipping free of Elora's desperate grasp.

"Marek!"

She tried to cross the broken threshold, but a cloud of ash and smoke pushed her back onto the walkway, coughing and gagging. She stuffed the vinegar-soaked cloth against her face and tried to move forward again. The ash seared her eyes, blinding her. She stumbled back and dropped to her knees.

"No..." Her throat tightened, and her face crumpled into agony.

A soft hand touched her shoulder. "Rhia, move back," Elora said. "You can't save him."

Rhia grasped her crow feather fetish in both hands, waiting for the rush of Crow's wings. If her Spirit had stolen Marek from her, after Nilik, she would renounce Him. Then she would curl up here on the ground and let Crow take her.

"Spare him," she prayed, though she knew all the pleas in the world wouldn't change Crow's flight.

A sharp bang made her jump. She wiped her stinging eyes and opened them to see another cloud of ash and smoke puffing out of the house.

The door slammed open from the inside, then fell from its hinges. From the darkness appeared a man holding a young boy, their faces smeared with soot.

Marek.

He staggered down the porch stairs, then saw Rhia and Elora. "Help him!" he croaked.

Marek laid the child on the ground at the end of the walkway. Elora went to work as the boy's mother shrieked instructions at her.

Marek straightened up and looked at Rhia. Before he could speak, she slammed him with the hardest embrace of their lives.

"Not dead this time, either," he whispered.

Elora spoke up. "Your son's going to be fine."

The woman clutched at the Otter's sleeve, sobbing. "Thank you." She wiped her face and looked up at Marek. "You saved his life."

He swallowed hard, staring at the child. Moonlight broke through the haze of smoke, and Rhia thought that Marek's blue-gray gaze had lost its haunted look. Perhaps for good.

Dravek wished he could see Sura in the full light of day, naked and perfect under his hands. But tonight, for a few minutes at least, they would revel in their Snake senses of exquisite touch and scent, while they still possessed them.

With his back to the wall, he drew her close and kissed her.

Her breasts pressed against his chest, where he could feel the tiny contours of her nipples. His fingers outlined the scar on her back, and his blood surged with the desire to protect her from suffering.

Her hands roamed his neck and shoulders, as though memorizing his shape. His skin came almost painfully alive at her touch, feeling it for the first time without the barrier of clothes. It seemed like an eternity since he'd first seen her in the forest and fallen asleep craving her body.

"Touch me inside," she murmured.

Her voice held an ache, as if she had an affliction only he could cure. He lifted her off her feet, sliding her up against his own body. Her knees grasped his hips, and he reached around and between her legs.

"Please," she moaned.

He slid one finger within her, then another. Sura clutched his shoulders, groaning and grinding against him, riding his hand with her tight, wet core. He curved his fingers, sending her into spasms of delirium that brought him near the brink himself.

Dravek turned them around to pin her back to the wall. "I need you now."

"Yes." She curled her legs around his hips. "No more waiting."

But he had to wait, one long moment to savor what was about to be, to bid good riddance to the endless aching void of denial. Then he sank himself deep inside her.

They cried out together, their voices bombarding the warm, dry air. Dravek pressed his forehead against her shoulder and fought for control as the sensations swept through him, pulsing hot. Every hour for a year he'd imagined this moment, but the reality of her body was another world beyond.

They remained still and silent, sharing shaky, astonished breaths. Waiting. For the world to end? For Snake to leave them? It was done now, and he wasn't sorry.

He brushed his mouth across hers, inhaling her scent, wishing he could taste every inch of her at once.

"More," she whispered, and slipped her tongue under his lip. The velvet shock flew down his spine, and he gasped with the effort to hold back.

He moved within her, slowly, their breaths mingling. The sinews of her thighs tightened in his hands as she rocked her hips against him.

"More." Sura clenched him with every muscle, and he groaned in wordless ecstasy, his control slipping away. They slid together, faster, harder, sweat slicking their flesh. His skin felt as heavy as a fur coat, suffocating him as their heat built higher. He began to struggle for breath, but couldn't care. Nothing had ever felt like this.

Something sizzled. Through the haze of pleasure, he realized it was their own sweat, turning to steam.

"Dravek?" Sura's voice slurred. "What's happening?"

"Burning...I have to..." He moved faster, desperate to end it before they burst into flames. His heat-possessed mind clouded and wavered, and he felt a blackness reach for him, ready to drag him into unconsciousness.

"Yes..." Sura pulsed and shuddered against him in a flaring orgasm he could feel deep in his own core. She screamed and clawed his shoulders, pulling him back to this world.

All at once he came, long and hot and loud, the blood boiling in his ears. He thrust into her again and again, clutching her body and gasping for the last few breaths of life. If he died right now, he would regret nothing. Sura knew he loved her.

At last the heat receded, and breath returned. Dravek realized he would live. He kissed her trembling lips.

She wrapped her arms around his neck. "I thought I was about to lose you."

He lowered her to the floor, knees shaking. "You almost did."

"You think that'll happen every time?"

"No." He gulped and struggled to put words in the right order. "Not unless I have to go another thirteen months...eleven days and...three hours without an orgasm." He sat gingerly on the bed, every inch of him exquisitely sensitive.

"You denied yourself because of our training?"

"Partly." He waited until he had a full breath to finish. "And I vowed that the next time I came would be inside you."

She laughed, a sound he'd sorely missed, then drew her fingers through his hair. Suddenly she gasped and pulled her hand away. "It's short again. Someone in your family—"

"No, we couldn't have made love if I'd been in my month of mourning." He drew her to sit next to him on the bed. "I cut my hair out of shame. For Kalindos."

She leaned against his shoulder and held his hand between both of her own. "You did what you had to do."

He kissed the top of her head, wishing the smell of her hair could blot out the memory. But they both carried the scent of smoke and ash.

"Where did you put the hamlet's heat?" she asked.

"There's an underground stream that lets out not far from here. Rhia showed me on the ride in."

She gave a light groan. "I wish I'd thought to look for something like that. I was too busy thinking about the fire." Her breath slid out over his skin. "I assumed I would die."

"I would never let you go," he said, though he knew he was powerless against the strength of her will. "Never again."

She nodded against his shoulder. "Next time I'm going with you."

"There won't be a next time. After Kalindos, I'm never using my powers to kill again." He traced the edge of Sura's face, studying its shape in the darkness.

Suddenly he realized how cold his hand was against her warm cheek. He drew in a sharp breath.

"Sura, do you feel that?" He cupped her chin in his palm.

"I don't—" She gasped and touched his hand, then his neck, chest and shoulders. "You feel different."

Dravek closed his eyes and searched inside himself for the presence that had inhabited him for over two years. The Spirit always lurked within, waiting to comfort and strengthen him.

She was gone. Snake had left him.

The chill spread through his body. "She died? Like Wolverine?"

"No," Sura said. "I can feel Her inside me."

Dravek's throat thickened. "She's abandoned me for what we did. Why not you?"

"Maybe She thinks I've been punished enough."

"You have." He touched her face. "I'm not sorry for what just happened." His hand went still on her cheek. "Unless you don't want me, now that I'm nothing."

"How can you think that?" The mattress creaked as Sura turned to face him. "I want to be with you, whatever you are."

He drew her into his arms and kissed her. The heat between them was that of nothing but lovers. He was only human now, but it was good enough.

Several moments later, he opened his eyes, amazed at how much time had passed. It seemed that sunset was only a few hours ago, but already the light of dawn shone through the window, glowing pale blue on Sura's face.

Or at least it should have been blue. This light was pure white—not even silver like the moon.

They turned their heads to the window.

"What is that?" Sura whispered.

Dravek stood up, holding his breath. Could it be a new Descendant weapon, a hotter fire than any he and Sura had ever extinguished? Whatever it was, it would have to go through him to get to her.

"Let's get out of here," he whispered.

The light brightened, giving him enough illumination to find his clothes. Sura rifled through the dresser of the house's former occupant and pulled out enough clothes to cover her, though the sleeves were too short and the shoes too big. As they dressed, Dravek stood near the window, watching the western sky turn a color he'd never seen before.

Or rather, *colors*. The horizon formed a glowing white canvas. Every hue played upon it, twisting and curling around and inside each other like ribbons made of air. It reminded him of his Bestowing, just before Snake appeared, when—

His heart stopped. It couldn't be.

"Can you see it yet?"

He turned to answer Sura, who was tying a loose pair of trousers at her waist. Only two words came out.

"She's here."

"Who?"

He couldn't speak the name, could only take Sura's hand and

lead her out of the bedroom, through the front door and out to the street. Others were gathering in the hamlet's central square, their clothes torn and covered in soot. He saw Rhia and Marek and Elora, but only spared them a glance as another extraordinary sight caught his eye.

A large scorched black circle lay in the dust where they had kissed. He pulled Sura to stand at the edge to await their people's salvation.

The light took the form of a giant bird, as he knew it would. Sura yelped, then dropped to her knees, yanking him with her. Everyone around them did the same, most of them pressing their foreheads to the ground. Dravek knew he should lower his gaze, out of humility and the desire not to be blinded. But he couldn't take his eyes off Raven.

As She approached, Her light illuminated the devastation, throwing long shadows of the shattered houses and charred bodies.

The Spirit of Spirits alighted in the hamlet square, in the center of the black circle.

"Greetings," She said in a voice that could shake the sun.

Dravek saw Rhia lift her head. "You honor us with Your presence at our hour of need," she said.

"I come to bestow My Aspect."

The crowd drew in a collective breath. No Crow offspring remained who had not already received an Aspect. Nilik had died, Jula was a Mockingbird and Corek was a Crow himself.

Unless…

Dravek looked at Rhia. Of course. *Born of a Crow in difficult labor* could mean a Crow person would transform into Raven in a time of great pain. A Crow like Rhia.

He smiled. The Spirits were clever, he had to admit.

Raven turned Her curved beak toward Dravek. "It's you I've come for."

The crowd went dead silent. Dravek's smile faded, and the blood seemed to stop flowing as he stared at the Spirit.

"What?" he said, ignobly.

"Must I repeat Myself?" Raven said with what sounded like a grin.

"But the—the prophecy said that the Raven child would be born of a Crow. My mother was a Spider, and my father—"

He stopped, remembering what Rhia had told him a few weeks ago. Everyone had a Guardian Spirit, even Descendants, whether they knew it or not.

His father was a Crow.

"No." He tried to get to his feet to run. Sura held his hand tight, keeping him on his knees. "Of all my people," he said, "I'm the least worthy."

Raven came closer, spiking the panic in his heart.

"Dravek." Her head tilted, gesturing to Sura. "You would have sacrificed your life to save this woman and your people. You gave up your Spirit in order to love her. You are not the monster you believe yourself to be."

Sura squeezed his hand. To his relief, she didn't say, "I told you so."

"Besides," Raven continued, "you have always been Mine. Perhaps it's why you and Sura loved each other, because something in you sensed you were not the same."

Dravek glanced around to see several nearby people giving them odd regards. There was no hiding their true feelings now, and no need to. He was no longer Snake.

He bowed his head. "What do You require of me?"

"That you accept My Aspect, and use it to do what only I can do."

Dravek had no idea what She meant. "When? Where?"

Raven enveloped him in Her light of every color. "You'll know."

Asermon Valley

Lycas tried to move toward the light. The crowd pulled him along, but every jostle spiked the pain in his chest. Each breath came shallower than the last. He wouldn't make it. He'd never see Raven.

Finally he veered away from the crowd, away from the dead and injured soldiers. The battle was over, and he wanted to be alone.

He found a pile of brush—discarded scrap wood from the hamlet's construction, no doubt—and collapsed behind it.

Sitting on the ground, Lycas watched the white and rainbow light glow against the yellowing leaves of the nearby maples. The hamlet couldn't be more than a hundred paces away, but it might as well be a hundred miles.

"You always were the lazy one," said a voice behind him.

Mali.

With the rest of his breath, Lycas suggested where she could stick her observations.

"Nice," she said, "and here I am trying to help you." She knelt beside him and took his arm.

"Mali, no," he said with as much force as he could. "If you pull me up, the pain'll make me scream."

She let go. Of course she would understand. He couldn't show weakness in front of the others.

She sat beside him. "Then we'll wait here together."

"No. You go see Raven. It could be your only chance."

"Eh. I'm sure it's not all it's touted to be. Besides, I hate crowds." She laid a hand on his shoulder. "Rest now."

The weight of her voice said she knew he was dying.

He tried to shift his position, but the movement jabbed the arrow deeper into his lung. He gasped in pain, which only made it worse. His next cough brought blood to his mouth.

"Lie on your side," she commanded. "I'll help."

She supported Lycas's arm as he lowered himself to the ground. The cool grass against his shoulder soothed the burning inside him.

Mali lay facing him and extended her arm to support the side of his head. The blood trailed from his mouth onto her skin, mingling with that of her vanquished foes.

The flickering light played over her sweaty face as her dark gaze traveled down his body. "I guess I can't punch you in the gut, like I've dreamed of doing for nineteen years."

They glowered at each other for a long moment, then the corner of his mouth twitched. Her eyes crinkled, and her thin lips tightened in a vague approximation of a smile.

"You look good," she said.

"You look terrible."

She nodded. "Thank you."

"Sura's in there," he said.

Mali's eyes widened, and he could tell she wanted to leap up and run to their daughter. But she stayed.

"She's a Snake," he told her. "I think she stopped the fire."

Mali smiled. "She was a good snuffer, even before she left Asermos."

"More than that." He closed his eyes. "I turned her into a weapon. My own daughter."

"You gave her the chance to help her people, something I was too afraid to do. I wasted her life protecting her."

He didn't want to spend another breath arguing. He never won with Mali, anyway.

"She named our granddaughter after you."

Mali's mouth opened, but for several moments no words came out. "Have you seen her?"

"Once. She's beautiful." *Just like her namesake,* he wanted to add, but knew he'd receive a fatal punch for it. "Red hair, black eyes. Striking."

Another stab inside, this time unprovoked. He gagged, and blood poured from his mouth, faster than before.

"Let me get you an Otter," Mali said. "They can at least take away the pain." She started to get up.

He clutched her hand. "Don't leave me." Lycas wanted to cringe at his own words. He was truly weak now, afraid to die alone. "I'm so cold."

She lay down again, her arm beneath his head. Behind her dark lashes he could still see the fierce young woman who'd always made him feel five seconds from a heart attack.

"I'm sorry," he choked out.

"Good." Her hand still in his, she blew on his forehead to shift the hair out of his eyes.

"Wish I'd been…anything else."

"No, you don't."

"Wouldn't have had to leave you."

She scoffed. "If you hadn't left, neither of us would have lived this long."

She was right.

"Besides," she said, "you've never been anything but a Wolverine since the day you were born."

Another pain skewered him, but this time not from his body. "I killed Him."

He wanted to howl his anguish to the sky, give his own life to bring back his Spirit. But nothing could ever do that.

Mali let go of his hand, then placed an object in it that was even colder than his fingers. He recognized the deer-bone hilt of one of his daggers, the one with the lock of Sura's hair inside.

He no longer had the strength to hold it. It slid from his grasp.

She replaced the weapon in his palm, then wrapped her hand around his to keep it there.

"You saved us," she whispered. "You honored Him."

He tried to believe it, tried to glimpse her eyes to see if *she* believed it.

But darkness stole his vision, and he slipped away, in despair.

Rhia stared as Raven stepped back from Dravek. He looked the same as before, in all ways but one: around his edges shimmered an almost imperceptible iridescent glow, trailing him as he rose from his knees. She wondered how long the aura would last.

One thing was for certain: he was no longer Snake. He had given up his Spirit to be with Sura.

Raven turned to the rest of the crowd. "I have also arrived to announce a fundamental change, from this point on." She looked at Sura. "Much misery has been caused by the progression of powers through reproduction." Raven raised Her head and addressed everyone. "There was a time long ago when it made sense, when your people were in danger of extinction. But now, despite the many deaths this war has caused, the land has as many humans as it can sustain.

"Therefore, We now decree that humans shall progress from the first to the second phase, and from second to third, when their Spirits deem them ready. This will end the perversion of powers that brings so much pain, and babies will be born to those who want them. Most important, those who cannot or choose not to bear children will not be hindered in their magic."

Rhia took in a deep breath. Marek smiled at her, teeth shining white against his soot-stained face.

"Power should no longer be an end in itself," Raven continued. "What Our people need now is not another military victory, but a spiritual revolution. The time for force has ended. The enemy must be won, not conquered. Most of you already have what you need to make this happen."

She looked at Rhia, whose heart tripped at the sight of the endless dark eyes.

Raven's light vanished. In place of Her many-colored feathers, sleek black ones appeared. The curve of Her beak straightened to a point, and She shrank until She looked just like—

Crow.

The crowd recoiled. Rhia realized that none of them had ever seen Him or ever would except at the time of their death.

"Be calm, everyone," He said in the most human voice of all the Spirits. "I'm not here for you." He looked at Rhia. "I'm here for her."

"No," Marek gasped.

Rhia smiled. Crow didn't mean it was her time to die.

The Spirit bowed gallantly. "Rhia, I grant you your third-phase Aspect, to enter the land of the Dead and bring a soul back to this world." Crow brushed His wing over her head, and she felt a surge of power course through her. Then He bent close to her ear and whispered, "You'll be needing it soon."

She shivered at the thought of wielding the ultimate magic of life and death. No one should have to make that choice, but she would now, again and again for the rest of her life.

"Choose carefully," Crow said, and then disappeared.

The crowd let out a sigh of relief. Though Rhia sympathized, she'd never felt fear in the presence of her Spirit. He'd been her guide and friend her whole life, even when she'd rejected Him.

With Raven and Crow gone, everyone stared at Dravek. He helped Sura to her feet, and they fell into a tight, wordless embrace.

"Mother!"

Rhia's heart stopped at the sound of Jula's screech. She and Marek turned to see their daughter lurching toward them down the main street of the hamlet. For a moment Rhia thought she'd been injured. She'd been given strict orders to stay with Corek and the healers, far from the battle area.

"It's Uncle Lycas!" her daughter shouted. "Hurry!"

Rhia was swept up in the crowd, as the fighters and the hamlet survivors together crushed toward the gate to see their leader. Jula waited for her and grabbed her hand.

"It might be too late." Tears choked her voice. "Corek's with him now, and Mali."

Rhia ran, her heart twisted in fear. Not again. She couldn't lose another brother to this madness.

They followed the crowd beyond the gate, down the hill to what must have been the battlefield, judging by the bodies strewn on the grass. She recognized several Bears and Wolverines, along with Vara the Snake.

The sorrow made her stumble. Marek took her hand and pulled her along.

"Over here!" Jula called from a nearby pile of refuse covered with honeysuckle vines. Someone stood near it holding a long torch. She and Marek pushed through the crowd, following the light, until they stood at her brother's feet.

Lycas lay on his back, eyes closed, hands on his chest, clutching his dagger. Her heart quickened with hope, for Crow's wings were silent. Perhaps her brother was out of danger.

Then Corek looked up at her from where he knelt beside Lycas. The torch cast grim shadows over his face as he slowly shook his head.

"No..." Tears spilled from Rhia's eyes. The monsters had stolen too much from her. Nilo, then Nilik and now Lycas.

Corek stood and let her take his place. She looked across her brother's body and saw Mali holding a blood-soaked cloth.

"We tried to clean him up before everyone came back." Mali nodded at Corek. "He already said the prayer of passage."

Lycas's clothes were spattered with blood, but held no

single pool indicating an injury. "Was he wounded?" Rhia choked out.

"Not today. He fought well, even without Wolverine. The bastards never cut him." Mali smoothed her hand over the broad chest of her former mate. "Maybe he broke a rib. The way he was breathing, it sounded like his lung was punctured."

"Not a rib." Rhia hung her head. "An arrow."

"Father!"

Rhia closed her eyes. In her own grief, she'd forgotten about Sura.

The girl broke through the crowd, Dravek on her heels.

"No..." Sura sank to her knees next to Lycas's head, fists clenched in her hair. She rocked back and forth, keening.

Mali waited a long moment before whispering her daughter's name.

Sura's head jerked up. "Mother..."

They embraced hard and fast, and Rhia thought that for the first time in her life, she saw Mali's eyes turn wet.

"I knew you'd survive." Mali stroked Sura's hair. "I knew it, I knew it." She looked over Sura's shoulder at Rhia, then down at Lycas. "Your father made you even stronger," she whispered to her daughter. "I didn't think that was possible."

Dravek's voice shattered the moment. "Bring him back."

Mali let go of Sura and turned to Rhia. "What does he mean? You're third phase?"

"As of a few minutes ago," Dravek said. "Rhia, hurry, before it's too late."

The crowd pressed in. "I'll pay the ransom!" a man shouted, and several people echoed him.

Rhia's mind wrestled with the possibilities. Without her

brother, the revolution would be weakened, perhaps irreversibly. If many volunteers gave time from their lives, each would feel little sacrifice, considering Lycas's relatively advanced age.

Tereus knelt beside Rhia and took her hand. His own eyes crinkled in grief. He'd known his stepson Lycas longer than any other living person had.

"I can't tell you what to do," he whispered. "But your heart knows, doesn't it?"

Rhia gazed down at her brother. His resurrection would provide inspiration to the resistance. And she would get to hug him and hear his teasing voice drive her crazy once more.

But for how long? Without his Spirit, he'd have little strength.

She looked at Mali and Sura. They exchanged a long glance, then shook their heads at Rhia.

"He was ready to die," Mali said. "He was finished with this stupid world."

Sura spoke in a whisper. "He hated living without Wolverine. If you brought him back, and he was still alone inside himself—"

"But we need him," Dravek said. "He knows that, and he'd want to lead us, no matter what."

Mali turned her sharp gaze on him. "Who are you? And why are you glowing?"

"This is Dravek, Mother," Sura said. "He's my mate. He's also the Raven."

"Oh." Mali looked at Rhia. "Do we have to do what he says?"

Rhia's eyes met Dravek's, which narrowed. For a long moment, she thought he would order her to bring her brother back to life.

Then he blinked and lowered his gaze. "Do what you think is right. You're the Crow."

Rhia touched her brother's cold cheek and struggled to listen to her own heart. What would Lycas ask of her? Did his wishes matter more than the good of their people?

She closed her eyes and felt for Crow. He'd given her a lifetime's worth of wisdom, but it all seemed feeble in the face of her sorrow.

First she considered whether it was even possible. He'd been dead much longer than Rhia herself had been when Coranna had brought her back to life. And she had little idea how to do the ritual. He might come back a shell of his former self. Her heart ached at the thought of her brother wasting away in a barely animate body, or with a half-conscious mind.

As a Crow, she'd been taught to hold the wishes of the departed above all else. Her first duty was to the dead.

Regardless of his wound's origin, Lycas had died on the battlefield after a hard-won victory. He'd died saving his people's lives and fighting for their land and freedom. He wouldn't want to come back.

Her tears fell as she whispered goodbye.

Mali let out a deep exhale.

"Thank you, Rhia," Sura said.

Rhia's gut felt full of lead as she stood and addressed the crowd. "We are deeply grateful for your offers of life to trade for my brother's. But he won't be coming back."

A collective wail of sorrow rose, but the faces of those nearby showed bitter understanding. Most people had never known anyone to return from the dead other than Crows themselves.

Tereus slipped his arm around Rhia's shoulders and kissed the top of her head. She buried her face in her father's chest and sobbed.

He rubbed her back in slow, soothing circles. "Your brother's at peace now."

Rhia wasn't sure that was possible, in this world or any other.

For the next few hours, Rhia walked through a fog, helping the dying cross over and assisting the Otters with the injured. The Bears and Wolverines guarded the Ilion soldiers who were still alive and walking.

At the first light of dawn, Mali took her aside.

"I've been thinking," the Wasp said. "This is the end for the Ilions."

Rhia stared up at her with exhausted eyes. "How?"

"I know it looks bad for us, but it's worse for them." She gestured to the smoldering hamlet. "This was an act of frustration. What would it accomplish, strategically? Nothing, and once word makes it back to Ilios of what they've done, their people will demand a withdrawal. I've read the headlines and opinions in the Ilion newspapers. They hate to see themselves as mass murderers. It offends their honor." She spat the last word.

Rhia thought about the Ilions' incentives to stay. "The vineyards are almost gone. Replanting them would cost a lot of money and time."

"They still have the quarries," Mali said, "but no one will work in them after this. It's either give up and go home or kill us all and start over."

Rhia quailed inside at the latter option. "We need a final blow, besides this. Something to convince them to leave."

"All we have in Asermos are a couple dozen fighters, plus the thirty I brought with me tonight." Mali frowned. "Most of our warriors ended up in Tiros, in jail or in the ground."

Rhia heard the sound of a trotting horse. She looked north past Mali at the hill they had descended to approach the hamlet.

A man was riding toward them at a brisk pace. He slowed to a walk as he neared the hamlet. In the light of the torches she could see his astonished eyes stare at the wreckage. Then he turned to the crowd.

"Message for Lycas."

The people parted for him, and he rode forward at a walk.

"Lycas is dead." Rhia walked up to him as his horse halted, snorting. "Are you bringing news from Feras?"

He handed her a scroll with a blue Bear paw seal.

"I followed your trails from Lycas's headquarters," he panted. "Feras asks for an immediate reply."

Rhia tore open the parchment and held it up, using the barest gleam of dawn to read the Bear's words:

Galen received Thera's message of Ilions burning hamlet. We moved battalion to besiege Ilion garrison west of Asermos. Descendants fought fiercely but eventually surrendered. Numerous casualties. Will stay and await your orders.

Mali read the parchment over Rhia's shoulder. "Excellent."

Rhia's mind raced. Could they strike the final blow today? Lycas's troops numbered in the hundreds, but they were dispersed all over the Kirisian Mountains and Asermon hill country. It could take weeks to organize them for an assault on the village. They could use Feras's troops, but the soldiers stationed within Asermos could fight them off. The last thing she wanted was to bloody the streets of her home village.

Unless…

She turned to Mali. "We take back Asermos now."

Mali looked at her as if she had lost her mind. "This minute? We have hardly any troops here. Our leader is dead."

Rhia remembered the words Lycas had repeated to her at least once a year since the war had begun.

"This isn't his revolution," she told Mali. "It's everyone's."

16

Asermos

Without a weapon, Rhia marched.

The sun rose behind the people of the hamlet as they walked, staggered, rolled or were carried into Asermos. The time for killing had ended. Now they would take back their land by the force of will alone.

Marek walked beside her, wheezing from the smoke of the fire. Like all of them, his clothes were covered in ash, smeared in soot. Let the Asermons—grape-heads and native villagers alike—see what the army had tried to do.

The road to Asermos curved along the bank of the sparkling Velekon River, and Rhia's heart ached to see it. She'd escaped the village at night after her prison break, and had not seen her home in daylight in over ten years. Despite the scarlet-and-yellow-clad troops who watched with suspicion as the throng passed through the streets, despite the strange temples the Descendants had raised every few blocks, dawn gave the village an aura of tranquility.

On Marek's left stalked Mali, as lithe and strong as ever; on Rhia's right, Dravek and Sura walked hand in hand. Behind them came Jula and Tereus. Only Corek and the Otter healers had stayed at the hamlet to care for the injured and dying Asermons and Ilions. All others who had survived the fire—men, women and children—were about to meet their would-be murderers.

The sun angled low and orange down the main street as they turned for the prison. Rhia's stomach turned at the sight of the place where they'd forced her to hear grown men beg for death. The towers loomed tall and silent over the street.

She could see the crowd now, over two hundred people gathered for Mali's execution. They milled about, restless at the delay.

One face turned their way, then another. Fingers pointed, and soon everyone was watching them approach, marching down the hill to take back Asermos.

They must have been a sight, a thousand sooty, bloody, bedraggled people, moving as one, without fear.

A line of about twenty soldiers stepped forward and drew their swords, blades glistening gold in the early-morning sun.

Several Ilions stepped onto a balcony on the prison wall. Rhia couldn't recognize them from a distance, but they carried themselves with the assurance of senior military officers.

Mali stepped out in front of their throng and sent a smirk to the officers on the balcony.

"Sorry I'm late, General Lino," she said, "but I had a massacre to stop."

"Arrest her!" he shouted.

The soldiers came forth, swords raised. On cue, Rhia and several other small, harmless-looking women stepped in front of Mali. They held up their hands, palms forward, to show they had no weapons, and to give the unmistakable message to *stop*.

The soldiers halted, confused, and glanced at the officer at the far right of their line. He looked up at the general.

Lino glowered back at him. "I said, arrest her, Lieutenant. Kill the others if you must."

The soldiers took another step forward, now only several paces away. Marek moved to Rhia's side, as did ten or twelve others, protecting Mali with a wall of flesh.

Rhia glanced at the crowd of Ilion settlers who had gathered for Mali's funeral. Though a few watched with anticipation, most wore creased brows and whispered to each other with worried faces.

Rhia took a deep breath and thought of Lycas. She needed his strength now. Her voice boomed forth, surprising her with its volume and force.

"People of Ilios, look. Your army won't hesitate to raise a weapon against unarmed women and men. How long before they raise it to you? How long before they burn *your* homes with *your* families inside?"

"Look at your neighbors," Mali called out, then gestured to the crowd behind her. "Herded like livestock into a hamlet, just to be set on fire."

"Like you did to our troops in Kalindos?" the general shouted. "Our brave soldiers?"

"*Brave?*" Dravek's voice shot forth. "A thousand men against a village half their size, sent to kidnap and enslave, like you did twenty years ago? You call that brave?"

Some of the settlers frowned and turned away at the mention of Kalindos. So they had some shame, at least.

"Lieutenant, arrest all of these traitors."

The young officer looked down the line at his men. "Stand down."

"*What?*" The general leaned over the balcony railing. "Obey my order, Lieutenant, or you'll be put to death for treason along with this Wasp witch."

"I'm sorry, sir." The young officer sheathed his sword. "You can't order me to break the law." Rhia thought she heard him add, "Not anymore."

Before the general could bluster further, Rhia spoke. "We're here to demand your complete and unconditional surrender."

The general and the other senior officers laughed. "Silly bandits, I could have an entire battalion here within two hours and crush your pathetic resistance."

Mali pulled out the second parchment Feras had sent, the one with the signed statement of surrender.

"You mean, the battalion at the Asermon garrison, the battalion led by Lieutenant Colonel Akero?" Mali looked up at Lino with wide eyes. "That battalion?" She folded up the parchment and handed it to one of the Ilion soldiers. "Give that to the general, would you please? Thank you."

The soldier hurried to the door of the prison and disappeared.

Rhia cleared her throat. "As you'll see in a moment, our so-called pathetic resistance has captured the Asermon garrison. We've also thwarted your attempts to roast our people at the hamlet." She looked at Mali, who nodded. She turned back to the general. "We're prepared to offer amnesty for your war crimes if you leave immediately, from here and Velekos." She looked at the grape-heads, who had suddenly grown restive. "Peaceful settlers may stay if they wish, but they'll provide fair compensation for stolen property."

The general turned to the door of the balcony as the soldier with the parchment appeared. He snatched the paper out of the soldier's hand and unfolded it hastily.

"Give me a moment." He and the other senior officers disappeared inside the prison.

The settlers were eyeing the Asermon natives with growing hostility.

Mali turned to Rhia and Marek. "We've got to do something about them. If they rush us, the soldiers will get involved, and things'll get bloody."

"We have no weapons," Marek said. "That was the point. Besides, most of our warriors' Spirits are dead, and the Ilions know it."

"We have a weapon," said a voice behind them.

Rhia turned to see Dravek staring into the distant woods, his eyes unfocused.

"Raven said the time for fighting was over," Dravek said. "We need to win them, not conquer them." He turned to them. "I'm going to call the Spirits."

A shiver went down Rhia's spine. "Here? Now?"

"The Reawakening," Marek breathed. "Yes."

"Do you think it'll work?" Mali asked.

"Raven commands the Spirits," Marek told her. "If anyone can do it, it'd be Dravek."

She examined the young man with a skeptical gaze. "How?"

Dravek searched the sky as if the answer were written on the puffs of pink and orange clouds. Finally he looked at them.

"I'll just ask them to come." He shrugged. "There's no ritual for this sort of thing. No one's ever been Raven before." He wiped his hands against the sides of his shirt, as if they were sweaty. "Anyway, it's all I can think of."

"You're forgetting one thing." Tereus stepped forward. "Four of the Spirits are dead. How can there be a Reawakening without Wolf and Wolverine? Or Cougar and Bear? Their people protect and feed us."

Rhia put a hand to her chest as she felt her breath escape. She knew now why Crow had given her the third-phase power.

"I'll bring them back."

Together, Rhia and Dravek entered the Gray Valley.

Within a few steps, she had forgotten the real world, where her friends and family shielded her and the Raven man from the prying eyes of the Ilions, and where Marek softly tapped two stones together to simulate the drumbeat. She'd been relieved that this journey had not required burning the thanapras herb, but she supposed that with Raven, all things were possible.

Speaking of which, Rhia looked at Dravek, who stared, slack-jawed, at their stark surroundings.

"People come here when they die?" he asked her.

"Just the bitter ones." She touched his arm. "Let's go."

As they walked through the Valley, she called the names of the four dead Spirits. Nothing but her own voice echoed from the high rock walls.

Finally Dravek stopped. "Maybe if I call the rest, the others will come, and you can bring them back."

She nodded. "Try it."

He brushed his hands together and muttered, "I have no idea what I'm doing."

"Raven chose you for a reason." Her tone, unfortunately, conveyed the fact that she couldn't fathom it.

He gave her a short, dark glance. "Right." He took a deep breath, then cleared his throat. "Spirits. All of you. We need you now like never before, and hopefully never again. We're on the verge of taking back our lands. Or we're about to lose everything. We need you."

They waited for several long moments, but nothing happened.

Dravek gave a harsh sigh. "I'm begging you on behalf of all my people, and even on behalf of the Ilions, who don't know how much they need you. If you accept them again as your own, they would love you as much as we do."

When nothing continued to happen, Dravek closed his eyes for a long moment, then took a step forward and raised his arms to the sky.

"I am Kalindon, and I am Ilion." His voice stretched forth. "I exist because of this war. Four Spirits died because of my part in it. If it's a sacrifice you want, if it's a life you need, then take mine."

Rhia put a hand to her mouth. Perhaps Raven had chosen well after all.

Silence reigned in the Gray Valley.

Dravek lowered his arms. "I don't know what else to—"

"Wait." Rhia held up a hand. "Do you hear that?"

From far away came the sound of wings and hooves and claws, flapping and pounding and scratching. Rhia looked around but saw nothing. No animals approached in any form. "Where are they?" she asked.

A slow smile crept across Dravek's face. "They're not here. They're out there."

She looked at the sky. It seemed as if the sound were coming from beyond it.

"Of course," she whispered. "The Spirits don't live here in the Gray Valley. They're not dead." She listened to the steady movement of the sounds from one horizon to the other. "They're going to our world." She turned to Dravek. "You did it. You called the Spirits."

His smile faded as he looked past her. "Not all of them."

She turned slowly, knowing what she would see.

Stumbling toward them, weak-limbed and wavering, were four animals. A wolf, a wolverine, a bear and a cougar.

Postures slumped, they dragged their feet, leaving trails of bloody paw prints. The wolverine looked the worst, its thick brown fur, black face and legs, all patched and tattered like an old coat. Each of its long claws was shattered into yellow splinters.

She readied herself to resurrect the Spirits, though she wasn't exactly sure how. And then she remembered.

There was always a price. For every moment of new life granted, another must be sacrificed. When she had died as part of her first Crow ritual and her mentor Coranna had brought her back, every Kalindon had offered a piece of his or her own life as ransom—what amounted to a month each, if she lived to Coranna's age of fifty-three.

But the Spirits were eternal. All the human life in the world couldn't bring them back.

Tears stung her eyes. It couldn't be done. There was no ransom large enough. Her people would have few warriors and hunters.

Even if the Ilions were Reawakened and became their allies, another enemy would come along later and prey on their weakness.

"I'm sorry," she whispered.

She turned to explain to Dravek, but he was staring over her head at the top of the cliffs.

She followed his gaze to see Raven. The Spirit of Spirits, the Mother of all Creation, was no longer glowing with feathers of every color. Instead She looked like nothing more than a raven, larger than Her brother Crow, with ragged feathers at Her throat, and a thick curved beak.

"If it's a ransom you need," She said with a voice clear and loud despite the distance, "I shall give it."

Rhia shook her head. "I don't understand. Whose lives do You offer?"

"The only one I can." She bowed Her head and ruffled Her wings. "My own."

"No!" Rhia shouted. "We need You."

"Yes, for this. Before, now and again one day."

Rhia looked at Dravek, who was gazing at Raven with misty eyes.

"She's right," he told Rhia. "She's played Her part, and so have I." He lowered his gaze to her face. "You'll have to take them across alone."

"You're not staying here." She looked up at Raven. "Tell him."

"Rhia's correct," Raven said. "Dravek, you must continue. Find another Spirit, one that's right for the rest of your life. Know that you have served Me honorably." She turned Her head to Rhia. "Take what I offer and give it to My children."

Raven leaped from the cliff and plummeted, wings tucked tight against Her body. Before Rhia could draw her next breath,

Raven hit the floor of the Gray Valley in a glorious white shower of sparks. The fire from the impact cascaded over the four injured animals, drowning them in flames.

When the smoke cleared, the bear, wolf, wolverine and cougar lay still. Rhia and Dravek crept closer.

The animals were whole now, and breathing slowly. Rhia slid her arms under the cougar and found it as light and soft as a blanket.

Dravek knelt beside the wolf and tried to pick it up, but his hands went through the fur as if the animal were made of air.

"Only I can take them across." Rhia nodded to their surroundings. "It's my Spirit's realm."

"Then I'll walk with you."

She smiled at him. "Thank you."

They made their way back to the dead tree. Rhia looked up at its branches, half expecting to see a leaf or flower growing at the tip of a twig.

It hadn't changed. Some things never would, she guessed.

She set the cougar down at the edge of the fog that led to the natural world. It stretched, bowing, extending each claw, toes flexing. Then it gave her an impassive look, as if to say, "Eh, not bad," before springing into the fog.

They repeated the action for the bear and wolf. They should have been too big and heavy for her to carry, but she managed it with ease—they were Spirits after all.

As the wolf trotted off through the fog, she motioned for Dravek to follow it. "I'd like to do the last alone."

He nodded. "But hurry. I have the feeling you won't want to miss this."

Rhia trudged back to the sleeping wolverine. She hesitated at the sight of its sharp teeth and long claws. Then she bent and picked up the strange animal.

"Thank you."

She whirled in her tracks, almost dropping the wolverine.

Her brother stood in the center of the valley, not ten paces away.

"Lycas…" Her throat tightened with tears. "You shouldn't be here. Go with Crow. Go to the Other Side."

"I will now." He stepped closer, and she longed to embrace him.

"Why are you here at all?" she asked him. "You died a warrior's death."

"I died from an old wound delivered by one of my own men, a wound that never would have happened if I'd been a better warrior. A nobler one."

"A noble war would have left us in chains."

He lowered his gaze to the bundle of fur in her hands. "He looks so harmless."

A smile twitched the corner of her mouth. "Not for long."

He gestured behind him, toward the fog. "May I go with you?"

"As far as you can, yes."

They walked together, ambling in a comfortable silence, as if they were back home on the family farm in Ascimos.

"I hate that you're gone," she said at last.

"Well, that's some comfort for me, knowing my death will eternally annoy you."

A laugh broke through her tears. "You never stop, do you?"

He didn't answer, and her heart grew heavy again. He would stop everything now, forever.

They reached the fog without another word. At the edge, she

set the wolverine on the ground. It snarled at her as it scrambled away, loping hunched over like a cross between a bear and a dog.

Lycas shook his head. "All my life, I've never seen one of those. Elusive little bastards."

She heard Crow before she saw Him, heard the great flapping of wings from far away.

"It's time for you to go," Lycas said.

"You first."

The Spirit landed beside them, then bowed, but said nothing.

"Goodbye," Rhia managed to choke out. She took a breath and steadied her voice. "I love you."

Lycas smirked. "I knew you'd say that."

She decided to let him have the last word, and merely smiled.

Lycas turned to Crow and nodded. A violet light shimmered around them, and they were gone.

In hope and grief, Rhia stepped through the fog.

She woke in the center of the village with everyone staring down at her. Dravek and Marek reached out and helped her to her feet.

"Are They here yet?" she asked.

Marek pointed past the crowd of settlers, into the place where the road curved up into a stretch of woods.

"They're coming," he whispered.

She looked where he was gazing and saw nothing at first. Then, bit by bit, another crowd came into focus.

Animals.

One of each kind, crawling, walking, flying, buzzing. Predators ambled side by side with their prey—cougar and deer, hawk and squirrel, wolf and rabbit.

Sura turned to her, wide-eyed. "What should we do?"

"Nothing." Rhia shook her head slowly. "They're not here for us."

The animals and birds, dozens of them, were all in full sun now, and everyone had fallen silent watching them, even the Ilion settlers.

When all the animals had reached the prison yard, they lined up and faced the group of settlers. Each person moved to stand in front of one of the animals.

A chestnut horse stepped forward. Its low, female voice rang out over the world.

"Greetings, people of Ilios."

The settlers looked at each other with apprehension, clearly unaccustomed to talking animals. The Spirits had chosen well in a speaker—Ilions loved and respected horses.

She continued:

"Many generations ago, We abandoned your people for what We saw as arrogance. You created gods in your own image and erected places that separated you from the earth."

Rhia thought of Leukos, the Ilion capital city. Its cold beauty made it feel far from home in more ways than one. But other areas of Ilios still verged on wilderness, and there her people's magic had thrived. It wasn't too late for that nation to turn back to the Spirits.

"We were too hasty in judgment," Horse said, "and far too harsh. Forgive Us. We want all people to be one again with the Spirits and with each other. Though this new Reawakening will not be complete for many years, We hope that one day all of your people will choose to accept their Guardian Spirits. Those who do will be bestowed with powers such as you've seen here in

Asermos." Her head bobbed, making the red mane shimmer in the early-morning light. "In return for such magic, you must honor and respect Us and the land from which We come. We cannot be separated from the earth, and neither can you.

"Believe in Us, and We will love you forever. Never again shall We turn away." She let out a small chuckle that sounded like a whinny. "Even Spirits can learn from mistakes."

The horse bowed, then returned to the mass of animals. Rhia walked into the square, closing the distance to the settlers by half. A few of the others followed.

Just then, the senior officers returned to the balcony. She spoke before they could deliver another threat.

"People of Ilios. We offer you the chance to stay, to learn and grow with the Spirits. We will train you in your powers, escort each of you to your Bestowing so that you may come into the fullness of your Aspects. All we ask in return is for you to watch, in peace, as your army leaves our shores." She turned to the officers on the balcony. "Today."

General Lino stared at the animals on the street. The enormous black bear reared up on its hind legs. The cougar roared, a sound that ripped the air, and crouched, muscles bunching, as if to leap onto the balcony.

"Do it," Daria whispered to her cat Spirit.

The general backed slowly away from the railing and drew a short, curved sword from his sheath.

Sura snorted. "Does he think he can kill a Spirit with a sword?"

Mali spoke softly. "That's not what he's doing."

Rhia saw jewels sparkle on the hilt as General Lino raised the weapon before him and spoke to her.

"Don't you understand?" he said. "I can't leave. My mission was to bring order to this land. I failed. I can never go home." He handed the sword to one of his staff officers and slowly dropped to his knees on the balcony. "May my life be sufficient payment for my dishonor. May the gods forgive me."

"No…" Rhia stepped forward as the staff officer pulled Lino's head back and sliced his throat. The general's hands went up at the last instant, and Rhia turned away.

Another death. She closed her eyes and prayed to Crow that it would be the final one of the war.

As if in response, the Spirit's wings rushed through her mind as He carried off the general's soul.

She opened her eyes to see the black bird hop out of the crowd of animals and stand before her. "You might like to know," Crow said. "For the first time since I created it, the Gray Valley is empty."

Rhia stared at him until he bobbed his head to confirm it. She shed another pair of tears at the thought of all the dead finding peace at last.

Then she wiped her eyes and regarded the bird. "Maybe you could take a vacation."

"Ha! You always had a sense of humor." The crow cocked his head. "Then again, I've been overworked lately. Perhaps a few days off would do wonders for my mood." He hopped away.

Rhia watched the bird go, then looked up at the balcony, which was almost empty. They had carried General Lino's body inside, and the last of the soldiers were filing into the prison building, hopefully to plan their voyage home.

Finally she turned to Marek, who was embracing his fellow Kalindons one at a time. She tried to freeze the moment in her mind, the looks on all her people's faces and the way they held their bodies.

They were free.

17

Asermos

Sura laid Malia in her crib, then drew the curtain against the afternoon light. The child had cried for two straight hours, no doubt missing her father and her home in Tiros.

Malia's home would be here now, in Asermos, with her mother and grandmother, at least until Kalindos was rebuilt.

The last month had brought a fragile peace and a teetering sense of stability. The day of the Reawakening, Feras had sent two companies of men from the Asermon garrison to escort the Ilion commanders to their ships. The new Asermon leadership had decided to accept General Lino's suicide as a sign of complete surrender. When faced with Feras's troops, none of the other Ilion soldiers contradicted this assessment. They left begrudgingly, and were soon followed by their counterparts in Velekos.

Sura tiptoed into the kitchen and shut the bedroom door softly behind her. The front door was propped open, letting in the cool breeze and golden light of the autumn afternoon.

She stepped outside to find her mother on her knees in the front garden, grumbling, as always, about the disrepair the house had fallen into during her imprisonment, as if that were its worst aspect.

Mali yanked out another weed and tossed it into a pile, then wiped her arm over her forehead.

"It's getting late," she said to Sura. "He should've been back by now."

"He'll be here."

Mali let out an incoherent mutter and turned back to the soil. She jammed a trowel at the root of another large weed, as if it were the base of Dravek's neck.

Most people who didn't know them had been confused at the course of events surrounding Sura and Dravek and his succession of Spirits. The only truth to all the rumors was that for a few hours, he had been Raven. He had started the Reawakening.

Dravek had spent the last month without a Spirit, as they had traveled to Tiros to fetch Malia and visit his son Jonek. Even as he lamented the loss of Snake and Raven, and they both mourned the death of their mentor Vara he had comforted her in her grief over Lycas. They had not made love, of course, since her month of mourning required that they abstain, but he'd lain beside her every night, a gift in itself.

Dravek had been the first person in years to venture to the Bestowing spot a day's walk from Asermos. The Ilions had prevented anyone from using the site for its intended purpose.

She took a deep breath, once again stunned by their new freedom. She'd lived under Ilion rule for so long, it would be hard to get used to walking down an Asermon street with her head held high, not checking over her shoulder for the red-and-yellow uniforms on every corner.

Sura reached inside the door and picked up a clean bucket. "I should heat water. He'll want to wash and have something warm to drink when he gets here."

Mali gave her a skeptical look but didn't protest.

Sura walked down the wooded lane to the pump, passing two houses that had once belonged to the Ilion settlers—or "grapeheads," as Mali still called them. Many had left for their home country, unwilling to give up their own religion despite the presence and gifts of the Spirits.

Those who stayed behind required training. Sura had a Snake apprentice of her own now, a woman twice her own age. With the new system decreed by the Spirits, linking magical progression to readiness rather than parenthood, many of the former Ilions would probably never reach the second phase. Which was just as well.

She pumped the water carefully, hoping that next year would bring more rain. The lands where the vineyards had sat were slowly being returned to their rightful owners, who would plant whatever crops they chose next year.

The bucket was almost full when she heard footsteps behind her. By reflex, she whirled and turned, fists raised.

It wasn't an Ilion soldier who stood there.

"I hope that's for me," Dravek said.

She reached behind her and lifted the pump handle to shut off the water. "I thought you might be thirsty."

"I am."

He took her in his arms and kissed her. His lips weren't dry at all, belying his words. She sank against him, feeling him just as warm beneath her hands as she'd remembered.

Sura froze at the realization of the heat between them. Had Snake claimed him again? Would they face the same choice of denial and misery or disobedience and disfavor?

She broke away from him. "What are you now?"

He stared at her, his gaze tinged with apprehension. "Does it matter?"

Sura stroked his cheeks, dark with five days' stubble. "No," she whispered. "I love you, and I'll stay with you no matter what."

A corner of one of his eyes twitched. "Are you sure?"

She kissed him again, to wipe away both their doubts. Finally he gave a great sigh and eased her away from him. "Then let's go home." He picked up the bucket. "I have an affinity for this stuff now."

She watched his smile curve in a tease. He was going to make her guess.

"You like water," she said. "Are you a Bear?"

"No."

"A Duck?"

He rolled his eyes and shook his head.

She tried the more obscure Animals, ones she'd never heard of anyone having their Aspects. "Trout. Salamander. Muskrat."

He pointed at her. "Close."

"Muskrat?" She stopped in her tracks and whispered, "Dravek, are you an Otter?"

He looked down, studying his hand. "Who would have guessed I'd one day heal instead of destroy?"

"The Spirits give us what we need." She stepped up to him, then rose on her toes to kiss his mouth. "I know I could use a healer."

He took her hand as they walked. Mali looked up at their approach.

She frowned at Dravek. "Well?"

"He's an Otter," Sura said.

Mali nodded, and her frown eased. "So was my mother. Not bad." Without another word, she entered the house and went into the bedroom.

Sura laid out a supper for Dravek while the water heated on the stove for his bath.

In a few minutes, Mali came out of the bedroom with a small pack on her back and Malia in a sling around her front.

"Rhia and I have a meeting," she announced, "and Malia needs to visit family." She stopped at the door. "It'll be a long meeting. We probably won't be back until morning." She glanced between Sura and Dravek. "Late morning." Mali walked out.

Suddenly nervous, Sura went to the stove without looking at Dravek. "I think your water's almost—"

The door slammed shut, making her jump. She turned to see Dravek fastening the locks—all three of them. Then he stared at her, his eyes as dark with lust as ever.

"Come here," he said.

Her tongue swept the back of her lower teeth. "But what about your bath?"

In a moment, Dravek was at her side. Hands beneath her hips, he lifted her, then turned and set her atop the table.

"Let's wait till we both need one."

He kissed her, deeply, slipping his hands beneath her shirt.

Her body flooded with heat, and she pulled him tight against her, erasing the distance between them.

Truth be told, Sura had often wondered if the intensity of their passion had been a result of their Snake natures. She couldn't imagine reaching the same explosive, consuming desire they had ignited on their first encounter.

The next several hours, however, erased those worries.

And that night, she did not dream of fire.

EPILOGUE

New Kalindos

"Nothing like a good old-fashioned bloodless coup, heh?"

Rhia laughed at Marek as they rode side by side on the forest trail. "After five years," she said, "I'd happily offer a little blood to anyone who'll take this job."

He turned to look behind him. "Any volunteers?"

"Jula said yes," called Corek.

"I did not!"

Rhia smiled. "It's never too early to start running for the next election. It'll be Velekos's turn."

"Hush," Marek said. "Don't give them another reason not to move home."

"Good point."

After the Ilion withdrawal, Jula and Corek had settled in

Velekos to be near his family—and so that Jula could eat her fill of oysters every night. Luckily Rhia's position as the Reawakened High Council leader brought her to each village several times a year. She was looking forward to a tranquil retirement with Marek on her family's old farm in Asermos, where she planned to breed sleek Ilion horses and scruffy Tiron terriers, and in her spare time, nag Jula to visit with her twin grandchildren, Nila and Lanek, named in memory of their parents' lost siblings. Rhia's ache for her son Nilik had never faded, though she knew he had found eternal peace on the Other Side.

She hoped the travel wouldn't be too much for Elora, the next High Council leader. Then again, Kalindos wasn't as far from the rest of the villages as it used to be. Immediately after the war, every Kalindon who could swing an ax began to rebuild the village in a new location, about half as far from Asermos as before—far enough that they could still claim their idiosyncratic independence.

Each election, the five-year High Council leader term would rotate among the four villages. Such an arrangement was the only way they could gain the cooperation of Kalindons and Tirons in the formation of a new regional postwar government.

It had taken nearly a year to hammer out the details of the Reawakened nation's constitution. Parts of it were modeled after that of Ilios, but with a much less centralized government. Those who had lived in that country during the rise of the militaristic faction claimed that the problem stemmed from too much power residing in the capital city of Leukos. Therefore, each of the Reawakened villages maintained their own Councils, and the High Council mainly served to address issues of nationwide defense and taxation—two subjects Rhia never wanted to think about again.

"Why did I think it would be fun?" she asked Marek.

"Wasn't it?"

"Compared to what came before, yes. Compared to what's ahead, I hope not."

"Especially tonight," he said. "I'm going to drag you through so many dances and pour so much meloxa down your throat, you'll fun yourself into a coma. Five years is too long to be sober."

"Maybe that should be our new national motto, instead of 'From the Spirits, For the Spirits.'"

"It will be, when I'm in charge."

She chortled at the thought. "People might feel nervous with a High Council leader who can turn into a fox *or* invisible whenever he feels like it."

"I probably wouldn't get as many bribe offers as someone who can bring people back to life."

She shook her head. She'd never used her third-phase Crow powers on a human, had refused to subject Corek to the same resurrection ritual her mentor had foisted on her and Damen. Crow didn't seem to mind, maybe because they'd all seen enough death to make it superfluous.

Strains of music came from up ahead, and she urged her pony into a faster walk, until his hooves clopped in time to the drumbeat.

A great cheer went up as they entered New Kalindos. From her vantage point on horseback, Rhia could see Sura and Dravek standing with Kara and Etarek, each holding up a frantically waving child. The four of them had built one of the largest tree houses in the village to hold them and their complicated little family, which had expanded as each couple added their own child to the mix.

A cluster of Velekons were crowded around one of the hickory trees, their backs facing outward. Rhia thought she saw the red hair of Damen's mate Nathas, but why wouldn't he and Damen turn to greet them?

Seeing Tereus approach, she dismounted and gave her father a kiss and a hearty embrace.

"You look relaxed as always," she said. Despite his gray head of hair, his visage held fewer lines than her own. "Being married to the High Council leader will change that."

"But the extravagant salary makes up for all the stress," Marek added, rolling his eyes.

Tereus smiled and took the reins of their horses. "Let me take care of these two, and hug my granddaughter and great-grandchildren while I'm at it." He jutted his chin toward the hickory tree where she'd seen Nathas. "There's someone you both need to meet."

"Who?"

"It's a surprise. Hurry, before someone spoils it."

Rhia took Marek's hand, and they made their way in the direction Tereus had gestured. Mali joined them, handing each a mug of meloxa.

"Long time no see," she said.

Rhia scoffed. "You were at our house last week."

"So I don't get a hug?"

"Nice try." She smirked at her former nemesis. "The last person you hugged when you were drunk spent three weeks in the hospital."

Rhia caught sight of a group of familiar Velekons ahead of her. Damen and Nathas stood in front, arms crossed. Clearly they were hiding someone behind them.

"We're here," she said. "Who is it?"

Damen held up a finger. "I'll give you three guesses."

"Forget it!" rang a voice behind him. "I can't wait anymore." A dark-haired woman pushed between Damen and Nathas and stood with her hands on her hips. "So, Rhia, Marek, how've you been? Any news? Children, revolutions, grandchildren, Reawakenings, that sort of thing?"

Rhia stared at her. The dancing black eyes were the same that had greeted her not far from this spot twenty-five years ago.

"Alanka…" she and Marek whispered together.

The Wolf woman flapped her hands. "So who gets to hug me first?"

Rhia rushed forward and drew her sister into a breath-stealing embrace. A moment later, Marek joined them.

Alanka sniffled. "I swore I wouldn't cry. That was a stupid vow."

Rhia hugged her harder and started to cry herself. "I've never missed Lycas so much as right now. He would've given anything to see you again."

Alanka laughed as she sobbed. "So he could tease me, right?"

"That's why they make brothers," Rhia said, or at least it's what she tried to say through her tears.

"My turn, Alanka," came a deep voice from behind them.

Rhia froze. It couldn't be…

She turned to see Arcas the Spider, her childhood friend and first love. He stood with his wife Koli, a Bat from Asermos who had joined their rescue team to save Marek.

"I don't believe this." And there was Filip, Alanka's husband, the first Ilion to be called by a Spirit. He'd been the first bridge between their people, but not the last.

She'd seen none of these people in twenty-four years, but it felt like yesterday. The world had turned upside down, and then right side up again, never to be the same.

"Don't take this the wrong way," she said, after she'd hugged them all several times, "but what are you doing here? I thought you were in Ilios."

Alanka sighed. "Others are continuing our work, including our two younger children, and the Spirit communities we started have their own momentum now. It's up to the Ilions now to turn one way or the other."

"It could fall into civil war," Filip added. "Or the Reawakening could reach its final completion there."

"As to why we chose now to come home," Arcas said. "Look."

He pointed to one of the tables, where Elora was embracing two men in their thirties, one after the other, then again, weeping as though her eyes were on fire.

Alanka put her arm around Rhia's shoulders. "We found the last missing Kalindons."

Rhia gasped. Elora's sons had disappeared in the first Kalindon invasion, when they were only fifteen and twelve years old.

"Nice timing," Marek said. "Think she'll celebrate hard this evening?"

Rhia kissed him. "I think we all will."

That night—or more precisely, early the next morning—Rhia lay awake in one of the tree houses, listening to the revelry below her. Between the arms of her husband and the embrace of the forest, she felt herself enter a deep, pure peace that had been scarce in the last two-and-a-half decades.

The five years of her tenure had felt like a long pregnancy and birth. She looked forward to watching the new nation grow and change under someone else's care, but her newfound lack of responsibility wouldn't keep her from lying awake at night, worrying about the future. It was one of her greatest talents, so why waste it?

If the Ilions chose to follow the Spirits, they could be their strongest ally. If they fell into civil war or chose a more reactionary path, the threat of invasion could resurrect itself. But next time—if there were a next time—her people would be ready for them. Unlike the people of her own generation, her children had grown up in a time of war and thus would be ever-vigilant. Whatever the future brought, her people would face it united.

A new song began, and Rhia sat up suddenly in bed. She shook Marek awake.

He stretched and stirred, then gave her a warm smile. "What can I do for you?"

"I can't sleep." She pulled him to sit up, then got to her feet. "Dance with me."

"The other thirty-eight times tonight weren't enough?"

"It's a new song."

"Well, in that case." He eased himself out of bed and gave her a deep bow. "Would you prefer visible or invisible?"

"Visible, please."

"Good, because I'm too tired for the other." He took her in his arms, and they began to dance. Their bodies moved together as easily as they had the first night they had met, and Rhia soon found herself wanting to do more than dance.

She drew him over to the bed. "When you say, 'too tired for the other,' you mean for invisibility, right?"

"Yes. I'm never too tired for the other 'other.'" He tugged her down into the soft blankets with him, then kissed her with a

Wolf's hunger. They discarded their clothes in a hasty pile, and she was happy to see him in all his visible glory.

"You know, you're right," Marek said as he pulled her close and kissed her again. "It is a new song."

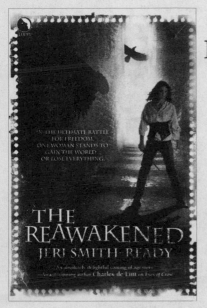

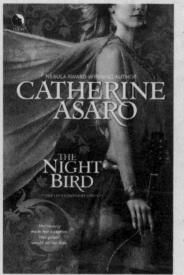

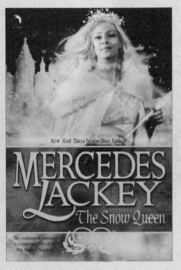

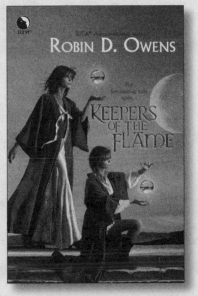